A JAMES RAKER MYSTERY

BREACHED

JOHN J. HOHN

ISBN: 978-0692250921

Produced by Publish Pros | publishpros.com

DEDICATION

In Memoriam

Joseph Matthias Hohn, DDS
July 18, 1904 – May 28, 1980

(Margaret) Ileen Carlon Hohn
April 6, 1904 – January 15, 1985

ACKNOWLEDGMENTS

As with my first novel, *Deadly Portfolio: A Killing in Hedge Funds*, I benefited from the help of many friends in writing this sequel. My heartfelt thanks go to Terry L. Dayton, a Vietnam veteran, who spent an afternoon with me sharing his combat experience and his struggles with flashbacks. Terry generously reviewed the passages in the book that deal with post-traumatic stress disorder.

I am deeply indebted to Ashe County Sheriff James Williams, Jefferson, NC, for the time he spent with me explaining many of the procedures his agency uses in their work. Lt. Grady Price was more than generous with his time. His input was invaluable to me. Dr. Terrance D. Bogard, MD, made many helpful recommendations, and I deeply appreciate his guidance on the anesthesia issues as related to treating comatose patients.

The women, who discussed their histories with me, as victims of childhood sexual abuse, may wish to remain anonymous. Neither they nor I knew I would one day write about childhood sexual abuse when I talked to them about their experiences. My thanks go out just the same to "B" and "M" in Winston-Salem.

A large number of books have been published on the subject of childhood sexual abuse. I found *Because I Remember Terror, Father, I Remember You*, by Sue William Silverman (University of Georgia Press, 1999) particularly moving, insightful, and compassionate. It was my major inspiration for creating Diane's story.

Thanks also to the Peacock-Neuman and White funeral directors, Southport, NC, for helping me with my questions about transporting a body. My son James M. Hohn drew on his years of experience in EMS work and firefighting to help me with the technical details of the fire scene. Professional Investigator Chris Miller provided essential background on many of the problems facing law enforcement in dealing with the trafficking of illegal substances. Alan Wease of State Farm Insurance helped me with insurance-related questions.

I failed to get the names of several helpful persons—including two members of the Southport, NC, police force—for the time they spent with me. Also, thanks to the three Brunswick County Sheriff deputies who allowed me to interrupt their breakfast at Locals Restaurant one Sunday morning with several questions about search warrants and search procedures.

My three first-readers were enormously helpful with their input: My wife Melinda reads dozens of crime novels every year. Her thoughtful recommendations kept me on track with my story. She has been steadfast in her belief in me. She is my muse. My good friend Joseph P. Frisina consented again to wade through an early draft and contributed to the editing of the story. A dedicated reader in her own right, my friend Betty Grigg shared several helpful ideas with me. To all three of these special people, I owe a debt of thanks for their support and encouragement.

I also want to send a special personal thanks to fellow author and friend Phil Kenney. His encouragement pulled me out of many a slump over the months of writing, and his insight into the creative process provided me with the reassurance I needed with the more challenging sections of the book.

My former colleague at Blue Cross and Blue Shield of Minnesota Jeannine Churchill challenged me with very insightful criticism and convinced me that an extensive rewrite of the last few chapters and the epilogue was necessary in order to draw my story to a more satisfying conclusion. Thank you, Jeannine.

Helping with the critical finishing touches, Martha R. Brown accepted my request to proofread the final manuscript. Martha has a keen eye for glitches of all kinds in a composition. She is also an author. Martha's book, *Holding Sweet Communion*, is an exquisitely researched, poignant portrait of how one North Carolina family lived through the Civil War. Her story is based on the letters of an ancestor who fought for the Confederacy.

CHAPTER 1

"I . . . I know this man," Art Nichols said as he and Detective James Raker drew closer to the body lying in the grass on the lee side to the dam. "It's Norm. Norm Dennison." Nichols's pace slowed until, with a final step, he knelt beside the body. "Ah, God, Norm. So this is how the anger ends."

"A friend?" Raker asked, standing at Art's side.

"We worked together on the property owners' association a few years back. I haven't seen him in a couple of years. I can't believe this. What happened here?" Nichols asked, looking up at the onlookers who had gathered around the dead man. "Is this an accident?"

Raker shook his head as he studied the victim. A high-caliber round had blown the back of the man's head away and splattered brain tissue all over the grass. Blood was pooling up beneath the victim's head.

Nichols stood up and looked around as if assuming command and suddenly shouted at the group of bystanders, "The rest of you, spread out! Whoever shot Dennison is still out there." He looked like a lumberjack foreman, broad shouldered, muscular even at sixty-two. A thick shock of brown hair flared out beneath the rim of his baseball cap. His gray eyes peered right through everyone he confronted. He grimaced, his mustache parting to display bright teeth that flashed with anger. He looked down the embankment to the shoreline, glanced at Raker, and then walked down to the water to wash the blood off his hands.

Neighbors had come running in response to the cries for help. Now they jumped back in alarm at Nichols's commands.

"I said 'spread out', goddamn it!" Nichols barked again as he turned around at the water's edge. "Get down below the ridgeline where you aren't so easy to spot."

Raker studied his friend as Art walked back from the water. Art's brow was furrowed. His face taut. Their eyes met. The detective could see Art Nichols was not in the moment.

"New kids!" Nichols cursed as he drew closer. "They're all gonna get themselves killed."

"Art?" Raker asked tentatively. "Art. They're not kids. Nobody's going to shoot. We're here . . . at the lake on the dam. You and I, Art. We just drove here in your Jeep and found this guy."

Nichols wheeled around looking at all the onlookers who had fanned out nervously across the road in response to his commands.

"No, Art. Nobody else. I'll check to see if anyone called law enforcement." Raker tried to put his hand on Nichols's shoulder, but his friend jerked away.

"Yeah, do that. We've got to move out. We're too exposed. Get everyone off this ridge!"

"Okay, Art," Raker said. The detective had heard about flashbacks veterans experienced years after combat, but he had never been in the company of a man who was overtaken by the phenomenon. Art Nichols was back forty years in time, in the dark mists of the Vietnam jungle.

Raker turned to the bystanders. Most were elderly. *Retirees,* he thought. Their eyes were following Art's every step. "The law enforcement people will not want traffic around the body," Raker said, hoping to restore a measure of calm. "Did anyone call the authorities?"

"Yes, I did," an older woman wearing gardener's gloves and a head scarf replied. "They're on their way."

"Anyone else know this man? Any of you?" Raker continued.

"Dennison. Norm Dennison! The new guy," Nichols shouted at Raker. "Now let's move!"

A siren could be heard in the distance.

"He wasn't supposed to be here. Why the hell can't people keep orders straight?" Nichols said, looking away.

"Did any of you see this happen?" Raker asked as the tension continued to build because of Nichols's behavior. Nobody responded. "Okay. Everyone please stay back. It sounds as though the police should be here shortly."

The siren drew closer, and the crowd turned to look toward the road leading around the lake, the only direct route to the dam. More people were crossing the dam to the scene of the shooting. Like those already at the roadside, most were elderly. Raker instinctively counted seven men and nine women.

It was an easy morning for folks to be up and about. The August sky was blue and clear overhead. Given the crisp mountain air, the sky would not turn milky during the day as it would in the summer heat and humidity at the lower elevations. The mile-and-a-half-long shoreline spread out in the shadow of the mountains that towered over the valley. A light breeze funneled through the peaks and rippled the surface of the lake. Raker was struck by the contrast of the bloody body lying on the grass in front of him and the bucolic setting.

Detective Raker was familiar with the behavior of onlookers around a crime scene. He had moved among them many times during his thirty-five years in law enforcement. Trim and athletic at five feet ten inches in height, he relied on his deliberate demeanor to establish control and earn the respect of any crowd. Knowing the scene should not be disturbed, he began walking slowly in a wide circle around the body. People watched him pass and stepped back even farther than they had in response to Nichols's commands. One glance into his hazel eyes and total strangers were taken in by the detective's quiet confidence. His full head of gray hair, strong chin and broad forehead gave him the appearance of a man who was comfortable taking charge. "You all live around here?" Raker asked, looking over the group. Several nodded. "But nobody saw anything?"

The bystanders looked at one another. "I didn't see it, but I was standing right over there when it happened. I heard him fall," a gray-haired woman said. She turned and pointed fifty yards down the road to the end of the dam. "I was out for a hike. I was so shocked. I was the one who yelled for help."

"We heard those guys shooting," an older man said. "They're down there three, four times a week. We always hear it. Then we heard her yelling and came down here as fast as we could."

The sirens grew louder. A cloud of dust followed the speeding car's progress as it raced along the gravel road that served the homes around Lake Hannah. A Baden County Sheriff's cruiser pulled to a stop on the gravel and two deputies jumped out. Their boots crunched in the rocky surface as they ran up to the group standing around the body.

"Step aside. Step aside," a heavyset middle-aged man in uniform demanded. "Get back, please, and stay back!" Deputy Rod Hurdler scowled through a thick mustache as his dark eyes darted from one onlooker to the next. "You hear me?" Hurdler shouted directly at Raker who had instinctively remained near the body.

"Yes, sir," Raker said, realizing suddenly he was also just another gawking spectator as far the officer was concerned. "I just wanted everyone to keep back. I know you have a job to do."

"How's that?"

"Retired law enforcement. Detective, Melville County. Raker. James Raker." Raker pulled his wallet from the back pocket of his jeans, flipped it open and showed Hurdler his retirement ID.

"Well, okay," the deputy said, looking up at Raker and nodding. Turning back to the bystanders, he asked, "Anybody see what happened?"

"I heard it," the elderly woman who had spoken earlier replied. "I didn't see it. But I heard the shot and then a . . . a muffled thud, and I turned to see this man had fallen to the ground."

"You heard the shot?"

"Yes. Down below there, in the woods," the woman pointed. "They were shooting down there where they always go for target practice. The poor man. I don't think anyone meant to kill him. To shoot him."

"Thanks ma'am. I am going to ask you to please wait here until we get a statement from you. Anyone else? Anyone else see what happened here?" Hurdler looked from one person to the next. "No? Okay. Y'all need to stay right here until we get your names and any other information you may have about this. This is Deputy Caleb Whitehead. I want you to give him your names and addresses so we can contact you later. Nobody leave until he has your information. Cal, start right now before anyone decides to drift away."

Raker realized his name meant nothing to Deputy Hurdler. The detective's role in solving the homicides of a serial killer in Charles City two years earlier was ancient history. The news of the deaths of three people who lived in the affluent lakeside community of Heron Lake, north of Charles City, and Raker's role in apprehending the killer, may never have reached Riley's Creek, North Carolina. *Just as well*, Raker thought.

CHAPTER 2

A Baden County ambulance pulled to a stop on the dam behind the sheriff's cruiser. A second county squad car pulled in behind it. The passenger's side door swung open.

"Hurdler, get this area cordoned off . . . now!" Sheriff Walter Grossman shouted as soon as his boots hit the ground. Grossman's driver jumped out of the vehicle and ran to Hurdler with a roll of yellow and black cordoning ribbon. Grossman, very agile for a stocky man of fifty, pulled his cap lower on his forehead to hide his pate. Gray hair at the temples made his green eyes all the more penetrating when he spoke.

"Yes, sir!" Hurdler snapped.

"I want the names of everyone here and whether any of them approached the victim. Gonzalez," Grossman barked to the deputy who arrived with him, "put the scene under custody. Get the names of anyone who is admitted behind the barrier."

"Yes, sir," Gonzalez replied.

"Whitehead is getting the names of everyone now, sir," Hurdler said. Gonzalez, a rookie and the only Hispanic on the force, paced off a large square surrounding the body with Deputy Hurdler, spooling out the yellow and black ribbon as they went. Gonzalez stationed himself at a corner obviously intended as the admission point into the cordoned-off area.

"EMS . . . one of you guys—check the victim," the sheriff ordered.

An EMS attendant gave his name to Gonzalez and knelt down beside the victim. He studied the man's wound and then, shaking his heard, got slowly to his feet.

"Never knew what hit him," the attendant said, looking directly at the sheriff.

"A retired detective, huh?" Deputy Hurdler hissed as he walked past Raker. "Big city, I suppose."

"Charles City," Raker replied with a smile.

"Okay, contact the hospital and let them know we are bringing the body in. And call the coroner; we need a death certificate," the sheriff barked at the attendant.

"This man's retired law enforcement, Sheriff. Melville County," Hurdler said, nodding in Raker's direction.

"These guys are going to take this over," Nichols whispered to Raker. "Nobody's going after the sniper. Let's get out of here. Take the men and reconnoiter down below."

"What brings you here?" the sheriff asked Raker without looking at him. He was focused on the EMS guy, making sure the man had understood.

"I'm a guest of one of the residents," Raker replied.

"What's his name?" the sheriff asked, finally turning to the detective.

"Art Nichols," Raker said, hesitant to introduce his friend given Art's present state of mind. "He has a place up on Rebecca Ridge. We were there when we heard the shots and drove down."

"See anything else?"

"No. But we heard the gunshots," Raker said.

"Okay. What about them?"

"They sounded as though they came from below the dam, as that woman said." Raker turned. "From the woods down there."

"Sounds can fool a person up here with the peaks and hollows; not the same as the big city."

"I understand. My experience is all metropolitan."

"Cities?"

"Yes. Detroit, Minneapolis and Charles City."

"Come on. Let's move out. This is just going to be chickenshit if we stay here," Nichols urged, continuing to whisper. He walked back to his Jeep and climbed in the driver's side. Raker followed around and got in the passenger bucket seat.

"It did sound like that's where the shots were coming from, Sheriff," a bystander volunteered. A Mercedes roadster skidded to a stop behind the last of the parked cruisers. A cloud of dust from the vehicle rose into the breeze coming off the lake and blew toward the people standing at the roadside.

"What the hell?" the sheriff called out as he shielded his eyes from the airborne silt. Everyone turned to see a short, middle-aged brunette step out of the roadster and run toward the body. "Hey, lady! Where do you think you're going?"

"I'm Helen Schreve. My husband's president of the property owners' association for this development. What happened here? I need to report it." Mrs. Schreve turned in time to see Gonzalez tie the yellow and black barricade ribbon to the guardrail as the EMS attendant left the custody area. "Do you mind?" she asked Gonzalez, as if she expected to gain access to the body.

"Stay right there, ma'am, please!" Sheriff Grossman shouted. "This is a crime scene, lady. You don't have any special privileges here. You'll have to step back from the area."

Mrs. Schreve spun around and searched the stout sheriff's chest for identification. Then she looked him in the eye and said, "Grossman, huh? Lots of Grossmans in Baden County. The county commissioners will hear about this."

"Yes, ma'am, Sheriff Walter D. Grossman, Baden County. You get that right when you talk to them," he shouted. "A man's been killed here. That's all you need to know. You're holding up an investigation. Now, please, stand off from the cordoned area."

Mrs. Schreve held her gaze on the sheriff a few seconds longer. He was head and shoulders taller than she. She wheeled about and stormed back to her car. The Mercedes kicked up another cloud of dust as it dug for traction in the gravel.

Nichols shielded his eyes from the dust. "Jesus, a chopper? Why the hell send in a chopper?"

"Who was that?" Raker asked, hoping to coax his friend out of the flashback.

"Who?" Nichols asked.

"The woman in the convertible."

Nichols clenched his teeth. *A woman in a chopper*, Nichols thought. *No, a woman in a convertible . . . a white convertible. There is no chopper. There is no platoon. Neighbors . . . only neighbors. We are not under fire . . . There's no danger.* Nichols stared through the windshield.

"You okay?" Raker asked.

"I guess," Nichols said without looking at him. He realized he was with his friend in his Jeep on the dam at Lake Hannah—Lake Hannah where he had found so much contentment since retiring. This is where he bought a cabin, on Rebecca Ridge, so he and Cheryl could have a glass of wine on the deck in the evening and look off for miles to the east, through the wooded valleys and the soft feminine contours of the Blue Ridge Mountains. Tears welled up in his eyes. He felt a tug in his gut. "Yeah, Jim . . . I guess," Art said, then groaned. He leaned forward to rest his head on the steering wheel.

"Bad spell?"

"Bad spell," Nichols replied. He raised his head from the wheel. When he turned, Raker saw the pain in Nichols's eyes, in the set of his jaw.

"Sorry," Raker offered. "It must be rough."

"Yeah," Nichols replied, shaking his head and then looking away to hide the tears. "I keep thinking . . . thinking it will go away some day. Stay away. Then there'll be a nightmare one night out of nowhere, and it's all back . . . right in my face. All of it. If I try to fight it, it gets worse. Fuck. That was forty years ago, and here I am and it's still with me. I get swallowed up in it. Jesus, do I carry this all the way to my grave?"

"I gave the deputy our names and your address," Raker said. "We don't need to stay around here if it troubles you."

Art reached down to start the engine. "What was it you asked me?"

"The little brunette woman who drove up? What's with her?"

"Helen Schreve, the wife of Frank Schreve, the president of the property owners' association here. That's their place on the lake on the east side there," Art said, backing the Jeep up to turn around. "It was vacant for years. Huge place. Bigger than anything around here. Schreve bought it and refurbished it and got elected to office by default. Long story. I'll give you the details some night over a beer. They're both a pain in the ass."

"Are you all right? Do you want me to drive?"

"No. I'm okay . . . It's just a hell of a shock. I knew Norm Dennison. I liked him. I can't quite . . . believe this. I didn't even know he was here. He hasn't been back in years. It could've been anyone on the dam this morning. But why him? Why today? They're having target practice down there all the time. Nothing like this ever happened."

"You going back to the cabin?"

"Yeah. Why?"

"Nothing. I want to make sure you're okay . . . and I was thinking maybe I'd come back down here. I want to know what's below the dam. I'd just like to get a sense of it."

"I'm okay; really. It just takes a little time. I don't have control when those things happen. Being afraid of them just makes them come on all the more. You want to head down below there?" Nichols nodded toward the tail waters of the dam and put the Jeep into gear. "Let's go. We can only get about so far on the right there. We may need to walk a little. The road on the left side runs out to a county road that isn't much used. What side do you want to try first?"

"Right. I just want a look. Just a hunch. The sheriff didn't give my opinion much credence, so I thought I'd just check it out."

"No problem." The Jeep turned onto a road marked Laurel Lane, which was nothing more than two tracks through the tall grass.

As the vehicle pushed through the trees, Raker could see why his friend did not want to drive into the wooded area very far. In the full shade of the valley below the dam, the air was noticeably cooler. Water gushing from the discharge pipe could be heard above the rustling of the wind in the trees. A jay took flight, calling out an alarm as it took off. Raker liked the quiet.

"I don't want to go any farther," Nichols said.

"That's fine. Let's stop and get out."

"Anything you say, Professor." Nichols jammed the parking brake into position, and both men dropped out of the Jeep onto the forest floor.

Raker studied the setting. "So what's your take on all this?" he finally asked.

"It's too much like the jungle for me to feel good about it. Just give me a sec. I know where I am. I'm just a little shaky is all. Dennison and I worked together on the POA board. He was a hard worker. Nice guy, but angry. He wanted to nail the developer."

"The guy . . . Dennison . . . getting shot is puzzling," Raker said emphatically. "Seems unlikely a stray round killed him. Someone was being very careless if that is the case. It's more likely it was a deliberate shot. The entry wound was clean. Not the kind of entry a ricochet round would make. If they get a forensic team out here, they'll probably find the shooter was below the victim. The shot entered his head at a point lower than where it exited . . . Where are we in relationship to the dam at this point?"

"To your left, and back a little. Maybe 150 yards."

"What will I find if I keep walking this way?"

"In about sixty yards you'll come to a stream that carries the discharge from the dam downstream. It used to be really good trout fishing, but I haven't tried it in years."

"Nobody lives down here?"

"No roads. They'd put them in if someone wanted to build, but people get discouraged. Nobody wants an area all grown over like this. Local people, folks who live here year round, know they'd need to get out in the winter when it snows, and they won't put themselves down here where they'd be isolated."

"But it's a good area for fishing, hunting, target practice . . ." Raker mused.

"Except for the noise, nobody gives a damn what goes on down here."

"The only road in is the one we came on, right?"

"Yes."

"So if somebody ventured down this far, they'd have to get out by going back to the dam. The shooter wouldn't do that. He'd get trapped in a dead-end," Raker said. "What about the other side of the stream? More of the same?"

"Pretty much. The road's a little better but nobody ever built on that side either."

"You notice there were no tire tracks on the trail we drove in on?"

"No, but it doesn't surprise me. Nobody ever drives down here. They walk. If they lived any distance from here, they'd park up by the dam and walk in."

"So you'd be seen walking in here, and it'd be obvious you had a gun with you . . . Let's go see the other side. Just for the hell of it."

CHAPTER 3

Frank Schreve heard his wife's Mercedes charge up the driveway and grind to a halt at the foot of the stairs leading to the deck.

"Frank! Frank?" Helen called out crossing the deck to the door. "You'll never guess . . . you'll never guess." She stopped one step inside the screen door to catch her breath.

"Norm Dennison got shot at the dam about a half an hour ago," Frank said flatly.

"How'd you know that? I just came from there."

"Highway patrol and county sheriff cruisers are all over the place. I just waved one guy down and asked him." At sixty-one, Frank Schreve still had a full head of hair and stood six-foot-five, but his rounded shoulders, high forehead and soft round face gave him the look of a submissive man despite his size. His jaw, resolute enough in his youth, had weakened in appearance by a neck grown flabby from too many dockside happy hours.

From his chair in the living room, Frank looked out lakeside windows that stretched to the rafters of the vaulted ceiling. In August, the lake had turned green with nutrient-rich runoff from the homes surrounding it.

"That's going to delay everything," Helen whined.

"I don't know why."

"You don't think for one minute they're not going to postpone the deadline now. They will!" Helen said. "The longer they delay, the more time people will hold out and then something will break against us. Just wait; you'll see. People are scared now. Two lots sold just last month. But they won't stay scared forever. This gives them time to plan. They didn't think the state is serious, but people are beginning to find out they are."

"Maybe. Maybe not. It might not be much of a delay. The guy's body isn't even cold yet. Don't panic," Frank said.

"I'm not in a panic. But it took forever to get the Department of Environment and Natural Resources to set a deadline for bringing the dam into compliance. It was only when we pushed for additional inspections that they came around. Government!"

"I'd be the last to defend them," Frank said, "but it's hardly likely they'll discredit their own man's work. Nothing's evident to the naked eye that the dam is going to fail. It takes a trained engineer to check things out. That's why Dennison was here. He wasn't going to go back and say they should extend the deadline. He'd be contradicting the reports of a colleague. You just kept raising so much hell in Raleigh that they sent another guy up here to make sure it was the right thing to do."

"Dixie States Development has been pushing the rumors that the state is going to condemn the dam. Dennison hated those people, the original developers. Dennison'd agree with the deadline out of spite, just to get back at Dixie States. He'd love to see all the lots they still own become worthless." Helen walked over to the windows overlooking the lake. "You're sure this is going to work out for us, that Palmetto-Atlantic will step in and buy up all of Dixie States' lots and repair the dam?"

"Absolutely. Palmetto-Atlantic has too much committed to let things fall through now," Frank replied.

"Well, you'd better be right. If the deadline for breaching the dam is extended one more month, then I'm taking this down to Raleigh myself. And I'm going to be at the county commissioners' meeting next week too. You should've heard the way that sheriff—Sheriff Grossman—ordered me around."

"A lot of good it did the last time you went into a commissioners' meeting. The leash law idea of yours got laughed out of the room. You can't get anywhere calling people rednecks. Please, please, just let it rest for a day or two."

"Oh my God! Did Art Nichols ever turn over those backup CDs to the dues billing program? He's got no use for them. I keep calling and calling . . ." her voice trailed off as she spun around and walked out of the living room into the adjacent kitchen. "Why can't people just see things through?"

Frank slumped back in his easy chair.

CHAPTER 4

Sheriff Grossman studied the body of Norm Dennison, a forty-six-year-old civil servant. The victim's gray hair was matted with oily, scarlet blood. "So, what've you got?" the sheriff asked Deputy Hurdler.

"Not much. Nobody saw anything. A couple of people heard gunshots. One lady was standing about fifty yards off to one side watching the birds on the lake. She turned and saw the guy had dropped. The shot came from down below somewhere. You can see that in the victim. I sent a couple men down that way to check it out."

"Did they find anything?"

"They haven't come back yet."

"Coroner notified?"

"Yes, sir."

"They can take the body in, then. You agree?"

"Yes, sir. Poor bastard catches a stray slug from some asshole practicing for deer season."

"An accident then?" the sheriff asked.

"Yeah, well, not too many people seemed to know the guy. We haven't found anyone who even knew he was here or what he was doing . . . You hear the rumors about the dam, that it's in danger of giving way?"

"They're not rumors," the sheriff said. "Property owners have ninety days to come up with a plan to bring the dam into compliance with regulations. But look at this structure. There's no seepage. No sinkholes. Looks like it would stand another hundred years." The sheriff looked down at Dennison's body one more time. "Get the body into town. That's a clean entry wound; not some wild ricochet," he observed.

"Yeah. One shot. Missed a target. Fired once . . . no backstop. The round kept coming, and this guy stepped in its way."

"Maybe. Let me know what your men find when they come back from below there."

"Yes, sir."

✠   ✠   ✠

"Okay, you want to see the other side of the stream below the dam," Nichols said, as if confirming direction from Raker. Art backed the Jeep onto the dam road and turned to cross to the opposite side. He nodded to Deputy Hurdler as they passed and noticed the EMS personnel had placed Dennison's body into a black body bag. When he reached the opposite end of the dam, Nichols turned the vehicle to the right onto a road that led to the valley below.

"I see what you mean," Raker volunteered.

"About what?" Nichols asked.

"The road. It's in better shape. Must get more traffic . . . Stop! Just for a second."

Nichols jammed on the breaks, surprised at Raker's request.

Raker lurched forward in his seat. "Whoa! I just want to get out and check the tracks in front of us." He walked around to the front of the Jeep and squatted to inspect tire tracks in the dust and gravel.

"Well?" Nichols asked when Raker got back into the cab.

"I can't tell anything. If it had rained or if it was graded recently that would help. But dry like this . . . who knows?"

Nichols slipped the vehicle back into gear and eased down the road until there was little gravel left on the surface. "This road continues along to a back entrance to the development. It doesn't get used much."

"Let's stop here then," Raker said. "This is about as far down the line as we went on the other side. I want to get out and walk."

The path extending into the woods was easy to follow. Raker noticed the poison ivy on the ground and its thicker vines clinging like huge millipedes to the trunks of the trees. The ground gave way underfoot, soft with rotted vegetation. In the shade, he could hear the water gushing out of the discharge pipe in the dam. The air was damp, scented by the green overgrowth.

"So, if you came down here for target practice, where would you set up?" Raker asked.

"Far enough to have a backstop for your shots," Art replied.

Raker nodded. "How far do we need to go to an opening so we can see the dam?"

"Not this way. If we went off to the right here, worked our way toward the stream, there's a clearing where the stream cuts."

The two men trudged through the underbrush until they could hear the gurgling of the stream ahead of them. They finally stepped into a small clearing that had been used as a campsite many times.

"There. Now you can see the dam," Art observed.

"Yeah, about 150 . . . 160 yards off," Raker said. "You can see the whole width of it. This a campsite?"

Art shrugged his shoulders. "I guess. Kids do a lot of drinking down here and smoking pot—messing up the place. There's no way to police it. The sheriff's people aren't going to run all the way out here to pick up a couple of kids."

Raker studied the ground around the campsite. *Too many footprints*, he thought. In the shade at the edge of the clearing he spotted a spent shell casing. He found a twig, inserted it into the open end of the brass casing, and held it up to his nose. The nitrate scent was still very sharp. *A 308*, he thought. *A sniper's round.*

"Stand where you are!" a voice commanded from the brush. "Don't move!"

CHAPTER 5

"This feels so Catholic," Diane Welborn said as she entered the church with Cheryl Nichols. At fifty-two, Diane was proud of her youthful, five-foot-two figure. Only an occasional gray strand appeared in her brown hair. Her fair skin and caramel-brown eyes added to her youthful appearance.

"It's an Episcopalian church," Cheryl explained.

"I know. I saw the sign. But it feels Catholic. The Madonna fresco. Episcopalians don't venerate the Virgin Mary, do they? Oh my God, she's pregnant!" The two women stopped halfway up the center aisle of the small church where they could see the full fresco of a several times larger than life pregnant Madonna on the wall to one side of the main altar. Diane looked at Cheryl. "Episcopalian?"

"Yes."

"My husband and I were Catholic. I wasn't born Catholic. I converted when we got married."

"Catholics and Episcopalians are a lot alike," Cheryl said. Cheryl was half a head taller than Diane. Jogging kept her trim, and she walked like a man, her blond ponytail bobbing with each step. "At least that's what I've heard. Art and I don't go to church. We aren't religious."

"Yeah." Diane sighed and turned to look down both sides of the center aisle. "Smell that incense? It just hangs in the air. Makes me sick to my stomach. It reminds me of when I was pregnant. I hated it."

"What about the frescoes, though? They're really famous. People come from all around—"

"I don't know. I just don't care for religious art."

"I'm sorry," Cheryl replied. "The frescoes are so famous. I just thought you'd want to see them. Part of the VIP tour." She forced a laugh.

"Oh, I'm sorry. No, I'm glad we stopped. It's just a thing with me. You know . . . Catholicism. I don't relate."

"It's Episcopalian," Cheryl said.

"I know. But it looks the same . . . it feels the same to me."

"Let's go then."

On the way back to the car, Cheryl wondered whether Diane would like anything without reservation. She and Art looked forward to meeting Diane, the first woman their friend Raker had mentioned since his wife Susan died almost two years earlier. The couple arrived late the previous evening. Given the hour, she showed both Diane and Raker to the guest room and wished both of them a good night of rest. The following morning, after breakfast, Cheryl asked Diane if she wanted to drive around to see the sights and perhaps take in a yard sale or two.

The town of Riley's Creek, North Carolina, was snuggled in the valley on both sides of the stream from which it drew its name. From the top of nearby Black Mountain, the tallest peak in the county, the valley looked like the crushed crown of a man's hat with mountains rimming the depression. The entire area was part of a land grant awarded by the First Continental Congress to a local man who made a name for himself in the Revolutionary War's Battle of King's Mountain, which lay miles to the south in South Carolina. Pioneers found passage through the Appalachian Mountain range much easier to the south, near Boone, or the north, near Damascus, Virginia. Riley's Creek and its valley were bypassed by early settlers as a result.

Settlers, nevertheless, migrated into the valley slowly over the years. Most were content to farm small plots of land. When the Civil War broke out, many were not in sympathy with the Confederate cause as they did not have slaves working the land. Riley's Creek became a stop on the underground railway for African Americans seeking their freedom in the North. It also became a haven for deserters from both armies.

The railroad crisscrossed the South by 1850 but did not extend to Riley's Creek until 1915. Timber and burley tobacco were the cash crops until Christmas tree farms took over in the 1980s. The natural beauty of the land attracted more residents as a result, and by the end of the twentieth century, hundreds of seasonal homes had been built by families seeking escape from the summer heat at lower elevations. Neighborhoods sprang up along the banks of the New River and on the surrounding heights, owing to the breathtaking views of the wooded landscape. At approximately 3,200 feet above sea level, summer temperatures in the drier mountain air rarely rose above 85 degrees. The winter season, though shorter than in the Midwest, could be very windy and cold with occasional heavy snows.

The stop at the church was the last Cheryl had planned. "Well, that's about it," she said as she started the engine in her Subaru. "Let's head home and see what the guys are up to."

"Fine. I think I'd like to lie down for a while if it doesn't interfere with anyone's plans," Diane said.

"That's fine," Cheryl replied, and the two rode on in silence for several minutes.

"You really haven't seen much of the area around Lake Hannah itself," Cheryl said as she turned onto Lakeside Drive. "Let's take the long way around. I can show you the dam and a few other places of interest."

"Good. I'd like to see it."

The car veered off onto a gravel road that dropped steeply away into a wooded area. "Art and I discovered this development about seventeen years ago. We came up here and found our cabin was on the market. The couple that owned it lived in Florida and spent summers here. Both of them died one winter just a few weeks apart from one another, and our cabin was offered for sale by their estate. We got it for a song."

"How tragic," Diane exclaimed.

"Tragic? Oh, yes, that they died. Well, they were elderly. We bought the place as is. Just the way they left it. All the furniture. One of them must have been having difficulty because we found oxygen breathing apparatus in one closet."

"Wasn't that weird?"

"Weird? No," Cheryl said. "We didn't find it that way."

"Moving into a house with everything arranged as if the previous owners expected to return. I'd feel . . . I don't know . . . intrusive."

Cheryl shrugged. "But we didn't know them. We didn't care much for their taste. They really liked orange. It was everywhere. Orange plates, tablecloth, curtains. And owls. Owl ashtrays. An owl toilet paper holder. Owl dish towels."

"That's what I mean. Sounds almost voyeuristic."

"Oh, I guess, but we went right to work and made it over the way we wanted it." Cheryl pointed ahead. "Look, we're coming up on the lake from the opposite side our cabin is on."

"It's so quiet down here. So cool. Isn't there anyone around?"

"Oh, there are probably ten or twelve cabins on this side of the lake, more up in the hills above us."

"My husband liked to fish," Diane said.

Cheryl glanced over and gently asked, "Divorced or a widow?"

"Divorced. He's remarried. Didn't take him long."

"Right after you divorced?"

"About two years after. Somebody he met after we split. My God, our divorce was final sixteen years ago."

"Just two years and he remarried?"

"I know. I think he wanted someone to help him with the children."

"They didn't stay with you?" Cheryl asked.

"The two oldest boys had graduated from high school. The youngest were with me—my daughter and my son—but they decided to move away with him when he took a job in Cincinnati."

"That must have been hard . . . being separated from the kids."

"I suppose. They weren't getting along too well with the guy that moved in with me. Even before my ex left town, one of the boys started staying most of the time with his dad."

"Where are the kids now?" Cheryl asked.

"All over. My oldest son lives in Richmond. He has a family. The next oldest never left Minneapolis. My daughter moved with her husband to San Diego, and my youngest son is in Cincinnati. He's married. He stayed close to his dad."

"Do you get to see them?"

"A couple of times a year. They've been good about either coming to see me or inviting me to visit."

"Art and I didn't want kids, but if we had children, I think it would be very hard to be separated from them like that," Cheryl said. "Did you all do any counseling to get through it?"

"Oh yes. We had someone we went to for help."

"Before or after you separated?"

"Before. And then again after."

"But you and your husband didn't get back together?"

"No."

"Do you mind my asking why?"

"Just one of those things."

"Okay, well . . ." Cheryl cleared her throat. "See that big place on the right we're coming up to? A couple named Schreve bought it. Huge place. Stood vacant for years and then they moved in and fixed it all up. It's the largest place in the development."

"Looks nice. My husband and I were building a cabin in Wisconsin when we broke up."

"Really. Do either one of you own it now?"

"No. He did all the work on it so he got it in the divorce. Then he had to sell it because he had trouble with his job and needed the money."

"What a shame. We enjoy our place so much. I would hate to run into bad luck and need to sell it."

"Well, I wasn't using it. He had the kids with him, and he moved away so I moved away too. To Arizona. The cabin was just sitting there. At least if he sold it, somebody got to use—"

"Jesus!" Cheryl yanked the steering wheel and the Outback station wagon lurched to the side of the road just missing a Mercedes roadster speeding toward them from the opposite direction. Cheryl leaned on the horn. The car roared past. A cloud of dust spread out over the road in its wake. "That bitch!"

"You know her?" Diane exclaimed, recovering from the alarm. "She nearly hit us."

"That's Helen Schreve. That big place we just passed is theirs. Drives around the lake like it was her own private park. I can't stand her."

"She'll kill someone driving like that."

Cheryl pulled her car back onto the road. "These roads are barely wide enough for two cars. You meet another vehicle coming from the opposite direction, you often need to pull to the side so they can get by."

The appearance of Helen's sports car broke up the women's conversation. Cheryl wondered how Raker found Diane. *Vacuous*, she thought. Not like him at all. He was always thoughtful. He volunteered more information whenever he felt he was not being understood. Not Diane. She was somewhere off in la-la land most of the time. Cheryl wondered how the two got along.

"We're coming up on the dam now. The lake's an impoundment. It was built to make a large millpond for a sawmill over 100 years ago. What's this?" Cheryl slowed the car as she turned onto the dam road. A highway patrol cruiser and two vehicles from the sheriff's department were parked on the side of the road. Their pursuit lights were flashing. To the left of the parked vehicles, an area had been cordoned off with yellow and black tape. Cheryl rolled down her window.

"What's the trouble, Officer?" she asked a highway patrolman standing near the edge of the road.

"A man's been shot. They took the body into town a few minutes ago."

"Shot! Murdered?"

"We think it's an accident, ma'am. Several people said that they heard gunshots from below the dam."

"Target practice."

"Yes, ma'am."

"Who was it? Anybody from around here?"

"Some guy the state sent up here to look at the dam. He was in the wrong spot at the wrong time." A sheriff's department four-wheel drive SUV pulled up behind Cheryl's Subaru. "You'll have to pull over, ma'am. The sheriff's vehicle needs to get by."

Cheryl maneuvered her vehicle to the side then looked up as the SUV crunched to a halt on the opposite side of the dam road. "My God, Art's in that truck! With Jim! What . . ." She opened the door and stepped across the road.

"Step back from that vehicle, ma'am," the highway patrolman ordered.

Cheryl stopped. The passenger's side door of the SUV opened, and a deputy got out.

"What's going on?" Cheryl demanded.

"Stay back from the vehicle, ma'am. Please!"

Art looked out the window at Cheryl and Diane. "It's all a mistake," he shouted through the closed window. The driver remained behind the wheel of the SUV. The air conditioning system was cutting in and out as the engine idled.

Cheryl stepped back in response to the deputy's commands. "Where are they taking you?"

Art shrugged. Raker turned and smiled and nodded toward the two women.

"Sheriff here?" the deputy asked Hurdler.

"He followed the body into town."

"What d'ya think? Take these guys to town?" the deputy asked. "Sheriff might want to talk to them."

Deputy Hurdler turned and walked over to the SUV. "Aw, for Chrissake Nathan, this guy's retired law enforcement. He was just here."

"Well, I didn't know. We found them down below. And look what he had." The deputy held up a clear plastic bag with two .308 brass rifle shell casings in it.

"Hold it as evidence. Probably doesn't amount to anything. Guys are down there all the time. What were you doing down there anyway?" Hurdler snapped at Nichols and Raker. The driver lowered the rear window of the SUV in response to Hurdler's question.

"Just having a look around," Art replied. "We didn't know it was off limits."

"Just couldn't leave it alone, huh?" Hurdler growled at Raker. "You have no authority here."

"My mistake," Raker answered. "We went down there out of curiosity. Nothing more."

"Whitehead, you got the information on these two guys?" Hurdler shouted over his shoulder at the deputy.

"Yes, sir."

"Why don't you just go back to your place wherever it is and leave this investigation to the responsible authorities? Nathan, you and Gonzalez go back down there and cordon that area off. The sheriff may want us to include it in our review of the scene."

Nichols and Raker climbed out of the SUV.

"What on earth?" Cheryl exclaimed and walked up to her husband and gave him a hug.

"Just a little misunderstanding is all," Raker said in answer to both of them as he walked over to Diane.

"Give us a ride down to where I parked the Jeep, and we'll tell you all about it," Art said.

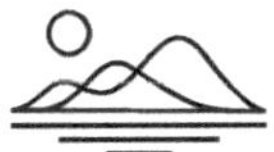

CHAPTER 6

"I could do that for you, if you want me to. It happened in my county. My jurisdiction," Sheriff Grossman said into his speakerphone. He shifted uncomfortably in the swivel chair behind his desk.

"No. No. Dennison was a good man. A little eccentric, but completely reliable. Didn't always get along with everyone, but he always did a good job. This is awful. An accident. Terrible." The man on the line was Gerald Baldwin, the director of the North Carolina Department of Environment and Natural Resources, Division of Land Quality—the department responsible for regulating dams throughout the state.

"An accident, yes. That's what it looks like at the moment. My deputies are still on the scene checking things out. We just started interviewing people. The body is at the hospital, and a death certificate is being prepared. We'll transfer it to the coroner. The family will need to make the arrangements to transport it back to Raleigh."

"Let me know when the coroner and the medical examiner are done." Baldwin sighed. "Damn, I don't want to call Marie about this. This is . . . worse than awful. He was only supposed to be up there for the day to check out the dam and the report Greg Lee filed a couple of months back. Lee

31

insisted the dam was in trouble. It's an old structure with a lot of problems. I just got through writing a letter to the property owners up there about it."

"I heard about the dam trouble. Everybody's alarmed," the sheriff replied. "You can't see any trouble, though. No seepage."

"I know. Dennison argued Lee's reports couldn't possibly be correct, and the dam couldn't deteriorate as quickly as Lee was reporting. Then Lee caught Dennison going through his desk right after work one afternoon and all hell broke loose. The two of them kept arguing about it. Then that Schreve woman shows up in Raleigh and raises so much hell about getting a deadline set. The governor's office finally said they wanted everything verified. Rumors about the dam failure were being used to pressure people into selling their properties."

"That's been going on for a long time. I can't see anything wrong with the dam, but I'm no engineer."

"That's why I sent Dennison up there," Baldwin said. "He knows the area. He went up there on a Saturday because he wanted to take the time to look up some people he knew. He had some kind of vendetta going against the developers. He felt his parents were conned into buying their land, which turned out to be impossible to build on . . . a ravine. Cost a fortune to build in it. He'd probably love to see the dam fail as a way of getting even, but he was an engineer. He argued with Lee about it until I finally told him to put up or shut up."

"I don't envy you the job of telling the widow. I'll call you when we're ready to release the body."

CHAPTER 7

"You said this road leads to another entrance to the development?" Raker asked after Cheryl let the two men off near Art's Jeep.

"Yes. It isn't used very much. We thought about closing it, but nobody wanted to spend the money to do it."

"Can we head out that way?" Raker asked.

"Sure. It leads to a county road, and we can take it back to the cabin." Art started the Jeep and crept forward in the grassy track that served as a roadway. After a few hundred yards, they rounded a bend in the woods and found a green pickup truck blocking their way.

"Shit," Art exclaimed, hitting the brakes. "Ramsay's fucking truck." He rolled down the driver-side window. "Hey Cleve," he yelled, "you don't own the goddamn road. Move this heap!"

A short man emerged from the brush carrying a shovel. "Keep your shorts on, Nichols." The man walking toward them had on camouflage fatigues and boots. His shaved head was uncovered, and he glared at Nichols through aviator sunglasses.

"Who's he?" Raker asked.

"Cleve Ramsay. An asshole."

"How the fuck would I know anyone was coming?" Ramsay muttered, tossing the shovel into the open bed behind his tool box and opening the cab door. He backed up several yards before finding a small dry clearing where he could pull off and make room for Nichols to pass.

"Thanks," Nichols said to Ramsay as his Jeep slowly pulled past the man's truck.

"Fuck you," Ramsay replied. "What the hell are you doing down here anyway?"

Nichols slowed to a stop. "Dennison just got shot down at the dam."

"Dennison?"

"Yes. He worked on the property owners' association before you bought in up here."

"So? They think it's murder?" Ramsay asked.

"That's yet to be determined. I see your deer rifle on the rack in the back of your cab. You been shooting around down here?" Art asked.

"No."

"I am going to tell the sheriff we ran into you and you had a gun in your truck. Just so you know."

"Fuck you, Nichols. It's a free country."

"Just thought you ought to know. See ya." Art released the clutch and his Jeep surged forward.

"Kiss my ass, do-gooder. What do I care? Go ahead and tell him."

"Who was that?" Raker asked as they pulled away.

"Just some redneck asshole that jumped up and nominated himself at a POA meeting a few years ago and got elected by acclamation. Then he started throwing his weight around. Got really abusive with people, and I took him on over whether he had the right to fire a duly elected officer. He wanted to go to an attorney for an opinion. That was okay with me, but I said I'd have to agree on the attorney we chose. At that, he just up and quit. Threw in the towel."

"Why would he be down here below the dam?"

"He bought up several lots here and wanted to put up some log cabins, some do-it-yourself kits of some kind. But he never got anything started . . . He's pissed at me. At the county commissioners. Got a chip on his shoulder."

"He had a gun."

"I know. He always has a gun with him," Nichols said. "I don't think he ever really quit the army when he was discharged."

"It was a rifle. It had a scope on it."

"Yeah. I saw that."

Raker studied him. "You are going to report that to the sheriff, right?"

"Yes. It'll make a lot of trouble for him, and that suits me fine. It's been almost forty-five minutes since the shooting, and if he was the shooter, he sure as hell wouldn't be hanging around down here. It's at least 700 yards back to the dam. He didn't have the shot."

"He could've gone through the woods and then retreated back to where we found him."

"You heard him. He didn't even know who Dennison was. I'll let the sheriff sort it out," Art replied.

"You know him. I don't," Raker shrugged. "He needs to be included among those the deputies question."

"Agreed," Nichols said, looking both directions at the intersection with the county road. "So what's with you and Diane . . . if you don't mind my asking."

"Nothing, really."

"It's none of my business, but—"

"I don't mind," Raker interrupted. "We kept running into one another at the supermarket, and one day I asked her to lunch. I hadn't dated anyone since Susan died. I was tired of being alone. I was getting depressed . . . drinking too much."

"I can't see you alone for the rest of your life. We thought about hooking you up with someone."

"Others have tried that. I'll get invited out to dinner and sure as hell there'll be an unaccompanied female there." Raker shook his head. "I want to go at my own pace. Anyway, one thing led to another, and finally one night, Diane asked me if I wanted to come into her place after a date. I decided to give it a shot. Big mistake. I started to get tense, started feeling as if I was being unfaithful to Susan. The more it didn't work, the more self-conscious I became. I'm sixty-two. I'm no high school kid ready to climb into the back seat with someone. Susan and I were used to one another. Now it's . . . it's just different."

"But you're still dating her?"

"Yes. She's been really gracious about it. She said she was okay with waiting. She said she wasn't looking for a fuck-buddy . . . a new term for me that kind of set me back. We finally made it happen one night, but it's only a now-and-then thing. That's my fault. I get what they call 'performance anxiety.' " Raker chuckled. "But I'm not in love with her. It's too matter-of-fact. We were still trying to make things work out when your invitation came along a couple of weeks ago, and I asked her if she wanted to come up here with me."

"She seems nice from the little I've seen of her. She's cute."

"Too spacey for me. I've got to break it off. She's had a rough history. Her first marriage ended in a divorce after she had an affair. She's a little out of touch with herself."

CHAPTER 8

"Who got shot? And what on earth were you guys doing in the sheriff's van?" Cheryl asked the minute the two men entered the house.

"Norm Dennison," Art replied. "He's dead. Jim and I went below the dam to look things over, and a couple of deputies picked us up thinking we had something to do with the shooting."

"Norm Dennison?" Cheryl asked.

"Yes."

"The guy that started the lawsuit against Dixie States Development?"

"The very same."

"He tried to nail those people for the way they mislead folks about the property here and not keeping promises about the roads and the water system."

"I remember," Art said. "He was really pissed about the way his parents were screwed. Obsessed is more like it. He kept wanting to go after Dixie States. Everybody else gave up and tried to forget it. Then he just gave up too. Stopped showing up for meetings. Never came around anymore."

"I keep trying to piece this together listening to everyone," Raker interjected. "It's beautiful up here . . . very nice . . . but this is a fairly primitive development compared to most. Somebody must have tried at one time to make a go of it."

"A rip off from the get-go," Art said. "The map the Dixie States showed people made these tiny lots look like an acre or more because nothing was to scale. The map didn't show the topography either. Some of the lots were nothing more than cliffs or swamps. People thought they had something. Then they'd come up here and realize they'd been ripped off."

"They bought sight unseen?" Raker asked.

"Most of the buyers were from Florida. They bought lots thirty-five to forty years ago. It's a full day of driving to get here from Florida, longer if you're coming from Miami. The nearest airport is either Charles City or Winston-Salem, and then you need to rent a car and drive for two hours. Dixie States put out a couple of newsletters with attractive photos of the place, and they were able to convince buyers that everything was on the up and up."

"Same with Dennison's parents," Cheryl explained, looking at Raker. "They bought four adjacent lots—all of them worthless. Dennison's father went back to Dixie States to see if he could trade his lots in for something he could build on. Dixie States refused. Dixie States held the mortgage. Dennison's dad stopped making payments, and Dixie States foreclosed on him. His credit was bad overnight. His father had a heart attack over it."

"They had to be doing business across state lines," Raker said. "Did anyone advise the federal authorities?"

"They may have. By the time we moved in here, it was a closed chapter in the history of the place. Nobody talked about it anymore. I found out only after I got to know people better," Nichols replied. "The homeowners sued Dixie States and won, but Dixie States was the mortgagor, and the court ordered all payments go toward retiring the mortgages. Dixie States lost the legal battle and had to forgive the mortgages. The people who sued them ended up with the land but owed nothing on it. It didn't solve any-thing. The property owners want to be awarded damages for the promises that were not kept. Then the roads could be completed. The water system would be extended so it serviced the entire area. But none of that ever hap-pened. All anyone got out of it was their mortgages were forgiven."

"Dennison vowed he'd get even," Cheryl added. "He got transferred down east, and we didn't see as much of him. A new guy came up here on inspections, Greg Lee." She pointed at her husband. "By the way, you've got a message on the answering machine, Art. From Helen Schreve. You need to listen to it. She's goes on and on until she's bleeped off the line."

"She can go to hell."

"No. You need to listen to it. She's hysterical."

"About what?"

"The property owners' backup CD to the billing program. She wants you to take it over to her house so that she can turn it over to the new treasurer."

"I told her I want to hold onto it in case we ever have a dispute about dues. It's two years out of date, for Chrissake. She knows that. They always write me first because my name's on the bill."

"Why don't you just make a copy and give her the original," Cheryl said. "Then she'll stop bugging you. She says the new secretary/treasurer needs it."

"Why doesn't he ask me then? He's got a phone. She's not on the board. Just erase the message. I don't want to listen to it."

Diane turned to Raker and in a stage whisper said, "He likes bugging that woman. That's the real story."

The phone rang. "I'll bet that's her again," Cheryl said. "You know how persistent she is."

"Let the answering machine get it," Art directed.

When the machine completed its recorded response, a woman's voice came on the speaker. "Mr. and Mrs. Nichols, this is Carla Thompson. I'm a friend of Marie Dennison and I'm calling on her behalf. She just received word that Norm has been shot. Oh dear . . ." The woman pinched off her words and cleared her throat. "Forgive me. It's a shock. She asked me to call because she wants to talk to you."

Art lunged at the phone and picked it up. "That's fine, Ms. Thompson. I'll be happy to speak with her."

"Mr. Nichols, this is Marie Dennison—"

"Marie, yes. I am so sorry over what happened. How can I be of help?"

"I need to make arrangements to have Norm's body brought back to Raleigh. I want to use people we know here. They're sending one of their vehicles with a driver up to get Norm, and I want to accompany the body back. I'm going to follow the hearse in my own car. A friend has agreed to drive me. I just can't . . . can't let him come back without any family with him. I haven't told his mother yet."

"I understand. How can I help?"

"Norm always said to contact you if anything ever happened to him. He said you could be trusted. He liked you. He liked you very much."

"I liked him also, Marie. We worked very well together."

"I have all his papers. He worked so hard to document everything about his parents' land up there and that company in Florida. I want to bring all his files with me tomorrow. Can I meet you somewhere and turn everything over to you?"

"I'll be glad to meet you. How about the Baden County Hospital? That's likely where you'll be picking up the body." Art hesitated before adding, "But, Marie, really, I am no longer an officer in the homeowners' association. His papers should go to one of the officers. I can deliver them to somebody for y—"

"Oh, no. No! Norm hated those people. He said you were the only honest man there. He told me to give the files to you. You alone. It's almost as if he knew something would . . ." Her voice broke off.

"Okay, Marie. Please, don't give it another thought. I'll be glad to take charge of his files."

"I'm so pleased," Marie said. "It'd be a comfort to me to know that I did as he wanted me to . . . Where should we meet at the hospital? In the parking lot, or is there a gas station nearby or something? I don't know the area like Norm did . . ."

"Why don't you call me when you get into town? It'll take you about four hours to get up here from Raleigh. I'll wait until I hear from you."

"Okay, yes, that's fine. And thank you! This means so much to me. It would mean a lot to him too."

"I understand."

"We'll want to come back to Raleigh as soon as we have Norm's body. The funeral director won't want to wait for me, and I do want to follow the hearse on the return trip. You understand?"

"Perfectly," Art said. "I'm only ten minutes away, and I'll come just as soon as you call."

"Fine. Fine. Thank you, Mr. Nichols." She took a deep breath and thanked him one more time before hanging up.

"What do you suppose that was all about?" Cheryl asked as Art walked back to his chair.

"What a shock that would be. God, Dennison couldn't be more than forty-eight or forty-nine years old. I feel sorry for her."

"Do they have any children?" Diane asked.

"No. They tried to adopt some years back. I remember him talking about it, but they weren't successful."

"Just don't—promise me!—don't get involved again," Cheryl pleaded. "It won't be good for you. Those Schreve people . . . they're horrible. Arrogant. Irritating. Promise me."

"I won't get pulled into anything. I'm just doing this for Marie. Who knows what she has? Probably nothing. Norm just kept getting dirt on Dixie States. I'll turn it over to somebody else. I don't want anything to do with Schreve or any of them. I did my time."

The phone rang once more.

"What the hell?!" Art said.

"Let the machine get it. It's probably Helen Schreve again," Cheryl responded.

"Mr. Nichols, this is Sheriff Grossman. I understand from my deputy that a Detective James Raker is a houseguest of yours this weekend. Please call me back. I would like to talk to Raker before he returns to Charles City."

Art picked up the phone. "Sheriff, yes, Detective Raker is here with us. I'm sorry, I was in the other room. Would you like to talk to him? He's right here, but now that you're on the line, you should know Raker and I ran into Cleve Ramsay below the dam after the shooting. He was down there with a rifle. I told him I'd be reporting it."

"He'd be questioned anyway if he lives anywhere near the dam," the sheriff said.

"He doesn't. He lives down 221, near Todd."

"Cleve Ramsay . . . Okay, I've made a note. Now, can I speak with Raker?"

Raker chatted briefly with the sheriff and hung up. "He wants to see me in his office," Raker said.

"Now?" Cheryl asked.

"Well, tomorrow is Sunday, and we'll be driving back in the afternoon."

"Okay, listen," Art said, "I'll drive you there, and the girls can join us afterward for dinner. We wanted to take you guys out anyway. Cheryl can bring Diane into town, and we can meet up."

CHAPTER 9

Art delivered his friend Raker to the front door of the Baden County office building. "I'll be waiting for you in the lobby," he said as Raker got out of the car.

The sheriff's office was on the second floor of the building—a new facility that had opened a few months earlier. The air inside was thick with the scent of carpet adhesive and fresh vinyl wall covering. Raker was directed by the receptionist to the office on the opposite side of the waiting area.

"Thanks for coming in to see me on such short notice," the sheriff said, extending his hand.

Raker noticed the office was set up to impress. Framed pictures lined the top of the credenza behind the sheriff's desk, most of them showing the sheriff shaking hands with other local and state political figures. At the center was a color picture of President Clinton shaking hands with the sheriff when Clinton visited the county to speak at a ceremony designating the New River as a wild river.

"Have a seat, Detective," Grossman said, gesturing to the chair across from him. "I just got off the line with your old boss, Sheriff Johnston. He sends you his best."

"I guess we parted friends." Raker smiled, noticing how precisely the sheriff's desk was organized: the inbox was empty, and the outbox was stacked neatly with several files. *Probably a demanding guy to work for*, Raker thought.

"So, you were the guy who broke the case at Heron Lake a couple of years ago?" Grossman asked.

"I've always considered that case a failure," Raker replied.

"I understand you're head of security with Southern World Textiles. Is that correct?"

"Yes."

"We've got a common problem. I called your home office late on Friday and found out you're the guy I needed to talk to, and then your name popped up with the people at the dam this morning." The sheriff leaned forward and rested his forearms on the blotter of his desk.

"So this is not about the shooting?" Raker asked.

"No. Why? Did you have anything more on it?"

"No, I just assumed that was the reason . . ."

"I'm going to hold the case open until we've questioned everyone out there," Grossman said, "but at this point it looks like an unfortunate accident."

"Any reason why that man would get shot? Was he involved in anything in the area?"

"No. He was up here just for the weekend. He works for the state. No record. Why?"

"His widow called my friend and wants to deliver a box of her husband's files to him. They were both involved with the property owners' association."

"I see. Probably has something to do with their work together then. Let me know if there's more to it than that." Sheriff Grossman sat up straighter, "The reason I called you is your company has a plant here in Baden County, a finishing plant. We are closing in on one of the employees there, a man we suspect is selling meth, or 'home stone' as some call it up in Virginia. Things have progressed to a point where you need to be brought in on it, and it seemed like the kind of conversation we should have in person rather than over the phone."

"I agree. Is this guy selling on the premises?"

"We think so. We also think he might be working with some of the truckers coming in to pick up and deliver product elsewhere in the Southeast. We think he has a fairly big operation. We've got problems like this all over the county. Years ago, it was moonshine. Now it's pot and meth. Hardly a month goes by that we don't bust up a lab or find a bumper crop somewhere up in the hills."

"You know who he is?" Raker asked.

"We've narrowed it down. The kids call him 'The Southern Source,' and that's helped. You might not think it in a small rural area like this, but there is a lot of traffic. A whole network; a chain of command in place. This 'Southern Source' is near the top. He puts out the stuff down the chain from him. They cut it. They distribute further and maybe sell some direct."

"So, like in a city."

"The same."

Raker nodded. "What do you want from me?"

"Just let your people know. We want this guy. We know he's there, but he's been very careful. Most don't know him by his real name."

"How much does our plant manager here know about what is going on?"

"Nothing."

"He's under suspicion?"

"We don't know who to trust out there. We think this guy works on the plant floor. Do you know the manager?"

"No, but I'll have him checked out. Depending on how that turns out, we may need to bring him in on what is going on."

"I know," the sheriff replied, "that's the reason for this meeting . . . to get the ball rolling. The management people out there are well-known in town and respected. Nothing has turned up that would implicate any of them. We've been working our way up the distribution chain. All those clowns say they'd take jail any time rather than roll up on a supplier. But once we bring them in, the story changes. They'd give up their own mothers if it meant things would go easy for them." He sighed and tossed his pen on the desk. "Nobody we've picked up so far knows who the Southern Source guy is, but one dealer reported a gal who supplies him deals with the Southern guy direct. She knows him by name. We want to pick her up and see if she'll tell us who he is. See if she'll roll up on him."

"I understand. I'll talk to President Becker on Monday. Here's my card. My cell, work, and home phone numbers are on it. Call anytime. I'd rather have a call that turns out to be nothing than miss something important," Raker said, standing up from his chair.

The sheriff pushed back from his desk and stood to shake Raker's hand. "You get anything direct from your company, let me know. We'll keep you in the loop and won't make a move without you knowing about it, okay? Thanks again for coming."

CHAPTER 10

Nichols parked the car and walked back to the sheriff's office. Events had moved so fast during the day that he and Raker did not get the chance to visit as they had anticipated. Forty-eight years had passed. They parted company the evening of their high school graduation, and their paths never crossed again until nearly a year ago, when out of the blue, Raker called. Art had been surprised. The two were not great pals in high school. Raker was the quiet, brainy guy who got elected to office, a champion debater—not one of the gang on campus that Art usually hung out with; Raker was not one of the jocks. In fact, after-school jobs kept Raker from competing in any sports.

Years earlier, Nichols had heard Raker lived somewhere in the Melville County area, that he was in law enforcement, but he never made contact with his former classmate.

"You'll never find my place," Art said when the detective called. "We're way back in the hills. It's all wooded, and people get lost coming here for the first time. Why don't we do this . . . I'll meet you in town at Frazier's, okay? You can't miss it. It's right on the main drag, on the left as you come into town."

Nichols recognized Raker immediately. His friend would stand out anywhere because of his full head of thick gray hair. He might have been somewhat shorter than Art remembered, but he looked fit and ten years younger than his age. Art pulled his car over to the curb and got out. Raker greeted him warmly.

They caught up over a long lunch. As Art had suspected, Raker had completed four years of college at the University of Iowa and went into the service. When he was discharged, Raker found his parents had moved again. His father had lost his battle with the chain stores to keep his small hardware store going, and he collapsed into bad health from exhaustion. Raker knew his parents could not have saved enough to manage well during retirement, and he decided to do all he could to help them. He put his plans for graduate school on indefinite hold and signed on as a rookie with the Minneapolis police department.

Nichols also did not consider graduate school. He set out to be a high school coach, football, basketball, maybe field and track. He was recruited to play football for the St. Leo's University, a Catholic, Division III, men's university located in south-central Minnesota. The only other school to express interest in him was St. Thomas in St. Paul. After visiting both campuses, Nichols enrolled at St. Leo's as a business administration major which seemed, at the age of eighteen, to be the start at a management career when he graduated.

Nothing worked out as planned. He reinjured his shoulder during football practice—an old, painful injury of the rotator cuff to his left shoulder. The trainers fixed a brace for him so he could continue to play, but the apparatus was too restrictive. Never fast on his feet, the limited movement in Art's left arm slowed him down all the more, so he eventually ended up quitting. The coach urged him to work hard at physical therapy so he would be ready to go the next season, but Art knew he was through with football.

The college game was much quicker than he remembered high school football to be. There was more competition for starting positions. At six-feet-four and 220 pounds, Art was no longer a big guy on the team. He was going up against upperclassmen who outweighed him by fifty pounds and beat him by five yards in the forty-yard dash. He wasn't playing for his hometown. Art couldn't walk downtown on a Saturday morning and have businessmen pat him on the back to congratulate him for his performance under the lights the night before.

Nichols managed to attain honor role grades in high school without ever learning how to study. Two years of accounting were required for a degree in business administration. He found it confusing. Double entry systems were more complicated than fitting a set of headers onto a flathead Ford V-8. Confusion led to bewilderment, bewilderment to frustration, and when he logged a C for the first semester, Art knew he would never satisfy the prerequisite for his major. He switched to liberal arts at the start of the second semester.

It was a good choice. He had always liked history and literature. He could teach English, history, or social studies at the high school level and still get on a coaching staff somewhere as an assistant. Graduation was a long way off. He began to enjoy college. His grades improved. He became a staff reporter for the campus newspaper. Everything was getting easier.

Nichols, as required, had registered for the draft upon his eighteenth birthday. Friends enlisted in the National Guard to avoid being called up while the Vietnam War was going on. Art knew he had a college deferment. Because St. Leo's was a land grant school, students were required to take two years of Army ROTC. Nichols enjoyed the classes. He had been interested since boyhood in World War II. Now he had a uniform, an M-1 rifle, and could drill with his company once a week.

"Yes, you've got a deferment while you are enrolled in college," the campus recruiter told him. "But you're single. You'll be subject to the draft as soon as you graduate. They draft the oldest eligible first. You'll be . . . what? Twenty-one, twenty-two? They are not drafting under the age of nineteen right now. Companies aren't going to hire guys who are subject to the draft. Get your service out of the way first. Serve out three years active duty, and you go into the reserves. You won't be subject to a call up again unless it is a real emergency. You go in as an officer; not as an enlisted man. The army can help with your college expenses the last couple of years."

So, Art enrolled.

Nobody was in the reception area of the sheriff's office as he stepped off the elevator. He picked out the nearest chair. So many years had gone by. Raker seemed like a different guy, still quiet and thoughtful, but easier to talk to. Raker had been in service also, in Germany, where he had avoided combat.

Everyone changes. Vietnam changed Nichols's life. He no longer thought about how he had been swallowed up in the jungle and the firefights, the carnage, and the drugs. He served. He did everything that was asked of him.

The Veterans Administration had nothing to offer men like Nichols who came out of Vietnam changed by the horrors of dank jungle combat. His father's generous way with others, an openness and trust in the good will of friends and strangers, became a legacy of hope for Art. Instead of closing down, as so many men did to deal with the loss of contentment in their lives, Art became more available to others. He was confident he would recover from the emotional damages of combat more quickly if he dealt straightforwardly with others and sought friendship.

Art knew his former self only as a memory—the good-looking, broad-shouldered young guy, tan as a nut with a winning grin, jogging the last block toward home for supper as the town hall clock struck the hour. His past was stored away like an archived Technicolor movie. He could view it, but he could no longer feel it.

To distance himself from the trauma, he dedicated himself to working with others who needed to rediscover a capacity for joy. He jumped at the chance to attend a workshop conducted by Tory Pace, a nationally recognized motivational speaker whose message emphasized freeing oneself from the constraints of self-defeating beliefs.

Pace was electrifying, funny, and profound. "That was great. That was just great," Art gushed when he intercepted Pace in the hotel lobby. Pace stopped abruptly and shook Art's hand. "I'm Art Nichols, Mr. Pace."

"Of course you are," Pace snapped back with a broad grin. "And what are you all about, Mr. Nichols?"

"I work with a lot of veterans, and there was so much in your speech for the guys . . . God, enough material for a whole year."

"You work with veterans?" Pace asked quickly.

"Yes."

"In what capacity?"

"It's all pretty much *ad hoc*. Churches, VFW, that sort of thing. The Veterans Administration isn't doing much to help guys adjust when they come back. Communities are wary, because the war was unpopular. There's a lot—"

"Here's my card," Pace interrupted. "I want to talk to you more about this. You live here? In Minneapolis?"

"Yes."

"Call the number on the card and ask for Sherrie. She'll set up a time for the two of us to get together."

Art's reverie was interrupted when he heard the door open to the sheriff's office. Raker stepped into the reception area.

"That's it?" Art asked, looking up.

"Yup. Let's go join the girls."

CHAPTER 11

"So, did the sheriff say whether the shooting was an accident or not?" Cheryl asked when the waitress set the coffee in front of them. The couples were seated in a booth at The Chop House, a popular restaurant on the northeast side of town.

"I'll take that whenever you're ready," the waitress said, placing the bill on the table.

"I've got it," Raker said, snatching the register printout.

"We said we'd take you out," Nichols countered.

"You guys got breakfast. You put us up. My turn," Raker insisted.

"Well? Was the shooting an accident?" Cheryl asked again.

"They're still investigating," Raker responded.

"What do you think?" Cheryl persisted.

"It isn't my case."

"Okay . . . so, suppose it was?"

"I'm sorry. I learned a long time ago not to comment on investigations being conducted by someone else. I don't want to be quoted anywhere. I don't mean to be abrupt."

"I won't breathe a word," Cheryl teased.

Raker already liked Cheryl. She had a quick wit and an easy way about her that matched her bright smile and warm brown eyes. She pulled her blond hair back into a ponytail that reminded Raker of a college girl. *There,* he thought, *why not one like her.* Cheryl must have been five-foot-eight because she came up to Art's shoulder when they stood side-by-side and, like him, she had a healthy aura about her, trim and athletic looking.

"I know you won't. It's just my policy. No offense intended."

"Okay, I understand. So, Diane, you've been awfully quiet," Cheryl observed.

"This has been so pleasant," Diane said with a sad smile, "being in the mountains like this, seeing those churches this morning. You guys are so lucky."

"More than you know," Nichols responded.

"Well, it's just so peaceful. So quiet. I didn't know where I was for a minute when I woke up this morning. I listened to all the birds outside and the wind in the trees."

"I figure I'll live at least ten years longer because we have the place here," Nichols said.

"Can I ask you something?" Diane said, looking at Art.

"Only if I don't have to answer if I don't want to."

"That's fine. You walk with a hitch in your step. At least, that's what my daddy called it."

"Vietnam."

"You were wounded? In the leg?" Diane asked.

"Yes."

"How awful! It must still bother you."

"I hardly notice anymore. It's part of me," Art said. "I never took up running or anything like that so it isn't a handicap of any kind. I got hit with shrapnel when I ran out to rescue a couple of cases of Coca-Cola sitting on the tarmac at an airstrip."

"No, you didn't!" Diane giggled. "You're kidding me."

"No. No. I'm serious. We had incoming. Mortars. We were all hunkered down in a dugout, and then someone noticed a pallet of Coke had been offloaded and left out in the open when the shelling started. The guys were afraid it was going to get hit, so three or four of us took off on a run for it. We couldn't get the whole pallet, but each of us tucked a case of cans under each arm and tried to run back. That's when I got it. Shrapnel in the right thigh. Really heroic stuff, right?"

"You must have felt awful. I mean, for something trivial like that," Diane said.

"Everything was trivial. It was insane. I was lucky I didn't get hurt worse when we were in the field. We were young. We didn't know any better. We were just there, and we did what we were told. I don't mind that you asked, but I'd rather not talk about it anymore."

"I'm sorry," Diane demurred.

"No. That's fine. People notice. I'm used to it." Drawing a deep breath, Art noticed the dining room had emptied of customers while the foursome was visiting. "About time we head back anyway."

Once back at the cabin, the couples retired to the deck overlooking the valley and the lake below as dusk softened the shadows. The quiet brought back memories for Diane of the evenings in northern Wisconsin when she and her husband spent summer weekends with their children building a cabin. Tom had always been so enthusiastic. Always took on more than he could handle. And the cabin was yet another monster project he barely had time to complete. He underestimated the cost. But they worked on it anyway. Worked each day until the sunset. Worked by the light of a campfire, and then went to bed looking up at the stars in the clear Wisconsin night. They completed the exterior, but the inside remained unfinished. The studs were exposed with only the subflooring in place.

When they split up, Tom moved to Cincinnati, Ohio. He came back for the kids who had lived with her for several months after the divorce. The children packed up, her daughter and her youngest son, kissed her goodbye, and she watched them drive away until the U-Haul trailer blocked her view of the rear window of their car. "I got hit by two empty rooms," she wept to a friend who called to see how she was doing. None of what was happening seemed real. None of it was turning out the way she thought things would.

"I thought maybe your pride would be hurt, but that's all," she remembered telling Tom during a counseling session.

She was surprised at how upset he became when she told him about her affair. Tom was away from home so much. He never had time for her except on weekends. She grew to enjoy the independence and having the children. She didn't want anything to happen between Neil and her, but it did, slowly, one cup of coffee at a time, until one day Neil admitted quietly, "You're really on my mind a lot."

"I know," Diane sighed. "You're in my thoughts all the time too." Neil was one of Tom's best friends. The two men had taken their sons camping and fishing together. Neil's wife, Louise, was a friend of Diane's also. They saw each other frequently at church. Life with Tom was no longer comfortable, and when the two couples were together, the tension was almost intolerable for Diane.

Tom sensed something was wrong. Diane tried to keep up a front, tried to keep him from suspecting anything, but it wasn't working. "You take the kids and go to California on this trip," Tom said one night after dinner about a vacation they had planned. "I don't feel like I'm a part of things any more. I feel shut out."

"But the children will want you. They won't go without you. You need to go for their sake," Diane argued. "I can't think of taking the big vacation you planned for us and not having you along." She couldn't trust Tom to understand. She couldn't tell him anything. What she was going through was not about Tom. It was about her. She never had any choices. She gave up college to marry Tom. Became Catholic to marry Tom and had four kids to show for it. She was thirty-four and had never had a chance to choose for herself or to decide what she wanted to do with her life. She was still young. Her life didn't need to be over. She didn't need to be standing by and waiting for the day the kids walked out the door for the last time.

Tom agreed she should go back to school to become a nurse. The kids were all out of the house during the day. But being in school reminded her of what she had missed. Everyone was younger, younger by as much as sixteen years. They were having fun, dating, going out after class, grabbing a beer and hooking up—for the fun of it. No commitments. No big emotional hang-ups. It was a part of life she never knew.

Then along came Neil. He paid attention to her. He was nice enough looking, a little older than Tom perhaps, but he had not gained weight the way Tom had. His body was vital and toned. She realized she had fallen in love with Neil while she was on vacation in California with Tom and the children. She missed Neil. She was sad without him and sad, too, that she was not enjoying the children. Tom was drinking too much. Every night!

Almost as if he felt he had to be as miserable as she was. When they returned home, she told Tom she wanted to go pick up Toby, their pet beagle, from the kennel. It gave her a chance to get away and meet with Neil so she could tell him how much she had missed him and how good it felt to be held by him again.

A couple of days later, she decided she could not let things go on as they were. Tom was not scheduled to leave town for a week, so one evening she told him she wanted some time alone with him. He agreed.

"What's this?" Tom asked entering the living room and noticing two of the dinning room chairs in the center of the room facing one another.

"This is an exercise I learned in counseling class," Diane replied, somehow embarrassed she had to explain it to him. "Please sit here and face me. I have something to tell you."

"Okay." Tom sat down and looked at her.

"We call this an honesty exercise. This is honesty night," Diane said, noticing the apprehension in Tom's face.

"Okay."

"I'm in love with someone else, Tom. I'm sorry, but it just happened. I didn't want it to happen, but it has. That's why you feel shut out. That's why things have been so strained these last few months between us."

"I knew it," Tom grumbled. "I knew something had to be going on."

"I'm sorry. I am, but I don't feel the way you want me to feel toward you anymore."

"Have you guys . . . slept together?"

"Only once. Just once." She could see Tom did not believe her. "We were riding around in the car one day, just talking. We drove by a motel, and he just sort of nodded toward it, and I nodded back. That's all." She could see her explanation was not helping. Tom was far more distressed than she thought he would be.

"Hey! Where have you been?"

The question startled Diane. Cheryl had spoken to her.

"We've been over here chatting away like magpies, and you're so far away." Cheryl studied her guest for a moment. Diane didn't smile often, but when she did, her face lit up, her brown eyes gleamed so that her complexion seemed even creamier. Cheryl understood why Raker would be attracted to her.

"I'm sorry," Diane said. "It's so peaceful here. Listening to night sounds as if the woods are drifting off to sleep. I just got pulled into all of it."

"It can happen," Cheryl said smiling. "C'mon. Tell us a little about yourself."

"There's not much to tell."

"Jim said you just moved to Charles City."

"Yes. That's right. I was working in Miami at a retirement village. I was the home visiting nurse. The village provided the service to the residents. It was really a way of keeping medical costs down. But I enjoyed the work. I liked the people . . . older folks. Most were very nice. Very appreciative."

"Why did you move?" Cheryl asked.

"A disagreement with the people who owned the place where I worked. Palmetto-Atlantic Development ran the retirement center. They have properties all over the Southeast. They wanted me to report more services for Medicare reimbursement than I was performing and to put in for services that were more serious procedures than what I provided. I thought it was dishonest. The company was run by a guy named Vernon Brost. A real bully. I didn't like him, so I quit."

"Good for you," Art said.

"And once I quit, I thought I'd move so I could be a little closer to my children. I have a son who lives in Virginia. A job came open in Charles City, and I applied for it."

"So where are you working now?" Cheryl asked.

"I'm still looking for a job. When I got to Charles City, the people said there had been a misunderstanding and the position I thought I was being hired for was filled. I was really bummed."

"I can imagine," Cheryl said.

"I had some money set aside so I started looking for something in rehab or being a home visiting nurse again, but I haven't found anything just yet. I can hold out a little longer and keep looking."

"Good luck. I admire your gumption," Cheryl said.

"I don't know about that. I can always find a job as a nurse. I just want something I think I'll like."

"At least you got away from those people. You'll never need to deal with them again," Art said.

"Yes. Thank goodness. I'm glad of that," Diane said.

CHAPTER 12

Deputy Hurdler saw Ramsay's pickup in the driveway as he approached on Highway 221. *Good. He's home*, he thought. Hurdler did not like chasing after people. He hoped checking around after the shooting at the dam was something the younger guys could handle, but the sheriff asked him to check out Ramsay. Apparently, the retired detective from Charles City and his friend had some kind of run in with Ramsay after the shooting, and the sheriff wanted special handling because of it.

Hurdler knew Ramsay. He had seen him around town and had spoken to him on occasion, but otherwise they did not have much to do with one another.

As Hurdler pulled his cruiser up the long gravel drive, Ramsay appeared on the front porch.

"What do you want?" Ramsay asked, as Hurdler walked up to meet him.

"Just routine, Cleve. You were down at the dam this morning, right? You were seen."

"Yeah, so?"

"You had your rifle with you."

"I always have my rifle with me. In my pickup. Fucking Nichols said something didn't he?"

"I just know you were there, and the sheriff sent me out to see what you were up to. A man got shot there this morning."

"Yeah. I heard," Ramsay replied.

"Can we go inside?"

"No. You can say what you have to say right here."

"Okay," Hurdler said, glaring at Ramsay, "what were you doing down there in the woods below the dam this morning at the time of the shooting?"

"I didn't know there was a shooting until Nichols told me."

"My question is what were you doing down there at that time?" Hurdler repeated.

"Checking my property."

"Checking it for what?"

"Surveyors' stakes. They did a shit job laying out all those lots way back when. Sometimes you can find a property line. Sometimes you can't. It costs $1,500 to get a survey crew out there. Surveyors hate the place. So I thought if could find the stakes, I could avoid hiring anyone."

"How many lots do you own below the dam?"

"Ten."

"What kind of rifle do you own?"

"A thirty-ought-six and a .22."

"Any other firearms?" Hurdler persisted.

"Only side arms."

"What side arms?"

"I've got a Ruger single-six .22 that I use for target practice and a Smith and Wesson snub nose .38."

"How long were you in the area below the dam?"

"From about 8:30 until 11:00 this morning. I gave up on finding the stakes."

"That's all flood plain down there anyway," Hurdler volunteered. "You might as well wait until the dam gives way 'cause it'll flood. Then you can build."

"Thanks for the free advice," Ramsay said. "I don't know the guy who got shot. Never heard of him."

"That was my next question. You have never had any contact with Norm Dennison, the victim?"

"I just said I never heard of the guy, for chrissake. No. I have never had one goddamn thing to do with him."

"Okay, that's it. Do you mind if I take a look at the rifle in your pickup?"

"Look away. You can see it through the back window. I don't have anything to hide."

Hurdler walked over to the pickup and saw that the rifle on the rack in the back was thirty-ought-six as Ramsay had said. "Unlock your truck, please," Hurdler yelled over his shoulder to Ramsay.

Ramsay trudged over to the pickup and opened the passenger's side door. Hurdler lifted the gun from the rack, pulled back the bolt to open the chamber, and sniffed. "Okay," he said and put the rifle back on the rack. "You let us know if you plan to leave the area," Hurdler said, turning back to Ramsay.

"You're shitting me. You guys think somehow I might've had something to do with this?"

"You were there," Hurdler replied flatly. "The sheriff's department is checking everyone who was in the area."

"Hadn't been for that asshole Nichols, nobody'd even known I was within miles of the place. What? They think it's a murder?"

"It's an open case."

"So . . . what? I'm supposed to stick around until you guys decide?"

"No. Just let us know if you're going to leave the area and when you'll be back."

CHAPTER 13

"Well, how the hell would I know what kind of information that woman has, Vernon? I don't even know her. Never met her. Dennison was no longer assigned here by the time we moved in. I guess I could be available . . . you know . . . introduce myself on behalf of the property owners' association . . . condolences and all that."

"Put it on the speaker!" Helen whispered loudly.

Frank waved her away.

"No. Do it! I want to hear!" Helen insisted, still whispering.

Frank turned his chair to put his back to her. He had taken Vernon Brost's phone call on his business line in his office, a room at the back of their lakeside home with its own entrance from the outside.

"It's tomorrow! My God, that's short enough notice." Schreve whirled around in his chair only to see his wife straining to hear both sides of the conversation. "Can you hold a minute, Vernon? Just a sec." He cupped his hand over the mouth piece and looked up at his wife. "This has nothing to do with you. Now, please, get out of my office. If you need to know any-thing, I'll tell you when I'm done. But get out now so I can concentrate on this call."

Helen glared at her husband. He was always fussy about his office and his privacy. She would find out, of course, somehow, even if it meant sneaking back into the room while he was gone and searching through his files. She closed the door behind her and waited to see if she could at least hear Frank's side of the conversation.

"Now, can you tell me?" Helen demanded moments later as her husband opened the door to his study.

"Dennison's widow is coming to accompany the body back to Raleigh tomorrow. He wants me to go into town and extend condolences to her."

"Why? My God, the man's parents sued Dixie States."

"A little PR never hurt."

"Like poking a hornet nest. You don't know her; what you say won't mean anything."

"From the property owners' association, not from me personally. It seems like the right thing to do," Frank said with a sigh. "Besides, someone told Brost the widow may bring up the dead man's files, and they may have a bearing on what we are trying to do with the development. Brost wants me to intercept the files on the grounds they belong in the hands of the POA."

"Well, when this blows over, the funeral is out of the way and all that, then I'm going back to the governor's office and push for a verification of the report on the dam."

"No. No, you're not. You will let matters take their own course. You've pushed this thing around too much already. You've made a nuisance out of yourself. People are fed up with you."

"Who's fed up? Who'd you hear that from?" Helen spun around and looked up at her husband.

"I don't suppose you thought for one second you were also responsible for that man getting shot yesterday," Frank sneered.

"Me? Why . . . that's ridiculous. Completely ridiculous. What an awful thing to say!"

"Yeah, well, who kept raising hell down in Raleigh? You! That's who. Couldn't let it ride. Kept yapping at the people . . . even the governor's office for chrissake . . . about the dam. Everybody was fine with the first report until you jumped in. That poor bastard Dennison was only here because of you. You just should have let it go." Frank turned as if to walk back into his office.

"Don't you yell at me and walk out like that. That's an outrageous thing to say. I . . . I just wanted the property owners to have some assurance . . . to know the truth. That man being here . . . his getting shot . . . I had nothing to do with that," Helen shouted.

"Don't shout at me either. You should've left well enough alone. At first I thought, yeah, hell, why not. She's the wife of the property owners' association president. Let her run. It demonstrates being involved . . . in caring. But would you let up anywhere along the line? Oh no. You keep pushing and harping and driving people nuts. That's the only reason they give in to you—they can't stand you anymore."

"So you say. Well, the owners have rights too. I was acting in their best interests, on their behalf," Helen snapped.

"And who the hell asked you anyway? You're not on the board. You're not an elected officer. It was the county commissioners all over again. You went down there about a leash law and insulted everyone. Pissed everyone off. Gave the whole development a bad name, and now we can't get shit done through them. They won't give us an ear on anything." Frank turned away from her.

"Don't change the subject. You always change the subject," Helen cried.

"I'm not changing the fucking subject. You are the subject. You've got the public relations skills of a rattlesnake. Your path is strewn with pissed-off people. People cross the street to avoid meeting you. I'm not changing the subject. I am telling you . . . for once and for all . . . back off, damn it. Just back off."

"That's not fair," Helen stammered.

"The damage you've done around here isn't fair to the people who go around patching up after you. Now that's my final word. I won't back you on anything anymore. As far as I am concerned, you're acting without backing by the board or the sanction of any of its officers, especially me. Got that?!" Frank walked into his office and closed the door.

"That's not fair, Frank. That's just not fair," Helen yelled at the closed door.

"Life isn't fair. Or hadn't you heard."

CHAPTER 14

"Do I get a hug, at least?" Diane asked, looking up at Raker.

"Of course," he replied. "A friendly hug."

"Yes. A friendly hug." The two embraced in the hallway leading to the guest bedroom in the Nichols's cabin. She tried to relax her body into his so he would feel her hips and her breasts.

He pulled back slightly, patted her on the shoulder, and said, "Good night."

"Good night," Diane sighed and dropped her gaze to the floor. "I can wait up for you."

"Good night," Raker repeated. "I'll be along later. I'll try not to wake you." He turned and walked back toward the living room. He wanted more time to visit with Art, but he also wanted Diane to be asleep when he eventually turned in.

Diane felt a sting of regret for suggesting she'd wait up for Raker. He had been clear since their first date about how uncomfortable he was about having sex, how he enjoyed her company but he had been married so long that he needed time. He had never been part of the wide open seventies,

67

the Me Decade, and he confessed he had been so happy with Susan all those years that he never felt he had missed out on anything.

She walked into the darkened bedroom and retrieved her floor-length nightie from under the pillow where she had placed it in the morning when she made the bed. Raker warned her that nights in the mountains were cooler. At least they would share a bed. Maybe something might happen. *One of the most decent guys I've met*, she thought.

The counseling she and Tom decided to try—with their minister and at the Bach Institute in Minneapolis—never worked out. Tom always won over the counselors assigned to them. At the Bach Institute, the therapist decided to separate them from the first, working one session with him and one session with her, but she could see the therapist was taking Tom's side. She told Tom she was quitting, that the counselor was incompetent, that he could continue if he wanted, but she was finished. She was not going to be judged without having someone on her side, without someone sticking up for her. Tom and the therapist could work together if he wanted. She wasn't going to admit she did anything to hurt anyone. She was hurt, too, and nobody seemed to care. Nobody cared she had been living a life that didn't feel like hers most of the time. Nobody cared she had given up so much or that she missed Neil.

"You've got a lot going on in your life," Trudie said early in Diane's individual therapy sessions. Diane found Trudie without consulting Tom and made an appointment with her. Trudie would be Diane's exclusive therapist. "Your feelings change so often on important subjects," Trudie continued, "like your marriage, your relationship with Neil, and your future. What can we do to sort out all those conflicting feelings? What do you think?"

"I don't know. They all feel real to me," Diane replied.

"Oh, I think they are real too," Trudie said. "But when I listen to you, it sounds like you are undecided about so many things. Do you think you are undecided?"

"Sometimes."

"Like when?"

"Lots of times. I mean, I had a hard time deciding what to talk to you about when I drove here this morning. My mind just rolls around and shifts from one thing and then to another."

"That sounds like a good description to me. That's how it seems when I'm listening to you. How does it feel to you?"

"I think my brain is a ball," Diane said with a laugh. "Just rolling around, but it hurts in some places, and I want to move away from where it hurts."

"I see. I can imagine."

"I had a little game when I was a girl. I could hold it in my hand. It was about the size of a postcard, and it had a picture in it under glass. The picture had holes in it and a little silver ball that I could roll around under the glass. Roll it from one little hole to the next. That's how life feels to me. Get stuck. Get unstuck. Get stuck again."

"That's a wonderful way to describe it, Diane," Trudie said. "Can you tell me about the holes where the ball comes to rest?"

"Sometimes it feels so wonderful to be with Neil. I'm as happy as I can be. I like being stuck there. But when I go home and see how distressed Tom is, I feel bad. I don't like being stuck at home anymore. I told Tom I'd stay so he wouldn't feel angry and hurt all the time, but I told him if Neil ever showed up on his motorcycle and asked me to leave with him, I would."

"You told Tom that?"

"Yes."

"And what did he say?"

"Nothing."

"Do you think he thought that was reassuring in anyway?" Trudie asked.

"No. But it was the truth. It seemed to me he should know."

"I see," Trudie said with a nod. "What are some other places the ball can get stuck in?"

"There's my mother. I don't like being with her, but I feel obligated. My daughter, Carolyn . . . I really enjoy my daughter. We laugh a lot. We laugh a lot at Tom. He gets angry and leaves the room when we do."

"How do you think your daughter feels about Tom?"

"She loves him, but she thinks he's funny too."

"How about the other children? Do they laugh at their father?"

"No. I mean, only when it is really funny and Tom knows it and he laughs too."

"You mean when the laughter is not at his expense?"

"He can take a joke. He's good-spirited usually. He's really good with the kids. I told him I loved him as the father of my children."

"What did you mean by that?"

"What? That's plain, isn't it? He's a good father. He's gone from home a lot, but he lets the kids know he loves them. He calls them when he is out of town. He does things with them when he comes back. Takes them fishing and out to games. He's very affectionate. Very nurturing."

"You admire that."

"Yes. Very much."

"So maybe there are at least two places where the ball comes to rest for you that involve Tom. One is with the good Tom who you love for the way he is with the children. And the other is the Tom you want to get away from, because he seems hurt and angry."

Diane squirmed in her chair. "Hey," she said suddenly, "maybe I'm the ball!" She laughed again and forced a smile. "And there is no place for me in the game except to go from one spot to the next."

"You think so?"

"Don't always do that. Don't always just ask me what I think, especially when I asked you what you thought."

"Okay. I simply want to be sure I understand because sometimes you sound distressed as you keep moving from one place to the next. Don't you find it that way?"

"Sometimes. But when I get to a good place, it's fine."

"So getting back to the good places, that's with Neil, and your daughter, and Tom as the father of your children. Are there other good places?"

"Work. I really enjoy my work and the people there."

"Nursing. I can see you as a nurse. And you like your associates at work?"

"Yes, very much. But I always need to go home afterward. I mean, sometimes I go out with the guys coming off shift and we grab a bite, but I ultimately need to go home."

"And that is not a good place."

"It's okay when Tom is not there."

"But not when he is," Trudie said.

"No. He waits for me. One night he prepared snacks for when I came home, and I was really late. He just tried to make me feel guilty about it."

"He was waiting up with a surprise and you didn't expect it. Is that it?"

"I guess, but it all turned out bad. The stuff he heated up cooled down and got mushy. Egg rolls. Ugh. They looked like dog turds on the plate. I think he did it on purpose, just to make me feel bad. I mean, why couldn't he just go to bed and let things be?"

"You didn't like disappointing him?"

"I didn't like that he did it—period! He set it up so it would fail. I know he did. But that's what I mean by rolling around. At times like that, I just hate it. I hate being where I am."

"I don't know Tom, but couldn't it be that he knew when you were getting off work and timed everything for when he thought you'd return?"

"I don't care what he thought. I didn't ask him to do it. I didn't want him to, you know. It's such a goddamn bother. Always a fuss. That's what I mean about the places I don't like being in. That's why I feel like my brain is a ball rolling from one hour to the next, day after day. Can you see that?"

"Yes. Yes, of course I can. I think it is a very good description of how you see your life at this time. You find yourself moving in and out of different situations. Some are pleasant. Some are distressing. Most of us experience those kinds of changes every day."

"So I'm not so different then. I'm not so different from other people."

"Everyone moves from one situation to the next every day. What matters is how you feel about moving from place to place . . . from situation to situation."

Trudie waited for Diane to respond. "There are too many sad places in my life," Diane finally said in a hoarse whisper. "My mother. Tom. Even Neil when I am away from him and not knowing from one day to the next. That's why I think my life is the ball . . . just rolling along, one day after the other. That's my life." She sighed.

"I see that too. Moving in and out of relationships and each one is different. Each one asks something different from you. Maybe the question we need to explore is, what causes the ball to roll? What causes the little card under the glass to shift so the ball changes direction and moves from one place to the next? One of these days we need to get in touch with the hand holding the game and hear what the hand has to say about why the ball is moving around the way it does."

"That's crazy." Diane giggled.

"Sounds funny, doesn't it? Well, it's an idea. You think about it, and we will talk about the hand next week. Okay?"

Diane left the session confused and angry. She thought about quitting. It would be hard to tell Trudie that she was going to quit. Maybe she just wouldn't show up for the next session. Trudie was turning out to be just like the other counselors she and Tom had seen over the months. Trudie wasn't on her side either.

Diane had never lived her life as if it belonged to her. Since childhood, she yielded to her father's intrusions at night while her mother waited in the hallway and pretended nothing was happening. Diane froze with horror at his nightly visits and the game of mousy he played with her. She cringed and shrank down to a tiny stone and saw herself lying at the bottom of a river of darkness flowing over her. Then it happened. One night, as she despaired at her daddy's approach, she left her body. She drifted away, pulled away by a warm unrelenting wind. She couldn't stop it. When it released her, Diane became the light of her own little body. Her voice belonged to someone else. The light of her withdrawn self cast a shadow of the body of the girl on the bedsheets as Diane hovered above it. She knew that night she could never stay on the bed again for her daddy. She would always choose to drift away in the warm wind when he came to her bedside.

Her withdrawal had frightened her the first time it occurred because she did not know what was happening. When he returned on subsequent nights, she slipped away again and again. After a while, she stopped noticing it was happening. She drifted up to the headboard of the bed and let the other little girl lie there and allow daddy to play. Diane even stopped looking at the girl on the bed. She gave the girl on the sheets a name. Her name was Margie. Margie seemed somehow to know about Diane. Margie knew she was helping Diane. Margie was proud of looking out for Diane. After a while, giving way to Margie was nothing at all, and Diane could easily ignore everything that was going on when Daddy was in the room. Diane didn't feel pain anymore. Margie felt it all. Margie knew it was how sex should feel. Margie turned the pain into passion. She turned the pain into sex.

The sound of people talking in the front room broke into Diane's reverie. *My God,* she thought, *why try so hard to please another man?* She walked over to the bed and sat down.

Diane made a big mistake when she called the minister during the period that Tom and she were counseling with him. She wanted to know what her pastor thought if she accepted an invitation from a guy at the hospital where she worked to go to New Orleans with him. She and Tom were separated at the time.

"Do you think we should let Tom in on our telephone conversation?" the minister asked her at the beginning of their next session.

"If you think we should," she replied.

"Do you want to tell him . . . or should I?" the minister asked.

"You."

"Diane called to ask me if I thought it was okay for her to go to New Orleans with a friend of hers, a man she knows from work. Isn't that about it, Diane?"

"Yes."

"Good thing I didn't say 'No' isn't it?" the minister directed at Diane.

Tom wanted to leave the room, but there was nowhere to go except a small kitchen off to one side. She could hear him pounding on the counter. She could hear him crying. But he finally returned to his chair and sat back down.

"I can't believe this," he said. "I'm working my ass off in what I think is a good faith effort to work things out between us. You mean you had to call our counselor to know whether it was okay or not to shack up with this guy? Couldn't you decide that for yourself? Going off for a weekend with some other guy? No moral conflict here? Right? Doesn't it put what we're doing here in any jeopardy? You didn't want to be responsible for your own decision?"

"I just thought I should ask," Diane countered. "I did not want to do anything that would affect our counseling here."

"Good thing I didn't say 'No' isn't it," the minister repeated.

"I decided not to go. Doesn't that count for something?" Diane pouted.

Tom had moved out at that time, and he kept traveling to one city after another, week after week. Why shouldn't she have a chance to get away? But she asked at the wrong time. They were supposed to be working at reconciling their differences and perhaps getting back together. Her question ended their sessions with the minister.

"You can help him move," the minister had said in an earlier session. The way he said it made her think he knew more about what was going on than he let on. The children came together one evening, and Tom told them they were going to separate. Tom crossed the room from one child to the next, trying to explain, trying to console but offering none of them any hope life would go on as it had always been. The older boys were resigned. The younger ones cried.

Diane remembered she dropped her head as Tom moved from one child to the next, and hiding her face in her hands, cried, "Oh God, I'm causing all of this."

She slipped her nightgown over her head and let if fall to her feet. During the summer so many years ago, when the kids were young, all of them slept in the same unfinished room at the cabin on the lake in Wisconsin. Tom made love to her quietly one night so none of the children would hear. During those days, when they were all together as a family, she never thought things would ever change. She never thought her life would be as it was now. She was older, not as attractive, just another face in the crowd, just another unhappy woman well into middle age.

CHAPTER 15

"Nightcap?" Nichols called down the hallway, hearing Raker on his way back to the living room.

"Think I'll pass."

"Just one. With me. For old time's sake."

"Well, if you put it that way," Raker conceded. "Got any brandy?"

"Oh yeah. Two fingers?" Nichols went to the kitchen and retrieved a beer from the refrigerator and then snatched an open bottle of brandy from the counter. "We really haven't had much time to get caught up with one another given all the extracurricular activity today."

"I know." Raker sat down in a recliner near the fireplace and took the snifter from his friend. "I don't have anything that exotic to report. Susan and I thought we had made it to the easy part of life when we moved to Charles City. Then she found out she had cancer, and in a little more than a year-and-a-half, I was alone. Life's not been the same since."

"And things with Diane are not going to work out."

"No. She's a good person. There's just no connection. She'll sit across the table from me, and I feel like I'm working as hard as I can to keep a conversation going. She's intelligent, but there's no meeting of the minds.

She's always in a different place. She kind of slides around on me. I can't figure out who she is. That doesn't work for me."

"Another Susan then?"

"I don't think there's another Susan anywhere. I can't imagine it. What we had . . . well, one in a million I'd say from talking to other guys. Maybe because we never had kids. Just the two of us. We had time for one another and we clicked." Raker looked into his snifter and shook his head.

"I'd be lost if something happened to Cheryl," Nichols replied. "I don't know why she took up with me. I had nothing to offer."

"She told me she thought you were cute," Raker chided.

"Yeah. I know. Hobbled ol' Vietnam vet, and she thinks I'm cute. The woman's got no taste. We'll disagree on something, and she'll say, 'If only you weren't so cute,' and that will be the end of it."

"Where's Cheryl now?" Raker asked.

"She always reads before going to bed. She's in the bedroom. She wanted me to say 'goodnight' for her."

"You're lucky, Art. How long have the two of you been married?"

"Twenty-three years."

"So you were in your forties when you met."

"Thirty-nine."

"Still young. Still vital," Raker observed.

"I guess. Seems like really young now at any rate."

"It was really young. Never thought about it at the time, but it was. I was still working out in those days, cardio, the weights, the whole bit. I felt like I was twenty-five and could maintain that kind of vitality for another forty years if I had to."

"My leg kept me from doing a lot," Art said. "I could manage the elliptical machines, and I worked the weights some. God, I look at some of the guys our age, and it's really sad, man. Overweight. Diabetic. Heart trouble."

"Cheryl's younger than you?"

"Oh yeah, by nine years."

"How'd the two of you meet?" Raker asked.

"At work. I was traveling with a company called Pace Learning Systems, a real slick outfit selling management and sales training systems to insurance companies and banks. Cheryl joined the company when we got a big contract with Bell Systems. Mobile phones weren't around then. The government broke up the Bell System into several regional companies, and Pace saw an opportunity in it. Pace found Cheryl working for Northwestern Bell in Minneapolis and hired her away to get someone on staff who knew the baby Bells and how to market to them."

Art shook his head. "She got off to a bad start, though. She didn't realize she came in as an outsider right over the heads of several people who had been working at Pace for years and looking for a promotion. Tory Pace, the guy who owned the company, was very impulsive and often failed to consider others in the decisions he made. She made matters worse when she bought a bright yellow Cadillac DeVille within a few days of starting the job. I tried to tell her that her ride was too damn snazzy . . . We struck up a conversation, and I asked her to go to lunch with me. One thing led to another, and we started dating. The rest is history."

"Great story," Raker said, swirling his snifter and taking a sip. "There's only one gal I'm really attracted to . . . we work together."

"Who's that?"

"My boss. She's about twenty years younger, is all, and way above my pay grade. We'd never hit it off as a couple, but she's attractive."

"Sounds like you think it's hopeless?"

"It is. But it's great watching her walk down the corridor."

The next morning—Sunday—Marie Dennison asked her friend to wait for her in the waiting room and went immediately to the morgue, escorted by the coroner and Deputy Hurdler. The driver had parked the hearse near the emergency entrance and waited there to begin the return trip to Raleigh.

Marie tried to prepare herself for the scene that she had viewed so many times before on television. She just had never imagined herself as the grieving party.

The coroner had time to make Norm's body more presentable, but the wound, especially where the bullet exited in the back of the head, was so gaping that little could be done. Marie gasped when the coroner pulled back the sheet.

"Yes," she nodded and gave way to her tears.

She struggled to recover her composure as she walked back to the waiting room. Frank Schreve was waiting there for her and walked up to greet her.

"Mrs. Dennison, I'm Frank Schreve, president of the Lake Hannah Property Owners' Association. I want to extend my condolences. This must be a terrible . . ."

"No. I don't want to talk to you," the widow snapped. "I know who you are. I don't want anything to do with you,"

"I just wanted to extend condolences on behalf of the POA . . ." Schreve persisted.

"I think Mrs. Dennison would like you to leave," Art Nichols said upon entering the room.

"But she has come all this way . . ." Schreve continued.

"Please, Schreve, you're not wanted here. Do the courteous thing and leave," Nichols said, taking a step toward the man.

Schreve turned and walked back to the door. "The Dennison family has been part of the development from the beginning," he said, looking back over his shoulder. "I just thought . . ."

"Never mind!" Nichols interrupted, and Schreve opened the door and walked out.

"Horrible man," Marie said. "Norm didn't like him. Didn't like the things he was doing. Didn't trust him."

"I'm not surprised," Nichols said. "How are you? I'm Art Nichols, the man you talked to on the phone."

"I thought so. Thank you so much, Mr. Nichols. I was afraid I'd run into somebody I didn't want to see. And, look at that, I did. I'm so glad you are here."

"Art, Mrs. Dennison, please. Just call me Art. This must be very difficult for you."

"Yes. Yes, I just want to get back to Raleigh." She turned to Deputy Hurdler and said, "Thank you, officer. You've been a comfort."

"Yes, ma'am. My condolences," Hurdler replied. "I'll be taking my leave, if you don't need me any further."

"No, officer. And thank you again."

Hurdler bowed, turned, and walked across the waiting room to the front door.

"You said you had some files or something you wanted to leave with me . . ." Nichols said.

"Yes. They're in the car."

Nichols, Mrs. Dennison, and her neighbor walked out into the parking area. Nichols saw Frank Schreve walking to his car farther down the lot. Schreve turned when he heard the trunk pop open on Mrs. Dennison's vehicle. Nestled to one side of the trunk compartment was a lidded plastic file storage box.

"I don't know anything about what's in there. Norm wanted me to be absolutely sure you got it. Nobody else. He made me promise. I wanted to deliver it to you personally. I don't care what you do with it. It all made Norm very unhappy. I wish we'd never had anything to do with any of it . . . the property . . . the associations . . . those people." She nodded back toward Schreve who was watching them from across the lot.

"I'm going to put it in my car, and that's the last you'll ever see of any of it," Art said.

"Fine. Fine."

✢ ✢ ✢

Raker's Camry was parked in the driveway to the cabin with the trunk open. Raker and Diane appeared in the doorway as Nichols pulled to a stop.

"You guys all set to hit the road?" Nichols asked as he stepped out of his Jeep.

"Just loading up," Raker said. "We didn't want to head out until you got back from town."

"Turned out to be quite a weekend."

"Well, couldn't be helped. Here, let me get the door," Raker said as his friend moved toward the front porch with the box Mary Dennison had given him. "This the mystery box?" Raker asked.

"Yes. I don't know what I'm supposed to do with it. I don't want to have another damn thing to do with the Schreves, the association, or any of it."

"You're at least going to look through it, aren't you?" Raker asked, following his friend into the cabin. "I mean, the dead man . . . he was a friend."

"I guess I'll look through it . . . but not anytime soon." Nichols put the box on the dining room table. "Cheryl won't want it there. Shit. I don't even know where to store it."

"Mind if I take a quick look? Just curious," Raker asked.

"Help yourself."

Raker stepped up to the dining room table and opened the lid to the file box. "Wow. This guy was neat," Raker exclaimed. The box held a series of file folders, each labeled. In addition, there were several loose-leaf binders, again each labeled. Raker's eyes fell on a folder labeled *Lake Hannah Dam Inspection Reports* and opened it. "Look at this. He's got this all redlined with notes in the margin."

"Some other time. You look it over if you like. Take it with you. You're the detective, not me."

"That widow said you were supposed to have it."

"I know. I know she doesn't want it to fall into the wrong hands, but that's not the case here. I'm serious. You want to look it over, take it. Bring it back the next time you come back this way. You'll be coming back won't you? Our bucolic lifestyle hasn't scared you off, has it?"

"You're sure?" Raker questioned, turning to look at his friend.

"Yes. I'm sure. Take it. I'd be glad to be rid of it. If you don't think it means very much, just let me know. You won't even need to bring it back. Just take it."

CHAPTER 16

Deep shade hung over the black asphalt mountain road as Raker drove toward Wilkesboro on Highway 16. The mountains to the west blocked any view of the sunset. In the higher altitude, the air cooled quickly.

"They're really nice people," Diane finally said, breaking the silence. "It was so peaceful being there. It reminded me of a cabin we owned once in the woods of northern Wisconsin. There weren't any mountains there, of course, but the same peacefulness. The same quiet. Do you think they will invite us back again sometime?"

"I wanted to talk about that, Diane. I thought driving back to Charles City together would give us the time."

"Oh . . . oh!" Diane said. "That doesn't sound very good. You're breaking up with me, aren't you, Jim?"

"Yes."

"That's all? Just 'yes'?"

"Yes . . . No . . . I mean I want to explain myself. I've always wanted to be straight with you. This isn't working out for me, Diane. I'm sorry."

"I see." Diane dropped her head and stared into her lap. "I guess I knew that. I sensed it. I was just hoping . . . wishing . . . that it wasn't so."

Raker kept his eyes on the road. He did not want to turn to look at her. He had given their romance a chance. He had tried to keep things sorted out, to keep Diane separate from the memories of Susan. He could allow another woman to get close, to be a friend, intimate and loving—a love mate like Susan had been. Susan was bright. Available. He knew who she was. Not so with Diane.

"I'm not smart enough for you, am I?" Diane asked, as if she had been reading his thoughts. "I'm just a nurse. I didn't get a liberal arts degree. But I read a lot, Jim. I read a lot, and I have a lot of other interests."

"Don't do this," Raker said, finally turning toward her. She had not wiped the tears from her cheeks. "I keep expecting things . . . things that are not coming true for me."

"Like what?" Diane pouted.

"Intangible things. It's hard for me to say, really, and I've thought about it, and for me, it's a matter of comfort . . . of ease . . . that's not there when I'm with you. We have very different histories."

"Oh God," Diane said with a sigh. "Try to compete with a dead woman. There's no way."

"No. No, that's not it. I don't want you to be Susan. This can't be explained away. I don't believe in trying so hard that I turn myself inside out. I don't think we've struck a middle ground. Something needs to be there. And that isn't happening for me."

"I know about the physical thing. I don't care. I don't think we need sex right now to make a relationship work. That'll happen when it happens."

Raker slowed as his car entered the heavier traffic moving through North Wilkesboro. He was glad for the distraction. They were more than ninety minutes from Charles City.

"I just thought," Diane started again softly, "this time would be different. This time would be something like you had with Susan. Like I had with my first husband, the first ten years or so . . ." Her head snapped up. "Oh!" Diane almost shouted. "That's it, isn't it? That I broke up with Tom. I should never have told you that. About the affair that broke us up. That's it! I know that's it. You've got to tell me if I'm right . . . please? Is that the reason?"

"You aren't listening to me," Raker said quietly. "I'm trying to tell you it is not one thing. Don't go looking. I'm used to one thing, and I can't help looking for it. This, with you, isn't working for me. And if it isn't working for me, then I don't see how it can be working for you either."

"Okay, but what makes you, you? You know. Things that you like. Things that you don't. You're so straight that you didn't like knowing I had been unfaithful. That's just a big fucking check mark in the wrong column, isn't it?"

"It happened a long time ago."

"But it mattered."

"If it mattered, it's because I don't know how to deal with it. It's so totally outside of anything I've been concerned with in my relationships . . . in my marriage. I mean, I've heard of affairs. I know guys who cheat. I don't know that I ever knew a woman who cheated. I was never aware of it . . . as something they'd tell me."

"Be honest." Diane turned in the bucket seat and looked directly at Raker. "You said you need to be honest."

"Okay, it bothered me. I don't know what to do with the information. I know it happened a long time ago. I know you have changed and have paid for your mistakes, but what it really represents is what I said earlier. Our histories are very different. We are who we are. I can minimize what you did, but it's just another thing that doesn't fit for me."

"Shit. That's easy. To you, it means I can't be trusted. Isn't that right? You can't trust me."

"It's unsettling. Suppose I cheated on Susan."

"But you didn't."

"But suppose it was true and I told you."

"All guys cheat."

"Not this one," Raker said.

"Aw fuck. You're just like Tom. He didn't cheat either."

"So you've got ghosts to deal with too. See! Can't you make allowances for mine? You can't love a person . . . be devoted to them for years . . . and then wake up one day and say, 'Well, that doesn't matter anymore.' Humans aren't built that way," Raker said.

"I paid and paid for what I did. I lost day-to-day living with my kids under the same roof, lost the fun in the hubbub of getting them ready every day and tucking them in for the night. I lost my best friend. I endured an abusive relationship with another guy for years because I thought I deserved it. Yes," Diane shouted at Raker who turned to her in alarm. "That son-of-a-bitch would hit me, and I thought I had it coming. I suppose I shouldn't have told you that either."

Raker swung onto Interstate 77 and for several minutes they drove listening only to the whir of the tires on the pavement.

"Our lives have been very different," he said almost in a whisper. "I've been a cop all of my life. I've seen human nature at its worst, but my own life has been quiet . . . almost sedate. My home with Susan was a refuge. A retreat from the rest of the world. I miss her. I will probably always miss her. I'm sorry it has gone as badly as it has for you. I can't imagine what it would be like to feel the way you say you felt, so bad about myself that I felt I needed to be punished."

"I never knew anything would cost so much. That the price would be so high," Diane said, turning to look out the passenger's side window. "A fucking tug-of-war between anger and despair . . . every day. Maybe I only had one shot and I blew it. I thought Neil and I could take off. I could leave Tom. Neil would leave Barbara. The children would see we were happy together, and they'd be happy for us. Hell, Tom was unhappy with me. I could see that. He was just too Catholic to do anything. He had the money. He could do just about anything he wanted to do," she said. "You know," she added wistfully, "sometimes you're sweet just like he was. Oh, he could be a real asshole sometimes. Too loud. Clumsy. Swore too much. I didn't like being around him when he was mad. Neither did the kids."

"Where is he now?" Raker asked, surprised at Diane's sudden change in mood.

"He's married. Married two years after we broke up. Someone he met after we split. That's maybe fifteen or sixteen years ago. A really, really pretty woman. The kids all like her. I see them and him at family affairs—the weddings, the graduations. Divorced people act like they're friends on those occasions, all smiles and asking about one another like everything is finally okay between them. It seems cool . . . so mature. But I see how happy he is. He's still really handsome. Very successful. I see how the children are with him, and the grandkids love him. They love him to death, I swear."

"But you never talked things through. Never tried . . . what? To reach an understanding?"

"No. Not really. Neither one of us could say much about what happened. You know, the kids this and the kids that, but nothing about one another."

"That would be tough. I don't know how I'd handle it," Raker said.

"Aw, shit, you'd do fine. Tom could do fine, too, if it wasn't so awkward for me. You know, the day before I was to go to court for the divorce, I got all panicky and decided I should go see Tom, maybe ask him if he still wanted to go through with it. We'd been separated almost two years. He was so surprised to see me show up at his apartment. We sat down. I looked at him and asked whether we should go through with the divorce.

"How stupid. He'd been mad as hell at me for having guys sleep over with the kids at the house, for having them take his place at the family dinner table, but he didn't say anything at first. He didn't even act surprised. He said he thought we should get the divorce. If it was meant for us to get back together, we'd get back together afterward. Funny, that kind of made sense to me. I just looked into his eyes long enough to see if he meant it. There was no warmth there anymore, just a flat, matter-of-fact stare."

"Damn," Raker confessed, "I never had anything like that happen to me. My life hasn't been very complicated. I lost Susan. That was painful, but my life has been pretty straightforward, even bland."

"I could settle for bland," Diane answered quietly.

"I mean unexciting, as in 'nothing dramatic.' "

"I could settle for that. Do we have to break up, Jim? That sounds so final. We can still be friends, can't we?"

Traffic was growing heavier as they approached Statesville and the intersection with Interstate 40. Years of police work had taught Raker to listen to others. Felons lied. They were accomplished at it. He knew how to avoid being taken in by them. Diane sounded sincere. She was close to pleading, and he was uncomfortable with the turn in the conversation. He had worked with women during his career. His relationships with them were defined. But what Diane was asking him to consider seemed impossible.

"I don't have women friends," he said bluntly.

"So?"

"So nothing. I don't know how to do what you are asking."

"Afraid it'll get serious?"

"No. The things that get in the way of our having a relationship are the same things that would get in the way of our being friends."

"Like what?"

"Ah, God, Diane, this is just going around in circles. I keep to myself most of the time. I have all of my life. I get lonely, but there is nothing more lonely than feeling I can't be myself."

"Look. I can accept anything but a door slammed in my face. Maybe that's what you're trying to do in a nice way. We could have lunch a couple of times a month. Maybe go to a Panthers game together, or I could call you just to say hello. Why does it need to be all or nothing? Damn," Diane said, her voice softening. "I must sound desperate. This is humiliating."

"I don't want you to feel that way," Raker insisted. "That's not what I mean. You want to call once in a while, fine. Maybe a lunch now and then. But no dates. We're not a couple. And if this doesn't work, then a clean break. No more long conversations like this. Never again. Okay."

"I could call you if I needed help with something?"

"Like what?"

"Like where to take my car if it breaks down? Or whether I should use Turbo Tax or get an accountant? Things like that."

"Okay."

"You like me a little, then?"

"A little, but if we keep this up for the rest of the way to Charles City, that could change."

"But a call now and then is okay?"

"Yes," he said simply.

CHAPTER 17

Raker waited in the car for Diane to open the front security door to her apartment building. She turned and waved. He nodded, and once she was safely inside the foyer, put the car in gear and drove off. *It might have been a mistake*, he thought, *giving in to her insistence they could be friends.* Their lives may have been lived worlds apart, but her fear of loneliness touched his own. *A phone call once in a while would be okay. She was right. They found it easy to chat when they first met. The trouble . . . the discomfort . . . began when being together was supposed to become more than it could.*

He could not remember when the awkwardness shouldered its way between them. He pulled into his own garage, hit the remote to close the door, and walked into the house. Home! He was accustomed to the silence. The emptiness. The grief in not having Susan there to meet him had finally eased some.

He opened the cupboard door above the refrigerator and pulled down a bottle of Jameson. He could have turned into a drunk during those first few months. He remembered the night he stopped. On that evening, he had poured a second stiff one and realized it would be his last of the night. He did not want a third. The evening was still ahead of him. He'd be able to concentrate on his reading after his evening meal. He'd awake in the morning and remember what he had watched on TV. Life was better with less.

The quiet was always there. Susan's chair became just another chair. Her toiletries were gone from the bathroom. He replaced her towels and washcloth with something more masculine from Belk. He remembered shopping for them. Picking things out for himself was difficult. He resented the time it took but realized making the place over as his own required more than a long list of strong dislikes. His choices were safe, and he knew it. Susan had always made the household furnishing decisions for both of them.

He kept a picture on the spinet piano of the two of them. Her piano . . . the piano he never played. He would sell it one day. He put the picture of her that had been on the nightstand in a drawer and out of sight. It was enough in the morning to get up to an empty house.

Back in the kitchen, he picked a Swanson bag dinner from the refrigerator. Preparation required eleven minutes. He glanced at the clock on the stove. *Plenty of time.* He picked up his drink and walked into the living room. He would need to tell Ms. Becker in the morning about the drug dealing. That could be interesting. They had a few problems at different operations in the Southeast. Shrinkage mostly. Stuff disappearing. Sometimes tools. Sometimes fabric. Some of the stolen goods were traced to a flea market outlet near High Point. The message light was flashing on his landline phone.

"Raker, this is Gerald Ferguson. Becker wants to meet with us first thing in the morning. We had one of our truckers arrested in Florida on a DUI. He got tagged with intent to sell also. She wants to go over everything." Ferguson was vice president of operations for Southern World Textiles.

There was a note on the door to Diane's apartment when she stepped up to unlock it.

The Painters Will Be On Your Floor Beginning Monday. Your Apartment Is Scheduled For Wednesday. The Job Will Take Four Days. Please Secure

All Fragile Items To Avoid Having Them Damaged When Furniture Is Cleared For Painters. Thanks. –The Management.

"Shit!" Diane exclaimed. Over the weekend, she had forgotten about the painting. The scent of latex had drifted up the stairwells from the floor below and hung thickly in the corridor. The odor gave her a headache. *I'll die with it right here in my own place*, she thought.

Her apartment was a tidy, four-room layout—galley kitchen, combined living/dining room, bedroom, and bath. A veranda off the living area provided a view of a small park four floors below. Most mornings, as she awoke, she could hear children at play in the parochial elementary school less than a block away. The yelling reminded her of her own children when they were young and how she and Tom always attended the teacher conferences together. How she resisted the tears the first time she went without him. How lonely it felt.

"You're the most nurturing man I have ever known," she told Tom on more than one occasion. She was never dissatisfied with him as a parent. Other women complained of ex-husbands failing to pay child support and forgetting the children; not Tom. She was grateful he continued to take as much interest in the children as he always had.

His frequent travel took him out of town so much that the kids grew comfortable with him away from home for long stretches of time. She became the head of the household. She had to deal with the problems of kids charging headlong through puberty and into rebellious, hormone-fired adolescence. Despite herself, she grew to resent him for being gone.

Tom would fly back into town on a Friday, arrive after dark at the airport and expect to be picked up. Then he wanted all the attention. From her. From them. He wanted to show how much he missed them. Everyone gathered around the television in the family room, *because Dad was home*—as if evenings would always be that way if he had a regular job in town, like most fathers, and would be home every night. She tired of it so much that she was almost glad to see him go on Monday morning.

Then there was Neil. All of the crap—the kids, the chauffeuring, the arguments and tantrums, and the loneliness—then there was Neil. The excitement in having Neil near grew until it was undeniable. She did not want to fall in love, but she did want to feel loved, feel appreciated, and feel special. Neil gave her that.

"Fuck," Diane shouted out in the dark as the floor lamp flashed and then died. The bulb had burned out. "I can't stay here with the stench of paint. I can't. I won't." Anywhere else on her floor would be almost as bad. No point in asking her neighbors. She had only been in the apartment a few weeks. *Why the hell wouldn't they tell me when I first saw the place?* She was too new to the city to know anyone else well enough to ask.

"When is it my turn?" she snarled as she opened a kitchen drawer in search of a replacement bulb for the lamp. "When do I stop paying for my fucking sins?"

She popped a burrito into the microwave, poured herself a deep glass of red, and sat down. Downing a gulp, she was ready to accept she was hurt. Raker was a great guy, quiet but nice. A gentleman; considerate, kind. She liked him. Maybe she'd made a mistake trying to get him to lighten up a little. He usually didn't laugh that much.

"It isn't happening for me," Raker had said.

What, for chrissake? What does it take? I've still got my figure. I'm willing. I don't need to throw myself at the guy. He doesn't want to take one step my way. She needed to come up with a reason to keep the communication open, to give everything a little more time.

As she had grown to expect, Margie showed up as she was about to drift off to sleep. Daddy was dead, but Margie was still there. Sometimes Margie took over, but never during therapy sessions.

Therapy! A lot of fucking good . . . navel gazing . . . that's all.

Diane found it easy to let Margie take her place. Margie endured everything for Diane. When Daddy came into the bedroom and started little mousy up her leg under the covers, Margie took over. Margie was the only one who could allow mousy to go anywhere. Margie would be Diane's forever friend. She would never refuse Margie. Never. Margie never looked down at the hairy hand. She just stared at the sliver of light shinning through the crack in the door from the hallway outside the bedroom. Margie was brave and could let the hand touch her anywhere. Margie would not let the hand touch Diane. Margie even saw Mother's shadow block the light as she passed back and forth in the hallway. Margie grew to know Mother would never come into the room. Diane came to know that was true also.

CHAPTER 18

"The trucker was arrested Saturday. He was from our Riley's Creek finishing plant. He left there on Friday bound for Miami," Ferguson said in response to President Becker's request for the details. "He was pulled because he'd been driving erratically. The breathalyzer was fine, but other indications suggested he was under the influence. At first he refused a urine test, but in Florida you can't refuse without losing your license. One of the patrolmen noticed a 35-millimeter film canister on the seat within reach. He checked it. It was meth. Enough for a charge of possession with intent to sell." Ferguson put his notes down with a sigh and then glanced at Raker who had taken a seat next to him.

Becker, dressed in a snug-fitting black suit that complimented her figure, leaned back against her desk. *Looks great,* Raker thought.

"Has legal been brought in on this?" Becker directed at Ferguson.

"Corporate has. Our people only deal with in-state concerns and property."

"Any word from them?"

"No. Except to say that the guy can sit in jail until they get the background on him."

"Jim," Becker said, shifting her weight, "the guy's from Riley's Creek. Any concerns?"

"Yes. Just a coincidence, but I was up there for the weekend visiting an old high school classmate. I met the sheriff in connection with a shooting near my friend's cabin, and he told me he was closing in on a dealer working out of our plant. I was going to report the sheriff's concerns first thing this morning when I came in, then this came up."

"So what's your take on everything?" Becker asked.

"The sheriff was concerned about our trucks coming and going at the plant. Whoever the dealer is may have a network set up using Southern trucks to transport. Nobody knows what the scale of the operation is."

"What do you propose?" Becker asked.

"Sheriff Grossman is a savvy guy. He knows what's at stake for us. He wants me in on everything . . . working with him. Everything's still very confidential. Not even our management up there knows what's going on because the sheriff doesn't know who to suspect. I think I'd better go back up there."

"Can't stay in touch from here?" Becker asked.

"Maybe, but there'd be no interface with our people once things start to break. The sheriff thinks he has a lead on a guy and can get one of the people down the food chain to identify him."

"If it turns out to be someone in management, I'd better be brought in right away," Ferguson interrupted. "Don't you agree, Denise?"

"Absolutely. If it turns out to be someone in management, then yes, Vince, but I can't see sending you up there until we know more about the situation . . . So, Jim, call the sheriff and make your arrangements. I'd feel better with you there on the scene." Becker lightly thumped her desk. "Ugh!" she exclaimed, surprising both men. "I can just see the headlines now."

"Where are you going?" Schreve demanded of his wife.

"To sit in on the meeting of the county commissioners."

"Like hell you are."

"Don't take that tone with me. The auction for the lots that are in arrears on taxes is scheduled for the first Tuesday of next month. That's too early. We don't—"

"You stay away from there. Those people see you coming, and they'd just as soon take the opposite side of the argument out of spite."

Helen Schreve slammed the door. Frank shrugged. All he needed to get Helen to act on anything was to take the opposite view. He watched her back the Mercedes out of the drive. The yard bristled with signs that read, No Trespassing, Private Property, Keep Out. Helen posted them when she found two beer cans near their dock, an obvious sign someone had trespassed on their property. The signs were an embarrassment to Frank. Neighbors respected the property of others, but the prevailing attitude was casual with regard to lot lines.

Dogs roamed freely from one yard to the next as did the children at play. Helen, incensed that a dog had entered their yard one day, raced out with a can of pepper spray and sent the mutt yelping on its way back home. On another occasion, at her insistence, Frank picked up his air rifle and shot a dog in the hind flanks as it was digging near Helen's flower garden. The owner reported the incident to the animal control office, a well-run county agency.

An eight-year-old girl had seen Frank shoot the critter. She was not allowed to accuse Frank, however, because her mother told her that ". . . those horrible people would get even in some way."

In Durham, the Schreves had made a name for themselves in the real estate business. Frank's height and relaxed manner served him well as he progressed through the ranks at the franchise office of a national realty chain. He was eventually promoted to manager of the local operation. Durham was a large enough city so Helen's antics were absorbed as eccentric. The couple went through a succession of friends until they found themselves without table partners at the country club—an outcome that had Helen indignant over being snubbed by many they had befriended. Her anger registered on her face, and everyone steered clear of her because of it.

Frank thought of leaving Helen several times over the years. He eventually decided the financial consequences would be too severe, and he could find his escape in his work. Real estate sales afforded an excuse for being away from home at any time during the week. Frank was often in the field helping close a deal or hosting an open house.

As he made his way back to his study, Frank acknowledged that their marriage was a stalemate. For months, he had allowed himself to get lost in the project to take over the Lake Hannah Development. Once that was completed and the money came pouring in, perhaps then he would decide whether his marriage to Helen was worth the bitterness and daily strain.

CHAPTER 19

The message light was on when Raker returned to his office after meeting with Becker and Ferguson. It was Grossman.

"Didn't mean to push you," the sheriff said as soon as Raker opened the conversation. "But we have moved in on the woman we think can lead us to the guy at your plant. How soon can you get back up here?"

"Right away," Raker replied. "We had a driver arrested in Florida with enough on him to hold him on a charge of intent to sell."

"You've told your people then . . . the management level?"

"Yes."

"But nobody up here at the plant level?"

"No, and the folks I talked to here know better than to say anything. I told them you didn't know who to trust at the plant."

"Good. That's still the case," Grossman said. "Need any help booking a place to stay?"

"They handle that for me here, thanks."

"Good. Call me when you get in."

"Okay," Raker said, hanging up the phone. He wasn't eager to leave town right away again. He had been looking forward to spending time getting caught up at his own desk, checking with his staff, and generally letting life settle back into the routine that had slowly established itself with his new position at Southern World Textiles. He thought of calling his friend, Fred Wirth, just to chat for a minute. The two men usually had breakfast together every other week, and they were due to meet again.

He thought of Diane and wondered whether he should call her before leaving for Baden County again. Her lonesomeness was not so different from his. *Misery loves company*, he thought with a smile. Somehow, he didn't want her to think he ran out on her by returning right away to Baden County.

"Diane. It's Jim."

"Oh . . . Hi . . . Gee, this is unexpected."

"Yeah, well, I've got to go out of town again right away, and I thought I'd just let you know so if you tried to reach me, you'd know what was going on."

"How sweet."

"No. It's not that. It's just that . . . well . . . you made a case for our being friends yesterday, and I thought . . . I thought . . . I just didn't want you to think I dropped out of sight suddenly."

"I have your cell phone number."

"Guess I didn't think of that."

"When do you leave?"

"This morning."

"How long will you be gone?"

"I don't know. A couple of days at least. Maybe the rest of the week."

"Can I ask a favor?"

"As long as I have the right to refuse."

"Can I stay at your place while you're gone? The landlord is having my apartment painted . . . everyone's on this floor, and I can't stand the smell. It gives me a splitting headache. They'll be done in a couple of days. What d'ya think?"

"I guess that'd be all right. I'm leaving right away. How will I get a key to you?"

"Can you leave it somewhere?"

"Let's see . . . Susan had a small frog statue she kept in the flower bed near the front door. I'll get it out of the garage and put it near the porch.

The key will be under it. When you leave, just put on the night lock and leave the key in the house."

"Okay."

"Good. I'd rather have someone in the place than have it dark anyway. I'll check with you in a few days. Okay?"

"You're sweet."

"No, I'm just being a friend."

"Well, you're a really sweet friend."

"Goodbye, Diane."

"Goodbye, Jim."

"You were staying with this guy Nichols when you were here for the weekend, weren't you?" the sheriff asked as soon as Raker entered his office. The drive back to Baden County had taken a little over two hours.

"Yes. Why? He's not involved in any of . . ."

"His wife called here and reported their home was burglarized. Ransacked. I sent some men out there to investigate. If you need time to look in on this, I can wait with the other thing. We've got all the information we need from the woman who knows the guy at the plant. She's still in custody. We can hold her for a while if you want to call out there first and check on your friends?"

Raker heard the panic in Cheryl's voice on the phone and knew he needed to get out to the cabin as soon as he could.

Cheryl ran up to meet him as he drove into the driveway. The two hugged. Two county sheriff's cruisers were also in the driveway. Art was standing just outside the front door looking back into the house.

"I'm so glad you're here," Cheryl said. "They completely wrecked our house. I can't stand to look at it. We went into town first thing this morning and returned to find this. And Art, my God, Art's lost it. He's not himself. You'll see."

Nichols turned to watch both of them approach. "My safe haven!" he blurted out. "My serenity! Here . . . this place . . . my place! How the hell did they know about it? How? It doesn't figure." There was panic in his eyes.

"I'm sorry," Raker said. "I can't think of what else to say, except that I'm so very sorry."

"No! Goddamn it. Now they can find me anywhere. They're still out there. Hiding. Hunkered down. Little fuckers! Just waiting. Just waiting for the right moment. God, this is what I hate most about it. Not when the shooting starts, but waiting for it. Wondering where they're going to come from. Wondering who's going to catch one without any warning. Sneaky fucking little bastards. I hate this!"

"Art . . . Art," Raker said, trying to soothe his friend. "Look around, man. This is the mountain. Rebecca Ridge. Your mountain. There's nobody here."

"Naw! Fuck! That's what I hate the most. Looking at something and knowing I can't trust it. VC. VC. You never knew when one was and when one wasn't. You never knew who you could trust. Nothing ever was as it appeared. Nothing, man. I mean nothing!"

"You want to pipe down out there!" a voice called from deep inside the house.

"Fuck you!" Art yelled back.

"Okay, cool it. We've got work to do. We don't need the hassle," the voice replied.

"They've been here almost two hours already," Cheryl explained, looking up at Raker.

"Yeah. There's nobody in there and it looks like we took incoming. We came back from town and the place was all torn up!" Nichols shouted so the men inside could hear him.

"They're processing the crime scene," Raker tried to explain. "Do you mind if I go in?"

"No. Hell, why would I?" Nichols replied.

Raker stepped into the doorway. "Hey, fellas," he shouted. "Sheriff Grossman sent me out here from his office. I'm retired law enforcement. Can I take a gander?"

"No disrespect, sir, but not until we finish."

"How long will that take?" Raker took advantage of his position in the doorway to view as much as he could of the interior of the cabin. Whoever entered the premises was looking for something. The couch had been overturned. The drawers to Cheryl's prize antique secretary had been pulled out and smashed on the floor.

"They hit every room," a voice called back. "This is going to take a couple of hours at least."

Raker looked up and saw Deputy Hurdler come into the doorway to the front room. He was shaking his head. "This is vandalism, pure and simple. They left valuables in favor of just wrecking the place."

"Okay, let us know when we can come back into the house," Raker said and stepped back from the doorway to join Art and Cheryl. One look at Art and he knew his friend was struggling to hold out his memories of murderous combat in Viet Nam. "They're going to be a while," Raker said quietly.

"They can take forever for all I care," Nichols growled. "They've ruined it. They found it now. It'll never be like it was. They have the coordinates. Sighted in. They can drop a round in here any goddamn time they want, and we can't do shit about it. We gotta move on."

As he was talking, a Lexus SUV drove up and stopped in front of the house. The driver's side door opened and Frank Schreve stepped out. Nichols looked up in alarm and ran to his Jeep, reached behind the front seat, and pulled out his Browning automatic twelve-gauge shotgun.

"You get out of here, you fat fuck! Nobody needs you around here." Nichols held the gun aloft.

Schreve froze one step away from his vehicle.

"I just wanted to see what I could do. I heard the sirens . . ."

"Get your flabby ass back in that vehicle and get the hell out of here. There's nothing for you to do here. You're the reason things are the way they are. We had no business out here in the first place. You hear me, asshole?"

Schreve got back into his car and rolled the window down. "You don't understand . . ."

"I don't need to understand. I don't take orders from you anymore, sir! I'm out! Now! You understand? Out! You understand?"

"Now see here . . ."

"Fuck you." Nichols fired his shotgun into the air.

Schreve jammed his SUV into gear and tore off.

"What the hell?" Deputy Hurdler yelled from the doorway. "Put the firearm away, or I'll put you under arrest."

"You can't arrest me, asshole. You've got no authority here. I'm not taking orders from anyone anymore."

"I can arrest you for assault."

"Fuck you. I haven't assaulted anyone."

"I heard you threaten that guy . . . that guy in the SUV. That's enough to haul you into the magistrate."

Raker took advantage of the moment Nichols was distracted by the deputy to walk over to his friend and grab the shotgun. "Come on, Art. This isn't going to help. Look, Cheryl's right here. See how frightened she is, Art? Cheryl wouldn't be anywhere in combat. She'd be here, in the mountains, with you. You don't want to do anything that'd hurt Cheryl. You know you wouldn't."

Nichols looked at Raker and then at Cheryl and back to Raker and a look of abject dismay overtook his features. He released the shotgun to Raker, who took him by the arm. "Let's go over to the porch and sit. What d'ya say?"

Nichols did not reply. He stared at Cheryl who took a step toward him and tried to smile through the tears toppling down her cheeks. "Oh God," Nichols moaned.

They sat for several minutes saying nothing to one another, Raker and Cheryl both hoping the sound of the deputies inside the house would not upset Nichols.

"This is so hard," Nichols finally said softly. "So fucking hard to hold everything in place. And the harder a guy fights it, the worse it is. I know. I've run groups where guys dealt with this. It's all about belief. I know what's happening, but that doesn't stop it. A guy wants to believe what he sees. Wants to trust it. That's what 'Nam took away from everyone. A guy can't trust anything anymore. A dead buddy's body can be booby trapped. The kid that brought the water into camp every day for weeks, one day comes in with a bomb and three guys get blown to bits along with the kid. Everyone liked the little shit, and he blows himself up just to get a couple of our guys. Your own guys drop rounds in on you because they think you're VC. You can't trust anything, no matter what it looks like . . . and that stays with you the rest of your life. Not being able to trust is a kind of madness. Fear is right there. Right on the edge of the minute. This was my place. This is the place I learned to take things for granted. Can't you see?"

"Yes. Yes. I think so," Raker said.

"No, Jim. You can't. I've seen guys do horrible things. I don't condone them, but I understand it. A guy walks up to a Vietnamese farmer. The poor old fart owns only one thing in the world—his goddamn water buffalo, and the guy shoots the beast dead for no fucking reason at all. He looks at the old man and walks away. He can't trust anything. He can't even trust himself. He doesn't even know himself anymore. He's not some kid from a small high school in Iowa anymore. Just a fucking grunt in a jungle with no idea why he's there or what's going to happen next."

CHAPTER 20

"Okay, we're through," Deputy Hurdler said, stepping out onto the front porch. "The cabin is a mess. You've got a big clean up job ahead of you."

"Got a minute?" Raker asked Hurdler.

"I suppose."

"Let's walk over to your cruiser," Raker suggested. When they were out of hearing range, Raker asked, "Vandalism? You're sure?"

"What else? The woman said both computers . . . laptops were taken. But that's it, at least as far as we could tell. They passed up a lot of valuable stuff. The guy's gold Omega watch was right there on the dresser untouched."

"Any evidence? Prints?"

"No. The forensic guys were pretty thorough. They have a few prints to check, but a lot of the stuff that was thrown around didn't have any prints on them at all. That's what you'd expect to find. Chances are the prints they picked up belong to the people who live there. No footprints."

"So whoever the intruders were, they were careful," Raker observed.

"I'd say. We've lab work to check out but, as of now, I don't know. You know this guy, the owner, right?"

"Yes. We went to high school together."

"Seems pretty volatile . . ."

"I know. He suffers from post-traumatic stress disorder. He's been settling down now since he's had a few minutes on the porch."

The deputy turned and walked back to the porch where Art and Cheryl were seated. "You know anyone who'd have a reason to do this?" he asked, directing his question at both of them.

"No," Cheryl said, after pausing for Art to reply.

Nichols simply shook his head.

"Anyone who'd have reason to do this? Anyone who has it in for you?"

"I didn't exactly make a lot of friends while I was on the board of the POA. I put a lot of pressure on people to get their dues current. But, shit, that goes back two years or more," Art said.

"So, it's not likely anyone would carry a grudge that long?"

"Why would they take your computers?" Raker asked.

"No idea. There's nothing on them except personal stuff. Bills. Taxes. That sort of thing. Correspondence."

"Anything controversial in the correspondence?"

"No. I deleted all that stuff from the POA after I resigned. I did have a backup CD of the billing system. I don't know what anyone would get out of that," Nichols said.

"How about this guy you ran off?"

"I wasn't myself. I thought he was someone else."

"Who was he?"

"Frank Schreve. He runs the POA now."

"You don't like him?"

"No. I don't like him, but it's no big deal. He knows that."

"He might think it a big deal now after pulling a gun on him. He can press charges. That's in the books as misdemeanor assault. Who'd you think he was anyway?"

"Look!" Nichols said, staring the deputy in the eye, "I have trouble. Everyone knows it. Schreve knows it. I came back all messed up from Vietnam. I was fighting to get control of what was going on with me when I got that gun out."

"Didn't look like you were getting the job done," the deputy observed.

"I think we can leave it at that," Raker said suddenly. "We can set things straight with Schreve later. Maybe he won't press charges. Pursuing this now isn't going to get anywhere."

Deputy Hurdler shrugged. "Okay, but it's going in my report to the sheriff."

"I understand," Raker replied. "Tell the sheriff I'll be in later, and I can add to the story."

"Whatever you say." Hurdler nodded to Deputy Whitehead who had been standing near one of the cruisers throughout the exchange. Whitehead got into the vehicle and started the engine. Hurdler looked back once at Raker and then got into the second vehicle and drove off.

"Well," Cheryl sighed as the car disappeared into the wooded slope of the mountain. "I guess we'd better take a look."

"I don't know," Nichols said. "I may not be ready for this."

The trio stepped back up to the front door. "Let me go first," Cheryl insisted and stepped into the doorway. The scene inside the cabin, if anything, was more chaotic than when she and Art found it earlier in the day. "Oh God," she said with a sigh. "This is going to take so much work. I'm going in to check on the bedroom. If it looks as bad as the living room does, we can't stay here tonight." She disappeared into the house.

Nichols peered in. "My sanctuary," he groaned. "My safe place. My serenity. Jesus. I . . . I can't go in there. It's not safe. Cheryl shouldn't be in there. Anything could happen. Get the hell out of there, now!" he yelled suddenly so that Cheryl would hear him at the back of the house.

"Come away," Raker said, putting a hand on his friend's shoulder. "You don't need to see it this way." Nichols turned, and Raker could see the struggle taking place in his friend's mind.

"Those guys should never have been digging near a tree, the three of them. We told them to come over close to us. One round hits the tree, and you got twice the shrapnel. They caught a round. A direct hit. Now you're telling me we got to go over there and pick up what's left of them. Body parts. In the tree. All over the ground. We got to pick them all up, bag 'em and send them back? I'm not going. Send someone else, Lieutenant," Nichols said, staring vacantly at Raker. "I've had too damn much of that kind of duty. You can't even tell whose parts you're putting into what bag.

When they bury one of them back in the states, they won't know it, but they'll be burying parts of all three guys. Shit. It's a lie. It's all a lie."

Raker held his gaze on his friend and watched for signs he was coming back around to realize where he was. "Okay, Nichols," he said, "you don't have to go this time. At ease. Stand down."

Nichols dropped his head, turned, and went back to the rocker on the porch.

Cheryl had witnessed Art's outburst. She crossed to the doorway as her husband turned away from Raker. "There's no way," she whispered to the detective. "Everything's so torn up. Every room. Come see for yourself. We can't stay here tonight. Surely not until everything gets put back the way it was." Cheryl stepped aside to let Raker pass.

"Stay with Art," Raker said and walked into the living room.

Cheryl was right. Every room had been trashed. Dresser drawers had been removed in the bedroom, and their contents dumped on the floor. In Art's den, all the books had been pulled from the shelves. His desk drawers were pulled and dumped. In the kitchen, all the cabinets stood open, their contents on the floor. Broken glass littered the entire area.

"You two stay at the motel in town tonight," Raker said, rejoining the couple on the porch.

CHAPTER 21

Raker made sure Nichols was settled at the motel before he returned to the sheriff's office. Cheryl called two of her friends from the motel to ask for their help in putting the cabin in order, and she made arrangements to meet with their insurance agent to review the damage. Nichols assured them both he would be okay. The motel offered cable TV service, and he said he would tune into a baseball game and watch for the rest of the afternoon.

The receptionist told Raker the sheriff had somebody in his office but wanted him to go in as soon as he returned.

"Assault with a deadly weapon, Sheriff! Assault with a deadly weapon. That's the charge. He pulled a gun on my husband and took a shot at him!" Helen Schreve was shrieking at the sheriff when Raker entered the room. The sheriff looked up at Raker and rolled his eyes.

"He did not take a shot at your husband." Raker surprised Helen who whirled about to face him.

"How do you know?"

"I was there. Your husband had no business being where he was. Technically, he was trespassing. Nichols fired the gun into the air when your husband refused to get off the property."

"So he *did* take a shot!"

"No. He fired the gun safely up into the air. Your husband was acting as if he wasn't going to leave the premises."

"That's not what my husband says."

"I don't care what your husband says. I was there. I saw it. I'm a witness."

"Who are you, anyway?"

"James Raker, Detective, Melville County Sheriff's Office, retired."

"Oh. More good ol' boys close ranks and stick together. Well, I'm not done with this. I've just come from the county commissioners' meeting and gave them an earful about scheduling the real estate auction on the courthouse steps too early. They can hear about this too."

"Fine, Mrs. Schreve. Now, if you have charges to file, see one of the deputies outside. The receptionist will summon one for you, and you can make a statement to him. We will give it every consideration. Otherwise, if you don't mind, I have other pressing matters that require my attention, and I'd appreciate it if you would leave now," Sheriff Grossman said, hoping to terminate the exchange.

"Ha!" Helen exhaled. Then pointing at Raker, she added, "You've got no authority here. None! We'll see about this." She stomped out of the office.

As soon as she closed the door, the sheriff buzzed the receptionist on the intercom. "This Schreve woman is headed your way. Get a deputy to take her statement. Sounds like misdemeanor assault to me, but have the deputy report to me as soon as she leaves." Looking up at Raker, the sheriff said, "I don't know your roots, son, but in these parts that's what we call a Yankee bitch." The sheriff lowered himself into the swivel chair behind his desk. "She drives everyone nuts. She's the reason your friend Nichols pulled out of the homeowners' association. Bugged him to death. Everything had to be her way. Impossible woman."

"She's wrong about Art assaulting her husband," Raker said. "It didn't happen that way."

"I know. I know. I'd never take that woman's word for anything . . . ever. Her husband is a stuffed shirt and can't handle her. It'd been something if he'd been shot. My deputy said he didn't witness the incident." The sheriff sighed. "The men out at the Nichols's place didn't turn up a thing. What's your take on it?"

"I don't know," Raker replied. "I'm just getting to know Nichols again myself. We hadn't seen or had any communication with each other for over forty-five years. I called him about a year ago, and we started talking again. A couple of weeks ago, we decided to meet up here for a weekend, but I don't know his habits or his associates."

"So you think maybe he's involved with something that could be a motive behind his place getting sacked."

"I don't know. He's a fiery guy. He could've made enemies. Whatever's behind it, it didn't come immediately to mind for him. He's badly shaken. Has problems with PTSD."

"Yes, yes," the sheriff said with a brisk nod. "Everyone around here knows that. Otherwise, he's well-liked and doesn't give anyone any trouble. Maybe it was kids . . . kids raising a little hell."

"Could be. I'll talk to him later," Raker said. "Are you going to bring him in to complete your report?"

"Yes. If that woman files charges, we may need to arrest him and bring him before the magistrate. I'd like to give him a day to settle down and get control of himself. Not to change the subject, but we've got the statement we wanted from the woman we picked up."

"Who is she?"

"Local woman, twenty-eight years old, maybe twenty-nine. Skinny little thing off a small farm north of town. Her folks didn't amount to much. One brother is serving time for grand theft auto. Name's Frieda McNaughton. She's just another one of the wasted souls in this community," Grossman said.

Raker knew about not being able to trust others. Truth meant nothing to addicts and dealers. They were always insistent they were sincere. When mock sincerity wouldn't work, they made a plea for sympathy, but for Raker, they moved quickly beyond his willingness to care. He knew the sheriff cut a deal with Frieda to get her off on a lighter charge. That was how it worked. The code was nobody ever rat on anyone else, but what comes first is avoiding incarceration and being denied access to a drug of choice. Frieda rolled up.

"If she isn't lying, your guy is Gus Turcotte. I want to respect your concerns on this, but I also want to move as quickly as we can. The state bureau of investigation wants to go old school with someone in deep cover at the plant. We don't know how big the network is. One more arrest won't mean anything if we lose a chance at cracking into a regional operation with possible national connections. We need to set things up so we can pick up Turcotte in the act of selling or at least with enough in his possession to make the intent-to-sell charge stick. We need to get an observer on the floor of that plant where he works—someone who appears legit."

"I understand. I need to call my operations VP and bring him in on everything. How soon is soon enough?" Raker asked.

"We can slap a bond on Frieda she won't be able to meet and hold her for trial, but word will get out soon enough for Turcotte to get suspicious. Nobody trusts anyone, you know. He probably has two options. Either quit and move his game somewhere else, or just lay low. My guess is he'll move. We only have as much time as it takes for him to close up shop, because he'll find out soon enough that we got the woman in here."

"Can he do that? I mean, he's a supplier, right? Can he just up and move?"

"Yeah. There'll be pressure on him to keep a supply chain going. The dealers he keeps in business will know how to get to him. Cell phones make it so easy anymore."

"Is there that much of this sort of thing in this quiet little county?"

Sheriff Grossman nodded. "I'd guess at least 500 people in this county wake up every morning with only one thing in mind—where to get their fix for the day. Let me know what your guy says. You'll call right away?"

"Right now."

"Good. Let me set up an office for you. We've got a spare room you can use."

CHAPTER 22

Becker and Ferguson agreed Raker should continue to stay in Riley's Creek to work with the sheriff in setting up the inside man at the Southern World Textiles' plant. Raker's first job was to talk to the plant manager, Norman Greason.

"Right here? In our plant?" Greason asked incredulously when Sheriff Grossman explained the reason for their visit.

"The sheriff's department is very sure of their information," Raker said, intervening on the sheriff's behalf. "I've talked to Ms. Becker and Mr. Ferguson about everything. They want you to cooperate fully with the sheriff. Everything is to remain confidential. None of us knows who is involved yet, so even your most immediate management staff cannot be told."

"I understand," Greason replied. "Seems to me this would work best if it doesn't look contrived. I mean, it would be great if we have an opening in the area one of the sheriff's men could fill without creating suspicion."

"Exactly," the sheriff said, obviously pleased with Greason's attitude.

Greason buzzed his assistant on the intercom. "How many positions are open on the plant floor right now? Good. Bring in the job descriptions so I can see firsthand what we're looking for."

Greason read over the job descriptions. "We're in luck," he said, looking up at Raker and the sheriff. "I've got an entry-level spot open in the same area where Turcotte works—basically, an unskilled nonexempt position."

"We've got a man ready to go," the sheriff countered. "It can't be one of my deputies, obviously. He'll need to go through the usual channels to get employed. Pulling strings might tip our hand. You can't take too much interest in the hiring," he cautioned. "Makes it tough because we want to move quickly."

"I can bring a little urgency to the situation without making it too obvious. We've been under the gun here to increase output. Manufacturing keeps complaining they need to slow their production because they have to wait for us. I don't like that. It's my performance that's being questioned," Greason said. "You can bring your man in this afternoon, and I'll have him on the floor in the morning."

"Naw. She went down there and raised hell about scheduling the auction so early, and she pissed everyone off the way she always does. They refused to move the date back. We got exactly what we wanted." Frank Schreve was on the phone to Vernon Brost, president of Palmetto-Atlantic Development. The call was on speaker because Schreve did not like holding the instrument to his ear, and his wife was not at home.

"You hear from anybody about the search of Nichols's cabin yet?" Brost asked.

"Nobody told me anything. Only that it was going to happen. I'm glad I don't know who did it. It's not information I'd want to have."

"They didn't turn up anything. Tore the place apart and found not one fucking thing," Brost said.

"Well, it damn near got me shot. The guy's crazy, you know—Nichols. He's a Vietnam vet who has been big in the campaign to help vets with post-traumatic stress disorder. Suffers from it himself—big time. He pulled a gun on me when I went up there."

"Did you see anything? Anything inside the place?"

"No. I couldn't get close enough. They say they didn't find anything? He had picked up the box less than 48 hours earlier. I saw him take it from the widow," Schreve said.

"Well, it has to be somewhere. They checked his Jeep and his wife's Outback. Nothing. Both vehicles were unlocked. You said it was a large box, right? Too big to hide easily," Brost asked.

"Not that big. A standard-size plastic file storage box. Nothing in either vehicle. I don't know what to say. Could he have trashed it all? He got pretty fed up with the homeowners' association before he quit . . . vowed he'd never have another thing to do with it."

"We can't take that chance," Brost answered. "Those files are somewhere."

"Okay, just doesn't add up," Schreve concluded. "Doesn't make any sense, but you suppose he could have turned it over to the guy that I saw up there with him?"

"Someone other than law enforcement people?"

"Yes. He was there with Nichols and his wife. I don't know who he is but I could sniff around and find out."

"Do that. Let me know who he is," Brost ordered. "If this stuff turns up in the wrong hands, it's all over, and we've flushed millions down the drain. You've got a lot at stake in seeing it work out too . . ."

"Okay," Schreve said, then hit the off button on the speaker.

CHAPTER 23

Diane packed her suitcase for at least a three-day stay before leaving for the two job interviews she had scheduled. After the second one in the afternoon, she drove directly to Raker's small home in one of the older neighborhoods of Charles City. The place was familiar to her. She remembered how excited she had been the first time Jim consented to having her stay overnight. He was so modest. He went into the bathroom and closed the door to put on his pajamas while she boldly undressed and simply pulled the sheet up over herself to wait for him.

She heard him brushing his teeth. The door to the bathroom opened, and he turned off the light. The bedroom was lit by a table lamp at the bedside. He walked over to it without as much as a glance at Diane to turn it off.

"Leave it on," Diane said softly. "I like making love with the lights on." Raker walked around to the opposite side of the bed where Diane was lying and slid under the sheet without pulling it back far enough to uncover her.

"I don't know," Raker said tentatively. "This is very awkward for me. I warned you."

"I know," Diane reassured him. "You warned me, and now it's time for me to show you that you have nothing to fear." She slid over next to him and pressed her breasts up against his side, nestled in under his arm and began unbuttoning the top to his pajamas. He shifted his weight. She slid her hand underneath his pajama top onto his chest.

"Hold it. Please. Just stop," Raker said quietly.

"Okay," she cooed.

"You're going too fast for me. Can't we just hold each other for a few minutes?"

"Sure. As long as you like." She rested her head on his chest and laid one arm around his middle. She felt reassured when he pulled an arm out from under his head and held her.

Raker did not want to disappoint Diane. She was easy to look at with a good figure. But Diane was not Susan. Her body did not feel like Susan's. She didn't sound like Susan. He had thought about Diane in bed, thought she would be good to be with, but it was all too soon. Making love meant a commitment. He wasn't ready. He wasn't sure. All of their conversations were disconnected and superficial. He didn't have a sense of who she was. He didn't want to measure every woman he met against how he remembered Susan, but he did want to feel at ease with someone else, feel as if he could be himself and relax.

He missed the serious side of Susan, the Susan he could talk over the events of the day with and the things that troubled him. Diane was always dismissive, as if what he was doing every day, what he was thinking, had nothing to do with the two of them.

"The last thing I want to do is disappoint you," Raker finally whispered.

"You can't, sweetie. There's nothing in the world you could do that would disappoint me."

Raker was put off by her reassurance. He sensed Diane remained poised to move without hesitation, to do anything to draw them closer. She was not going to give anything enough time for him to feel comfortable. "It's just that my mind is racing. I can't get out of my head. You understand?"

"Of course I do. There's no hurry, Jim, sweetheart. If not tonight, then some other night. I'm not going anywhere."

"Do you mind then? Do you mind if we wait for another night. A better night for me?"

"No. That's fine," Diane said. Raker thought he heard a hint of impatience in her voice. She threw back the sheet, pulled away from him, and walked over to her night case that was still open on the stool by the dresser.

Raker looked at her. She was trim but he was struck by the vulnerability in the way she carried herself, in the paleness of her back, the slight sag to her butt. He turned away.

She slipped into a floor-length nightie, turned off the light, got into bed, and kissed him. "Sleep tight," she whispered.

The 'another night' they had both agreed to finally did come along, but Diane recognized Raker was not bringing any passion to the encounter. Perhaps he had too much to drink, but he worked away at making love until he finally climaxed and then dropped back, sweaty and spent, beside her. She knew they had a long way to go before their relationship was going to be anything close to what she hoped it could be.

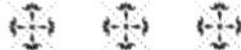

Raker wondered whether he should call Diane as he stepped into his motel room but figured she would call if she couldn't find the key. It had been a long day. He was impressed with Art's struggle to regain control and how his friend had worked hard to overcome an affliction that serving his country imposed on him.

"It was all a lie," Raker said. He sighed, thinking about Vietnam and all the conflicts in the Middle East. And Art was only one guy. Thousands of men and women came back from the conflicts crippled physically or psychologically. The country generally refused to face the economic cost of the wars and the cost in human suffering, including the civilian casualties—the deaths that were never reported.

Raker had tired of politics years earlier. He was convinced thoughtful men didn't stand a chance of being heard going against the vested interests of the politicians and the people with money who backed them. He decided not to distress himself over events he could not influence or control. Nichols's troubles struck close to home for Raker, however. Art had grown up in the same setting, and Raker knew Art was a man who tried to do what was right. Nichols wanted to believe in his fellow man, perhaps even more so than Raker, who was tainted by his years in law enforcement.

He thought also about Diane's story and how she had stumbled along through the years without finding any contentment or fulfillment. The only time in her life she looked back upon favorably were the years she was married to her first husband, and she broke that up with an affair of her own, an affair somehow prompted by the thought she could be happier than she was.

Earlier in the day, Raker thought he might call her just to see if she had settled into his home comfortably. It was the kind of thing he would have done for Susan. It was the kind of thing that came naturally to him, but he did not want to complicate his relationship with Diane. Being friends was all new ground for him. He felt unsure.

A maid had turned back the covers on the bed. He hoped he would fall asleep quickly.

"Jim? Jim? Is that you?" Diane called out from bed. She heard something in the front of the house. Awakened, she remembered Jim was out of town and he had let her stay in his home while he was gone. It couldn't be him, not unless he returned unexpectedly for some reason. Suddenly the noise stopped. She had heard something. She was almost sure that she had. She turned on the table light next to the bed. Maybe whoever it was would be frightened away. She waited, and she realized she would not be able to go back to sleep without investigating.

"Hello. Is somebody there?" she called as she got out of bed. She heard nothing. She picked up the phone. "I'm calling 911 so if anyone's there, you'd better get out." She started to punch in the emergency number and then stopped. Jim had a gun in his dresser. She came upon it once while putting away laundry.

"Yes, it works," Raker had told her at the time. "Be careful with it. I keep it loaded. It doesn't have a conventional safety. It'll fire when you pull the trigger. The safety is this little first trigger in front of the main trigger," he explained, pointing out the features of the baby Glock to her. "As soon as you put your finger into the trigger guard, you're set to do business with it. I keep it here by my bedside in case someone comes around here looking for me. I made some enemies when I was in law enforcement," he concluded and put the Glock back into the drawer where she had found it.

Diane opened the dresser drawer and lifted the pistol. *What if nobody was there? What if she had been dreaming?* She couldn't be sure. She didn't want to call the police only to have them show up at Jim's house and nothing was wrong. They might know Jim from when he worked as a detective. It might embarrass him. *Okay, here goes*, she thought, stepping out into the hallway that led to the living room in the front of the house and turning on the overhead light.

"If anyone's there, I want you to leave. I have a gun. I won't hesitate to use it." Her pulse raced. Midpoint down the hallway, doorways opened on either side; one on the right to a second bedroom in the front of the house that Raker had turned into a study and the opposite into a bathroom. *I'll check the study first*, she thought, feeling it far more likely that an intruder would hide there. At the door to the study, she reached around the door jamb for the light switch. As she found the switch, she felt something move behind her. A bright light flashed suddenly.

CHAPTER 25

Raker was about to go next door from his motel room to see if Art and Cheryl were ready for breakfast when the phone rang. It was the sheriff.

"Not too early for you is it, Detective?" the sheriff said in greeting.

Raker looked at his watch. Five after eight. He had slept late. "Almost," he chuckled. "What is it?"

"The guy we want to put on the plant floor with Turcotte is being processed as a new employee this morning. He's been trained by the state bureau of investigation and reports to Tim Moran. Moran's the one who insisted on going old school. I like the idea. This way if anything goes wrong, it's not on my doorstep . . . or yours, if it matters."

"Watch Moran," Raker said. "He's looking to make a name for himself."

"I've worked with him before; I know how he operates. We get along."

"Good. Thanks for letting me know."

"Sleep okay?" Cheryl asked Raker when she answered his knock at the door to the couple's motel room.

"Well enough. You? How'd the two of you do?"

"Okay," Art shouted from the bathroom. "Made love all night. Couldn't you hear us next door? Something about motels gets Cheryl really hot. Flashbacks from an earlier life."

"Guess who's feeling better?" Cheryl said with a smirk.

"Let's get some breakfast," Raker suggested. "They've got stuff in the office area."

"No way," Art said, emerging from the bathroom. "The Winners' Circle restaurant at the Best Western has the best breakfast in the county. It's all the way across town, but the drive is worth it."

"Okay," Raker replied. "What are you doing for the rest of the day? Are you going to stay checked in here?"

"Not sure," Cheryl said. "Art wants to see what happens if he goes back to the cabin. It looks better because I had help all yesterday afternoon to get things cleared up. It doesn't matter one way or the other. Our insurance guy said our policy covers temporary living quarters."

"I just want to give it a look," Art said. "Go easy. I know what to expect now. It was a shock at first, but I think I can handle it today."

"Okay, I need to check in with our plant manager right after breakfast. I'll follow you over there but, after we eat, that's it for me. I've got too much to do. You have my cell phone number."

✠ ✠ ✠

"This is Raker," the detective said, answering his cell phone as he stepped into his temporary office.

"Jim, this is Denise." Raker was surprised to hear the company president on the line. "Something terrible has happened, and I think you'll need to return right away to Charles City."

"Okay," Raker said tentatively.

"There's been a fire at your home. The area of your house where your study is located has been badly gutted, but the house is still standing. I haven't been to see it so all my information is secondhand."

"Did this just happen?" Raker asked.

"No. It happened during the night. Your place is all cordoned off now. But there's . . . a woman was injured, someone who was staying there."

"Diane Welborn."

"Yes. She's in very serious condition from burns and a head wound," Denise said. "You knew she was staying there, I presume?"

"Yes. Yes. Her apartment was being painted, and she wanted to stay at my house while the work was being done."

"I see."

"I'd better get back there. Things are all set up here now. The SBI is involved. Sheriff Grossman has a secure grip on things. They've got my contact information. I'll only be a couple of hours away if they need me to get back here."

"Do you mind my asking if your friend is a special person?"

"No. She's a friend. That's all. We dated for a while but nothing came of it."

"Is there anything I can do before you get here?"

"Could you have flowers sent to her room for me?"

"Of course. Consider it done. She's in a coma, Jim, in intensive care. You need to be ready for that. They're also having a difficult time finding any family members."

"She doesn't have anyone in the immediate area. She has four children . . . adult children, but they're scattered all over the country. I think I have contact information on them. If not, I'll see if I can get into her apartment and can find it among her things."

"Very well. Call me when you have a minute once you get back and have a chance to see everything. I'm sorry, Jim, to give you such terrible news."

"Thank you. I'd better get going."

Raker went immediately to the sheriff's office and explained to him and Agent Moran what had happened. They agreed there was no reason for him to remain on hand until something developed on the drug case. He called Cheryl and explained what had happened and said he had no other choice but to return to Charles City. Cheryl reported Art was much better, and he was inside the cabin helping with the cleaning.

Once on the road, Raker's mind raced. His home was built in the late 1970s when construction codes had been updated with regard to electrical wiring. His stereo, a small TV, his computer and printer were all in the study. None represented a fire hazard. He missed his inter-agency radio that he was required to turn in when he resigned. He decided to call Sheriff Johnston in Charles City.

"I heard about it, Raker, but the local police are handling it. Let me see if I can get one of the local guys who's familiar with the situation to give you a call," the sheriff replied. A few minutes later, Raker's cell phone vibrated.

"Raker."

"Jim. This is Fletcher. Sorry for the reason for this call . . . I've thought of you many times since you retired."

"Good to talk to you, Fletch. What's going on?"

"As far as we know, a neighbor across the street thought he heard a gun shot around 2:00 a.m. last night. He got up and looked out across the street, saw two men running from your place. They got into a pickup and drove off. He saw the flames were spreading very quickly and called 911. The firefighters pulled a middle-age woman out of the blaze. She was unconscious in a center hallway, next to a room where the fire was the worst. An ambulance took her to the hospital."

"Any word on her condition?"

"She's in a coma," Fletcher said. "The hospital announced her condition as 'critical.' She sustained a very serious head wound, a hell of a blow, before the fire started. We're puzzled because there was nothing in the area where she was found that could have been the cause—no falling beams or fixtures or anything like that. The fire barely reached the area where they found her."

"Any word on the cause of the fire?"

"They're trying to determine that now. Where are you?"

"Coming up on Statesville on I-77. I should be there in about an hour or so."

"Let me know if there's any more I can do."

"I will," Raker replied. "I'm going to the hospital first and look in on Diane. Are you assigned to the case?"

"No. Not yet, at least. Mike Pleasants has been assigned. Do you know him? He may ask for me since you and I worked together for a couple of years."

"No. Never met him."

"Good man. Great guy. He'll do a good job."

"Okay. Listen, when I'm done at the hospital, I'm going to the house. Call if there are any new developments."

"Roger that, Jim. Good luck."

"Yes, she's here," the nurse at the station replied when Jim inquired about Diane. "Are you a member of the family?"

"No. I'm a friend. She was staying at my home when she got hurt. I was hoping that I could see her."

"I can't give you permission as long as she is in intensive care since you are not a member of the family."

"How serious is her condition? Can I talk to her doctor?"

"I can tell you only that the hospital has announced the patient is in serious condition. Her doctor is on duty now. An emergency physician treated her when she first came in, and another doctor took over when she was transferred to this floor. But since you're not a member of the family, neither doctor can discuss her condition with you beyond what I've already told you. I'm sorry. It's hospital policy."

"I understand," Raker acknowledged. He asked the nurse for a number he could call to check on Diane's progress and headed for his home.

He tried to picture how his place would look from what Fletcher had told him, but he was not prepared for the shock when he arrived. The center of the house, where his den was located, had been gutted, the window glass shattered. The eaves and the roof had been burned away almost completely. He could see into the attic on either side of the burned-out portion of the roof. A fire marshal's van was parked in the driveway—the arson investigation team.

CHAPTER 26

Raker identified himself to the fire investigators, and he was allowed to move into the areas of the house that had not been touched by the fire. His life had been violated. His personal possessions were exposed to passersby. His attachment to the furnishings broke away. Even the picture of Susan, barely touched by smoke, seemed remote and out of place. His furniture lost all character, as if it had detached and assigned itself to an anonymous owner.

He stepped tentatively down the hallway from the living room. "Is this where they found the woman?" he asked.

One of the investigators turned to him. "Yes, sir. We were not first on the scene. But that's what we were told. Please don't come any further until we've completed our work."

Raker nodded and stepped back. Most of the door and the door jamb into the den had been burned away. The walls and ceiling of the hallway were blackened. The wooden floor molding was partially burned away, and the carpet had fused into a plastic mass. "Can you tell yet what caused the fire?" Raker asked.

"We're not finished with our findings, but it's clear an accelerant was used—gasoline. We found an empty gas can in the front yard." The man pointed to a plastic gallon container that had been set to one side. Raker had filled it the week before to have it on hand for his lawnmower. Whoever set the fire must have retrieved it from the garage at the back of the house.

"How does it look in there?" Raker finally asked, frustrated by not being allowed to get any closer.

"Nothing left. The floor held up, or we couldn't be working in here, but everything else is toast."

"My desk?"

"Nothing left but scorched hardware. This was a hot fire."

"My files?"

"Gone, sir. There's nothing here. The fire crew must have gotten here very quickly because this fire appears to have been hot enough to spread more than it did."

"Okay, thanks. When will you turn in your report?"

"As soon as we're done, sir. We can get done more quickly if we're not interrupted."

"Sorry. I'm going around to the back so I can look into the bedroom. Will that be okay?"

"Yes, sir, that's fine. Thanks for letting us know."

Raker walked through the garage into the backyard and around to the bedroom window where Diane would have been sleeping. The bedsheets were turned back as if she had just gotten up. The drawer where he kept his baby Glock was open. *She must have taken it*, he thought. *Time to check with Fletcher again.*

"Yes," Fletcher replied. "Diane had a gun. It appears to have gone off accidentally because the bullet grazed her left forearm and then went into the wall. We don't think anyone else was hit. As soon as the fire guys are through, our forensic people are going over the scene because this has already been declared arson."

"Anything else?" Raker asked.

"Pleasants is going by the book. I've been assigned to the team, at least initially. I need to get out there now and start interviewing neighbors. Late at night like it was, though, I don't expect we'll turn up much. The guy that reported the fire said he saw two men running out of the house and get into a stretch-cab pickup. It was dark. The truck was probably black or green. He thought one of the guys had a limp. As I said, it was dark."

"Do you guys have her personal stuff down there? Her purse and personal belongings?"

"Yeah, it's all here. She had an address book with the names of what appear to be family, kids maybe. But none of them have the same last name as hers. Do you know her children?"

"They're all over the country, but I don't know any of them."

"We called a guy named Howard Brooks in Richmond. She had him down as an emergency contact. Turns out he's her oldest son. He volunteered to contact the others. There's nobody here in town we know of."

"She's new in town. She hadn't found a job she liked yet but was looking. I'm waiting to get into the rest of the house. The fire guys are keeping me out at the moment. Did my gun turn up anywhere? My Glock?"

"No. We didn't pick it up. You might want to check with the guys who are there now."

"Call me if anything breaks."

"Roger that."

Raker holstered his cell phone and walked back to the front of the house. "Hey, can I bother you guys one more time?" he shouted to the men who were examining the scene of the fire.

"Yeah. What's up?" one man answered.

"Did you guys come across a gun? A Glock?"

"No. We didn't."

"It's missing then," Raker said. "Keep an eye out for it."

"Okay, we'll let the station know if we come across it."

"Thanks."

Raker remembered Denise Becker wanted him to call when he got back into town. He paced as he reported all that had transpired.

She assured him she wanted him to take as much time as he needed. "So, how is your friend, Jim?"

"She's still in critical condition. I can't get any information other than that. It's terrible this happened to her . . . I need to get my stuff out of what's left of the house because the place is not secure. I also need to find a place to stay and contact my insurance agent."

"I understand. Let me know if there's anything we can do here."

As Raker walked back to his car, he glanced across the street and wondered which one of his neighbors had reported the fire. He decided to investigate. The home directly across the street from his was owned by Dwight Kohorst, a friendly middle-aged man with three teenage sons.

"Hey!" someone shouted as Raker crossed the street. He looked up to see Kohorst dressed in a bathrobe and slippers standing just inside the front door to his home.

"Good morning," Raker replied.

"I don't mean to be inhospitable," Kohorst explained as Raker mounted the steps to the porch, "but I have one hell of a cold . . . Sorry about your place. What are you going to do?"

"I haven't figured it out yet," Raker replied. "One thing at a time."

"How about the gal that was taken away in the ambulance? Is she all right?"

"It's pretty serious. She's in a coma. I'm on my way back to the hospital next."

"I hope she's all right. If it hadn't been for this damn cold keeping me awake, I would've probably slept right through everything . . . at least until the fire trucks arrived."

"I'm glad you were awake," Raker said, standing at arm's length from his friend. "Can you answer a few questions for me?"

"Glad to. I want to help if I can."

"The officer I talked to said you saw two men running from the house."

"Yes," Kohorst said. "They came out of the side door, the kitchen door, and ran across the front lawn to a truck parked at the curb in front of the house next to yours."

"Did you get a good look at them?"

"No. It was the dead of night. The street light cast long shadows, and I couldn't make much out. I gave a description to the other officers."

"Right. They went over their report with me. You said one of the men had a limp."

"Yes. That's right. The other guy pitched a gas can . . . not a can really but a plastic container. Red. You know. Like everyone uses. He tossed it into the yard. I guess the police took it away because I didn't see it later."

"Did anything else strike you about the two men beside the one guy had a limp?"

"No. Not really. It all happened so fast."

"Take your time. I don't want to keep you at the door like this, but I need as many details as you can recall."

"I understand."

"How tall were they?" Raker asked, hoping to jog Kohorst's memory.

"One guy was at least six feet. He could look right over the top of the cab on the pickup. The other guy was shorter but faster on his feet. Oh, yeah, the bigger guy was carrying a crowbar . . . small wrecking bar . . . you know for pulling down boards. When he got to the pickup, he popped the lid on the tool box in the back and dropped it in there."

"How big was the crowbar?"

"At least a foot-and-a-half long. Yeah. At least that. It had the curl at the end, you know the kind."

"Yes," Raker agreed. "Did you tell the police about it?"

"No. It just came to mind now somehow as I was thinking about it."

"Did the investigating officer leave a business card with you?"

"Yes. It's on the dining room table. You want to see it?"

"No. But I want you to call him and report the crowbar. Tell him what you told me, okay?"

"Yeah, okay."

"What kind of truck was it?" Raker asked.

"I didn't see that. It was a dark color . . . maybe black but it could have been a dark blue or green."

"Did you see the license?"

"Yeah. I'm pretty sure it was North Carolina. I told the officer that."

"Did you catch any part of the license number?"

"No. Not the number. But I did catch the first two letters on the plate. XR. That's all I could see. I told the police that also."

"Anything else? Anything at all?" Raker persisted.

"Gosh, no, Jim. I think I've told you everything. I'd better get back inside. No point in tempting fate with this cold."

"Yes. Thanks. Thanks very much. This has been very helpful. Please call the investigating officer and tell him everything you told me, about the crowbar and the license plate. I'll see you again soon . . and get over that cold!"

"I will, Jim. Take care."

Raker planned to check with the hospital every day or so, hoping he would be allowed to see Diane once she was released from intensive care. Fletcher called and reported all of the family members had been contacted, and the oldest son was being dispatched from Richmond to look in on his mother. He would report to the rest of the family on her condition.

"She may not be able to identify her attacker," Raker ventured to Fletcher over the phone.

"There's no way of knowing until she comes out of it. We don't know how long that'll be or even if she will pull through."

The acrid stench of smoke from the fire permeated what was left standing of the house and everything in it, including Raker's clothes. An insurance adjuster surveyed the place and said he would be working up an estimate. In the meantime, he assured Raker the cost of temporary housing was covered, and Raker decided to pack the little he could use from his home and move into a residence motel on the northwest side of town. It would be a good jumping off place for Riley's Creek whenever he needed to go back.

The insurance company reported it would take at least four months to repair all the damage to the house so he could move back in. They also arranged to have his furnishings cleaned, deodorized, and moved into storage until the house was ready. Nothing remained of the furniture in Raker's study. He would need to buy new. Arranging for the contractors, securing permits, and scheduling the repair work would all be handled by the insurance company.

Once in his new quarters and with time on his hands, Raker decided Wednesday morning to check in with everyone. Word from the sheriff in Baden County was the SBI man had taken his position in the plant, but Turcotte had been very cautious in getting acquainted with him.

"He's playing his cards close to his vest," the sheriff explained on the phone. "Moran says he wants his guy to take it slow, naturally. Get to know the suspect first before trying anything. It's going to take a while. No need for you to rush right back up here as long as you got so much trouble down there." Raker thanked the sheriff and made a point of telling Ms. Becker how grateful he was for the patience the company showed him.

Raker was eager to see Diane, but as long as she remained in critical condition and in the intensive care area he would not be admitted. Fletcher was able to give him some details, at least as they appeared on the police report.

According to Fletcher, Diane apparently surprised the intruder or intruders and was struck on the head. She fell to the floor unconscious. She landed on her right arm when she fell, and the gun she was holding fired a round that grazed her left shoulder and arm. Powder burns on her clothing and chest established that the wound was accidental and self-inflicted.

"We're trying to get the Motor Vehicle people to track the license information. All we know at this time is the first two letters were assigned to two western counties and one of those is Baden County," Fletcher said. "The DMV is so slow, so very slow. It's damn near impossible to get anything out of them."

"They know it's a pickup truck, right?" Raker asked.

"Yes, but not the make."

"But a dark color. That has to narrow it down some."

"They don't record color on a registration. What we'll get is a list of vehicles described as pickup trucks for the two possible counties. That could be a pretty damn long list," Fletcher explained.

"But it's a start."

"Agreed."

Fletcher did not have any current information on Diane's condition. Settled in the residence motel, Raker tried to get back into his usual routine as much as possible—if for no other reason than it would help time pass. As he sat at his desk in the office, a sense of urgency was building in him. He resisted feeling he was responsible in any way for what happened. He pulled out a yellow legal pad and began to make notes.

"Why Diane?" he scrawled on a top line. *Did somebody know she was there?* He had not told anyone. Perhaps she did. But the information on her whereabouts could not have been spread among too many people. There had not been enough time for word to get around. He didn't know any of Diane's friends. More likely than not, nobody knew she was there. Whoever broke in must have thought the house was vacant. The intruders must have known Raker and wanted something he had in his home.

"Assume Nobody Home," Raker scrawled on the pad. A couple of lines beneath it, he wrote, "Why my study?" The focus of the intruder's interest was his study. Diane must have heard someone in the house, gone to investigate, and been hit on the head to keep her from discovering who it was.

"Diane saw intruders???" Raker wrote the question on the pad. *Won't know until she recovers.*

For years, he dreaded something might happen to Susan because he was in law enforcement, because someone he had helped convict wanted to even the score and get back at him. That dread came back to him now that Diane was in the hospital. All of his years of police work and nothing happened as he feared it might. Now somebody has struck when he was the least concerned, when he was the least aware.

The most recent criminal case in which he had played a part had been closed for almost two years, and the guilty party was still incarcerated. There had been no loose ends. Three people had been killed, but nobody walked away from that horrible story with a grudge. Perhaps somebody from Minneapolis had tracked him down. But who? Most of the cases he worked on in the Twin Cities were clear cut. *Ancient history, all of them*, he thought. *No threats from anyone about getting even.* The people he helped convict may have been bitter, but he could not recall anyone so angry at him personally that he would be targeted.

Besides, it was not an attack on him. If the intruders thought nobody was there, the attack was on his home. *But why?* He needed to make several assumptions in order to give any plausibility to what had taken place. First, whoever broke into the house must have known that he was not there. Second, whoever it was did not know Diane had moved in for a few nights. They must have thought they would be able to search the home undisturbed, and then Diane surprised them when she suddenly showed up in the hallway. *Why the hell didn't she just call 911 from the bedside phone?* Raker decided she must not have been sure herself that someone was in the house. Rather than call and be embarrassed if the police showed up on a false alarm, she decided to investigate.

So burglary, he decided. "What did they want?" Raker wrote in the middle of the page. He would not know whether anything was missing until the arson report was completed. Even then, the fire consumed his files, his furniture, and the other articles in the room—books, papers, tax returns.

Why set the place on fire? Nothing added up. Art's mountain place was ransacked the previous day. Years of experience taught Raker to be suspicious of what may appear to others as coincidence. If Diane was going to continue to be confined to intensive care, perhaps he should go back up to Riley's Creek and look for a connection, however implausible.

Thinking about returning to the hospital brought back memories of when Susan had been confined there before coming home to be watched and cared for by the hospice people. With Diane's condition uncertain, everything felt too familiar. He smoldered. He had been down this road only too recently. He never wanted to go through anything like it again. But here it was . . . in his face.

CHAPTER 28

"There's a man waiting in your office," Jeannine, Raker's administrative assistant, said as he walked up to her desk. "He's been waiting since nine o'clock this morning."

Raker looked at his watch. It was 9:45. "Did he have an appointment?"

"No."

"Who is he? Does he work for us?"

"Howard Brooks. No. He just came in and asked for you."

"Brooks," Raker repeated aloud as he walked toward the door to his office.

The man stood up as Raker entered the room. "Howard Brooks," he said, extending his hand.

"What can I do for you?" Raker said as he sat down behind his desk.

"I understand you know my mom . . . that the two of you are friends. She was hurt when your house caught fire Sunday night . . ."

"Diane? My God, I heard you were coming to see her. Brooks; her first marriage."

"Right," Howard smiled.

"I know her as Welborn, of course," Raker said, motioning to his guest to take a seat. Raker could see the resemblance. Same brown eyes. Same clear skin. Trim. Balding with a clean-cut mustache and goatee. Probably in his mid-thirties.

"Yes. She went back to her maiden name a few years ago. I got into town late yesterday and spent most of the night at her bedside. She's in a coma."

"I know. I went to check on her right away, but not being a family member, I couldn't get in to see her. They wouldn't give me any other information on her condition."

"Well, I've seen her. She looks really bad. It's hard to see her like she is . . ." Brooks cleared his throat and then straightened up in his chair. "Would you mind telling me what your relationship has been with Mom? Why was she in your house when you weren't there?"

"I've known your mother for about two months. We were dating." Raker looked Brooks directly in the eye. Jim cleared his throat. "We broke up last weekend, but we decided to stay in touch as friends. Good friends but nothing romantic anymore. She asked to stay at my place because her apartment was being painted, and I agreed because I expected to be out of town."

"So, you were not engaged or anything?"

"No, nothing like that," Raker conceded. "I like your mother. I think we gave each other a good chance at having something become more permanent . . . more substantial between us, but it just wasn't there. I think she might have been hopeful, but I wasn't. At my age, you get to know what to expect."

"She never mentioned you in any communication with anyone in the family," Brooks said. "The police said they thought she may have surprised a burglary in progress and that's how she got hit on the head."

"That's what I understand also. How is she? As I said, nobody will tell me anything."

"Pretty bad," Brooks said, trying unsuccessfully to strike a casual note. "I had a long talk with one of the physicians. It doesn't look good." Brooks broke off.

"Well, this is really awkward for me. I may not feel anything especially romantic about your mom, but I care about her. I am concerned. I lost my own wife over a year-and-a-half ago, and this is feeling pretty bad for me," Raker explained.

Brooks held his gaze on Raker for a moment and then looked at the floor. "There isn't much good news to report," he finally said, looking up. "The blow on her head fractured her skull. Bleeding inside her skull had to be relieved because it was putting pressure on the brain. She has deep burns on one side of her face . . . the side that was exposed . . . and the same on one arm. She looks bad." Brooks choked.

Raker saw tears welling in the man's eyes.

"Her . . . her hair is singed. Her eyebrows. It's a good thing according to the doctor that she is unconscious because the burns are deep enough to involve the nerves. She might have some scars, but she won't be badly disfigured. That is, if she recovers. She may not."

"I see. I know it must be hard . . ."

"Yes," Brooks said, anger ringing in his voice. "It's very hard . . . to see her like she is. The only good thing was she was on the floor or her burns would have been much worse. She inhaled some smoke but not as much as she would have if she hadn't been knocked to the floor where the air was cooler. The doctors don't believe she inhaled any large amount of toxic fumes. The head injury is their main concern."

Given his visitor's angry tone, Raker was not sure how to respond. He waited until he was certain Brooks had stopped talking. "I am," he began, "grateful that . . . even though it is terrible news . . . you took the time to find me and come see me. I want to know what I can do for her. For you. For the family."

"Why?" Brooks ignored the tears streaming down his face. "Why would that happen to her? I mean, I know why she was in your house . . . and that's okay with me. Everything you said is okay with me. You're okay with me," Brooks said through a sad smile. "The police all said you can be trusted. I just don't understand why this happened. Do you have enemies in the city? Was somebody after you, and she got in the way?"

"I've been asking myself the same thing over and over. I don't think I have any enemies who would break into my house. I'm not in law enforcement anymore. If I were, I'd do whatever I could to apprehend whoever is responsible. All I can do now is think about it and use the limited authority of my civilian role here at this company to do whatever I can."

"You've been in touch with the police then."

"Yes. And I'll stay in touch. I have friends there. They'll keep me informed. Besides, it was my house."

"Okay, I need to ask you something. See, I can't stay in town here indefinitely. I need someone here who has an interest in how Mom is doing. I'll probably be here through the end of the week, but I have a family and a job to get back to myself. Once I go back, will you keep me in the loop? Will you check up on Mom, talk to the doctors, and keep me apprised of what her condition is and what the prognosis is? Is that asking too much?"

"I'll do everything I can, but they won't let me in to see her while she's in intensive care, and they won't give me any information."

"We can change that. I have power of attorney. I can get things set up so you stay informed."

CHAPTER 29

"God, I'm actually glad they took my laptop. This one's so much faster," Art Nichols yelled to his wife from his study in their mountain cabin. The claims adjuster from the insurance company agreed there were a few items lost or destroyed in the vandalism of their home that could be replaced immediately and made an advance to help cover the cost of buying them. New laptops were high on the list for both Cheryl and Art.

"Mine too. Did you see the notice about the property owners' association meeting this Saturday?"

"What about it?"

"It's some kind of emergency meeting. Everyone's been ignoring the date the state set for bringing the dam into compliance. Nothing's been done. The meeting's to get people organized to do something."

"I couldn't care less," Art shouted back to his wife.

"You're not going?"

"Why the hell should I? That asshole Schreve will be running things. He wouldn't acknowledge anyone from the floor he doesn't want to speak. It'll be a travesty. Fuck 'em." Art looked up and noticed Cheryl had abandoned her laptop and was standing in the doorway to his study.

"Did you read it?"

"Read what?"

"The notice."

"Why would I read the goddamn notice if I wasn't going to attend the meeting."

"Because it says some things that pertain to us."

"Like what?" Art growled.

"Like the dam is going to be breached if action isn't taken."

"Who cares? We're up here where it doesn't matter. I've never stuck a toe in the lake. Let them turn it into a stream. It's just attracted a lot of beer-drinking kids who raise hell at night anyway."

"Rumor is some outfit is willing to fix the dam, but it wants control of the development before it's going to back it. They've been pressuring people to sell to them, and then they will lease back. If too many sell, then they'd own the majority of the lots. Anyone who lives here like we do would be at their mercy," Cheryl said.

"It'll never happen."

"You don't know that."

"Ah c'mon, Cheryl, Schreve is just trying to sensationalize everything to get a turn out. Something's going on that we don't know the first damn thing about, and it can stay that way for all I care."

"Well, the last thing I thought I'd ever do is try to talk you into doing anything with the POA, but you know so much. You wouldn't need to participate. Just get a sense of what's going on. I don't want to see our dues go through the roof. They're too high now. I don't want to see someone running the place without regard for the long-term owners. We have enough of that now. It doesn't help to just turn our backs. They win that way without our saying anything."

Art closed the lid on his laptop, turned to his wife, and stared at her.

"Don't give me that look," Cheryl protested. "Maybe there's some connection between what's happening and what happened to our house. Getting ransacked like it was."

"Like it still is, you mean," Art said, looking around at the room that was still sparsely furnished because the damaged furniture had not been replaced. "Fuckers!"

"So. See. Maybe you'd find something out."

"I don't see the connection."

"You were the secretary-treasurer for three years. You know a lot. You had a lot of records from when you were in office. You still have the backup files that Helen Schreve keeps bugging you about."

"Okay, okay, a connection." Art stood up. "Not a great one. But a hunch. And if being at that meeting blows my program, then what?"

Cheryl did not want Art to get upset. She thought, however, that the situation would just get worse if they did not get involved, at least to the point of knowing what was at stake. Their retired life at the cabin was very important to her.

Cheryl and Art had been an unlikely match when they first met. Cheryl couldn't help noticing Art's rugged good looks, his thick dark curly hair. He was a big man, a head taller than her five-feet-six inches. He had broad shoulders and strong arms. She found out after they met that he was something of a gym rat, taking time every day to work out. At first, he didn't appear to be her type.

She grew up in Edina, Minnesota, the middle child of Wade and May Carlson's three daughters. Her father, an attorney, moved his practice into the high six figures early in his career when he was hired to handle the Broderick estate. Broderick—a lifelong bachelor, bank president, and legendary miser—left millions to a long list of charities.

"I wonder if a review board ever looked at the way the Broderick estate is being handled?" she overhead a man say on the putting green at the country club one afternoon. "Carlson's getting a percentage cut of everything going into the trust and everything going out."

The other man laughed. "Yeah, and he's probably getting a cut of everything that stays in it also."

Her parents were socially active. Their home was spacious and well furnished. A hired woman came in every afternoon to help with the housekeeping, and a yard man appeared two days every week to keep the grounds neat and tidy.

Cheryl realized at a young age what her parents expected of her. She was to be perky, polite, and cute to her parents' friends. She enjoyed the role until somewhere during her high school years it began to feel phony. A woman was growing up underneath the starched blouses. She wanted to know who that woman was and to stop being Doris Day for her parents.

She attended Augsburg College in St. Paul, preferring to live on campus even though she could commute. She settled on English as a major her junior year.

"Good choice," her father said in a rare approving mood. "Those are good credentials for law school."

But Cheryl did not want to go to law school. She did not know what she wanted to do when she graduated and seriously considered postgraduate work to give herself more time.

During the spring of her senior year, she began interviewing with various recruiters visiting her campus. She sat down with a young man representing Northwestern Bell Telephone in one such interview. He allowed he had only been working with the company a few years himself, but he liked it. The company was looking for candidates who would enter their sales training program to become communication consultants. Cheryl liked the sound of the job, going from company to company to review their communication needs, then recommend a system, support the installation, and train employees on how to use it. When offered, she accepted the position.

Her father was dismayed with her choice. *Good*, she thought. Her training began in Minneapolis, and she moved out of the house when she received her first check, taking an apartment in Bloomington with another young woman she met on the job.

Cheryl progressed up the ranks at her company very quickly. The Doris Day upbringing was paying huge dividends, and her girl-next-door good looks were a winning asset. She was eventually promoted out of sales and into sales training.

Pace Learning Systems was conducting a pilot seminar for the sales representatives of Northwestern Bell Telephone in the hope the company would be interested in buying their program and instituting it for all sales personnel. Cheryl was invited to attend and help evaluate the program. She took advantage of a break in the proceedings to seek out Tory Pace and introduce herself.

"Hi, Mr. Pace," she said, beaming as she approached. "I'm really enjoying the seminar. I'm Cheryl Carlson."

"Of course you are," Pace said in his usual flippant manner.

Pace was older than she, but she found him exciting and was attracted to him. He propositioned her twice; once to join his company and then to go to bed with him. She was excited by the first offer and accepted it but declined the second.

She met Art at Pace Learning Systems. He was a marketing specialist to the military. They met by chance in the parking lot one morning as she pulled her bright yellow Cadillac into a corner space and got out.

"Some snazzy ride there, girl," Nichols said.

The car had become an embarrassment to her. She bought it dreaming of the day she could pull into the driveway at her folks' house for the first time. Her dad would see she was doing well, if not better than she ever would have as a lawyer.

Nichols's friendly manner was a relief. She agreed to have lunch that day with Art. She found she could drop her defenses with him. He was older, sure, but very understanding and kind. He wasn't afraid of his feelings and she liked that. As they dated, she learned from him how to relax into herself, become more authentic, trash the Doris Day shtick, and be more her own person.

"I don't want to bring children into this world," Art said one evening as they were discussing getting married. "I have seen too much of it. It's bad now. It is only going to get worse."

Cheryl respected Art's experience. She ached when he suffered from a painful flashback and always wanted to do more when they occurred. Art was nothing like her father. He was caring, considerate, and affectionate. She had never considered having children. It was not important to her. She never wanted to live an Edina lifestyle again—ever.

As they both worked out their careers at Pace Learning, Art came up for retirement several years ahead of her. She decided to resign when he retired. The years at Pace Learning had been good for both of them. Money was not a problem.

Art had traveled extensively in the Southeastern states and had grown to like the Blue Ridge Mountains of Virginia and North Carolina. After vacationing in the area over several summers, Cheryl and Art decided to buy a home on Rebecca Ridge, located a few miles east of Riley's Creek, North Carolina.

CHAPTER 30

"You're the reason they called the meeting," Frank Schreve yelled at his wife. Helen was in the kitchen adjacent to the dining area where he was drawing up notes for the presentation he knew he would have to make to the membership.

"You can't say that, Frank. That's just not true," Helen shouted back.

"You bugged those people. Bugged them to death. You kept calling them and then you made that disastrous appearance at the commissioners' meeting and pissed everyone off. I swear. You never know when to let up. You've never learned about winning people over. You just push and harp, push and harp. It's too much."

"If they have that meeting . . . if they go through with auctioning off the property in arrears in taxes and if people sell out so that the dam will get fixed by Palmetto-Atlantic, they'll change the character of this development forever. People who bought in years ago are going to lose their investment. They're going to be railroaded into doing whatever the new developer wants."

"I can't think of anything I'd rather see happen," Frank replied. "Place is owned now by a bunch of deadbeats. They don't pay their property owners' association dues. They're getting a free ride off of those who do pay."

"I suppose you want to get booted out of office. Lose control. That's what'll happen, and then they'll rewrite the bylaws. Make everything more restrictive. More expensive. I've heard they're going to put gates at the three entrances. You'll need a card key to get in. They want a golf course. Who needs a golf course? We have two in the county already."

"Rumors. Just rumors. Don't believe everything you hear. I'd like to see the area in the hands of somebody who knows what they are doing . . . knows how to plan something and then run it. Bunch of amateurs trying to make a go of this place. One big pissing contest. People are always getting angry . . . worked up about something or the other, and then every couple of years, the officers get fed up—and who can blame them—and a new group comes in. Everything starts all over again. The same issues. Nothing changes."

"I just don't want to be in a situation where we have no say. Have you thought about what happens to our investment in this place if the worst thing happens?" Helen asked.

"The worst thing? What's 'the worst thing'? That a developer would take over and make this into a great place to have a second home?" Frank got up, folded his notes, and walked into the living room as he talked. "I'd guess the value of this place could double then. Maybe more. Maybe two-and-a-half million."

"But you can't say what will happen. Everything will be in the hands of the owners. They'll widen the roads and cut into our yard. They'll pass an ordinance against golf carts. Who knows?" Helen said, following her husband out of the dining area.

"Look," Frank said, wheeling around to face her, "the worst thing that could happen to this place is everything goes on as it has. Nobody with money is going to buy in here. We got those goddamn double-wides out there at the entrance look like shit, all rusted and faded. It's a turnoff to anyone who wants a nice place . . . a place with some class to it. If things keep going as they have, this whole area is going to look like something right out of *Li'l Abner*—fucking Lower Slobbovia."

Helen pulled short. "What's the matter with you today? We always see eye to eye."

"The hell we do," Frank roared. "We always see things as you see them.

But this time, it's not going to be that way. This time it'll be something I can accept rather than something I allow just to keep you happy . . . just to keep you from harping on and on about things."

Frank saw the surprise in his wife's face. She studied him quickly, then turned and walked back to the kitchen. Frank was never like this. *Not her Frank!* Big, easy-going, considerate. "Mild as soap," one of his associates described him. Always good on his feet, Frank knew what to say and how to say it. She could be so proud of him when he gave a speech or had a meeting to run. She could help. Put the agenda together so that the issues appeared as they both wanted them. Write the minutes to emphasize his contribution and temper the impact of the arguments from those who opposed him.

She knew how to fight. When she was a girl, she marveled at how her mother ran things. Her father, a copywriter at a local newspaper, always took a supportive role, and while she loved him, she learned quickly to look to her mother for permission to do anything and for advice. She found as she matured that her father moved farther and farther out of her affections until she treated him with reluctant respect but little else.

Howard Brooks was scheduled to leave town on Friday so he set up a meeting with Diane's doctor on Thursday afternoon and invited Raker to sit in.

"She has a long road ahead of her," began the doctor, a wiry, intense man who had a disconcerting habit of staring just off to the side of the person he was addressing, his eyes narrowing as if he wasn't sure of his next word. "Her burns are going to be painful as they heal. They were not deep enough to destroy the nerve tissue. However, our major concern is with her head injury. It is severe. Her skull has been fractured. Fortunately, no bone splinters have penetrated brain tissue, but internal bleeding was putting pressure on the brain, and we needed to relieve it by venting the skull. It remains to be seen if she has suffered any permanent damage." The doctor paused as if he expected questions.

Brooks and Raker said nothing.

"One of our most immediate concerns is, because she was in a fire, if her lungs might have sustained injury. An infection could set in, which would be very difficult to treat," the doctor continued. "We will watch her condition, but with each passing day, we grow in confidence that her lungs will be fine. We're also closely monitoring her blood pressure. If it drops too low—and we are keeping it lowered to prevent an onset of cranial bleeding—kidney failure can result."

"Sounds complex," Brooks observed. "What about the coma she's in?"

"As she gains strength from one day to the next, her recovery becomes more certain. She is immobilized because she's still recovering from the head trauma. There are risks involved in keeping a patient immobilized for any extended length of time. Embolism, for example. We want to maintain her as she is for her own comfort and to keep her stable."

"How do you do that?" Brooks asked.

"Medically."

"Drugs?" Brooks asked again.

"Yes. Lorazepam and an analgesic. It's difficult to say how long it will be necessary to maintain her in her current condition. She'll develop a tolerance for the anesthetic and the depth of her coma will vary, at times becoming more shallow. We need to monitor how she's responding and regulate her dosage. We are going to keep her on a ventilator for the time being." The doctor looked at the time. "Well, that's about it for now, gentleman. We have contact information and will get in touch with you if anything unexpected happens."

Howard had cleared Raker so he could visit Diane while she was in intensive care. They both decided to look in on her after meeting with the doctor. Brooks had prepared Raker for his first visit, but he was taken aback by Diane's appearance. The tubes and monitor sensors were alarming in themselves. The burns on the face were beginning to heal, and her skin was discolored, yellowed and scaly under the ointment. She was oblivious to their presence.

"Why is there tape over her eyes?" Raker asked.

"To keep her cornea from being scratched accidentally. She doesn't have normal reflexes," Brooks replied.

"I can see why this is difficult for you," Raker said softly. "She mentioned you and her other children, but she never talked much about any of you."

"I'm not surprised," Brooks replied. "Each of us made it a point to go see her at least once every year or so. It was always awkward. She'd be with one guy and then another. Usually he'd clear out when one of us showed up. There's so much that was always left unsaid."

"It's that way with all families," Raker observed.

Howard grimaced. "But ol' Dad never said one thing about her, and she never said anything about him. Here they had all these years together, had all of us kids, and one day it just falls apart and nobody ever speaks of it. She betrayed him, you know? She drove him out of the house with her late nights away from home. He finally couldn't take it anymore and just moved out."

"There's no need for you to tell me this," Raker interrupted. "It's not anything I need to know. Water under the bridge."

"I know. But then again, it's not. I look at her lying there. She's my mother. I love her and I want to be kind to her and yet there's all this unfinished business. We had a good family. I thought we were happy. For years, that's all I focused on . . . the good times growing up."

"She might be able to hear you," Raker said in an effort to get Brooks to be quiet.

"My younger brother told me Dad was a little drunk one night and came into his room crying, all upset that the family had broken up. Here it was, two . . . maybe three years later . . . and he's still hurting over it, and he was getting ready to remarry."

"It takes a long time to get over some losses," Raker said. Brooks's behavior puzzled him. He wondered whether the man had been drinking.

"No. You know, for years I never looked at what happened. Then one morning, I realize I'm thirty-six years old, raising a family of two sons of my own. And if my wife came home one night, the way Mom did, and told me she was with some other guy, shit, I'd go nuts. And I've never done what Dad did. He took it all on. Married right out of high school. A straight-up guy. I made some unfortunate choices along the line, but I was free to make them. Dad wasn't. He shaped his life around being married to her. He was trying . . ."

"Just . . . just hold a minute, Howard," Raker said, raising his voice slightly to interrupt. "We don't know what your mother can hear. And this is really family stuff that doesn't involve me."

Raker pulled Brooks by the upper arm and turned him. The young man looked directly into Raker's eyes.

"Okay," Brooks demurred. "But let's step out then. I can't just leave things like this."

The two men turned and walked out of the room. "I'll be right back," Brooks said over his shoulder as if Diane would hear him. Once in the corridor, he turned again to Raker. "Look, I trust you, Mr. Raker. I . . . this may be the last time I'll see my mother alive. I'm glad you're here. If she comes out of it, you've got to tell her I was here. Tell her I'll be coming back to see her."

"I will. I assure you," Raker said.

"See, it's always like this. All of us kids, we wanted Mom and Dad to know we love them. As a kid, you go along. You have to. They're the parents. They're running your life for you, but somewhere along the line, when you look back, there's this big hole when everything came apart. Your parents are running around like they have no sense at all. You ought to get a chance to say something, something that's real, something that's happened. I mean, I've been angry too. She wasn't the only one," Brooks said, nodding back toward Diane's room. "Everyone was hurt. Dad moves away with my younger brother and sister. Seeing Mom move. I don't get it. Now, suppose she dies. Nothing's ever explained. Nothing gets talked out after what we've all been through?"

Raker could see how shaken Brooks was. "This is not the time," he consoled softly. "You need to be steady for her. Whatever worked up until now has to be the rule from here on out. I hope your mother makes it. If she does, that'll be your chance. She might surprise you."

"Yeah, if? And if she doesn't, that's it. We just keep thinking the best. God knows we're good at it." Brooks looked down at his feet. Then he sighed and looked up and said, "I . . . I'm sorry, Jim. Forgive me. I . . . I gotta leave first thing in the morning. If she dies while . . ." Brooks swallowed hard. "I don't want her to die. I . . . I've said too much. Forgive me." Brooks did not immediately notice Raker extended his hand as if to bring the conversation to a close.

"There's nothing to forgive," Raker said. "Maybe in time you'll find the answers. At least an answer for yourself," he ventured. "She may have her own regrets, things that aren't easy to talk about. I doubt she wanted to hurt anyone, least of all her children. She doesn't seem like that kind of person to me."

Brooks nodded and said nothing further. The two men stood quietly in the corridor.

"I know this is difficult," Raker said finally. "I wish I could do more."

"No. You've been great. I'll say goodnight to you now. I'm going back to be with her for a while longer, sit at her bedside. I'll look at her not knowing what to think. I'll miss her. I love her, yet without a clue about who she really is—just what I've wanted her to be." Brooks choked off his own words. "You know," he said looking up suddenly with a chuckle. "Maybe she didn't think anything at all about what she did. Maybe, sometimes, people just don't."

Brooks declined Raker's offer to drive him to the airport the next morning, explaining he had a rental car to return. The two men exchanged telephone numbers and email addresses and parted company when Howard walked back into his mother's room.

The residence motel furnished Raker with everything he needed, including the table and dinnerware for meals. He had replaced his laptop and was relieved to find nearly all of his websites had retained his previous entries, addresses, and other information. Nothing of consequence had been lost. He kept his correspondence in LockBox so he could retrieve it if necessary from his computer at the office.

Raker realized that there had been no word from Sheriff Grossman in two days, but he knew the sheriff would call if an arrest was made. His concerns for Diane, her son, and the meetings with the insurance adjusters, however, overtook Raker's thoughts, and he had not considered further why his place had been burglarized. He still could not tie it to any case or cases he had been working on prior to leaving the sheriff's office. There was nothing with the new position at Southern World Textiles that suggested a connection. Perhaps the license plate information would lead to something, but Fletcher was not optimistic that anything would be forthcoming very soon. The truck may not have been from Baden County at all. Cars can be purchased and licensed in one county and end up in another. People move from one county to the next. The possibilities were too numerous. The intruders may even have entered the home by mistake.

CHAPTER 31

Wave after wave of light passed over Diane. Voices boomed and faded. She heard them but didn't understand. Margie was there with her. But neither Margie nor she found the strength—the energy—to push through the haze and wake up. At times, she could begin to feel a faint heat, a burning sensation, in her face and her arm. She wondered groggily if she was too near the radiator in the room where the light came through the crack in the door, the room on the other side of the hallway from where her mother and her father slept. A wave of deep fatigue overtook her and she drifted off, away from everything, from the echoing voices she could not understand, from the waves of light that splashed across her closed eyes, from the brittle pinches of pain she felt in her face. The darkness would be there waiting for her whenever she tired of trying to understand.

At one point, she thought she heard Jim's voice. It reached her as if she were down a long hallway. She recognized the baritone overtones, the silken sound of his masculine voice. She wanted to rouse herself but did not know how. She wanted to reach out to him, but could not move her arm. Her body refused to respond. Margie, too, was quiet. Margie seemed pleased to hear Raker's voice.

When Howard came into the room, Margie went away. Diane, only Diane, wanted to hear him. His voice was more distinct than Raker's, but she still could not make out what he was saying. She felt safe when Howard was there. He would make sure everything was okay, and she would not need to worry or be afraid. She felt him touch her hand and wanted to respond, but her hand refused her most concerted effort. She quickly tired of trying. The heavy fatigue took over, and she fell back under its weight, back with the hope she would find Jim and Howard at her bedside another time. The lights washed over her again. The sounds of people coming and going faded away.

"She betrayed him, you know." Howie's voice reverberated. "She drove him out of the house . . ."

CHAPTER 32

Art Nichols awakened slowly. The night before, he fell asleep listening to the insect chorus emanating from deep in the darkening woods surrounding his cabin. The rhythmical spiny chattering—*chi de de chit, chi de de chit*—was like a chorus, with one side of the forest singing the phrase and then pausing as the other side responded. He listened as to a lullaby.

He rolled over to see that Cheryl was still asleep beside him. He studied her face. Her short blond hair was disheveled, with strands lying loosely on her forehead—she was the picture of contentment as she slept. He acknowledged his love for her, and he filled with contentment as he looked at her. She was, in moments like this, the heart of his serenity. He relied on her, on her clearer vision of the world, of life itself. A light morning breeze spilled across the window sill and flowed over both of them and, eventually, she stirred.

"Oh," she yawned. "Hi there, big fella!" She smiled and reached up to put her arms around his neck and pulled herself up to him. "How you doing this morning?"

"Just fine. So fine. When I look at you, girl, I feel just fine, fine, fine. You are the center of my life. You know that? The center."

Cheryl kissed him on the neck and whispered, "You sweet, sweet man. I'm the luckiest woman."

"All this time together . . . all these years, and I am so grateful to you . . . so appreciative."

"We're lucky, that's all," Cheryl replied. "We're just really lucky."

"I'm so sorry for the rough times. I can't help it when they come along. I wish I could. I wish I could stop them once and for all," Art whispered.

"Not to worry," Cheryl cooed, and stroked the back of his head. "I know nothing you do is directed at me. I just feel bad that you have to deal with it." She paused. She could hear the eastern towhee singing in the yard, the cardinal near the feeder on the deck. "It's getting better, don't you think? I mean it's not as frequent. Not as harsh . . . as hard on you?"

Art sighed. Pulling away from her, he sat up on the side of the bed. "Yeah, I thought so, too, until this happened, the raid on the house. I felt I was standing on *terra firma* here. Now the ground feels like it is shifting beneath my feet. Like it's ready to give way on me at any moment."

"I thought you said it helped to put things back in order . . . to get out in the yard and walk around a little. Get back the feel of the place."

"It has. Every day that goes by, I feel stronger. More myself. It would help even more if I could figure out why these guys came in here and tore everything up the way they did." Art walked over to the closet and picked out his shorts and a shirt for the day.

"You may never know," Cheryl said, her eyes following her husband. He still moved like a young man, she thought. Still loose and agile at the age of sixty-two. "It could've been kids with no reason."

"I still feel somebody was looking for something. You know, from the way things were thrown out into the middle of the room everywhere. Like they're digging for something," Art said.

"But what? We went over this a dozen times."

"I know. I just want the peace of mind in knowing they . . . whoever it was . . . had a reason for coming in here like they did."

"Do you think whoever it was knew Jim and his girlfriend were here?" Cheryl asked.

"I doubt it. I mean, they'd have to be watching the place or followed Jim . . . something like that. We don't have neighbors who could see anything going on here. Maybe the house above us, but they don't have much of a view, and they've been there all along. We don't have any issues with them. We hardly ever talk to them."

"What about the visit to the sheriff's office? Maybe something happened when he was there," Cheryl offered.

"Possible, I suppose. Maybe I could call him. He didn't have much to say after he went into town. Yeah, I'll call him just to see."

Raker was thumbing through interoffice mail when Art's call came in. It was the first time the two men had spoken since Jim had returned to town, and Art was shocked to hear about Diane and the fire.

"You don't think there's a connection do you?" Art finally asked. "This is just too strange."

"It passed my mind, but I've been busy here, worried about Diane, meeting her son, moving . . . there's been a lot on my plate."

"Suppose there's a connection; suppose someone knew you were here. Maybe you had something they wanted and that's what's behind this. Nothing about me and Cheryl."

"I suppose that's possible," Raker conceded. "But I didn't tell anyone I was going up to your place. Nobody would've followed me up there from here, not from Charles City."

"And why take our laptops, Cheryl's and mine? They were both older models and couldn't have been worth much."

"I know. It doesn't add up. Did you have anything valuable on either machine? They may have thought you had some information they were looking for. I know that's a stretch, but consider it," Raker suggested.

"I will, but back to my initial point: Maybe they were after something of yours. Something you had that they needed. Who up here would have known you were staying at my place?" Art asked. "I mean, if you are convinced nobody from Charles City knew, maybe it was someone here."

"The only people who knew were the sheriff and those guys investigating the shooting at the dam."

"Okay . . . You went in and saw the sheriff. Then I went into town to meet with Marie Dennison the next day and you waited for me to return to the cabin before leaving for Charles City. Wait. How about the box! If they're after information when they took the laptops, maybe what they really were after was the file box that Dennison's widow gave me! You took it with you. You still have that box? Or did it get burned?" Art asked.

"No. It's been in the trunk of my car all this time. I never bothered to look at it. I saw it when I got my bag out, but I never thought another thing about it."

"Did you even open it?"

"No. I left it right where it was. Never made the connection. Listen. I'll get it and check it out. Can I call you back in an hour or so?"

"I'll be right here."

"What d'you have there?" Raker's assistant asked when he walked back toward his office with the file box.

"I don't know, but I'm going to find out," Raker replied. He set the box down on his desk and began sorting through the contents. There were several files of what appeared to be official inspection reports. He pulled one and opened it. *Only an engineer would understand these*, he thought. He pulled all the folders labeled "Reports" and stacked them on the side of his desk. Next he looked through several folders that were not labeled. They contained correspondence that dated back several years. Raker realized it would take several hours to go through all of the material. He pulled the unlabeled files out of the box and stacked them on the other side of his desk. A USB flash drive lay at the bottom of the empty box. He plugged it into a port on his own computer but could not access it when it asked for a password, so he turned to the correspondence files and leafed through several folders.

The correspondence was generally in chronological order, the earlier letters dating back to 1974. He thumbed through several pages and noted many were on North Carolina Department of Natural Resources letterhead. Most were photocopies.

Raker pulled a letter at random from among those with a more recent date. The letter was from Lester Hunsinger, president of Dixie States Development Company in Miami, to Gerald Baldwin, head of the Natural Resources Department. Hunsinger was complaining to Baldwin about Norm Dennison, stating Dennison's reports were suspect and cited the legal action Dennison had taken against Dixie States: "I view the history of animosity and the actions taken by Dennison against Dixie States to be such that, in speaking for our shareholders, I cannot see any reason why Dennison's reports on the condition of the Lake Hannah Dam should be accepted as objective and free of bias. I am, therefore, respectfully requesting some other qualified party be assigned to the Lake Hannah Dam."

Raker recalled what Nichols had told him about the lawsuit Dennison had filed against Dixie States and how he had campaigned to get owners to join in the class action suit against the company. *No wonder,* Raker thought. *I'd want him replaced also.*

As he continued to check the correspondence at random, Raker realized he did not fully understand the issues in them because he did not know the development or the people named in the correspondence. He knew Art Nichols would understand and decided the box and all of its contents should be taken back to Art.

Raker recalled from a management meeting that Southern World Textiles employed an engineer on staff to oversee several of the company plants that were constructed decades earlier to provide power to run their mills in several locations throughout the state.

"Yes, yes. He's right here in the home office," the vice president of operations said over the phone in response to Raker's question. "We don't generate our own hydropower much anymore, but we need to maintain the dams, and we got a guy qualified from our regular staff to oversee them. It's cheaper than hiring a consultant firm to come in whenever one of the states wants us to conduct some kind of compliance exercise."

"Can I ask him to look at these files, just to get an opinion?" Raker asked.

"Be my guest. His name is Wilson, Craig. He's on the third floor."

Wilson agreed to look over the inspection reports and told Raker he would get back to him that afternoon. Raker's next call was to Sheriff Grossman.

"I've been concerned about you, Raker. I heard all about the fire at your place and the woman getting hurt. How are you dealing with all that?" asked the sheriff.

"I'm holding up, thanks," Raker replied. "The metro police are working on the case. It's clearly arson. The woman was a friend who was staying at my place while I was there in Baden County. I don't think anyone knew she was up. She surprised the intruders."

"How she doing?" the sheriff asked.

"She's in a coma. It's touch and go."

"I'm sorry."

"A witness said two men ran from the house and got into a late model stretch-cab pickup truck that was parked down the block. The first two letters on the license plate indicated the plate could have been issued in Baden County."

"They'll play hell getting anything out of motor vehicles. It's the worst-run agency in the state."

"That's what I've heard. But it's a factor," Raker persisted.

"Well, keep me posted."

"I will. Now, anything going on with the dealer at the plant?" Raker asked.

"No. He hasn't been showing up for work the last couple of days. He got hurt and hasn't reported in. Turcotte is cagey. Our guy reported he's on casual terms with him, but not to the point where he can make a move. You got to remember most of Turcotte's dealings are down the network to dealers he supplies. We don't know how much direct dealing he does on his own."

"Has our management tried to contact him about being absent?" Raker asked.

"Yes. There was an accident with a forklift and a pallet dropped on his foot a couple of days ago. He reported to first aid and went home. The McNaughton woman is out on bail. He may have figured she rolled up on him and got suspicious."

"But he's expected back at work?" Raker asked.

"He hasn't reported in, but they haven't terminated him."

"How about the shooting at the dam?" Raker asked. "Anything new there to report?"

"Still an open case. We completed interviewing people in the area. Nobody reported anything suspicious. Why?"

"Just curious. I was one of the first guys on the scene. Nothing for me then from the sound of it."

"Nope. By the way, your friend Nichols was brought in on a misde-meanor assault charge because of that incident you witnessed. We had a warrant issued and were going to have him appear before the magistrate, but Schreve, the husband, called and recanted. His wife was the one who signed the complaint, but he didn't want to press charges. Sounded like he had enough on his hands and didn't need more trouble out there at the development."

"I'm glad they let the matter drop."

"Yes. Me too. Thanks for checking in."

Raker hung up. Instinct told him to withhold the information about the box that Dennison's widow had left with Nichols. Art was right. The only people who knew Raker was in Riley's Creek were the guys with the sheriff's department. Schreve may have seen him there when Art ran him off the place, but Schreve had no way of knowing who he was.

"Who saw you pick up the box from Mrs. Dennison?" he asked Nichols just as soon as his friend picked up the phone.

"Geez. The coroner, of course. I mean, he took her in to identify the body. He saw me when she came back to the waiting area. He may or may not have known. That one deputy from the sheriff's was there also . . . Hurdler. Guy's name is Hurdler. But you know who else was there? Schreve. Mrs. Dennison wouldn't have a thing to do with him. She was actually hostile toward him."

"Okay . . . You doing all right with this so far?" Raker asked.

"Yes. Why?" Nichols replied.

"I think the box Mrs. Dennison turned over to you is a key to everything . . . ransacking your place, torching mine, the attack on Diane. Art, you need to see the correspondence in the box. I don't know the people who wrote the letters or those mentioned in them."

"Okay."

"I'm waiting now on word from our own engineer. He's studying the technical reports. When he's done, I'll call you back. And by the way, the two guys running from the fire were driving a dark-colored stretch-cab pickup with a license that might have been issued to a Baden County resident. Didn't that guy we saw in the woods after the shooting drive a dark-green pickup?"

"Ramsay. Cleve Ramsay," Nichols said. "Son-of-a-bitch!"

"Don't jump to conclusions. Could just be a coincidence."

"But the guy is two-thirds asshole and the rest of him is worthless," Nichols said.

"Just let it be for now, okay? Don't mention it to anyone. Let's concentrate on the contents of the box."

"You got it. Man, I'd sure like to have everything in hand for the property owners' association meeting this weekend."

"When is it again—Saturday; day after tomorrow?" Raker asked.

"Yeah."

"I don't know. There's a lot of stuff to go through, and Wilson's doing it as a favor. He's got his regular work to do, too, you know."

"It'd be nice, but . . ."

"I don't think you'd want to say anything about this at the meeting anyway," Raker cautioned. "Not until we know who is after the box."

"I see your point. Okay, I'll wait. Thanks, Jim."

"You're welcome. Given what happened to my house and to Diane, I've got my own reasons for wanting to get to the bottom of this . . . I'll talk to you later."

CHAPTER 33

Raker was pleased Craig Wilson called the very next day to say he had concluded his review of the reports on the condition of Lake Hannah Dam.

"This is intriguing," Craig exclaimed, looking over the top of his reading glasses at Raker. The engineer was a marathoner, pencil-thin and all sinew. The skin on his face was drawn tightly across his high cheekbones, giving him a look of intensity even when he was relaxed. "The more recent reports don't add up," he said. "Up until about three years ago, the reports from Norm Dennison are pretty routine. Nothing out of the ordinary. He was watching the seepage. Had the trees cut down on the downstream side of the dam. Flows were constant. Nothing seemed out of line. Then, for no reason, this guy Greg Lee takes over and things begin to deteriorate . . . things you wouldn't expect."

Craig paused, as if he were trying to come up with the right words. "I don't want to get too technical," he said, "but Lee gets critical of the seepage very early . . . starts citing a deviation in the toe of the dam—that's the downstream side—reporting it out of compliance, which in itself is not critical, but the next thing he begins criticizing is the spillway. Now the spillway has been there for 100 years. It's not even a spillway but a large depression without a control gate to regulate the discharge downstream—very typical of dams the size and age of this one. If the lake reached a critical height, it would wash over the depression and follow the channel created for it to a flood plain for a nearby creek or stream."

Craig stood and began to pace around Raker's office. "Lee also starts questioning the height of the overflow shaft. He thinks it should be lowered to reduce the pressure of the reservoir on the dam, which is something that could be causing the increased seepage he reports. Then he gets into the records . . . goes back to the 1800s . . . to find the history of precipitation in the area—rain and snow melt. He constructs a worst-case scenario to demonstrate mathematically that the overflow shaft is too small, that it needs to be lowered and the opening to it increased in size. Lee then insists an actual concrete spillway is needed in the event of major inflows." He looked at Raker. "Follow me?"

"I think so. It's not exactly rocket science is it?" Raker said, motioning Craig to sit back down.

"No, not really," Craig responded as he took his seat. "Not once you translate all the technical stuff into layman's language. I see why you had trouble with the reports."

"They made no sense to me," Raker acknowledged.

"Actually, they're more technical . . . obtuse . . . than they need to be. My guess is Lee didn't want a layman to understand these reports if they should fall into the wrong hands. A person can hardly make heads or tails of them without doing as you did . . . turn them over to someone who could decipher them. Did you look at some of this correspondence?"

"I saw the one where Dixie States Development wanted Dennison taken off the dam and someone else assigned."

"Yeah, I saw that too. I can see why someone would want Dennison off the site, but I still suspect Lee was doing someone else's bidding—making the worst possible case for the dam," Wilson said. "The deterioration in the condition of the dam is too accelerated. It could all happen just as Lee reports, but it'd take years, not months the way he has it all drawn out. Dennison's notes challenge Lee's conclusions. He documents his argument very well. I found them convincing. Some of Lee's observations could only be true if the reservoir was much, much larger and deeper than it is. You should go over the emails carefully to see if they might suggest something."

"Okay, thanks. I will. I really appreciate this. Is there some way I can reciprocate?" Raker asked as Wilson stood again, this time to leave.

"Just let me know how it all comes out. I'm really curious."

"Will do."

"Oh," Wilson said, "Ferguson wanted me to tell you some guy named Turcotte was going to be let go at the Riley's Creek plant. He's going to be terminated for failure to report for work."

Raker called Ferguson to get the details on Turcotte's termination. Company policy dictated that anyone failing to report for work in five consecutive days was subject to termination. Ferguson said Greason had discussed the termination with Sheriff Grossman, and both agreed making an exception for Turcotte would be the wrong thing to do.

At least that's one less thing, Raker thought with relief. He had lost interest in the Turcotte situation in the wake of everything else that was going on. He closed his office door and began looking through the correspondence. Everything added up as Wilson had told him. He wondered how Dennison was ever able to collect all of it. Someone was guiding Lee in the work he was doing. The emails suggest it; emails should never have been exchanged between a state employee and a private party with a vested interest in what was being done on an inspection site. Raker opened his address book and reached for the phone.

"Mrs. Dennison, how are you, ma'am? This is James Raker calling. I've been asked to look into the box of material that you delivered to Art Nichols."

"I don't know anything about that, Mr. Baker. I don't think you should have that material. It was supposed to go only to Mr. Nichols."

"Yes, ma'am, I know. And the name is Raker, with an R. I'm a retired police detective, and Mr. Nichols asked me to look through all of this material."

"Raker. I see. Ah, well, Mr. Raker that doesn't change anything. I don't know anything about that material. I don't think Norm wanted me to know about any of it. It was always so secret, so hush-hush."

"Hush-hush?"

"Well, yes. Someone walked in on him once when he was looking through another man's computer files," Mrs. Dennison said. "It was reported to his supervisor and he was reprimanded for it. That really upset him.

After that, he'd go down to the office on weekends . . . or sometimes late at night when nobody would be there. He'd return after an hour or two and go directly to his study here at the house. Sometimes he was upset, but he wouldn't talk to me about it."

"Do you think he was at the office to copy material for these files?"

"Oh, Mr. Raker, I can't say. It was an obsession with him. He'd be so distracted, I decided to say nothing because it was the only way I could get him to relax. He'd go down there . . . to the office . . . late and then be distracted for a couple of days afterward. I just let him be. He would eventually come out of it. If I tried . . . if I pried into what was bothering him, it made matters worse. He'd get cross and moody. You know how those things go between married people."

"Yes. I do Mrs. Dennison. I have no more questions for you. You've been a great help, and thank you for taking the time to talk to me."

"Oh, you're welcome. I don't know what I said that could've been of any help, but you're welcome."

Raker hung up and stared at the box that Wilson had placed on his desk. He had failed to acknowledge his reaction to the contents when he first opened the box. It felt like the work of a person obsessed. Too much detail, as if there could never be enough.

Raker thumbed through the correspondence files. Everything was as Wilson reported. The only correspondence, up until the time Dennison was withdrawn from the assignment to the dam, dealt with the lawsuit against Dixie States. Dennison had requested a transcript of the trial and annotated it thoroughly with comments in the margin.

When Greg Lee took over, emails to the department supervisor began suggesting that Dennison had a vendetta against Dixie States Development, the original developers who were the current owners of the unsold lots and common areas. Gradually, the inspection reports from Lee became more critical—at least to the extent Raker could tell from Craig Wilson's notes.

Raker was convinced that Lee was coached; emails provided the evidence. Lee received messages hinting that a gradual escalation in the severity of the trouble at Lake Hannah Dam would make his reports more credible and less likely to be challenged. Lee had more than three years to work with his assignment, and, sure enough, the reports became more and more critical of the dam's condition as time wore on.

Raker wished he knew the password to the USB flash drive. There should be a clue to it somewhere. Dennison wanted the right person to know the contents. *Dennison would be smart enough not to use his own name, birth date, or that of any family member*, Raker thought. A clue to it was probably in the correspondence somewhere. He wanted to go through everything again to look for it, but the morning was almost gone. He had enough information now to make his case. His case, he laughed to himself. "I don't have a case. I'm not in law enforcement anymore," he said out loud.

There was a knock at his door.

"Yes," Raker replied.

The door swung open and Denise Becker stepped into his office. "Oh," she said. "I thought you had someone with you. What's all this?" she asked, noticing the files spread out on Raker's desk.

"It's all stuff that has something to do with the fire at my place and the woman who is in the hospital."

"Looks very detailed," Denise said.

"Yeah. It is. I need to put it up and focus on a few things. I know I haven't been much good around here for the last few days," Raker admitted.

"You know you have my support for whatever it takes to set your affairs straight following the fire," Denise said.

"You've been great. It's been a tough time for me."

"You get things worked out and let me know when everything is back in order."

"Okay, yes. Thanks. That's great."

CHAPTER 34

"I'm having a change of heart," Cheryl said as her husband negotiated the sharp curve in the gravel road leading away from their cabin to the highway into town.

"You were the one who thought I should go in the first place," Art said.

"I know. Just, please, don't let it get to you. Don't lose you temper. Promise," Cheryl pleaded.

"I promise to do my best," Art said.

"Not good enough."

"I promise."

"Good!"

The Subaru pulled onto Nettle Knob Road, which skirted the north side of Lake Hannah. The sun had dropped behind the mountain, casting the entire valley into shadow. The lake was still, without a ripple. The soft sunlight painted the peaks that stood as sentinels on the east side of the valley, crowning them with a yellow and orange light. On the horizon, brilliant cumulus clouds billowed thousands of feet into the blue sky. As the evening progressed, they would reflect the last light across the floor of the valley in the pink, purple, and blue of the sunset.

The Lake Hannah Property Owners' Association held a meeting once a year, usually in the spring when owners, who lived at a distance and had children in school, would find it difficult to attend. The meeting served one purpose—to fulfill the one clause in the bylaws that required an annual meeting of the members. A quorum was never present. Out of 1,257 lots, fewer than 120 owners would attend. Voice votes were taken, and close calls were decided by the president.

A special meeting had been called this Saturday to discuss the pending condemnation of the dam at Lake Hannah.

As Art and Cheryl entered the restaurant, they were greeted by their friends and took their places in the cafeteria line to order barbecue and sides. The aroma of hickory smoke and barbecue sauce whetted appetites of everyone waiting to fill their plates. They carried their steaming trays into the meeting room at the far end of the building.

President Schreve called the meeting to order.

"I'm pleased to see so many in attendance," he said to open the meeting. "Unless there's an objection from the floor, I'd like to waive the reading of the minutes and the treasurer's report from the annual meeting we held in June. Both are on the agenda as usual for the next annual meeting." Schreve surveyed the crowd. More were present than he had anticipated—nearly 200 people packed the room; some struggling with dinner trays stood in the back of the hall.

"We have only one reason for calling this meeting and one reason only. We need to discuss the dam," Schreve announced.

"What about the guy that got killed out there?" a man called out from the back of the room.

"If you want to be recognized, please raise your hand. And by the way, if you aren't current with your dues, you cannot participate in the discussion or vote on any issues that come up." Several put their hands up immediately, including Art Nichols. Schreve glanced over the audience in search of a friendly face. "Neville Duke."

"I think that's fair," Duke said. "Some people in here haven't paid their dues in years. Yet, they come and argue about everything. I say if you don't pay, you have no say." Several people laughed.

Nichols did not wait to be recognized. "Mr. President, there is no provision in the bylaws for restricting any property owner from voting. There is no provision in the bylaws authorizing the association to assess and collect dues. These issues have all been discussed . . ."

"Out of order!" Schreve shouted over Nichols. "Sit down, sir."

"No, sir! I'm going to say my piece, dues or no dues," another man said. "I've withheld my dues because in nineteen years the association has never done anything to maintain the road leading to my place. It's the association's road, but I pay to have it maintained. You start maintaining my road, and I'll pay my dues."

"Out of order! You have not been recognized. I'm going to ask everyone to save these issues for the annual meeting, which is the proper forum for them to be discussed."

"And everyone with an opposing view will be squelched then too," someone from the back of the room called out. "You're dictating everything, and everyone knows it. You and your wife there, who isn't even an elected official. She gets to talk any damn time she pleases without being recognized by you or anyone else."

Schreve turned to his wife who had jumped to her feet. "Stay put," he said quietly. Turning back to the crowd, he said, "The slate of officers was elected in June. If you don't care for the way things are being run, you can either start impeachment proceedings or vote them out of office next year. We'll be here all night if we start on all of these issues again."

The crowd, perhaps because everyone considered the issue of the dam of uppermost importance, or perhaps because they recognized the truth in what he was saying—dues and bylaws being perennially controversial issues—quieted, and everyone one who had a chair sat back down.

"Sheriff Grossman is here tonight to bring everyone up to date on the shooting. Sheriff," Schreve said, yielding the floor.

"First of all," the sheriff said, rising out of his front row seat and turning to the audience, "I want to thank everyone for cooperating with the deputies when they came around to interview each of you. As things stand right now, the case is still open, but we're considering it an accidental shooting. Many of you know or knew Norm Dennison when he lived here. You may even know his folks who own property out at the lake. He tangled with Dixie States Development a few years back, but as of now we are considering that a nonfactor."

The sheriff peered around the room. "Along those lines, many of you have complained about the shooting that goes on down below the dam. Some of you, for years now, have wanted it stopped. I'd like to do every-thing I can, but there's no law against discharging firearms in this county. If there's destruction of property or a threat to life or limb, that's different. Then call my office, and we'll dispatch a car to investigate and make an arrest if necessary. Meanwhile, as my deputies have been telling everyone, if you remember anything you think might have a bearing on the shooting of Mr. Dennison, please let my office know. Thank you." The sheriff sat back down.

"Any questions at this time," Schreve asked. He paused and surveyed the room. "All right. Moving on then. I wanted to get Gerald Baldwin, director of the State Department of Natural Resources, to come up here and talk to us, but he's a very busy man. He did send a letter, however, that I think makes the most logical place to start with our discussion. It reads as follows:

"Dear Mr. Schreve,

I regret that I will not be able to accept your invitation to speak to the Lake Hannah Property Owners' Association because of other commitments. It is my hope that the matter of the Lake Hannah Dam can be resolved without further controversy or concern. The officers of your association were informed several months ago that the state considers everyone living downstream from the dam to be at risk, and that the dam is perilously close to failing. Unless the property owners of the area take immediate action to bring the dam into compliance, the state is obligated to make a controlled breach in the structure and drain the lake.

The owners should know the deadline can no longer be postponed. An unexpected breach would lead to possible loss of life and severe property damage downstream. Your organization must act now, or we will be forced to step in and alleviate the risks to all involved. To that end, I respectfully reiterate the following:

Lake Hannah Dam no longer meets the standards for an impoundment of its kind with a reservoir of its capacity. To bring the dam back into com-pliance would require the following:

- *The reservoir must be drained.*

- *The current spillway must be reengineered to increase its capacity and lower the level at which water will flow over it. A concrete spillway needs to be constructed with controlled floodgates so that the discharge in an emergency can be regulated.*

- *Spillway discharge can no longer be routed to the floodplain for Beaver Creek. Beaver Creek, due to landfill operations along its banks, can no longer handle the capacity of a large runoff without causing serious erosion that threatens state highways 163 and 16. Rerouting will require the purchase of land from current owners.*

- *The current discharge flow-through culvert has developed a serious deflection causing excessive wear on the structure. The culvert will give way in time, and erosion will undermine the dam from within.*

- *The toe, the downstream side of the dam, needs to be excavated and filled with rock to provide for permissible seepage through the structure.*

- *Draining the reservoir is likely to reveal other structural weaknesses that cannot be evaluated at this time.*

In summary, the dam needs to be extensively reengineered. The cost will easily run over a million dollars, perhaps twice that amount. My office will gladly assist you with the preparation of the specifications for sending out requests for proposal to qualified companies doing the kind of work required for this project.

Time is of the essence. The conditions reported by our inspector grow worse at an accelerated pace. Any unforeseen natural calamity, such as high snow melt, hurricane, seismic activity, or heavy rains, like those on record for 1940, could threaten the structure to the breaking point. Barring anything cataclysmic, the structure has only months before the erosion undermining it will cause a breach.

In closing, let me reiterate that my office is at your disposal. My staff has the professional credentials to help your people assess the situation and develop a plan to address all the issues enumerated in the foregoing."

Schreve put the letter down on the podium and looked up at the audience. "We have been on a collision course on this issue for months. Some have chosen to ignore it. Some have not believed the reports. Now we are required as a body to act. Lake Hannah and the dam are property held in common by the association. The floor is open for discussion."

The crowd in the room was silent. "Come on, now. You see how serious the situation is," Schreve said.

"Let's get a second opinion," one of the owners in the front of the room said, looking directly at Schreve.

"We've looked into that. A second opinion, a survey by a professional outfit who do this kind of thing, would cost us at least $30,000, maybe more," Schreve said. "Perhaps I made a mistake waving the treasurer's report. That would be our entire budget for road maintenance for the year. And what if anyone we hired came up with the same conclusion? It'd be money down the drain. We'd need to contact firms that are qualified and then decide which one to hire. We may not have the time to go through all of that."

"Why the hell didn't someone bring this up earlier then?" a voice called out. "Why, all of sudden, is it an emergency? I don't trust what's going on here."

"I can't account for what your previous board did or didn't do," Schreve said. "I looked through the correspondence, and inspection reports were routinely furnished and on file. They document that the dam was trending toward a crisis."

"I can tell you what the previous board did," Art yelled, jumping to his feet. "We wanted to raise the money first, without creating any alarm. We felt publicizing the issue would affect property values. Nobody'd want to buy in here. That's why the dues went up. That's why we put an amnesty program in place, so people in arrears could get caught up and stay current. We raised a lot of money. We've got more money coming in now than at any other time in the history of the organization."

Art took a deep breath and shook his head before continuing. "There's no continuity in the administration. The previous board was voted out. The current board took over, and all momentum on these issues was lost. It happens like that all the time. That's why I wanted to have a vice president/president progression. Then we'd have continuity. But everyone has his or her own ax to grind, and nothing of a serious nature ever gets taken to a vote as it should. Sometimes, it doesn't even get discussed!" Art sat back down.

"You're not laying this at our feet!" Schreve stormed.

"Shit, Frank, it was the first thing I told you and the treasurer when you took over two years ago," Art said. "You and your wife didn't even attend the board meetings for the year before you were elected, so how the hell would you know? Your wife wouldn't let me put it in the minutes. She wrote the goddamn minutes the way she wanted them to read. It's that simple."

Cheryl reached up and tugged at Art's sleeve. "Easy," she whispered. "Easy."

"You told me to take the minutes. You told me to do it," Helen Schreve shrieked, surging toward the podium. "I was helping you out. Everyone knows about your problems. Your health. And, no, I didn't give the notes to you. You were the outgoing secretary-treasurer. It was . . ."

"Right," Nichols shouted over her, "I was the outgoing secretary-treasurer. Thanks for noticing that. The outgoing secretary-treasurer is responsible for the minutes of the annual meeting conducted while he was in office."

"You wouldn't be in office when the minutes came out."

"You weren't in office at any time. I'm talking about the way it has always been done. You left out all mention of the dam problems in the minutes."

"Order!" Schreve shouted. "Helen! Helen, sit down. This is not the issue. We won't get anywhere this way. Wasting time trying to blame someone for the problem doesn't solve anything."

"Yeah, right, especially if the current board needs to answer for a few things," someone said in a stage whisper.

"Order," Schreve shouted again. "We . . . we have a simple decision to make. We either drain the lake and let the area return to wilderness, or we fix the dam."

"Drain the lake," an owner shouted. "It only matters to you wealthy guys who live by it. My property is up on the mountainside. Lake or no lake won't affect it one damn bit."

"We need to stick together on this," Helen Schreve said, still standing at the podium by her husband.

"Yeah. We need to stick together when the issue is important to you. You've got the most expensive place in the area. When the issue is the roads and erosion on the side of the mountain, then it's suddenly every man for himself," a homeowner yelled, taking the floor in the middle of the crowd. "For the past two years, the only thing that gets done is around your side of the lake, around your big place. People are getting pretty damn sick of it."

Schreve raised his hand to his wife to indicate he wanted her to break off the discussion. "The longer view . . . the longer view that involves everyone in the development is that the lake should stay. Others will move in here and build because the lake is there. If we get better fishing by stocking, better swimming by enforcing runoff ordinances, it'll be all the more attractive. As others build, the property values for those already established have only one way to go—up!"

"The guy's letter said 'a million dollars' to fix the dam," another owner shouted. "Let's say it'd cost that in round figures. You know the current developer is broke. Dixie States won't belly up. Only about 30 percent of the owners pay their dues now. Some don't even pay their taxes. My bet is that probably only about fifteen or twenty of us will have to bear the entire cost. So, do the math." He paused. "That's more than $50,000 if all twenty chip in!"

"Suppose it costs less?" Schreve countered.

"Suppose it costs more?" someone else replied. "Once you start a project like this, you can't walk away from it. And we don't have that kind of money. We're working people."

"We'd borrow the money," Schreve replied immediately, "and pay back over time, maybe ten years."

"Yeah, well, you wealthy people with your summer homes might be comfortable throwing that kind of talk around. I live here year-round. The county tax value on my place is $120,000. I can't see shelling out $15,000 to $20,000 just to keep the dam there. I don't fish. I don't own a boat. I say drain the lake and forget it."

The crowd began to stir as the man sat down. Neighbor turned to neighbor. The speaker had struck a nerve. Year-round residents of Baden County resented part-time and seasonal residents. A bumper sticker, "We Don't Care How You Did It In Florida," captured the sentiment.

"Order! Order!" Schreve banged the gavel again and again. "There is . . . people . . . there's another way to approach this."

"Yeah, what?" a man who had spoken earlier shouted, "keep the year-round people paying for you guys to vacation here and tear up the roads and keep us awake at night with your loud drunken parties? You know, this was a dry county until Yankees and Florida people kept putting on the pressure for liquor by the drink."

"No. No. You know that's not constructive," Schreve protested. "You drain the lake, and your property values will drop. It will be worth—"

"Your property values will drop," another man shouted angrily from the middle of the room. "I only paid $56,000 for my place twenty years ago. Lake or no lake, it'd sell for at least that much today, so don't mislead people. Most of us who have year-round homes would always be able to sell to others who want to work and live in this area."

"Yeah, you're just trying to get the working people pulling on your oars. You got the money. You pay for the dam."

Cheryl leaned over to whisper in Art's ear. "What do you think?"

"I think the guy's right," he whispered back. "Our place would sell—dam or no dam—at a fair market price because of the location and the view."

He rose to his feet. "I move we close discussion of the issue on the floor, and I move that the property owners' association votes 'no' to any special assessment or further action to finance repair of the dam."

"I second," another shouted.

"You are out of order with your second motion," Helen Schreve yelled at Art.

"You are out of order because the chair has not recognized you," Art shouted back.

"Order!" Frank rapped the gavel on the podium. "All those in favor of closing the discussion on financing the repairs to the dam, indicate by saying 'Aye.'"

The crowd roared their approval.

"Opposed?" A few nays could be heard. "Motion carries." The crowd applauded.

"All those in favor of dismissing any and all consideration with regard to repairing the dam, indicate with 'Aye.'"

The crowd roared again. There were a few dissenting votes. "Motion carries," Frank reported.

"Move to adjourn," Helen Schreve cried.

"Second."

"All in favor of adjourning this special meeting of the Hannah Lake Property Owners' Association signify by saying 'Aye.'"

"Hey. Hold it!" one man shouted. "You didn't call for any discussion."

"All in favor," Frank repeated.

"Aye." The crowd roared.

"Meeting adjourned."

CHAPTER 35

"Tom? Tom, is that you?" Diane tried to speak. She peered through the fog and realized she was on the back porch of their home in south Minneapolis, an older two-story family home on the corner of the block. Ancient elms shaded the house and yard, making it difficult for Diane to tell who was standing just a few feet from her. "Tom?" she repeated, but all she could see was a silhouette. The silhouette did not answer. It was Tom. It was his body, his way of standing.

She tried to raise her head to see more clearly, but her neck muscles would not respond. "Oh," she sighed, feeling strapped in place, "don't go. Please. I . . . I have so much I want to tell you. It's been too long. Way too long. Please . . ." she implored, but her mouth was not moving. She tired from the exertion. The shaded yard, its white fence, the breeze through the elms, the cool Minnesota morning summer air faded away. A heavy gray cloud moved into place instead. The door opened a crack to let in a slender shaft of light, the light from the hall that was always there, the hall where Mother paced waiting for Daddy to finish tucking her in.

Don't let him, Mama, please. Open the door on Daddy. See what he does to Margie, Mama. See what he does to make me go away, to hide on top of the headboard, the headboard with the two big round wooden breasts, harder than yours Mama, the breasts that poked out over Diane every night and guarded her from Daddy when Diane needed to let Margie take her place.

Mama never came. The door never pushed open wider to let in more light, to make her father stop what he was doing to Margie. To make him get up and go into his own room. To let Mama come in and kiss Diane goodnight. Mama never came in, never kissed Diane goodnight. Mama did not even know that Margie took Diane's place. Margie was strong. Margie knew how to let Daddy love her. Margie was love.

"Sometimes I think she's pulling out of it," a voice said in the cloud. It wasn't Mother. It was a lady in white. She was with another lady in white, like a nun. The nuns who had cared for Diane when she was first pregnant and sent away to have the baby by herself, away from Tom, away from Daddy and Mama, away to be with the nuns.

"The doctor wants her stable for several more days," a strong woman's voice emerged from the cloud. "Watch her closely. If she begins to come out of it, let the doctor know." The cloud thickened like smoke. Diane's head felt heavy. She faded away.

✠   ✠   ✠

"You did great," Vernon Brost roared over the phone at Frank Schreve. "You were right. You said the people on the higher elevations would say 'screw it.' I counted on that. And the year-round residents with lots well back from the lake joined right in. That gives us the pressure we were looking for."

"Well, we scared the hell out of the lakeside people. They don't want to cough up sixty grand or more to repair the dam, which is what it will take if the rest of the people don't go along," Frank responded as he walked over to the window in his study and looked out at the lake.

"Wonder how all those people will feel about having no say at all in the way things are run. We get the majority of the lots and the voting rights that go with them, and we can dictate our own set of bylaws and vote them in." Brost laughed. "Have you talked to our Mr. Commissioner yet?"

"No. I was waiting for the property owners' meeting to be over. Time to move on it?"

"Yes. Our man knows you're coming. We made an offer to Dixie States through a subsidiary to purchase all of the lots they haven't been able to sell. Of the 1,257 in the development, they still own 372, and they were asking an average of $5,000 apiece, or one-million-eight in round figures. They've had some of those on the books since the area was first surveyed in 1968. We offered $300,000, and it looks like they will take it."

"Okay." Schreve hung up the phone. He knew Dixie States would not back away from the sale. They might counter, and Palmetto-Atlantic could up the ante of a couple of hundred thousand and still make out like gangbusters. The only thing left for him to do was contact a county commissioner to get the commission to authorize the sale of all the lots in the development that were five years or more in arrears on their taxes. The county had never done that. There was no precedent. The commissioner could prove to his colleagues that the county would benefit from a huge windfall, especially important because of funding cuts at both the federal and state level. More than a big inflow to the treasury, the county would have a ready, well-qualified buyer; namely, Palmetto-Atlantic. Once the properties were sold, the county could rely on the new owner to pay the taxes regularly. That meant an annual increase in revenues. The package was too compelling.

"A slam dunk," the commissioner told Frank. "They'll see those dollars. They'll see that no local people are involved. Almost all the owners are out of state and are eager to dump their lots. Shit, most of the people bought those dinky little lots are dead now anyway. Their kids own them. They'll be relieved. They don't give a damn."

The county had passed an ordinance, four years earlier, which required a distance of at least 100 feet between a well and a septic drain field. Most of the lots in the Lake Hannah Development were too small to qualify.

"I think everyone can be persuaded to keep a low profile on this and put up whatever notices may be required in the shortest possible time period. Hell, we've only got one paper here, and it only comes out once a week."

The numbers are beginning to add up, Frank thought after hanging up the phone. The lakeside lot owners were isolated with their concerns. That was evident from the special meeting. Local year-round residents and those with properties situated well back from the lake were not going to help pay for the cost of repairing the dam. There were only about nineteen lakeside owners involved, but the group was critical. If they got together and raised the money to repair the dam, the plan would fall apart. Palmetto-Atlantic would be out nearly six million and not have the muscle to turn the development around and resurvey it into new, larger lots. It had to work.

It's got to come together, Frank thought. *It was always there right in front of everyone, but nobody took the time to see it.* Frank had taken the time. It had been his baby from the beginning. Vernon Brost liked to throw his weight around, but the idea had been Frank's from the start. He owned the largest place on the lake. He wasn't going to let the lakeside owners come to agreement. He'd sell his place to Palmetto-Atlantic, and the rest would follow in a panic fearing they would be left out.

Frank seldom drank during the day, but today was different. Today, everything was going to fall into place, and he decided he deserved it. He walked to the wet bar he had built into his study against Helen's wishes.

"I don't want you drinking during the day," she had said. "I don't want you drinking when you're alone. You start drinking, and nothing will get done around here. The work you bring up here for the weekend will just sit. You won't touch it."

But one week, when Helen could not make the drive from Durham, he came up to the construction site alone and told the contractor to put the wet bar in as planned.

She did not even notice it at first. Frank chuckled. She never noticed anything unless it was exactly what she wanted at the time. *Then there'd be hell to pay. She was a terrier bitch. Once she sunk her chops into your calf, you couldn't shake her, not until she got what she wanted.* He poured out two fingers of Glenfiddich, held it up to the light and said, "To the numbers."

Frank saw the numbers shortly after he and Helen began restoring the huge summer home on the lake. He didn't have the money to get things underway, but Vernon Brost did. Hundreds of lots that were on the books nobody cared about anymore. The original owners had passed away. Deeds transferred to their children, some of whom never bothered to drive to the area to see what they owned. County tax office records were public and could be downloaded in an Excel format. Once that was done, a mailing was quickly created and sent out with an offer to purchase the property. Most owners jumped at the chance. They were tired of being dunned for property association dues every year and dunned for the taxes. The mailings quoted the tax value of each lot. It didn't take much thought to see a lot worth $2,500 to the Baden County Tax Collector would not demand much of a price on the market.

The mailings also pointed out that the county commissioners had passed two ordinances that placed severe restrictions on the small plots of land. For one thing, building permits would not be issued for new residences without verifying the structure would be placed on at least one full acre of land. Further, any wells that were to be drilled were required, for obvious reasons, to be placed a minimum of 100 feet from the drain field for a septic system. Most of the lots in the development, being less than half an acre in size, would not qualify on either requirement.

The offers to purchase were mailed out from various peoples' names, most of them employees of Brost's Palmetto-Atlantic Realty and Development Company, to avoid creating the suspicion any one organization was behind the buying campaign. What the letter did not say, of course, was buildable land in Baden County was selling within a range of $14,000 to $70,000 an acre or higher depending on the location. The opening bid to purchase was $1,500 for a third of an acre; $2,000 for half an acre. Thus Palmetto-Atlantic and Schreve were acquiring land at a fraction of the price of what it was going for on the open market. *Five cents on the dollar*, Frank gloated. He couldn't help himself. He took another sip of his single malt.

The only thing left was to persuade the county to break with tradition and auction off the lots that were in arrears on their taxes. Palmetto-Atlantic could bring deep pockets to the sale. When the lakeside owners started to pull up stakes and get out, the other numbers would add up to more than two-thirds majority of the owners, the number needed to rewrite the bylaws.

Palmetto-Atlantic was prepared to purchase property from lakeside owners and offer a lifetime leaseback agreement. The lease could be passed in the estate of the owner to surviving family members. With the owners signed, Palmetto-Atlantic would repair the dam. It was a have-your-cake-and-eat-it-too deal. At least the owners would see it that way. The executed leases gave Palmetto-Atlantic ownership and the voting rights in the association. It would not take long to make the leases so expensive with assessments that most owners would gladly waive the terms to be released from their contract.

Frank walked over to his desk. Everyone thought Helen was the driving force behind their success financially. She was a hustler. She tore up the residential real estate market in Durham, and she made enemies out of nearly everyone who worked with her. Her persistence impressed sellers at first. Persistence, however, developed into annoyance, as Helen had no respect for the feelings of her clients, and annoyance grew into unabashed harassment. Clients prayed their homes would sell just to be rid of Helen. Buyers regretted ever contacting her. Listing clients never renewed their contracts when the initial ninety-day listing period expired.

Nickels and dimes, Frank thought. He had found the way to the big money, and Helen could go to hell. He just hoped she would never find out how he and the Palmetto-Atlantic people had used her.

CHAPTER 36

Raker took the file case with him when he left the office Friday afternoon. He felt he had a good grasp on the recent history of the dam from Lee's reports and Dennison's criticism of them.

With the weekend ahead, Jim decided he would make his new quarters as livable as possible. That meant at least a day shopping for groceries, stationery, computer supplies, and other incidentals for his suite at the motel. He also planned to visit Diane. He had not been to the hospital to check on her for a day. If her son called to inquire about her condition, he would not know what to say.

He introduced himself at the nurse's station. Diane was still in intensive care.

"There's someone with her right now, Mr. Raker. We don't want more than two people at her bedside at any one time," the nurse said.

"I understand. Who is it? Another one of her children?"

"No. Her son called to say we were authorized to let this man in. He's her ex-husband. His name is Tom Brooks."

"But I can go in to see her now?"

"Yes. If anyone else shows up, one of you will have to leave."

"I understand." Raker walked to Diane's room. The door was ajar. The man turned as Raker stepped in. "I'm Jim Raker, a friend of Diane's," he said, extending his hand.

"Tom Brooks," the man replied. "My son told me about you. It was your house where Diane got hurt, wasn't it?"

"Yes. I'm afraid so. I still don't know why it happened and very little about how it happened. She's been unconscious since the fire happened a week ago yesterday," Raker said, nodding toward Diane.

"Well, my son thought it'd be a good idea if I came by," Brooks said. "Diane and I haven't had much to do with each other over the years since our divorce. We'd see one another at the children's weddings, graduations, and that sort of thing. We tried to be cordial to one another, but we never did discuss anything of importance."

Brooks walked back over to Diane's bedside and looked down at her. "I don't think I'd have recognized her like this. Do you think she can hear anything we say?"

"Probably not," Raker said. "I've seen her stir a little from time to time, but the doctors want to keep her stable until all the tests come out as they would like and the burns heal a little more. She'll be in a lot of pain if they bring her out of her coma."

"I understand. The doctors told my son as much." Then looking up Brooks said, "Were you in a relationship with her?"

"We tried briefly to become important to one another, but it didn't work out."

"I see."

"I've felt responsible for her, because we had been friends and she got hurt at my house."

"Why was she there . . . at your house? You weren't home."

Raker shook his head. "Fate, I guess. Her apartment was being painted. I was going out of town, and she asked me if she could stay at my place until the painters were through."

"She always hated the smell of paint."

Diane's breathing continued at a steady pace. "You came all the way down here from Minnesota?" Raker finally asked.

"No. Cincinnati. I moved there years ago. I flew in this morning. My son thinks Diane's condition is critical. He thought that maybe . . . that there'd be some things that ought to be said between us if it was possible, but it looks like it isn't. I may have made the trip for nothing."

"Are you staying in town long?" Raker asked.

"Just overnight and then head back late tomorrow. It's impossible to time these things. I called and spoke to her doctor and asked about her condition, but he wouldn't give any information. I finally said I could afford to come only once, either immediately or in a week because of my work. He told me to come right away. I guess that was as close as he could come to telling me how serious she was."

Brooks looked back at Diane and shook his head. "I don't know what my son had in mind. On the way down here, I thought about what it'd be like to talk to her, but I felt really unsure of myself. It was a long time ago; you know . . . our divorce and the trouble that led up to it. Did she tell you anything about all of that?"

"No," Raker replied, "only that there had been a breakup. You guys were high school sweethearts and had to get married. I knew that. I knew you had children, although I have only met the one son who was here earlier. Seems like a great guy."

Raker stopped talking as Diane's breathing was interrupted again. This time a monitor sounded a quiet alarm. A moment later, a nurse rushed into the room and checked the screen next to Diane's bed.

"Her heart is giving her a little trouble," the nurse said, turning and looking first at Raker and then Brooks. "We didn't expect this, but . . . it's not serious. Just a little irregularity every now and then. Perhaps it would be best if you excused yourselves. We never know what a patient can or cannot hear. They usually can't recall, of course, when they come out of it, but that doesn't mean they don't react in the moment."

"You want us to leave?" Brooks asked.

"That might be a good idea for the moment, just to make sure she settles down. Perhaps you could come back in an hour or so. We'll be monitoring her, and we'll know whether she has stabilized."

"Do you have a minute for a cup of coffee?" Brooks asked Raker as they made their way down the hospital corridor to the elevators. "This is a little awkward, but I don't think Diane has anyone in town here except for you?"

"If she does, I don't know any of them," Raker said with a shrug. "I had the same thought myself. She hasn't been here long. She was looking for work. She thought she had a position when she came to town, but when she got here, she found there was a misunderstanding and the opening had been filled. She wasn't worried. She knew as a nurse she'd find work. She wanted to work with addicted patients. In rehab. She was making the rounds . . ."

The elevator door closed behind them. Nobody else was onboard. Brooks punched the button for the first floor where the hospital cafeteria was located and the car started its slow descent. Raker noticed Brooks was easily a head taller than he, with a full head of gray hair, strong chin, and clear hazel eyes behind his glasses.

"You must feel a little stuck then," Brooks observed, turning to Raker.

"Perhaps, but as I said, I feel responsible in a way. I lost my wife about two years ago. I don't have anyone else. I have the time. It's something I want to do. I'm leaving town on Monday after work though, and I'm not sure when I'll be back. Hopefully, in a couple of days."

"Well, I know the family appreciates what you're doing. I do, certainly," Brooks acknowledged.

There were only a few people in the cafeteria. Coffee service was set up on the counter as self-serve. The two men filled their cups and decided on a table at the far side of the room near the windows. The long shadows of the afternoon fell across the manicured lawn and gardens of the hospital. The crepe myrtle bloomed in the August heat.

"I can't stay beyond tomorrow," Brooks began as they took their seats opposite one another. "My wife understands that I wanted to be here, but I'm not going to impose on her patience by extending my stay. I felt that if I didn't come my son would be disappointed. We tried to keep the children out of the bitterness after the divorce."

Raker stirred his coffee. He liked it black, but the cup felt hot to his hand when he lifted it to his lips, so he set it back down on the table to cool. He looked up at Brooks.

"Do you have children, Mr. Raker?" Brooks asked.

"It's Jim. And no. Susan and I didn't have children. We wanted to when we were first married, but it just didn't work out that way."

"Diane and I had four very early. Married at nineteen and had four kids before either one of us was twenty-six years old. Felt like an okay thing at the time, but I look back now, and I can barely believe we knew what we were doing. We stacked up the responsibilities so high we were forced to do whatever expediency dictated just to get the bills paid, just to keep going. We tried . . . really tried . . . to make the best of it."

"You don't owe me any explanations, Tom."

"I know. I don't want to embarrass you."

"You're not. It's just that I don't think you need to explain anything to me personally. Diane and I were . . . are friends, but . . .."

"I realize that," Tom interrupted. "I was just leading up to ask you to do something for me. You see, there's no one else around for me to ask. But . . . but I don't want you to feel obligated. I'll understand if you refuse my request, okay?"

"Okay," Raker said.

"What happened between Diane and me is ancient history now. It was over seventeen years ago; at least that's when the trouble started. I hung in there for a couple of years, but we divorced fifteen years ago. You know when you marry as young as we did, you've got a lot to learn about yourself . . . about life and being an adult. You make your marriage carry it—maybe *hide* is the real word for it—your immaturity. You don't grow up. It just seems like you do."

Tom played with his cup for a moment. "When it turned up Diane had fallen in love with another guy, it tore me up. I wasn't myself for almost two years. I was angry. I was hurt. Even a little paranoid. I couldn't see things clearly. Years and years later, I still woke up in the middle of the night wondering how she could have done it, been with another man. We held physical intimacy sacred—the bond of the flesh." Brooks looked up apprehensively for some sign of how Raker was taking everything.

"So what was it you want me to consider doing?" Raker asked quietly.

"If she comes around while you're at her bedside, please tell her I came to see her."

"Okay."

"No. That's not all. Tell her I value the years we had together, and that I'm not angry anymore. I want only good things for her. Can you do that?"

"Of course."

"That won't be hard for you?"

"No. Not at all."

"I don't want to impose on you," Brooks insisted.

"You're not," Raker said firmly. "Diane and I have shared a lot with each other. I may not be here at the right time, though. You realize that?"

"But you'll have a better opportunity than anyone. My son may return to see her, if she improves, and I've asked the same thing of him, but neither of us can be here indefinitely."

"You could always write her a letter and leave it for her," Raker offered.

"I thought of that, but I'd never know for sure if she read it. If she's in and out of consciousness, she may not be focused enough to read it . . . It might get discarded inadvertently. I'd just like to know she finds out."

"Fine. Consider it done. You could leave a letter any way."

"Okay, I will write one tonight and leave it on her bedside in the morning."

"Was there anything else?" Raker asked.

Brooks hesitated. "You said you felt responsible for what happened to Diane . . . Do you think your relationship with her will ever, you know, rekindle? Become romantic?"

"No. I want to stand by her until she gets through this. I'm not thinking of anything beyond that point." Raker lifted his hands palm up from the table. "Who knows that far ahead of things? Look," he said with a touch of exasperation in his voice, "I want to assure you that I will do everything I can for her until she is able to make her own decisions and physically able to care for herself. That doesn't mean I'm going to care for her. Just that I'm going to stay involved until I'm satisfied her situation is being managed the best that it can. I don't think I can promise more than that to her or to you or to the family."

"Of course, of course. I didn't mean to press you in any way. I'm sure the children are very, very grateful for all you have done. Heavens, we're lucky to have you here and available. Not many men would do nearly as much. Please, you see . . ."

"Let's leave it at that, okay? I'm committed to seeing this through. I have no other priorities in my life at the moment. Only my work and so far I've managed without a problem," Raker said.

"You don't suppose she'll think nobody will ever be interested in her again because her face is a little scarred from the burns?"

"Tom, I don't know what she'll think. You can't know either. She's got a lot to get through, if she survives. I'm just taking things day by day.

Speaking of which, I had better get going. It's been good to meet you." Raker pushed his chair back and extended his hand. Tom pushed back also but reached into his suit coat pocket for his wallet.

"Here. Here's my card, in case you need to get in touch."

"Okay. Your son has my contact information, but here's my card as well. It has all my numbers. Don't hesitate to call if I can do anything," Raker said.

CHAPTER 37

"Raker, we got him. We got Turcotte," Sheriff Grossman roared over the phone to Raker. "We staked out a place, a double-wide, where we thought he'd holed up, and sure enough, he turns up. He'd tried to drive off, but we pulled him over, and he had enough on him to bring him in."

"He's no longer our employee," Raker countered. "We terminated him. He should've reported in for work on Saturday but didn't. He'd been absent without notice for five days."

"I know, I know. I talked to your manager, Greason, and he said to call you anyway. It's up to you. You want to be here when we question this guy, you're welcome. There could be others out at your plant. If you observed, maybe you'd give a little direction if something comes up that implicates your company. Greason is going to observe."

"I'll check it out."

"Fine, just call me back and let me know, as soon as you can."

"Will do."

Raker was pleased to have a reason to call his friend Art Nichols and tell him he would be back in Baden County in the morning. Telling Becker was only a formality. She would want assurance no other Southern Textile employees were implicated, and she would agree he ought to be in on Turcotte's interrogation.

"I'm going to bring this box back up there, Art," Raker said after the two men exchanged greetings.

"Like hell you are. I don't want the goddamn thing anywhere near here. When you said I should look through it, I thought maybe I'd come down to Charles City. I don't want that stuff up here. Look what's already happened."

"But you should see this stuff Dennison put together. He intended it for you," Raker argued. "Plus, I was thinking there must be a key in here somewhere for the password to a flash drive. I'm hoping maybe you'll spot it, that maybe it's in the letters somewhere, and I just don't know what to look for."

Nichols did not reply. Raker heard the anxiousness in his friend's voice. He did not want to put Art in a stressful position again.

"I don't know, Jim. Can we keep everything a secret? You know, the last time several people saw the box, those guys thought it was with me here at the house."

"I don't need to take the stuff out to your house. We can go over it in my motel room."

"I thought you'd stay with us . . ."

"Better not. No point in connecting the two of us if you want to be careful. As of this moment, I don't know who knows what's going on and who doesn't," Raker said.

"Ah shit!" Art exclaimed. "I don't need this. I just don't need this. Do you think someone is watching Cheryl and me? Really?"

"How can I say?" Raker said. "Of course it's possible. I just don't have a handle on things to know one way or the other. We need to be careful until things become a lot clearer."

"So if I go to your motel room, that doesn't make things any better, does it?"

"Well, it's still better than meeting at your place," Raker insisted. "Listen, Art, my reason for going up there is to see this guy that the sheriff arrested. I can't see that it matters. If you are being watched, they'll know we're together no matter where we meet, so let's just keep it simple and meet at my motel."

Art hesitated. "Okay," he finally said. "Call me when you get in, and let me know your schedule."

Diane would have a rough time once she recovered, Raker thought as he maneuvered his Toyota Camry through the midday traffic on I-77 heading north of Charles City. The troublesome file box with Dennison's documents was in the trunk. It could stay there until he met with Art in the morning. He shook his head. The Dennison murder was not his affair, not his case. Yet, he allowed himself to get pulled into it. Intuitively, he sensed everything was connected—Dennison's death, the ransacking of Art's cabin, the fire, and the attack on Diane. He couldn't walk away from any of it.

He passed Statesville and was pleased he had been able to get away early enough to make it to the sheriff's office by four o'clock. The sheriff could forgo any probable cause hearing because he had the indictments he wanted. Bond would be set, and Turcotte would be back on the street once it was posted. The next federal superior court date for Baden County would not be until October. It was a long time to have the man running around in the community.

Upon arriving, Raker went immediately up to the second floor to the sheriff's office.

"I'm glad to see you," the sheriff said as Raker walked into his office. "I've got news for you, but let me ask first, are you missing a firearm?"

Raker looked at him with surprise. "Yes. I am. My Glock was missing after the fire. Why do you ask?"

"We've got it."

"You?"

"Yes. My deputies picked up a baby Glock when they searched Turcotte's double-wide. When they brought it in, we noticed it had been engraved the way law enforcement guys usually do. We checked it out. Melville County came back and said it was one you registered with them while you were still active. It even has your initials on it. JPR, right?"

"I'll be damned. It was in my house. The woman that was staying there knew about it. We think it fired accidentally when she was attacked," Raker said.

"We want to interrogate the guy now. We'll ask him how he got it. You want to watch on the monitors?" the sheriff asked. "I'm not expecting we're going to get very far with this guy, but you never can tell. He didn't volunteer anything when we brought him in. He knows he's in big trouble. The deputies went out with warrants to his double-wide. A girl was there. She had to let them in. They found over a thousand grams of meth stashed away. He must've picked up a delivery recently."

"Any priors?"

"He's been picked up several times. Drunk and disorderly. Simple assault. Domestic stuff. He was charged with grand theft auto, but was acquitted. He's clever. Nothing's ever stuck."

"What else did the search turn up?" Raker asked.

"A 308 with a high-powered scope. He was in the army. Qualified for sniper training, but washed out." The sheriff stood. "We can go back to the monitor room."

Raker followed the sheriff around to the monitor. Two smaller widescreen digital monitors were set up on a table with a recording machine. Interrogations were video recorded and watermarked so they could not be edited or changed. Raker sat down in front of one of the monitors and settled in.

Turcotte was sullen. The officer conducting the interrogation asked several questions, but Turcotte either remained mute or responded he did not know. His attorney was present.

When the sheriff entered the viewing room, he signaled to the officer that the proceedings were being observed. Then turning to Raker he said, "I told the deputy you'd be looking in when you arrived, and you'd probably want to observe questioning related to the suspect's work at the Southern World plant."

The sheriff and Raker sat down at the monitors outside of the interrogation room. The interrogating officer had already begun.

"You're going to be tried in superior court as you have been charged. That's ten to thirty years if you're found guilty. We can work with you on this, if you'll work with us," the deputy said.

Turcotte nodded.

"Do you know a Larry Nolan?" the deputy asked.

"No."

"Nolan was a driver for Southern World Textiles working out of Riley's Creek. Now do you know him?"

"I don't have much to do with truckers."

"He had meth on him. We think we can trace it back to a batch we found at your place."

"So?"

"If we do, the FBI gets involved with your case. The feds, Turcotte. You still sure you don't want to make things a little easier?"

"Nolan . . . that was his name? I didn't know any Nolan. If he had something on him, he got it on his own. I don't know nothin' about it."

"Anything you want to tell us about the guys at the plant? The guys you worked with?"

"Good guys. What about them?" Turcotte replied.

"Any of them likely to turn up with the same kind of stuff Nolan had on him?"

"How would I know?"

Raker turned toward the sheriff in the viewing room. "Ask him why he hasn't been at work for the last week or so." The sheriff passed the question on to the interrogating officer.

"Any reason for your absence from work the last week or so?"

"Yeah," Turcotte replied. "I quit."

"You resigned?"

"No. I quit."

"That's funny. I don't think your supervisor knew you quit."

"I can't help what he knows and what he don't know."

"Your supervisor said you're supposed to call in when you're absent."

"I wasn't absent. I quit."

"He thought you'd probably show up and file a workmen's comp claim because of the accident that happened your last day on the job."

"I ain't filin' no claim," Turcotte said. "I got hurt. It was my fault. I quit. I ain't going back there for anything."

"So nobody at the plant knew you had quit, right?"

"How would I know?"

"How did this 308 Winchester come to be in your place?"

"Bought it at a gun show, Hillsville, Virginia."

"You bought it there?"

"Yeah."

"That expensive scope on it when you bought it?"

"Yup. Package deal," Turcotte said.

"What about the Glock?"

"Found it."

"Really?" the deputy asked.

"Yeah. Someone must have been out target practicing with it. Laid it down and walked away from it."

"Seems like an expensive gun to walk off on?"

"Yeah. That's what I thought. Careless."

"Where'd you find it?"

"Just out. Out where I target practice."

"How long ago?"

"Couple of weeks."

"Out target practicing?"

"Yeah, so, no law against it," Turcotte said.

"Where were you when you found the Glock?"

"West of Warrensville."

"You alone?"

"Yes."

"Can anyone verify that?"

"No. Not unless someone saw me driving out there or on the way back."

"You stop for anything?"

"No."

"Where were you on the morning of Saturday, August 16?"

"Saturday. What, two weeks ago? Shit, I don't know."

"I need to ask you to remember."

"Well, let's see. Ah . . . I was . . . yeah, that's the morning I went target practicing now that you mention it. That morning."

"You were target practicing."

"Yes."

"With the 308?"

"Yes."

"Down below the Lake Hannah Dam . . . right?"

"No," Turcotte growled. "I told you. Up the road from Sturgills."

"I thought you said 'Warrensville?'"

"Warrensville then."

"Why'd you go there?"

"I knew a place. A place that I used before with some guys."

"A long way to go just to target practice."

"Yeah. Well. I had the time," Turcotte said.

"We found 308 casings in a target practice area below Lake Hannah Dam on that Saturday morning. It'd be interesting if they turned out to be from your gun. What would you say then?"

"I'd say somebody made a mistake 'cause I wasn't there. I haven't been there in months."

"A man got killed out there that morning, Gus. Shot clean through the head."

"I heard about that."

"Might have been a 308 slug that did him in."

"You gotta respect guns, man. People can get hurt."

"We could be talking murder then, Gus. Whoever gunned that man down, accident or no accident, he drove off. That's more serious than just dealing, Gus."

"I guess it is, but I wasn't there, so it's no concern of mine one way or the other."

"Just remember you've got a window of time here when we can make things go easier for you," the deputy said.

"Not my concern . . . like I said . . . I was up near Warrensville. I wasn't anywhere near Lake Hannah."

Raker stood up from the viewing table. "I've heard enough," he said to the sheriff. "Are you going to check the casing we found to see if it came from that guy's gun? That would connect him with the death at the dam."

The sheriff nodded. "The lab's working on it right now. I don't know when they'll get back on it, but we've got a case with him dealing, whether he says anything or not." He blew out a breath. "Think I'm going to let the shooting thing ride for now and use it to scare him. We jump on the shooting case, and we'll never get the information we want about his network here in the county. He's probably hooked up with a bigger supplier up the line. He can lead us to his source and that would be a great bust. We've got all the paperwork. We can move on the shooting any time the case firms up."

"What about the FBI?" Raker asked.

"They're interested, but they're looking into the interstate side of the case. SBI's involved too because some activity in other counties may be related."

"What kind of vehicle does Turcotte drive?"

"A Ford F-250 stretch cab. Why?"

"Because the two men who were seen running away from my house after setting the fire drove off in a dark-green stretch-cab pickup," Raker explained.

"You suggesting he's tied into that?" the sheriff asked.

"He had my Glock."

"Okay."

"It's more than coincidence. The first two letters in the license number also suggest the vehicle could've been registered in this county."

"Why didn't I know about this sooner?" the sheriff asked.

"Charles City Metro has been treating the crime as a local matter. Nobody thought there was any connection. They need to be contacted now. If it hadn't been for the Glock showing up, I'd never have guessed at a connection either."

Sheriff Grossman shook his head. "Damn funny Turcotte didn't file off the serial number."

"He probably intended to but never got around to it. Did Turcotte have a phone or mobile phone?"

"No landline, but a cell phone. We checked it for numbers, but he didn't store any on it. He erased everything immediately. We're checking with the phone company for a record of his calls. They've not gotten back to us."

"I'll want to see that when it comes in. Southern World has plants up and down the coast. I want to know for sure no other Southern employee is implicated in any way," Raker said.

"Understood. Do you know who's handling the case in Charles City? I'm going to call them right away."

"Lt. Mike Pleasants. Great guy. Knows his stuff. I met him for the first time when he interviewed me about the fire at my place. You got anything else from Turcotte? Notes? Letters?" Raker asked.

"No. The guy wasn't much of a writer."

"I'm sure we have the license number of his truck in his file here."

"Great. Can someone look it up and let the Charles City Metro know also?" Raker asked.

"Say? Who's in charge here anyway?" Grossman laughed. "Keep this up, and I will need to swear you in."

"Sounds like a great idea to me," Raker said.

CHAPTER 38

Diane was in her 1974 Ford Falcon, on the road to her hometown. Trudie, Diane's psychologist, had supported her decision to confront her mother. As if prompted by the whistling of the wind, Diane recalled how Trudie had helped her find a way to talk about Margie.

"Margie's just another part of me," Diane explained. "I mean, I'm still me but I just give in to Margie. I'm being Margie, sort of, but all I feel is a kind of detachment. I don't feel a lot of different things then."

"So, Margie helps you avoid feeling things when she takes over?"

"Yes."

"When do you detach and let Margie take over for you?" Trudie asked.

"I'd rather not say," Diane said softly.

"And why is that?"

"Because . . . I don't know. It's like Margie really can't speak for herself. I mean, Margie says things, but Margie isn't a deep person, if you know what I mean."

"I think so. What kinds of things does Marie say?"

"Margie just gets excited. She gets passionate. She might say something like, 'I love you.' She moans and stuff. She breathes heavily. It's funny, kind of, but she turns my fear—me, as Diane—into excitement. Then I don't need to feel anything at all."

"Does she mean it when she says something, when she says, 'I love you?'" Trudie asked.

"Oh, yes. Margie's really passionate. She gets tense and out of breath, and she responds to all kinds of touching. I mean, it's exciting to her, really."

"But she doesn't say much?"

"No. She likes it when nobody is talking."

"Does Margie talk to you?"

"No. That's silly," Diane chuckled. "I know Margie is me. I mean, I know she is part of me. Everything she knows, I know."

"I'm a little confused," Trudie said.

"I knew you would be. That's why I didn't want to tell you about Margie."

"Doesn't it get confusing for you?" Trudie asks.

"No. It's very simple. Margie's the part of me who has sex." Diane giggled. "Margie loves to fuck. That's pretty simple isn't it?"

Trudie noticed a change in her patient. Diane's voice had become husky. "Can I talk to Margie, Diane? Will you let me do that?"

Diane laughed. "I just told you Margie doesn't like to talk. All Margie does is make love."

"Why don't you tell me about Margie then, since she doesn't like to talk?"

"I really don't want to," Diane said as tears welled up in her eyes. "Oh, I wanted so to keep her a secret. I feel so much safer when she's a secret. I kinda like keeping Margie a secret from myself even."

"I see."

"Do you?" Diane said, looking up at Trudie through her tears. "Do you think I'm crazy? Margie is so brave. Margie can do the things I can't. Things I'm afraid of. She's so fearless. She can get naked, and it doesn't matter. She can make love . . . you know, she can fuck!" Diane said angrily, "and it doesn't matter."

Trudie did not respond. Diane felt her anger melt away and she looked up again at Trudie. "Aren't you going to say anything at all?" she asked.

"I waited just to be sure you had told me as much as you wanted to about Margie," Trudie said quietly. "You have told me a lot. I'm very pleased. I can see Margie is very important to you. I can see she is brave and protects you."

"Good," Diane said and began to sob softly. She pulled out a hand-kerchief and blew her nose. "Nobody else in the whole world knows, you know. I never told anyone else."

"I'm glad you told me. I understand so much more now. I'm glad you trusted me."

Over the next several sessions together, Trudie and Diane worked to help Diane on her own without Margie's help, without Margie being part of things. Diane wanted to know what sex would be like without Margie. She wanted to experience orgasms and feel treasured for who she was. Diane grew to believe she could be the woman who experienced sex, the height of climax, and the joy of sharing bodies, instead of just enduring it.

The wind whistled past the Falcon's windshield. No traffic. Diane's car was the only one on Interstate 35 W. She liked being alone. Diane could feel Margie was pouting. Margie knew Diane was going to see their mother. Margie knew Diane was angry and hurt. Margie was only hurt when Diane ignored her as she was now. Margie knew Diane was weak. Diane got very angry when she felt weak. The Falcon sped toward Waverly.

The sign said *Waverly 63*. They were getting closer and closer. Mother would not know what to think. Mother would not know what to say. Diane had tried to show how angry she was with her mother by using foul lan-guage that would make her mother uncomfortable. "It's hot. Wouldn't you say, Mother? Butt-fucking hot," Diane had said on the way to the restau-rant to celebrate Tommy's college graduation.

"Stupid cunt," she had yelled at a woman who bumped into her on the sidewalk, loud enough so everyone on the sidewalk turned to look at her, her mother, and the children.

"Arrogant peckerhead," she had said in the restaurant about the com-mencement speaker who had offended her with his political views.

Her mother had tightened her lips and said nothing. Just as she said nothing when Daddy was tucking Diane in at night, sliding his hand up the inside of her thigh to her special place. Just as she did when Diane and Tom stood in the darkened hallway kissing and whispering to each other.

"Diane," Mother would say from the other side of the closed door. "Diane."

What was that supposed to mean, Mother? Come inside? Tell Tom 'Goodnight.' Then say it, goddamn it. Say it! Open the door on both of us. Tell me to come in. Tell me to get into the house. Tell Tom to go home. You're an adult. Kids take orders from adults. You know Tom fucked me one night in Mrs. Knevel's yard? You could've seen us right outside your kitchen window. I pulled up my pretty white summer dress with the smocking around the waist so Tom could pull down my panties and fuck me. And you didn't see it. You didn't want to see it just like you didn't want to see Daddy tuck me in, just as you didn't want to see Daddy poke me before I even had hair in my special place. It was so much easier to fuck Tom after fucking Daddy. Can't you see that, Mother? Fucking is love. It's the only love we knew, Margie and I, because you never gave us anything that felt like love. If you loved us, you'd never have let Daddy tuck us in and play with Margie. You'd have hugged us, and your hands would've been soft and warm instead of cold, your fingers like sticks. Your breasts would've been soft like pillows instead of wooden, like the breasts on the headboard of the bed. I never felt your breasts, Mother, never laid my head upon your soft breasts. You never stroked my head and held me against your chest. You never said I was pretty. You never said you were proud of me. You never said you loved me. You were cold, a cold mother. Always busy. Always busy.

Weakness is no excuse. Your fingers always showed your nervousness. What's it like to live a life where you're too scared to do the things that are expected of you?

The Falcon was racing over concrete. Diane was hunched forward in her seat, as if urging the car to go faster. Her mother would be stunned by Diane's words. The secret would be over between them. Diane had become a woman without her mother. Diane was no longer someone who was un-important, someone who would one day grow up and then all the trouble would go away because she was older, and the two of them—Mother and Diane—wouldn't need to speak of it because they were both grown women, women who knew such things happened in life, and it was best to forget them, to just let them go, to never ever speak of them. But Diane didn't need to protect her mother now. Her mother never protected her.

She won't understand, Diane thought. *Mother will just look at me wide-eyed, her thick glasses making her eyes so large she looks stupid. Mother didn't know any-thing. She didn't know how to love; how to express love. She won't know how to take what I want to say. She's never discussed a serious subject with me—ever. She won't understand. It won't make sense to her. I can tell Trudie I couldn't do it. Trudie will understand. There will be other times. It doesn't need to be now.*

The Falcon slowed. A cloverleaf was coming up, the perfect place to turn around and go back to Minneapolis. Margie was happy. Diane could feel her smiling. The Falcon dissolved into a smoky gray cloud. Two nuns approached.

"She's like this every now and then. Her respiration rate is faster. Her heart rate increases. And she twitches. Then she settles back again. I don't know what it means," one of the nuns in white said. They were there when Howard was delivered. Nobody else. Just the nuns.

CHAPTER 39

"I hate knowing that son-of-a-bitch is back out on the street," the sheriff said. "Who the hell posted bail for him? I thought we set that high enough so there was no way—"

"Some woman in Florida," Deputy Hurdler replied. Hurdler had rushed into the sheriff's office upon hearing the bail had been posted. "You think he's a flight risk?"

"How the hell would I know?" Sheriff Grossman growled. "I never thought anyone from out of state would post bail for him. If I put up that much bail for a guy, I'd have to feel pretty damn confident I could control him. Check it out. Find out who posted bail."

Hurdler turned and walked out. With Turcotte back in circulation, any number of things could happen. Frieda McNaughton, the girl who rolled up on him, was in trouble for sure. Turcotte would have time to tidy up his distribution network, get someone else in charge, and there was nothing that law enforcement could do to stop the flow of drugs into the county.

Raker called Lt. Mike Pleasants of Charles City Metro from his desk in the sheriff's office and brought the lieutenant up to date on the developments of the previous afternoon and the interrogation of Turcotte. Deputy

211

Hurdler reported Turcotte's pickup had a license that began with the same two letters the neighbor had reported seeing on the truck that drove away the night of the fire. Lt. Pleasants suggested he could assign an officer to review the traffic tapes from the cameras that were positioned at critical intersections close to Raker's home.

"There's always a chance we caught the truck on video. It would at least prove Turcotte's truck was in Charles City that night at the time the fire was started," Pleasants volunteered.

Raker looked up when the door to his office opened. The sheriff peered in. Raker put his phone on speaker and motioned to the sheriff to step into the room. "Lieutenant, Sheriff Grossman just came into my office. Sheriff, Lieutenant Pleasants of Charles City Metro is on the line." The sheriff nodded. "The witness reported," Raker continued with Pleasants, "that one of the two men running from the house was carrying a crowbar. He tossed it into the tool box in the back of the truck before they took off. We need to check Turcotte's truck for that crowbar. If it's there, we need to bring it in to the lab to see if any of the victim's blood or epithelial tissue could still be on it."

"Can you do that?" Pleasants asked. "I can get my captain to call."

"That won't be necessary," the sheriff said. "I'll get a man on it right away. Somebody posted bail for Turcotte. He was released late yesterday."

"We may both be after the same man," Pleasants said. "If you can pick up that crowbar right away, we'll make arrangements with the lab and have it checked out. You can send it overnight to our lab directly."

"Okay," the sheriff said. "The shell casing from the shooting at the dam was from Turcotte's 308. Ballistics just phoned. He may have been out near Warrensville when Dennison was shot, but his rifle was in somebody's hands out at the dam that morning."

"Sounds like things are beginning to come together," Pleasants replied.

"Motive," Raker said flatly. "How are Turcotte and the victim connected? We don't have that."

❖   ❖   ❖

As agreed, Cheryl and Art met Raker for lunch at Frazier's and then went to the motel room to review the contents of the file box. "I've tried everything

I can think of," Art said. "I can't come up with a password. I'm afraid to keep trying. Sometimes these things are programmed to erase if too many attempts are made at opening them."

The motel room was not a good choice for the meeting. The small table afforded only limited space for spreading out the papers. Art sat in one chair; Raker, the other. Cheryl paced the room. The air conditioner banged off and on.

"Let it go, then," Raker said. "Maybe we'll find a key in the documents, something you'd recognize but nobody else would. I thought the correspondence would reveal more. Most of this is interdepartmental stuff. Looks like Dennison at least tried to challenge Lee's earlier reports. There's no correspondence other than state agency memos. Lee must have had a personal computer. He wouldn't use the state's computer for any correspondence about what he was doing."

"It'd be easy enough to prove Lee's reports are false. All you'd need is a second opinion. A second inspection," Cheryl said.

"That came up at the property owners' association meeting, and they don't have the funds for it. Besides, Dixie States owns the dam. If they don't agree to an inspection, it isn't going to happen. The state thinks there's a threat to life and property if something isn't done soon. They aren't about to wait," Art said.

"Dennison's wife said he got caught going through Lee's desk. Whoever is after the box must assume Dennison found something out and can't risk the information becoming public knowledge," Raker said, pushing back in his chair and walking over to the window. He shifted the curtain to peer outside. "Then my gun shows up in the hands of a drug dealer here. There must be a tie-in there somewhere."

"Norm wasn't taking it all that seriously," Art observed.

"Why do you say that?" Raker asked.

"He wrote 'Life is like a box of chocolates' at the bottom of a couple of pages. He must have been laughing at himself."

"Forrest Gump, huh?" Raker shrugged.

"Not funny," Cheryl said. "What are we going after first? Find out how your gun got here, or find out who is after the files?"

"Could be one and the same," Raker said.

"You guys really need me here?" Cheryl finally asked.

"I hoped you'd help us second-guess ideas as they came up is all," Art replied.

"What ideas—" Cheryl asked.

"She's right," Raker interrupted. "We've been through all of this stuff. Dennison proves that Lee was falsifying reports. We know what the supposed cost will be to fix the dam. The letter for the Natural Resources Department reported it. They get the current owners to cave in, and the new company comes into the development, takes over the dam, and they don't have to fix anything because the reports were false all along. Slick deal. Crooked as hell, but slick. We know at least one party who has something to gain."

Raker yanked the curtain back and returned to the table. "Lee's reports hurt Dixie States. If everyone knew the dam was fine, which is what Dennison says, there'd be no crisis. If Dixie States is going broke, they'd welcome knowing the dam is in good shape. They might be able to hold things together until the economy improved."

"People are running scared. Dixie States Development is broke. People are hopping mad. With the threat of the dam failing, the property owners' association has been blown out of the water," Art added. "The people well back from the lake and at elevations on either side will go their own way. They won't pay to fix the dam. They never see it and probably never use the lake. Lakeside property owners need to foot the bill to fix the dam. Otherwise, they lose big time. Look at Schreve. He's got that great big place right on the shoreline. It's a white elephant now, but without the lake, it would be a monstrosity. A mansion on a mudhole in the middle of the woods."

"That's true, if the dam needs to be repaired. What if it doesn't? Dennison didn't think it did," Raker said. Looking at Art, he added, "Schreve knew Mrs. Dennison turned her husband's files over to you. When they couldn't find the box at your place, they went to my place."

"You are also assuming the fire was set by someone looking for the box. You don't know for sure," Cheryl cautioned.

"No, but that's good enough for now," Raker said. He walked over to the motel room door and opened it. Sunlight streamed in followed by a blast of hot air rising off the asphalt parking lot. The sound of second-shift commuter traffic from 221 roared into the room. He checked his watch.

4:21 p.m. They had been at it almost the entire afternoon. "I feel like we're going around in circles," Raker said, sighing. "I need my whiteboard."

"I don't know about the two of you," Cheryl said. "But I've had it. And we need to get back. I don't want another night at a café. Do you want to join us, Jim?"

"No, but thanks. I'm going to drive over to Walmart and get a whiteboard and some markers. You go ahead. I'll check with you in the morning. Just close the door when you leave. I have my key with me."

"What're you doing with my truck?" Cleve Ramsay yelled at Deputy Hurdler.

"Your truck?" Hurdle shouted back. "You mean Turcotte's."

"His is out there, at the ditch," Ramsay replied, nodding toward the gravel road in front of the house.

Hurdler had driven out to Turcotte's double-wide to pick up the crowbar the sheriff had asked him to retrieve. He noticed a second, nearly identical, green stretch-cab pickup parked in front of the yard and had assumed the vehicle in the driveway was Turcotte's.

"Okay," Hurdler replied, noticing Turcotte had come to the door. "What are you doing here anyway?" the deputy asked Ramsay.

"Came by for a visit," Ramsay replied. "What the hell is it to you?"

Hurdler ignored the two men and walked up to the second truck and tried to open the steel tool chest behind the cab. It was locked.

"Open this!" Hurdler said, turning to look at Turcotte.

"Why?"

"If you don't want me to bust the lock or impound the vehicle, then open it."

Turcotte thrust his hand into his jeans, stepped off the porch and walked across the lawn to the truck. "What is it this time?" Turcotte asked.

"Just open it." Hurdler opened the lid to the toolbox and inspected the contents. A large crowbar lay on top of the assortment of mechanic's tools. He picked it up carefully.

"Where you going with that?" Turcotte demanded as Hurdler walked back to his cruiser.

"You'll get it back. Just don't leave town. We may want to talk to you again." Hurdler looked back at Turcotte as he slammed the door to his Charger cruiser and started the engine.

Turcotte walked back to the porch where Ramsay was still standing.

"What was that all about?" Ramsay asked.

"Beats me," Turcotte said with a shrug. "Maybe he's got some home improvement job going and needs a crowbar for the afternoon."

CHAPTER 40

"Turcotte? Who the hell is Turcotte?" Frank Schreve yelled into the phone. Vernon Brost, president of Palmetto-Atlantic Coastal Realty and Development, was on the line. "I never heard of the guy."

"Yeah. Probably not. But the stupid son-of-a-bitch has been arrested. Quit his job and got arrested for dealing drugs," Brost replied. "It just put a crimp in our plans."

"I don't see how," Schreve said.

"It really doesn't concern you. I just want you on alert. Turcotte knows more about us than he should. We made the bail for him so he isn't pressured to say anything he shouldn't. You never know about these guys."

"What the hell is that supposed to mean? 'Be on alert.' Alert for what?" Schreve demanded.

"Cleve Ramsay just called me to say a deputy was out to Turcotte's place and picked up a crowbar. That crowbar can be really incriminating. They can use it to pressure Turcotte even more. Things could start to unravel and when they do, you'll need to cover your tracks."

"What tracks? I didn't leave any tracks," Schreve countered.

"There's very little to tie you into anything. Good for you. I wish I could say the same for everyone working on this. Turcotte is the big risk right now. We may need to do something about him. Everything else is falling in line. The numbers are looking better. Our kids have been able to locate more and more owners, second- and third-generation owners, and they're jumping on our buy offers. They're glad to be rid of the property. How's our commissioner doing?"

"Philpott? Just great. The announcement has been in the paper as required, but nobody's excited about it. Local people understand the Lake Hannah Development was a rip-off from the beginning. It's a laugher. I doubt anyone will show up for the auction," Schreve replied.

"The numbers are looking so good that we may not need to buy every lot that goes up on auction."

"We will though."

"Why should we?" Brost snapped.

"The shortest distance between two points. For every owner we need to convince after we have the majority of the holdings, you can expect a delay. The price will never be lower than at the auction."

"Okay, I see your point. I'll have our guys bid on everything. Let me know if anything takes a turn we're not anticipating," Brost said. "Okay?"

"Fine. Yes." Schreve hung up. He wondered what could go wrong at this late date. The dissension among the owners was fevered. Neighbors were not speaking to one another. Lakeshore homeowners were jumpy. As soon as he put his For Sale sign up, others would follow. There was no market locally, of course, but it really didn't matter. Once the tax auction was open, and Palmetto-Atlantic could go public with their numbers, they could make offers up and down the line. Only owners with big lots and expensive homes would hold on, but they would fit into the new scheme of things.

It had to work. Just two hours from Charles City and the same from Winston-Salem and Greensboro, the new development would be aimed at the high middle market: $300,000 to $650,000. It would appeal to a large market of buyers who were well off but would choke on a purchase at Blowing Rock, Banner Elk, and Linville.

Schreve strolled into the living room and walked over to the ceiling-high windows overlooking the lake. The lake was green from all the nitrate-rich runoff. That would be one of the first things to go. They would control the runoff. The streams flowing into the lake were crystal-clear mountain water. He looked across to the opposite shore. The hills would be sectioned off into large wooded lots, and the lakefront would be spiked by docks with fishing boats and sailboats tied up alongside.

Somewhere downstream, below the dam, they would put in a golf course. Then, upstream from the dam, they'd build the lodge with an Olympic-size swimming pool, tennis courts, a riding stable, and a zip line. During the winter months, buses would transport skiers to the slopes just thirty to forty-five minutes away with a cash bar onboard for the return trip. Cross-country running and skiing paths would track through the quiet forest for use year-round. A shuttle bus would serve the county airport, which was only twenty minutes away.

Frank smiled as he remembered his father's dreams to acquire a primitive cabin on a lake in southern Minnesota. His dad, Dennis Schreve, moved too slowly. His initial idea was good. The family became excited about the prospects of having a place on the shores of Silver Lake, just three miles from town. They drove out to the lake several times and peered into the vacant cabin through the windows. But something happened somewhere along the line. Dennis couldn't raise the money, or somebody outbid him. He never explained what went wrong. He just stopped talking about it one day, and nobody ever questioned him about what happened.

Now Frank had a place bigger than anything his father ever dreamed of owning. And he was going to make more money than his dad ever thought possible.

Raker found a whiteboard and markers and drove back to the motel. He was glad to be alone. Art and Cheryl were good company, but this was something he liked to do on his own. *Two heads are not always better than one.* Sometimes one more just added a distraction.

He was tired of the motel room, tired of not being at home. *What home?* He caught his breath realizing he didn't have a home anymore. He had been reclaiming the house as his own since Susan died, but the fire changed it—probably forever. Everything in his life had changed. At sixty-two, he didn't want to think about the future. He was treading water. Waiting for something to come along, something better. He didn't speculate. He would recognize it when it appeared.

He sat back down at the small table in the motel room and propped the whiteboard up so he could write on it. Art and Cheryl had cleared everything off the table. *That's funny*, he thought. *Art didn't want the file box at his place. He must have changed his mind.*

In the upper left-hand corner of the board, he wrote, "1. Who benefits from false inspection reports? 2. Who knew about the box? 3. Who knew Art had the box? 4. Who knew I had the box?"

Answers probably the same to all four, he thought.

After the first question, he wrote, "Any company interested in coercing owners to sell."

After the second question, Raker listed, "Art, Deputy Hurdler, Sheriff Grossman, Frank Schreve, Others(?)."

For 'who knew Art had the box,' he wrote, "Cheryl, Diane, Hurdler, Schreve. Others?"

But who knew I had it? Raker pondered, looking at his last question. Perhaps someone saw him carry the box to his car from Art's cabin, but it was very unlikely. *If anybody knew I had the box, then Art's cabin wouldn't have been searched. Not finding the box at Art's place, they must've decided Art had given it to his guest. They played the hunch.*

The answer to that last question would be anyone who knew Raker was staying at Art's place. Raker quickly jotted down his answers. "Sheriff Grossman, Deputy Hurdler *et al*, (gave my name at the dam as Art's guest), Diane, anyone Art or Cheryl told." *Someone who knew I was staying at Art's*, Raker concluded, and pulled his cell phone out of its holster.

"Art," Raker said as soon as his friend answered. "I know you and Cheryl are sick of this today, but I have two more questions."

"Yeah, fine."

"Did you tell anyone Diane and I were staying with you the weekend Dennison was killed?"

"No, I don't think so. We aren't exactly active in the social circles around here. We keep to ourselves."

"Well, think about it. I want you to be sure," Raker persisted. "How about Cheryl? Would she have told anyone?"

"I'll check." Art stepped away from the phone while Raker waited. "No. She feels pretty sure she didn't mention it to anyone."

"Okay," Raker said. "Keep thinking about it. Try to remember. It's important. Now, can you recall telling anyone I had the box Mrs. Dennison delivered?"

"No. I didn't give it another thought. Out of sight; out of mind," Art replied.

"You didn't tell the deputies that had the crime scene assignment?"

"No. Why would I? I was in bad shape. I was still in bad shape when you showed up. Remember? It never occurred to me anyone was looking for the box. I had one of my spells," Art insisted.

"Right. I remember. The guy that showed up . . . the guy you ran off with the shotgun, who was that?"

"Schreve. Frank Schreve, president of the property owners' association."

"It was his wife that drove up on the dam that morning your friend was killed."

"Yes," Art said.

"Okay, now that's beginning to add up. I want to make sure I know all the names of the people who knew I was staying at your place that weekend, so if someone else comes to mind, let me know."

"I will. Jesus, Jim, this thing really has a grip on you, doesn't it? Have you even had supper yet?" Art asked.

"When it gets like this, I can't help it. I need to move it along before I can get any peace of mind. So thanks. I didn't mean to interrupt your evening."

"You didn't. Anytime."

"Thanks for picking up everything before you left. I didn't expect you'd take the box with you."

"Um, we didn't pick up . . ."

"You don't have the file box with you?"

"No," Art said.

"Then someone's been in here and taken it. Shit! How'd they get in?"

"We took the Do Not Disturb sign off the door and closed it tight when we left. It was locked. I tried it . . . The only thing I've got is the flash drive. It was in my pocket. I put it there without thinking and found it when I got here."

"Well hang on to it. It's all we've got now. Okay? Don't let it out of your sight."

"Yes. Yes, of course," Art assured Raker. "I . . . I can't fathom this. Somebody must have known we were there."

"Looks like it. Keep that thought. See if you can remember anyone seeing you on the way here or if you or Cheryl said you were coming here. I'm going up to the front office and check with them. Maybe they saw something."

"Okay, Jim. Call me if you find out anything."

"You call me also. Okay?"

"Right."

The desk clerk had been on duty throughout the afternoon. Nobody had asked for the key to Raker's room. Nobody had asked about him or Cheryl and Art.

"You sure something's missing?" the clerk asked defensively. "Can I ask what it is?"

"A file case, a portable file case," Raker snapped. "How about your cleaning people? Have they seen anyone prowling around or in the parking lot?"

"I'll page them. How long ago was it you noticed the item was missing?"

"What difference does that make?" Raker barked.

"We have two cleaning women on until about twelve o'clock. Then a second one stays just to catch rooms that check out late. She's the only one still here at this time."

"Get her. I'd like to talk to her."

Gerta, a heavy, middle-aged woman, responded to the page. "I saw y'all leave," she said. "You'd been in the room all day long. You had the Do Not Disturb sign out. So when you left, I thought I'd hurry in there and clean. New towels and make the bed. You didn't notice when you came in?"

"All I noticed was that a black case was missing . . . a file case," Raker explained.

"Oh, that! Yah. I saw that. Such a mess of papers around the table. I said to myself that I should leave all of that alone. I didn't want to disturb anything. I just made the bed and then cleaned the bath. That's all."

"Did you hear anything while you were in the room? Did you see any-body?" Raker asked.

"I heard someone come into the room when I was in the bath. I called out. The manager here wants us to do that. But nobody answered. They should've seen my cleaning cart out front, but I called anyway so that they'd know I was there. Then I couldn't hear anybody anymore."

"You didn't hear the door open and close?" Raker asked.

"I always prop the door open so I don't need to keep unlocking it when I get fresh sheets and towels and my cleaning supplies."

"So somebody could have entered the room when you had the door propped open?"

"Yes . . . That's what we always do. We've never had trouble with that." Gerta looked up at the desk clerk.

"Did you hear anything at all? A cough? Anything?"

"Footsteps when somebody left the room, and when I came out of the bath, I heard someone running across the parking lot, but I didn't think anything of it. I thought somebody probably came back for the things on the table and left in a hurry. I really didn't think anything unusual was happening."

"Did you notice whether the black case was gone at any time?" Raker asked.

"The only time I saw it was when I first came into the room. I didn't see it when I came out from cleaning the bath. I . . . I just didn't see it, you know. I wasn't looking for it. I . . . I guess . . . yah . . . it wasn't there anymore."

"Okay, thank you, Gerta," Raker said.

"I'm sorry. I hope I didn't do anything wrong. I just did as I always do when someone wants the room cleaned late in the day. That's all."

It seemed to Raker there was only one place the file box could be. Two names kept showing up at all the critical points on the whiteboard: Sheriff Grossman and, now, Frank Schreve. He did not know Grossman that well, but his intuition told him the sheriff was trustworthy. *Schreve!*

CHAPTER 41

"Frank," Helen Schreve yelled from the kitchen. "Somebody's pulling into the driveway, Frank! Frank?"

"Yeah, so," Schreve called back from his study deep in the house.

"I don't know that car, Frank. I don't recognize it," Helen yelled again. "A man's getting out. He's the guy that was at the sheriff's office when I was there about Art Nichols threatening you. He's coming to the door."

"Well, answer it."

Raker knocked on the kitchen door to the huge lakeside home. Helen dried her hands, opened the door and greeted him. "Didn't you see the signs?" she demanded nodding back toward the road. "No solicitors. No salespeople."

"Yes, ma'am. I'm not a salesman. I want to talk to your husband. My name is Jim Raker. I'm with Southern World Textiles. Is he in?"

"Frank," Helen yelled. "He wants to see you. Says he's from Southern World something or other."

"What's he selling?" Frank yelled back.

"Nothing. He's not a salesman. Should I bring him to your study?"

"Yeah. Bring him back."

Raker followed Helen through the dining area and the living room with the vaulted ceiling to Frank's office.

"What can I do for you?" Frank asked, extending his hand.

"Well, I . . . ah," Raker stammered, realizing for the first time in his professional life he did not have a badge to produce or a law enforcement title to give Schreve. "I . . . was here the day the man got shot at the dam. Jim Raker. I'm with Southern World Textiles, head of security for them. And we suspect one of our employees may somehow . . . well, let's just say that I'm checking up on a few things."

"I know who you are. You were there the evening Art Nichols ran me off his place with a shotgun. My wife met you at the sheriff's office after the incident."

"Hardly the best of circumstances . . ." Raker said.

"What sort of things are you checking? Have a seat." Schreve nodded to a chair facing his desk. "You can go," he said to Helen, who was standing in the doorway. "And close the door behind you."

"Don't be long. Dinner will be ready in a few minutes," Helen said, pulling the door closed behind her.

"Speaking of Art Nichols. Talking to him, I understand you are interested, or at least expressed an interest, in the box of files Marie Dennison, the dead man's widow, turned over to him."

"No. No. You're mistaken. I had no interest in any box Mrs. Dennison had. None in the least. I was there as a representative of the Lake Hannah Property Owners' Association to express condolences on behalf of our members."

"Art's impression was you wanted Mrs. Dennison to give it to you, but she refused to hand it over. Art said she was upset."

"Yes. Well, you have to make allowances for someone who suffered the shock she did. Her husband getting killed that way. She wasn't herself. I'm having trouble seeing just how this can have anything to do with Southern World Textiles?"

"I'm accountable for the security concerns of my company and its employees."

"I don't see how your company has anything to do with this. Dennison was shot accidentally. He worked for the state. No one from your company is connected with him or with the accident . . . at least as far as I know."

Raker had to concede Schreve was right. Without investigator's credentials, he had no leverage in the conversation. He decided to push as far as he could.

"Why were you interested in the box Mrs. Dennison gave to Art Nichols?"

"I just said I wasn't interested. She gave it to Art Nichols? I didn't notice."

"Yes. Art said you called after the episode at the hospital and asked him for it. He said you wanted it because you thought it had something to do with the POA."

"Oh, right. I forgot. Well, that was my reason. Why ask if you already knew? I think this meeting is just about over, Mr. Raker. You've called at our dinner hour." Schreve stood up.

Raker remained seated, a tactic he learned years earlier when someone was trying to get him to leave before he was ready. "I just wanted to verify what Nichols told me. And I appreciate that you have."

"Nichols isn't on the most congenial terms with the property owners' association, Mr. Raker. He served as secretary/treasurer for a couple years a while back, and his time in office was . . . well, acrimonious. As for Dennison, a few years ago he stirred everything up with a lawsuit. Brought a lot of negative publicity to the development. If I had any interest in what was in that box, it's because I didn't want any old issues resurrected to stir up trouble. Things are running smoothly now. We have a few problems, but that's just the nature of the beast, you understand."

"Of course," Raker acknowledged, hoping a little flattery would alleviate some of Schreve's suspicions.

Schreve sat back down. "You know whether Art did anything with the contents of that box?" he asked, affecting nonchalance.

"No. As far as I know the box is missing. It may have been carried off by the burglars who ransacked his place a couple of weeks ago."

"Right. The night he ran me off," Schreve said. "He's not okay, that guy, you know. He had a bad time in Vietnam and has never gotten over it. Just another reason why I didn't want property owners' business in his hands. And that's why I didn't press charges for pulling a gun out on me."

"So you thought the contents of the box were property owners' business?"

"I thought," Schreve snapped, raising his voice, "there was a strong possibility the box could contain something pertaining to property owners' business. That's all. I thought it was my responsibility to determine that for myself. I could hardly take Art Nichols's word for it, and I didn't want any information in his hands. Isn't that clear? I didn't want any more trouble from him. And now, Mr. Raker, that is all. You never answered my questions about your interest in this matter. I think it is time for you to leave."

"As I said earlier, I want to be sure my company is not going to be implicated in any way," Raker replied.

"I don't see how that could ever be the case," Schreve said, getting up and walking toward the door. "You can tell your superiors that."

Frank saw his wife scurrying across the dining area when he opened the door for Raker. Raker extended his hand. Schreve shook it reluctantly and smiled as if annoyed.

CHAPTER 42

"I want your company to pay for a tubal ligation for me," Diane said, anger ringing in her voice. Diane and Trudie had reached a point in their sessions together where it seemed it would help to have Tom sit in. Trudie, Diane's counselor, was clearly surprised. Diane had not discussed demanding a tubal ligation with Trudie at any time earlier. She recovered her clinical composure quickly and looked at Tom to catch his reaction.

"Good God, Diane, that's not why I accepted your invitation to come to this session. What's that got to do with anything?"

Why did you say that, Cleo? Why? Cleo had been in charge that day. Diane and Margie had gone along for years without Cleo, but Cleo appeared when Diane passed her thirty-fourth birthday with a good figure—passing often for a woman ten years younger in age. Cleo sprang onto the scene as someone who withdrew from Margie. No longer a little girl, Cleo wanted to be recognized as a woman, and she tired of Margie's passivity. Cleo was angry. If Margie could turn Diane's fear into excitement and passion, then Cleo could put Margie into situations where the two of them would enjoy excitement. Cleo was angry about the missed chances, angry that there was so little left of her youth. And Cleo liked sex. She liked sex even more than

Margie. Cleo wanted to fuck and fuck often and fuck different guys for all the years that she had been faithful to Tom, for all the nights she spent taking care of colicky babies in poorly heated rooms and waiting up late into the night for teenagers to return home, for all the times her daddy would not leave her alone. It had all been unfair as far as Cleo was concerned. It was Cleo's turn, now before time ran out. Before her figure turned frumpy, and her face gave up its youthful look.

You fool, Diane tried to say to Cleo. *All you did by asking for a tubal ligation was tell Tom you wanted to go on being unfaithful. He'd never give you a tubal. That was stupid, stupid, stupid. You should've known he'd turn you down. All you wanted was to hurt him more, to let him know his tears meant nothing to you. You wanted him hurt, just like you wanted Daddy hurt. To get even. To get revenge. Painful revenge.*

Trudie said nothing at all. She sat quietly looking first at Diane and then Tom. Diane and then Tom. Later, Trudie would admit Diane and Tom were not making progress. She said she thought Diane was very close to coming into her own, to reclaiming her body, but not after this outburst.

"Explain it to me," Trudie demanded of Diane/Cleo. "You startled me and heaven knows what Tom must have thought. How did you feel when you had that outburst? Can you explain it?"

"He's never going to forgive me," Diane shouted. "I can see how angry he is. What's the use? He's never going to forgive me."

"Let's forget about what Tom is going to do? Let's focus on what Diane is going to do . . . what Diane wants to do?"

"I want a chance at my own life. Is that so hard to figure out?"

"No. That's not hard to figure out. You already have a life. You have children. You have a job. You have a husband who still seems interested in working things out with you."

"He'd be better off without me. Much better off."

"And the children?"

"Them too."

"Can you explain it?" the shadow of a nun asked the man next to her.

"From time to time anesthesia wears off, and you'll see signs as if she is experiencing REM sleep," a man's voice echoed through the room. "But she goes back under. The drip is set just about right. I wouldn't change a thing."

"You've been up in Baden County for two days this week already. Are you planning to stay the entire week, Jim?"

Raker heard a note of exasperation in Becker's voice on the phone.

"Vince Ferguson said you told Craig Wilson to find a reason for making a visit to the Riley's Creek plant," she added, before he could answer. "What's going on? Ferguson told me that the guy we're watching walked away from the job. He doesn't work for us anymore . . ."

Raker felt cornered. He wanted Wilson to drive up to Lake Hannah and inspect the dam. It was one way he could get a second opinion. Raker had hoped Wilson would jump in a company car and make it a day trip. He also hoped Wilson wouldn't tell Ferguson where he was going or why. But being a good company man, Wilson checked with Ferguson and Ferguson refused to authorize the trip. Then Ferguson told Becker. Now Becker wanted to know what the detective was doing in Baden County, given that Turcotte had been terminated. Raker knew explaining about his gun showing up here would not justify his absence from work. Becker was not about to allow that his presence in Riley's Creek was in the line of duty for Southern World Textiles.

"That's right. Turcotte was arrested but released on bail Monday afternoon," Raker replied, trying to buy time.

"Don't you think the company is out of it then, Jim? He wasn't on our payroll when he was arrested was he?"

"No. He was terminated for failure to report on Saturday. He'd been off the job the required five days. I wanted some time here in case Greason needed me, or there was any bad press that needed to be turned around," Raker said, his throat tightening as he spoke.

"You've been up two full days already," Becker repeated. "As long as the guy wasn't working for us, I think we're clear. You need to come back to the office. I've got several things I want you to take care of. I've had them on hold waiting for you to get back. Besides," Becker continued, her voice softening somewhat, "it'll be good to have you back where you're close at hand, and I can see you and you are part of things."

"There's one more thing. My gun showed up here, the gun taken from my home the night of the fire. I'd like to talk to the sheriff about it and see if we can find out how it got here. It could lead us to whoever set the fire and put Diane in the hospital."

"I don't see where that has anything to do with Southern World Textiles, Jim. I'm sorry. I know the fire has been traumatic for you, and I've tried to be as understanding and patient as I can. But what you're asking falls outside the normal lines of duty," Becker said. "You can check with the sheriff on the phone. People are asking me every day about things that are being held up because security has not signed off on them. I'd like you here in the morning."

"Okay, I'll be there," Raker said. He closed his cell phone. *Shit*, he thought. *I can't get everything done in the time I have left today*. The file box was missing. He could not possibly find it in less than a day. He was not accustomed to taking orders. As a detective, his superiors were interested in his work. They may have directed him to give one case priority over another, but he was usually left on his own to conduct his investigation, go where he wanted to go. This, like not having any leverage in questioning people, was new to him. He didn't like it. The thought flashed through his mind that he'd like to quit. Go back to law enforcement.

His life had changed. No siblings. No children. He had friends. He wasn't lonely; he was alone. And now he had a supervisor. For the first time in years, he had to take orders from someone. He bridled at being told what to do, and—yes—taking orders from a woman made it worse. He felt diminished; stripped of his self-reliance and, to a degree, his self-respect.

He pulled his Camry up to the traffic signal at the intersection of highways 163 and 221. He couldn't drive away from everything. *Becker can go to hell. This isn't going to work.* It was a realization that had been dawning slowly for weeks. His job was a bore. A vendor review of security cameras; then burglar alarms; then tailgate locks for semitrailers. He was being asked for opinions on subjects he knew nothing about. He remembered the day at a staff meeting when he finally blurted, "You guys are going to have to slow down for me. I'm not following most of what you're saying." It was true. He was at sea. Very little in police work trained him to be good at corporate security. He was an investigator first and foremost. Everything else was somebody else's concern.

The light changed. He wheeled to the right and headed for the sheriff's office.

As he pulled into the parking lot at the County Law Enforcement Center, his cell phone buzzed. Howard Brooks was on the line.

"Are you in Charles City?" Howard asked.

"No. I'm up in the northern part of the state, in the mountains. Why? Are there any new developments?"

"Yes. I just talked to the doctor, and he said the depth of Mom's coma varies, and she's getting closer to full consciousness. They've kept her unconscious to keep her stable, but they're not going to continue to do that," Brooks explained.

"Will she experience pain when she wakes up?" Raker asked.

"From the burns, a little, yes. The head injury is healing pretty well. They stopped bandaging the burns a while ago. They want the skin to breathe. At least, that's what I understood him to say. There's still some risk of infection, but it's not that great."

"Are you going to see her sometime soon?" Raker asked.

"That's why I'm calling. I can't get away. The doctor seemed to think it might help Mom get reoriented if there's someone in the room she will recognize . . . someone who's not a stranger," Brooks explained.

"I see."

"I can't get there until after a series of reorganizational meetings my company is holding that I have to attend," Brooks explained.

"So you want me to look in on her."

"Could you? I was hoping you'd be in Charles City. Are you going back soon?"

"I'm in the thick of things at the moment. I won't be back there until late tonight," Raker said.

"Could you look in on her tomorrow? When you get back?"

"I could. I can't stay long. I have a job, too, you know. I'm not retired," Raker said.

"Just so someone is there that she knows. They say she may recognize voices. It may even help her come out of it a little."

"Okay, I'll give it a shot. I can't say when, but I'll try."

"Can you call me afterward . . . I mean, if she wakes and is aware of her surroundings?"

"Yes," Raker said, "of course." *Good God Almighty,* Raker thought as he snapped his cell phone closed. He felt pulled in several directions—the missing file box, the gun, Diane, Becker and the job. "Not like I don't have enough going on right now," he said aloud. He got out of the car, slammed the door, and headed for the sheriff's office.

CHAPTER 43

"Can you deputize me?"

The sheriff was surprised by Raker's question. "Whoa! What's this all about?"

"I went out to interrogate a guy late yesterday, and I found myself instinctively reaching for my shield. Guess what?" Raker smiled, "I don't carry one anymore. I'm a civilian. I don't have the authority to ask people questions and expect they'll answer. That's why I'm asking. Is it possible?"

"It depends. How long have you been inactive?"

"My resignation was effective December 31, almost two years ago," Raker replied. "I'm on inactive status."

"You could be reinstated almost immediately. But that would be best done at the agency where you were working when you retired. I don't understand," Sheriff Grossman said. "How old are you? You must have a full thirty years in already."

"I do. I don't fit in the private sector, and I don't like freelancing."

"We aren't moving fast enough for you here?" the sheriff laughed. "What's behind this?"

"Let me lay it out for you. You know most of it anyway. Turcotte's possibly involved in the shooting at the dam and the burglarizing of my house because my Glock showed up in his possession. What's missing is a motive. I think everything that happened has to do with the property owners' association and the dam."

"Sounds like a stretch to me," the sheriff said.

"Dennison's widow brought up a box of files the husband had spent years putting together. She gave the box to Nichols. His house was ransacked because somebody wanted the box. They didn't find it because I had it. They went into my place looking for it and were scared off when Diane Welborn surprised them, and the gun she was holding went off . . . the same gun, the Glock. They didn't find the files so they torched my place. They ran out thinking that if they couldn't find the documents, the fire would destroy them. You know the rest of the story."

"That's a long string to tie up neatly, maybe too long," the sheriff observed, swiveling in his chair behind the desk.

"I was hoping I'd find a connection. I had everything in my hands twenty-four hours ago . . . a file box full of incriminating documents, but I got careless, and it was stolen from my motel room. I'm not getting anywhere without it. All I can do is play a hunch or two, and I really don't have time to pursue it. My boss wants me back at the office. I'm going back tonight. Turcotte doesn't work for us anymore, so I don't have reason for staying involved."

Raker blew out a breath. "But as a deputy, I'd have some authority in questioning others. I don't want to walk around as a private citizen with a sidearm under my shoulder. I can't request anything of the lab. I miss all of that."

"What about your job? You said your boss wanted you back in Charles City."

"I'm going to quit," Raker said. "I only took it because I wanted out of law enforcement at the time. My wife had just died. I'd wrapped up an especially sad, depressing case involving a couple of nice families, and I wanted to give it all up. I thought I could coast until I was ready to retire."

"I don't have funds in the budget to take on another man. Your best bet is to go back to Melville County to get reinstated. The crime, if the woman dies, becomes murder, and that'll be in their jurisdiction."

"I know. But the perpetrator is in residence here."

"We can coordinate that. Go see Johnston. I bet he'd be glad to have you back. What about your job with Southern? I don't see why you can't be content providing input. My deputies can check everything out," the sheriff countered.

"Can you bring Turcotte back in for more questioning?"

"We'll bring him in again and question him about everything you've told me, but it'd be great if we had more to go on," the sheriff said. "It'd be a whole lot better to wait until we have all of the evidence checked out. Have the lab reports in hand."

"Okay, I see that," Raker allowed. "I've got to get back tonight. I'll want to know what the lab finds on the crowbar. I just wish I could be here when you bring him in, but I can't stay. I owe my boss that much after all she has done during the last two weeks. One more thing. Did you find out who came up with Turcotte's bail money?"

"A woman in Florida. Miami. Probably a relative."

"Can you give me her name?"

"Yeah, I remember it. Amy Nederveld. We're having her checked out. I went through the SBI so that we get some action on it."

✥ ✥ ✥

Raker's cell phone buzzed as he was packing up his belongings at his office in the sheriff's department.

"The lab has the crowbar," Lt. Pleasants told him. "There was blood on it. It'll be awhile before we find out whether it was the victim's or not. The review of the video cameras hasn't turned up anything. We're still checking, but the suspects may have avoided the busy intersections with cameras. The doctors say the victim probably will not be able to recognize her attacker. Our own crime scene crew has been involved, and they feel she had her head turned when she was struck. The wound suggests she was struck from behind. You know about the license plates. We're trying to jack up the motor vehicle people to get a run on registrations with the first two letters on the plate and cross-reference to generate a list of trucks licensed with the same two letters. They're just slow, Jim. Really slow."

"Well, keep pushing it."

"I will. Check in with me in the morning," Pleasants said.

"You got everything?" the sheriff asked, as Raker was waiting for the elevator. "There's one more thing here you might want to look over if you have the time. The call records came in from the telephone company, and we've got some background on Amy Nederveld, the woman who came up with the bail for Turcotte."

Raker stepped back from the elevator and followed the sheriff into his office.

"This is interesting," the sheriff said, spreading out the call records on his desk in front of Raker. "It seems Turcotte and Ramsay are pals. At least they talk back and forth a lot. Other than that, Turcotte made a lot of calls around the county. I don't see much of a pattern."

Raker looked over the list. "There're several calls between Turcotte and Ramsay at the time of the shooting out at the dam . . . the day before and the day of the shooting. Art Nichols and I saw Ramsay in the area below the dam the day of the shooting. Do you think we could put in a request to look at Ramsay's calling record also?"

"Ramsay? You mean use the shooting as justification?" the sheriff asked.

"Yes. He was at the scene. He had a rifle."

"We can try," the sheriff replied.

"He has a green pickup also. Let's check it for a crowbar. Do you think we could get a warrant to do that as well?"

"No harm in trying. I'll get someone on it right away."

"Find anymore out about the woman who put up the bail bond money?" Raker asked.

"She claims she's Turcotte's aunt, but we haven't been able to verify that. What's surprising is that she's not wealthy. We don't know how she came up with the cash. She has a job for a company in Miami, Dixie States Development. She's an administrative assistant there. They could be the money behind the bail."

Raker sighed. "But stay with it. The bail money must have come from someone . . . maybe the dealer network." *What next?* He asked himself. *How many people are involved in this? This part of the drug dealing or something else?* "Okay," Raker said, breaking the silence. "Look, let's get Turcotte's bank records. There's a lot of telephone activity around the time of the shooting at the dam. Maybe there's money exchanging hands. What do we know about this guy, Ramsay?"

"Not much. He moved into a place south on 221 three or four years ago and then bought property in the development at Lake Hannah. He's been no trouble to anyone. He got the property owners all stirred up out there, but that happens every couple of years. I didn't make anything out of it."

"Okay," Raker said. "Let's get his bank and telephone records checked also. I need to hit the road. I'll call you as soon as something breaks."

"I'll do the same," the sheriff said, shaking Raker's hand.

CHAPTER 44

The nuns were back. Diane could hear them.

"She's coming out of it again. I thought she was going to wake up earlier, but she drifted off."

Diane didn't recognize their voices. She was alone again. She opened her eyes, but the light was too strong and she was forced to squint. She wanted to stay where it was light, to see what was there. A huge dark form leaned over her and blocked the light. *A priest. No. Not a priest. No! No! Not a priest!* she thought.

"There's nobody in town," Diane heard one of the nuns say. "No family. She has had visitors, but nobody is in town now."

"Ms. Welborn," the dark shape said. "Ms. Welborn, you have been asleep a long, long time, my child," the priest soothed.

"No!" Diane croaked. "No! No." She shook her head violently. Pain radiated from the top of her skull down to her forehead and temples and fired down her spine. "Get away from me." She tried to raise her hands to push the black form away. "Get away."

"There. There, now," the black form said.

Diane saw the Roman collar. It was a priest. *A priest! A priest leaning over my bed.* "No. Go away. Go away!" she said as loudly as she could. Her voice was weak and hoarse. "Mother's never going to come into my room. Never, but I don't need you in here with me. Not anymore! Mother may not come, but you need to go . . . to go now. I won't let you touch me. Never, ever again." Diane's voice gave out. She tired from her exertion.

The man stood upright and backed away from her bedside.

"You're not my daddy," Diane said weakly. "My daddy's dead. My daddy can't play with me anymore." She squeaked a laugh. She gasped for air and coughed. She drew a deep breath. "I'm not a child. Not. Not. Not. I've never been a child. My father ran his hand up my skinny leg and stole my childhood. He took it. Daddy took it. I'm nobody's child."

"You're still feeling the effects of the anesthesia," a nun said, stepping up to the bedside. "You don't know what you're saying, dear. You've been dreaming from the anesthesia."

"No!" Diane shouted at the woman. Her voice cracked. "You're a nurse. You're a nurse. You're not a nun. Good. I don't want any nuns around me. And you," Diane said, straining to see the man with the Roman collar and a black shirt and coat. "I don't want you here. I don't want any of you."

"Ms. Welborn," one of the nurses soothed. "You are coming out of a coma. Do you understand? A coma."

Diane struggled to take in all that was being said around her and to shake off her sleepiness. The memories of the voices came back to her. The memories of the big walnut bed with the scrolled breasts in the middle of the towering headboard. The sliver of light sliced through the crack in the open door to her bedroom. Her mother pacing in the hall as Daddy tucked her in and petted her. "No!" Diane cried. "I haven't been cared for. I haven't been protected. Not. Not. Not." She shook her head back and forth. A searing pain shot from the crown of her head down her cheeks to her jaw.

"I'm sure it must seem that way," an older nurse said, trying to calm Diane. "You've been unconscious for almost three weeks. You suffered a terrible blow to your head. But you're going to be just fine. The doctors have seen to that."

Again Diane weighed each word. *Three weeks. No. I've been in the darkness with the voices. With Tom and Howie and Jim. Jim. Yes, Jim. Three weeks? Not three weeks.*

"You have been away for a long time. You still will need to stay with us and get better. We will help you, dear. That's why we're here. That's what we do."

"Then tell him to go away!" Diane shouted and stared at the priest. The man nodded to the two nurses who stood by the bed, stepped back, and walked to the door.

"Her doctor needs to know she's alert," one nurse said.

The priest turned at the door and looked back at Diane in her bed. "I'm here for you, Ms. Welborn. You've been through a terrible ordeal. When the body suffers such an awful injury, it takes time to heal. The same can be said of the soul. It takes time. I will follow your recovery, and if you want to talk with me, let one of the good nurses know. Okay?"

"Never," Diane shouted. She let her head drop back into the pillow. The light in the room softened. She heard footsteps in the corridor. The footsteps had been there all the time. People coming and going. People coming and going with her mother. Coming and going where the lights stayed on.

The nurses did not go away. *Am I dreaming?* she asked herself. *Why was a priest at her bedside? Why would a man be there when I woke up in my room? Why, when I want to feel safe . . . at the only time of the day I felt safe . . . safe because Daddy was gone, and Tom was gone, and Diane could come down from the headboard, and Margie could sleep.* She turned and looked at the two nurses standing back from her bedside. The older one smiled.

"How long have I been here?" Diane asked.

"Almost three weeks," the older nurse said, looking down at Diane.

"How did I get here?" Diane asked.

"You were in an accident. You hit your head."

"I hit my head. I hit my head? How could I hit my head?"

"We don't know but you were very badly hurt. You are lucky to be here and to be awake."

Diane felt more of her body waking. Her face felt stiff and pinched as if someone was pressing against it. "What's wrong with my face? Why does my face feel stiff?"

"There was a fire, and you've suffered burns on your face and your arm," the younger nurse said. "They're healing now, but you suffered severe burns."

The hot, pinched sensation appeared suddenly in her arm. She raised it above her head to look at it. "Oh. Oh, that's terrible. That's terrible. It looks terrible." She felt tears welling up in her eyes. Then, in shock, she cried out, "Does my face look this bad? What about my face?"

"It is healing nicely," the older nurse said calmly.

"Does it look like my arm, all ugly and scabby?"

"All of that can be fixed in time."

"What does my face look like?" She reached up with her unburned arm to touch the pinched feeling in her cheeks.

"Don't touch it!" the younger nurse said, quickly grabbing Diane's arm. "You mustn't touch it while it is healing."

"I want to see it. I want to see it," Diane demanded.

"You need to prepare yourself, dear," the older nurse said gently. "You need to remember the scars can be removed, and everything made to look better in time. Your bone structure is as good as ever. Only the skin was burned."

"I want to see it," Diane cried. The younger nurse placed a mirror in Diane's unburned hand.

"Oh no. No. No. Oh dear God." The face in the mirror was not hers. Her stomach clenched in anguish. *That. That's not me. Not my face.* She saw her own mouth moving in the mirror. She saw the tears well up in her eyes and slowly blur her vision. *I must be in a dream—a nightmare, as all the other awful things had been:* She saw herself yelling at Tom again; felt her anger at her mother and her despair over losing the kids; the empty rooms and the big house with nobody coming home at the end of the day; being hit by men and getting up and being hit again and feeling she deserved every blow. She remembered the pain and the bruises she bore, thinking they were good, a badge of repentance for the pain she had caused others. That badge was permanent now. She was marked: One who hurts others; one entitled to her anger.

There'd be no escape now. No way to try once more. She might have had a life to start over again, to have a life with Jim or someone nice like him; someone who respected her and would not slug her and take her to bed where Cleo would turn it on so he could get his rocks off.

She saw the years ahead open like a long thin scroll stretching as far as her eyes could see. It was blank. Nothing was written on it. No dreams.

No other people. Blank. Day after empty day without others, without joy. Month after month of waiting each day out, waiting for it to come to an end. Her head dropped deeper into her pillow. She did not want to be awake anymore.

CHAPTER 45

Raker checked in with Becker as soon as he reported for work Thursday morning.

"Good. You're back," Becker said. "I hope there's no serious misunderstanding about my requesting you to return to work. I spoke to your admin. She has all of the priorities lined up on your desk."

"No problem," Raker acquiesced. "I have one priority to add to the list. I need to get to the hospital to see Ms. Welborn. Last time I checked on her was Sunday."

"Just read through what's on your desk first, Jim. I hope the trouble with her and the fire isn't going to drag out indefinitely."

"I'll try to confine my visits to my lunch breaks and after hours," Raker conceded. "I may need to make calls during the day, but I'll try to hold those to a minimum."

"Good. I'd appreciate it. I don't want to be unreasonable but—"

"You've been great," Raker interrupted. "It's just been a bad time for me. I'll look over everything first thing and make sure to communicate with people who are expecting something from me." He did not wait for Becker to respond but turned and left her office. He could feel her looking after him. He resented the tone she took with him. He wanted to keep on walking and leave the building, jump into his Camry, and forget all about Southern World Textiles.

Jeannine, his administrative assistant, smiled when he walked by her desk. He nodded. "President Becker asked me to put everything in order for you. Welcome back."

"Thanks," Raker grumbled as he entered his office. Correspondence and reports were neatly stacked in two piles on his desk. When he sat down, he noticed Jeannine had scribbled notes on yellow stickies, which she affixed to most of the documents. *Wants you to call ASAP*, one read. *Getting impatient*, read another. *Was pretty rude the last time he called*, was written in red ballpoint on a third.

Raker took them one at a time. He called the submitting parties about their memos and requests. He made promises to everyone who sounded as if the issue was urgent, and it was impossible to ask for understanding over any further delays. *I'm not cut out for this*. The thought reverberated through his head, and he realized he hated being ordered around and having department heads treating him like an errand boy. Corporate security was considered essential, but it was a service and did not bring in anything above the line. He missed the camaraderie that was always part of being with his fellow officers when he was in law enforcement.

"I may be late," he said to Jeannine when he broke for lunch. "I'm going to the hospital. I hope people will understand."

Diane was sleep when Raker entered the room. The doctor reported he was pleased that she had come out of her coma. He cautioned Raker that she would feel the effects of the drugs for hours, if not days. The nurses assured the detective that Diane's awakening moments were normal. "Patients go through a period of disorientation," the older nurse said. "It takes time, and it is very helpful you are here, but don't be surprised if she is angry or depressed. She seems especially upset over the burns on her face."

Raker looked at her as she slept. He shook his head slowly, realizing he barely knew her. She had been so eager to please him, so eager to become a couple . . . a serious couple. Now as he looked down at her, he wanted to feel more than a measure of compassion for her. He hoped to feel something similar to what he felt when he was at Susan's bedside, but he simply didn't.

He was concerned for Diane, dismayed at her appearance, and touched by her struggles. She might feel that all had been in vain, and he would understand it, but what he felt did not draw him closer to her.

Her eyelids fluttered. She squinted. "Jim? Is that you?" she asked.

"Yes. Yes, Diane. It's me."

"You're not a priest then?"

"No," Jim chuckled. "I'm not a priest. Not even close."

"Good. I don't want that priest hanging around here."

"I'll make sure he gets the word."

"I think I was awake earlier," Diane said.

"Yes. You were. Yesterday afternoon, as I was told."

"There was a priest here then. I told him to go away. I've had enough of priests. They always talk down to people. That's so superior when they say, 'my child.' That's what he tried to call me. I'm not anyone's child, Jim. I have never been a child."

"You were a little girl once upon a time," Raker said.

"No. No. I wasn't. I was little. But I was always afraid. Diane is so little, so very little she hides all of the time. And she's bad, Jim. She's a bad girl. I am bad, bad to the core." Diane sighed and drifted off as if to sleep.

Raker pondered her statement. He had studied criminal psychology. He recognized that drugs had taken Diane back into her past. He felt unsure about his responses.

"My face. My face looks pretty bad, doesn't it?" Diane asked, suddenly awake once again.

"It was a bad burn. It'll look a lot better when it heals completely," Raker replied.

"I don't care. I felt really awful at first, but I don't care now. I've been trying so hard, and I'd lose out, feel like giving up, but others around me seemed happy. I'd try again. My children saw that. They saw me trying. Did you know Howard came to see me? Howard. My dear Howie. Do you know I had him when I was all alone and away from my home? I was only nineteen. I was in Waterloo at a Catholic hospital." Tears welled up in Diane's eyes and toppled down the side of her face. "I was going to have him adopted out. I was going to give him up. Imagine. That's what my mother wanted to do. She wanted me to give him up. My life would have been so different. My sister had a child that she gave up. But Tom came to see me when I was in the hospital, and we decided to keep Howard. We decided to get married and keep him."

"He came to see you here too," Raker said after a long silence. "Howard, I mean. Well, Tom, too, for that matter."

"I know. I heard them. They must've seen my face. Did they say anything about my face?"

"No. Not to me. They both were very concerned about you."

"I heard them talking. Howard is mad at me. I know he is mad at me."

"I don't think that's true," Raker countered. "He's a fine man. He was concerned, very loving in his concerns. I enjoyed getting to meet him."

"No," Diane interrupted. "Howard is mad at me. Everyone was happy, but I broke it up."

"I doubt he meant it the way you have taken it," Raker stammered.

"No. He meant it. I know he meant it. Trudie . . . Trudie was my psychologist . . . She tried to get me to feel better about myself. She tried and tried and sometimes I would start to smile, and I'd see myself getting to be a bigger person, a happier person, but . . . you know . . . in the end, I just kept feeling I was pretty bad. Pretty damn worthless. I hurt people. I didn't tell Daddy to stop. I didn't push him away. I didn't ask Mother to help me. I've never done the right thing. Even with Neil, I did the wrong thing. They divorced, too, you know. Neil and his wife. They were a happy family once, and it all blew apart."

"You . . . you really need to stop thinking that way," Raker said. "What you say may be as you see it, but it may not be true for others. You weren't making the decisions for everyone. They had a role to play in what transpired. Maybe you should save those thoughts for a counselor, someone who can help you see things in a different light. There's probably one on staff here at the hospital."

"I'm glad my face looks the way it does. You know why? Because now I can stop trying. Ever see someone with a face that kept them from being attractive? You know, someone with a really homely nose, or something like that. I've wondered what that'd be like. Maybe then, people would see a person for who she is. Maybe then, I'd feel safer." Diane laughed. "Maybe then, little Diane could come down from the headboard. The portrait of *Dori-anne* Gray. Dori-Diane Gray, get it?" Diane laughed again. "Did you ever see that movie with Hurd Hatfield?" She chuckled once more. "That's my story, too, now. That was a good movie in black and white. Tom and I liked it so much. So much better than the remake of it. That's . . . my story . . . too . . . now." She slumped back into her pillow and drifted off.

CHAPTER 46

Raker needed to shake off the depression that overtook him as he watched Diane drift off to sleep. The feeling stayed with him as he walked to the parking lot, found his car, and drove to the Melville County Sheriff's Office.

"Look who the cat dragged in," shouted one of the officers announcing his arrival.

"Checking in with your parole office?" another called out, and the room filled with laughter. Officers and the clerks converged on him, greeting him and shaking his hand. He walked down the corridor to Sheriff Johnston's office and noticed his old office had been changed into a media room.

Sheriff Johnston greeted him warmly. "I can reinstate you to active status without any trouble at all," Johnston reassured him. You'll be the oldest guy in the place, though. You sure you want to do this?"

Raker shook the sheriff's hand and accepted the invitation to sit down. "Not only that, but I'd be another Yankee onboard," Raker chided, recalling how the sheriff had dressed him down once for not understanding the conventions of southern culture.

"I thought you were a Midwesterner. You kept insisting there was a difference between Midwesterners and Yankees," the sheriff kidded in return.

"You mean you haven't noticed yet. There's no hope for some guys," Raker replied. "Midwesterners are nice like Southerners. They just don't talk as funny." Sheriff Johnston chuckled. "Seriously, this is probably temporary, sir. I got into this thing up in Baden County, and I think I can play a role in a case the Metro Police and the Baden County Sheriff have in process. Lt. Pleasants is working it here."

"You have no plans to stay on then?" the sheriff asked.

"I haven't decided one way or the other. I know you're right. Guys my age usually bow out. Burn out is probably more like it. But I'd like to let that wait until we get through the situation I just mentioned." The sheriff nodded and Raker gave a full report of all that had transpired, linking the arson at his home, the attack on Diane, and the death of Dennison. "The first thing I need," he concluded, "is to know how the lab work turned out on the crowbar Pleasants had processed. If it has epithelial tissue on it and it proves to be Ms. Welborn's, then we know Turcotte was in my house the night it burned," he concluded.

"Nope. Not that easy," Johnston countered. "All we know is somebody about Turcotte's size and weight and driving Turcotte's pickup was in your house that night. We have very compelling circumstantial evidence, but we don't have a witness. Is the Welborn woman going to survive?"

"Yes. I just came from the hospital. She came out of a coma and is coming back into her own a little more every day."

"Did she see who hit her?" the sheriff asked.

"She said no when I asked her, but she doesn't recall a lot of what happened that night. She may know more as her memory comes back, but your forensic people think she was struck while she had her head turned away from her assailant."

"Okay, where do things stand now?" the sheriff asked.

"Turcotte's already been indicted on a charge of dealing. He's going to get put away one way or the other."

"So how do you see your role in all of this?"

"Liaison, primarily, with an investigative side to it, especially in Baden County."

"What about the Dennison death? Is that case still open? You said the casing found at the site came from Turcotte's rifle."

"Yes. It's all connected in some way," Raker replied. "It's complicated. My friend, Art Nichols, is helping me piece it together, but it looks like a conspiracy to defraud landowners in the development around Lake Hannah is all part of it."

"That won't involve my department," the sheriff pointed out. "Most of what you've talked about will involve the Metro people locally and maybe SBI at the state level."

"I know," Raker conceded. "It's a county case in Baden County and the sheriff is investigating. I can coordinate between our Metro folks and Baden County. But I won't be effective without the shield. The drug dealing is a county issue in Riley's Creek so I'd be back in my old role of coordinating between local police and county."

"Let's get you sworn in then," the sheriff said, standing up. "You can't have your old office back. We turned it into a media room, but I'll find a desk for you somewhere."

CHAPTER 47

"Yoo-hoo, I'm home," Cheryl called out, as she opened the front door to the cabin. She paused to listen for a response. "Can you help me bring in the groceries?" She cocked an ear, but again, no reply. Art's Jeep was in the driveway, but he must have gone out for a walk or to work in the yard.

She walked through to the kitchen and set a bag of groceries on the table. Jessie, the couple's golden retriever, came into the room wagging his tail. "Hey, sweetheart," Cheryl said, acknowledging her pet, "where's Daddy? Where did Daddy go, huh?" Jessie looked about, as if to wonder himself.

Cheryl enjoyed the weekly routine that Art and she had settled into upon moving into the cabin. She did not like driving mountain roads. She left negotiating them up to her husband. But once a week, she made the trip to Ingles's huge store on the outskirts of Riley's Creek and did all of her shopping for the week. Not wanting to make a special trip, she took thorough inventory in preparing a shopping list before departing.

Jessie had followed her back out to the Subaru, and she kicked the door closed holding a last armload of groceries and turned to the animal. "Go find Daddy, Jessie." The dog looked about again and then, as if catching Art's scent, bounded down the hillside toward the front of their property.

Jessie was attached to Cheryl. Art thought the animal was his dog, but Jessie always stayed by her when the three of them were together. Life was good on the wooded slopes of Rebecca Ridge, especially good for Art. He relaxed and took on projects around the place. The previous year it was a new stoop at the side door. The year before, he completely rebuilt one of the bathrooms right down to the floor joists, where he found one of them had cracked, creating a sag in the floor.

When Art was happy, she was happy. The disturbances of the past few weeks were an exception. They spent most of their time reading, walking Jessie, and catching up with their friends via email. Art had tried writing, but he found it very disturbing to remember his experiences in Vietnam.

"I'm not getting away from it," he exclaimed in exasperation one day. "Writing about it just brings it all back again."

"Then don't," Cheryl replied.

"I thought it would be therapeutic. It isn't. I started dreaming about everything again. I'm going to give it up. Stick to poetry. Stick to the here and now."

"Great. I love your poetry."

Cheryl turned at the sound of footsteps on the kitchen porch. "Out for a walk?" she asked Art as he stepped through the door.

"Yeah. Felt good," he responded. He walked over to Cheryl and kissed her forehead. "I thought I heard a couple of gunshots farther down the hill. I was curious. Whoever it was drove off. I caught sight of a green pickup, turning at the Ravens Wood intersection."

"Did Jessie find you?"

"No. He's out?"

"Yes. I sent him to find you."

Art turned and went back out on the porch and called the dog. "How long ago did you send him to look for me?" he shouted over his shoulder to Cheryl.

"Ten minutes ago. He always comes when he's called."

Art called again. This time he heard Jessie's distinctive bark down the hill at about the same point where he had heard the vehicle drive off earlier. "I'd better check this out," Art said and walked across the back of the lot toward the woods on the downward slope of the mountain. "Jessie? Jessie?" he called, making his way through the undergrowth.

Jessie barked each time he called and Art took a bearing from the sound. As he drew nearer, he heard the dog whimpering. "What is it boy?" he asked. Then he saw.

A man's body was lying in the woods. He had obviously been shot. Then there were wounded everywhere. He heard them moaning. Some called for a medic. Some called for their mothers. He hated coming onto the site of an ambush after a patrol had been gunned down. "Anyone else?" he yelled to the man's face as he knelt down beside him. A shotgun blast at close range had blown a hole in the man's chest. "Ah shit," Art moaned as he saw part of the man's heart exposed. It had stopped beating. *My carbine! Where's my carbine?* His thoughts raced. *Trust, damn it. Trust. What's going on here?* "I'd better get back to the others," he said aloud and ran back through the brush.

He didn't like to run. The brush was steaming. They could be any-where. *Pop up just as you run past from a firing pit and shoot you in the back.* He ran faster. He finally cleared the woods and sprinted as fast as he could, loping forward with his hampered leg.

"Art? What is it, Art?" Cheryl called as he mounted the steps to the porch.

"Ah," Art cried. "Ah. Okay, okay." He was on the back porch to his cab-in. He heard Cheryl's voice. Nobody was shooting. It was quiet. He could trust where he found himself.

"Where's Jessie? Oh, Art, don't tell me Jessie's hurt. Please, not our sweet Jessie," Cheryl cried in alarm.

"No. No, he's not. He's fine," Art said, catching his breath.

"Why isn't he with you? Why didn't he come when you called?" Cheryl demanded.

"There's a body down there in the woods. Jessie found it. The man is dead. He's been shot. Blown apart. Call the Sheriff. 911. Right away."

"Who is it? Who's been shot?" Cheryl asked.

"I don't know. Just call, please. Right now! I was out of focus."

Cheryl raced back into the house, grabbed her cell phone, and returned to the porch where Art waited, still trying to catch is breath. "Where should I tell them to go?" Cheryl asked, holding the phone up to her ear.

"The intersection of Sunset Drive and Ravens Wood. Tell them I'll meet them there. The body is just off the road above the intersection, but I'll meet them there."

The cruiser from the sheriff's office pulled to a stop on the gravel road when they saw Art's Jeep parked at one side. Art immediately recognized Deputy Hurdler and Officer Whitehead from the investigation of Dennison's death more than two weeks earlier.

"This way," Art said.

A second cruiser pulled in behind the first. Two officers jumped out. All four followed Art down into the ditch and up the back to the steep wooded hillside.

"When did you find him?" Deputy Hurdler asked.

"About twenty minutes ago," Art replied without looking around. "My dog found him. I heard some shots earlier; sounded like a shotgun. Didn't think a thing of it at first—figured someone was shooting varmints—but then I went for a walk out of curiosity. Didn't see anything, but when my dog didn't come home, I went out again looking for him."

The brush parted. Jessie was still seated at the dead man's side. Deputy Hurdler pulled up behind Nichols and stopped abruptly alongside of him. "No fucking way!" Hurdler exclaimed.

Art turned to the deputy. "What? Who is it?"

"Gus Turcotte. A lowlife drug dealer. We've been trying to find him. Whitehead, call the medical examiner." Hurdler knelt on one knee beside the body. "He's dead all right. Never knew what hit him. Must have been at really close range. Okay, everyone back away. This is a crime scene. Let's get it cordoned off and go by the numbers. You know the drill."

"All I can tell you is what I said earlier to the deputy," Art said in reply to the sheriff's questions. Sheriff Grossman had sped to the scene as soon as he heard the victim's name. "I heard two shots and then a vehicle started up and drove away. It was a green pickup. I just caught a glimpse of it through the trees."

"You own a shotgun?" Grossman asked.

"Yeah. You want to check it out? It's in the back of my Jeep."

"This is just procedure, Mr. Nichols. If it'd been a rifle, we'd want to recover the slug. Shotgun's another matter. I just want to know if it's been fired recently." The sheriff followed Art to the Jeep and then stepped ahead of him to look for the shotgun. "Where'd you say the gun was?" the sheriff asked, backing out of the Jeep to look at Nichols.

"On the floor behind the seat. I keep it resting on a blanket."

"I see the blanket, but there's no gun here."

"There's got to be." Art's mind raced. Once Cheryl had placed the call, he decided to drive down to the area where the body was, rather than go through the underbrush and woods again. He had no reason to check to see if his gun was behind the seat. He was not in the habit of checking for it.

"There's no gun," the sheriff repeated, shaking his head. "Maybe you had it inside your cabin or something. Any chance of that?"

"It's got to be there," Nichols said. "I always keep it in the same place."

"Well now, how do you explain this?" the sheriff asked. The sheriff pulled on a latex glove and picked up a small ziplock plastic bag and held it up to Nichols. Art drew closer to look at what the sheriff had found. "This has to be at least six ounces of pot," the sheriff exclaimed.

"Hey, Lieutenant, I've got something here," an officer shouted at a distance in the ditch. Officer Whitehead, who had begun cordoning off the area, turned and beckoned to Deputy Hurdler.

"Just stay right here," the sheriff ordered Nichols. He turned and followed Deputy Hurdler down the road to the officer. A shotgun was lying in the weeds at the bottom of the ditch.

Hurdler pulled on latex gloves and bent down to inspect the weapon. He opened the chamber and sniffed. He lifted the muzzle to his nose and sniffed again. "This has been fired recently," he said. Then turning and looking up at Nichols, he asked, "You recognize this gun? Come on down here a look at it."

As Nichols drew near, the deputy picked up the shotgun and held it out for Nichols to inspect.

"Yes," Art answered. "It's mine. At least it looks like mine." Art shook his head. "But . . . but how the hell did it get here? I haven't had it out of the truck in a couple weeks."

"It appears to have been fired recently. You're sure it's your gun?"

"Absolutely."

"You'd better come with me, sir," Sheriff Grossman said to Art, nodding back toward the vehicles. "Just take a seat in my car there, if you will. I need you to wait there until I clear a few things with my deputies." The sheriff opened the door to the back of the cruiser and put his hand on Art's head to make sure he stooped low enough to get in. "Okay? Whitehead," the sheriff called, closing the door to the car, "keep an eye on this guy while I talk to Hurdler."

Hurdler and the sheriff walked down the gravel road far enough so that Nichols could not overhear them. "You know this is the same guy that lost his head and pulled the gun on Schreve. They dropped the charges, but it's the same guy."

"I know," Hurdler said. "He has a reputation for being kind of unstable."

"You were assigned to inspect the burglary at his cabin. Did you come across anything that would lead you to suspect this man uses drugs or has them in his possession for resale?"

"No. And we went through his place thoroughly. No evidence."

"That's pretty much what I thought would be the case. He had about six ounces of pot in the back of his Jeep."

"Really!"

"Yes. I think it's a plant. I think this whole thing was staged to get him into trouble. Pretty clumsy job of it too."

"He's the guy who found the body, called us. He's cooperated with us every step of the way. Be pretty stupid to throw his own gun in the ditch right at the scene if he was guilty, but shit, sir, he's been trouble in the past. You know, post-traumatic stress disorder. He just goes off from time to time. No telling what he'll do."

The sheriff walked back to the car where Nichols was being held, opened the door, and asked him to step out. The roadside was in shade as the sun had dropped below the crest of Rebecca Ridge. The thin mountain air began to cool almost immediately. The leaves on the oaks flickered in the fading afternoon breeze. "I need a few questions answered here, Mr. Nichols. Why don't we take a walk together?"

Art got out of the back of the cruiser. "My deputy says you don't know the victim. Is that right?'

"That's right. I don't ever recall seeing him before."

"Any reason why he'd be out here on your property?"

Art cleared his throat. "He wasn't on my property, Sheriff, but the lot abuts up to mine. My property ends in the woods about halfway down between this road and the road my cabin is on, Tanglewood Drive."

The sheriff looked up the side of the mountain. Nichols's cabin jutted out like a stubborn man's chin through the pine and oak forest. "You must have quite a view up there. What's the elevation?"

"About 3,800 feet."

"Can you see this road from up there?" the sheriff asked.

"No. The trees pretty much block the view. There're a couple of openings where you catch a glimpse of a car passing."

"But you can hear one going along the gravel here?"

"Yes. I heard an engine start up after the shots were fired and caught sight of a pickup driving off."

"Must be really quiet," the sheriff observed and turned to look Nichols directly in the eye. "So peaceful."

"Yes," Nichols replied. "We were lucky to find it when we bought it. We love it here."

"So your dog found the body?"

"Yes. I kept calling him, but he wouldn't come. He just kept barking back at me, so I walked down here to investigate . . . and this is what I found."

"Whose property is this, if it isn't yours?"

"A woman owns it. Cutlip's her name. I tried to buy it from her, but she wants too much for it."

"Any reason why Turcotte'd be in the area then?" the sheriff persisted.

"None that I know of. These two lots where he was found . . . they're not advertised for sale. I know everyone in the development from when I was the secretary/treasurer of the property owners' association. He's not a resident and doesn't own property as far as I know."

"You know all the owners on sight?"

"Oh no. I see what you're saying. No. I haven't met everyone. There are hundreds of owners."

"You heard the gunshot and the vehicle drive off but you didn't see anyone?"

"That's right. I didn't think anything of it. The gunshot didn't sound close because it was below me and the woods muffled the sound. I saw a truck make the turn through the trees, a green stretch-cab pickup, but I couldn't see the driver."

"When was the last time you used your gun?" the sheriff asked. "I don't believe anything is in season right now."

"Oh, God," Nichols sighed.

"That's what I thought," the sheriff said knowingly. "You pulled a gun on Frank Schreve on Saturday a few weeks ago. A complaint was filed," the sheriff continued.

"Yeah," Nichols said quietly. "I . . . ah . . . was having a bad day that day. My place had been trashed by intruders. It set me off."

"Anything set you off today?"

"No, Sheriff. I was out for a walk. When I got home, I called the dog. You know the rest."

"Not a chance you had a spell then . . . one you can't remember?" the sheriff asked.

"No. I'm sure." Nichols looked up into the sheriff's eyes. "I don't exactly black out. I mean, it isn't as if I do something and later can't recall. I can always recall. Sometimes I wish I couldn't. But I can always recall, and it embarrasses me." Nichols studied the sheriff's face for a moment and then dropped his gaze.

"That Jeep your vehicle?" the sheriff asked, looking back up the road.

"Yes."

"Own a pickup truck by any chance?"

"No. I had a little Toyota a few years ago, but I traded it in."

"Okay, let's go back and join the others now. You're involved here so I don't want you to leave Baden County without notifying me."

"I understand."

"That just blew the shit out of our case," the sheriff said to Deputy Hurdler as he got into his cruiser. "Make sure this gets processed, and then come see me back at the office. No need for me to stick around."

CHAPTER 48

"I think I've taken care of the priority items," Raker said, taking a seat in Becker's office. "You know, a lot of what was waiting for me in this office could have been handled by someone else. There are guys around here that know a lot more about security than I do, especially the kinds of concerns that come up."

Becker looked up from her desk. "I know you've been on the steepest part of the learning curve here," she said, smiling. "But, really, I have no complaints."

"There's part of that curve I don't think I'll ever get up," Raker said. "Listen, I know there are politics everywhere—we had them in the sheriff's office, but I was mainstream there. I had a reputation and a good record. I had the respect of my fellow police officers. The politics here are just beyond me."

Becker chuckled. She tossed her pen on the desk and leaned back in her chair. "You're not part of the politics here, Jim. You're staff, not line. I thought we both saw this as a sort of last chapter for you until you retired. You know, no aspirations. Just do your best for the company and ride out the last few years with us before retiring."

"That's just it," Raker said. "I don't like riding things out. I never have. When I was with the department and stationed out on Heron Lake, I was riding it out, and I damn near went nuts until a case finally opened that I could take an active part in solving. This . . . this work here doesn't mean anything to me. I don't like being staff. I'm a line guy in a staff job, and I don't like it."

"You're not qualified for anything else, Jim. You certainly aren't going into the management training program. I can't offer you anything else."

"I know that," Raker said. "This just isn't working out, ma'am. I got sworn in this morning at the sheriff's office. I need to tender my notice. I'll stay on the job as long as you want, but I need to resign."

"Okay," Becker said abruptly. "Take all your files to Ferguson. He can evaluate what needs to be done and who can do it. You can go whenever he says." Becker stood up and walked around her desk. Raker jumped to his feet. "I wish you the best, Mr. Raker," Becker said and extended her hand.

"I want to thank you for all that you have done for . . ."

"That's fine. It probably wasn't a very good idea in the first place. Mac McAllister thought you were a good bet. I should've kept my own counsel. Public sector people never work out in the private sector. It's just a plain, simple fact. I'll call Ferguson and let him know you're meeting with him."

The meeting with Ferguson lasted only twenty minutes. Ferguson was dismissive. "We can get all of this cleared up by the end of next week," he said after closing the last file. "As they say, 'It ain't rocket science, is it? You can clean out your desk and go. Becker said you get two weeks' severance. Call the human resources officer about your benefits and COBRA."

When Ferguson remained seated, Raker realized no cordiality was expected in parting.

"Did you see the letter here on the table beside your bed?" the older nurse asked Diane.

"No. Who's it from?"

"You'll have to open it to know. I think that nice man that flew in for a day from out of town left it there for you." The nurse handed the envelope to Diane, who tore it open and began to read.

Dear Diane,

So many years have passed. So many things left unsaid between us. Yet even as that is so, I hardly know where to begin. I don't want to pretend. I want to be truthful.

I came to see you because Howie wanted me to make the trip. You were in a coma during the time that I was here. I am so sorry you have met with such a terrible accident. It grieved me to see you so badly injured. I hope your recovery goes smoothly and you are back on your feet soon. Had I been here when you awakened, I would have tried to tell you what I am writing.

We were both so very, very young when we married. In our desperation to be together, we gave up the years most kids have to try out different things, to recover from a broken heart, to launch a career, and to make the best of their talents and find themselves in their life's work. You and I did not have that. We did what expediency dictated. We never checked to see what was possible.

Remember the evening we went for a walk, shortly after we were first married. We looked up and saw a woman, somebody's mother, standing in the kitchen window of the home. She was probably doing the dishes or some other simple task. Looking up at her, we both had the same thought, "We are on our own now." We didn't have parents to fight anymore. Nobody was waiting for us to return home. We were through being kids. We went back to an empty apartment, and our lives were what we could make of it on our own from then on.

I wanted a successful career—position, recognition, and comfortable income. I kept changing jobs in order, as I remember saying, "to be compensated at a level commensurate with my talent and willingness to work hard." I didn't mean to withdraw from you in that effort, although I know now, looking back, that I did. I was gone from home far too much. My absence meant less and less to the children and ultimately to you. It was important to get my earning power up for the kids and you, but what was more important to me was I could achieve as if I had been left alone to pursue my career without the encumbrances of family.

Some days, I am astonished at what we accomplished. Some days, I am amazed everything came crashing to an end as it did. Most of the time, however, I need to remind myself that we did what we could for as long as we were able and life caught up with us. I wanted to be successful. You wanted to be loved. It's a mistake to imagine everything would have turned out any better had circumstances been different—had we chosen an alternative path. The road less traveled has as many perils in it as the one chosen. (That's a stupid poem, by the way.) Nobody can tell, looking back over the years, whether he or she turned out the better for what happened in the past. What I need to accept is, I am the person I am today because of what happened. I wouldn't go through it again for anything, but then I can never be the same man I was when I went through it the first time.

Things could have been infinitely worse. Things could have been better, but what is the measure? How much a person suffers at the time? Or how much a person grows through the recovery? It is impossible to know.

I would like to try to be friends. I don't know what you will think. Perhaps you are fine with the way things have always been. The children and the grandchildren are still ours to share.

Best wishes,

Tom

"Oh God, Tom," Diane sighed, putting down the letter. "You're still the same gigantic pain in the ass you always were. Sanctimonious, narcissistic, self-absorbed, boring pain in the ass." *I'm supposed to be a better person because my father abused me and my mother didn't protect me. Tell me how that makes me better than a pretty little girl who gets treated with love and respect. We don't turn out better. We just turn out. Otherwise, we'd look for trouble. The more trouble, the more pain. The more pain, the better by overcoming it. Bullshit!* "Friends? Never happen. No way!"

CHAPTER 49

"I know. I heard," Jeannine said, when Raker told her he was leaving the company. "It's been so nice working with you, Mr. Raker."

"I'm just going to pack up my personal items and clear out," Raker said. "I guess Ferguson will take all the calls about the requests you had sorted out on my desk."

"I . . . I know, Mr. Raker," Jeannine said, following him to his office door. "Mr. Ferguson just called. He said he'd have a replacement for you in a couple of days, and I should just be patient until that new person arrives. I . . . I put a box on your chair for your things."

"Fine. Fine, Thanks," Raker muttered as he began clearing out his desk drawers and stashing everything into the cardboard file storage box that Jeannine had provided. *She's been through this before*, he thought. When the phone rang, he looked up to see Jeannine scurry back to her own desk.

"Corporate Security, Jeannine speaking."

That was quick, Raker thought. *I'm not even out of the building yet.*

"It's for you, Mr. Raker."

Raker looked up and shrugged.

"No. No. It isn't a business call. It's a Lieutenant Pleasants."

"Thanks." Raker picked up the handset. "Mike, how are you?"

"Great, Jim. And congratulations are in order. I understand you are back on the county force. Great."

"For now, anyway," Raker said. "What's up?"

"I've got some good news, and I've got some bad. What do you want first?"

"Good news."

"The epithelial tissue on the crowbar is a match with the victim. The only prints on the weapon are the suspect's, but then it was his tool. They could be there from normal use. There are no other prints."

"That's okay. That puts his truck at my place the night they torched it. What's the bad news?"

"Turcotte's dead. I got a call from a Deputy Hurdler earlier this morning, and he said the man had been shot at close range with a twelve gauge."

"Shit! Really? Just as we're closing in on him."

"Yeah, the Baden County people are really pissed. They thought they had the guy that could take them up the line on the drugs entering the county up there. No way now."

"Do they have any suspects?" Raker asked.

"Yes and no. A gun was found at the scene, and it belonged to an Art Nichols, a local guy. The victim was shot out near Nichols's place."

"I know Nichols."

"He's not been arrested, but he can't account for the gun. He's threatened people with it in the past, so I don't think he's in the clear."

"Art Nichols never threatened anyone with a gun. He shot one up into the air a couple of weeks ago to get some guy to leave his property. Jesus, people make so much out of things."

"All I know is that a complaint was filed and then recanted."

"Okay, anything else?"

"Nope. I'm still waiting on the traffic video review and the license plate trace. Turcotte may be dead, but two men were seen running from your house. We're still looking for the other guy."

"Okay. This is the last call that I will be taking at this number, Mike. I resigned today, and they let me leave right away. Use my cell phone number from now on. I want to go back up to Baden County as soon as I can. Nichols is a friend of mine, and we have other troubles up there that

I would like to sort out. I'll talk to Johnston about it before I take off. Thanks for this."

Raker tucked the box of his personal items under his arm and walked out of his office. "Thanks for everything, Jeannine. You've been a great assistant. When I first came in here, I had almost no idea of what this job was all about. I couldn't have gotten along without you."

"Good luck, Mr. Raker. Is it okay for me to give out your mobile phone number if anyone calls?"

"Yes, fine. Good luck to you also." Raker nodded, smiled, and stepped back. He felt a load lifting off his shoulders when he slid the box of belongings into the back seat of his Camry. He called Art, but Cheryl answered, and reported that Art was handling everything well. Raker assured her he was on his way back up to Riley's Creek, and he would check in with them in the morning.

"I see you read the letter," Raker said. He was pleased to see Diane was sitting up with the aid of her hospital bed.

"Oh, that. I wish I hadn't," Diane said. She looked at the detective and gave him an impish blink. "It's awful thinking that Tom came by. I would not have been in any mood to see him. Did you read his letter?"

"No, of course not," Raker said flatly.

"Did he tell you what was in it?"

Raker shook his head. "No. He just wanted me to make sure you got it and to tell you that he was here to see you if the letter got lost somehow. He seemed very self-conscious about asking me to do anything, as if he thought he was imposing on me or taking my relationship with you for granted."

"That's Tom."

"He wanted to know if I was comfortable telling you everything. He said to tell you he wasn't angry anymore. That he forgave you and hoped you had forgiven him."

"What's the point in forgiving someone for something I've forgotten?"

"You're sure you've forgotten?"

"God, Jim, it's thirteen years. I'm amazed it's still on his mind."

"Well, he seemed very sincere. You need to remember he thought you might not recover . . . that you were on your death bed. Can you see it in that light?"

"I hear his voice in his letter. He writes just the way he talks, introspective sort of. He's a good guy. He tried hard enough. We had good years. So much came back to me while I was unconscious. It came back like dreams. I remembered times when I was married to him. They were good times. We were so goddamn young when we got married. Where were our own parents? I mean, God, you have to wonder."

"Others have married at the age you did," Raker said.

"I know. He writes that in his letter. Ah, the betrayed and the betrayer. One's him. One's me. It must be hell to be betrayed. Being the victim is so fucking noble. There's nothing noble or redeeming in being the one who betrays. The Judas. The destroyer. Shit," Diane slumped back. "See what I need to do. I can't allow myself to say that the years I had with Tom were any fucking good, because that automatically means I trashed it . . . all of it. I've been running from that, you know. You and I talked about it, coming back from the mountains."

"I remember."

"I did find a counselor here. She's really good. She's helping me. The thing that gets me about Tom's letter is he says we're better people now for what we've been through. That's bullshit. What we went through was just fucked up. That's all." Diane dropped her gaze and shook her head. "You didn't come in here for this though, did you, Jim? Dear, faithful Jim, friend of the woman with the burned face."

"Ah come on," Raker said. "That kind of talk gets nobody anywhere."

Diane could see he was uncomfortable. "You're right. I'm sorry. I'll save it for my therapist." She gave Jim another big blink and a slight smile played on her lips. "It still hurts to smile," she said. "The monster from the blue lagoon."

Raker smiled. "It looks like it's healing nicely. I don't know about such things though. Are you pleased?"

"Pretty much. I've run up a huge hospital and medical bill. I have insurance. I took COBRA coverage after I quit my last job, and it has several months to run. My doctor says I can go home the first of the week. He's already called in a plastic surgeon to see what can be done with my face."

"Will you be able to get by?" Raker asked.

"Get by, yes. Do much, no. I need to take it real easy and check in with my doctor every few days, but I'd rather be in my apartment. I guess they're through painting by now."

"I'm headed back to Baden County for an indefinite period. I really came by just to tell you I was going to be away for a few days. I think your son plans to come back over the weekend. We talked on the phone. I quit my job at the textile company today."

"You did! Not because of me, I hope."

"No. It wasn't right for me. I didn't think they'd show me the door the day I resigned, but that's fine. My heart wasn't in it anymore. I've got trouble up in Baden County, but I'll tell you about it someday. It does have to do with the fire the night you were hurt, but you aren't the cause of anything. Be assured of that."

"Good. Please call me when you get back to town . . . just check back with me in a few days."

"I will," Raker said. "You can count on me."

"I know that. I really know that." Diane blinked at Raker one more time. "I'll be waiting."

CHAPTER 50

A full moon peered over the peaks as it rose in the east and bathed the valley with a soft lemony light bright enough for the trees in the meadows to cast shadows. Raker felt tired. He knew he was pushing the limits of his stamina by trying to get back to Riley's Creek by midnight. He had packed in a hurry.

"Saturday, Sunday, Monday, Tuesday, Wednesday," he counted aloud, tossing five pairs of boxer shorts into his suitcase. Five T-shirts. Five pairs of socks. Five handkerchiefs. And so on until the case was brimming. Pajamas were a last-minute addition. *Good!* he thought, *they'll be right on top.*

Someone could be trying to frame Art Nichols for Turcotte's murder. The box of documents was missing. It had to be in the hands of whoever was threatened by the contents. They knew Dennison was building a case to debunk the reports that the Lake Hannah Dam was about to fail. *Why give a shit? Diane was recovering. I'm out of a boring job.* All of his working life, he felt he was making a contribution and helping others and his community. Working for Southern World, with all the arrogant ambitious people in the upper levels of management, didn't give him that gratification. *Fucking errand boy!*

"Most guys your age bow out," Sheriff Johnston had said. *Bow out? Bow out to what? An empty house, once it's put back together?* He didn't have a hobby. At one time, he liked helping Susan with the yard. A kid from the neighborhood took care of it for him now since she died. He had never taken up a sport. Until the McAllister woman's body drifted ashore and he got involved in her death, he was a fifth wheel at Melville County. Now that he was reinstated, he was the oldest guy in the agency. He remembered how he felt about the officers on the brink of retirement when he was younger. They were considered a liability. They couldn't move quickly anymore. They didn't take chances. They became intellectually lazy and weary of the pursuit.

Sixty-two felt a lot younger to him than he thought it would. He had stayed in shape, but he knew he was not as quick on his feet as he had been even ten years earlier. His wits were sharp. He could eliminate a lot of wasted effort by using his experience and showing the younger guys how to move a case along. *If they'd listen.* He remembered he didn't. He wanted to stay positive. "Ah shit," he found himself saying aloud. "You want to mean something to somebody." His throat clenched. Tears pushed up under his eyelids. In the dark and the moonlight, all alone on the mountain roads, he knew he had tapped into an ache; one he kept thinking was grief for Susan. The ache now was for him.

He checked into the motel, lugged his suitcase into his room, grabbed his cell phone, and punched a quick dial number. "Hey, Matt. It's Jim. Not too late for you, is it?" he asked Fred Wirth, his retired friend on Pelican Bay.

"It's a little late, but you caught me still up. I had to see a Braves game through to the bitter end. What's up?"

"Well," Raker said, clearing his throat, "I just realized it's been three or four weeks since I talked to you. I'm in Riley's Creek, and I thought I'd give you a call . . . you know . . . just to check in."

"I'm glad you did. We've let some time go by. I've got a phone, too, you know. I could've called you."

"I quit my job at Southern World, Matt. I quit today."

"Whoa. That's sudden. You're not the kind of guy to act on an impulse. You weren't let go, were you?"

"No. It'd been coming on for a long time. That job wasn't for me, Matt. Do you know what the range of tensile strength is for semitrailer locks and how resistive one needs to be so that the standard bolt cutter won't get through it?"

"Ha!" Fred chuckled. "I see. I still think it was a good place for you after all that happened out at the lake in the summer of '08. You took that very hard. You thought you should've been able to keep that awful tragedy from happening. You needed a place to let life settle out for you."

"I know. But . . . well, maybe it's too late . . . I, ah . . . things are a little tough right now for me. I'm pushing ahead one day at a time . . . and that's okay if it's got to be that way. Trouble is, I can't see an end to it. I mean, is this . . . is this going to be it the rest of the way out?"

"I don't want to offend you, Jim, but have you been drinking?"

"No. Oh God no. I can see why you'd ask, but no. Something just hit me driving up here. This motel room is depressing. I've got a job to go to in the morning, and I want to get to the bottom of something up here, but when that is over, wow, I can't see what happens after that. I'm coming up empty on what to do next."

"Okay, I hear you. Most guys in your line of work would be all covered up by your age, crusty, cynical, and pessimistic. You didn't go that way with yourself."

"I'm not sure it changes anything."

"Listen, it's tough discussing something like this on the phone. I hate to put you off, but let's pursue this when you get back to town. I know what you're going through. You're right on schedule. We live most of our lives completely confident that we've got plenty of time to get where we want to go, that the people we love will be with us forever, and then one day the string comes up short. Life turns into a treadmill. Everything that you've worked for is behind you. Right?"

"I'm there."

"Well, hold on. Get through whatever you've got to do up there. Don't make any more major decisions, and we'll go for a long breakfast or something as soon as you get back. How does that sound?"

"That sounds great, Matt. Really great. Thanks."

"Good to talk to you."

CHAPTER 51

"I thought we agreed nobody'd ever, ever come to my house," Frank Schreve shouted on the phone. "I don't want to get mixed up in the dirty work. What the hell am I supposed to do with this goddamn box anyway? It was here in the house when I got back from town."

"Cool down," Brost said. "Have you looked at the files?"

"Yes. It's a bunch of technical reports on the dam. They're all marked up, and there's some copies of official memoranda also. These must be the same files Mrs. Dennison brought up here when she wanted to accompany her husband's body back to Raleigh. The reports refute the dam's in trouble. Dennison debunks everything Lee wrote up."

"Take it all, and get it overnighted to me. I couldn't trust Ramsay to know what any of the contents meant. That's why I had him take them to you after he got away from the motel. Get them to me right now, as soon as we hang up. I don't want to take anymore chances of having this fall into the wrong hands. Then get rid—"

"Frank! Frank!" Helen shouted as she came in the door.

"Hold it, Vernon," Schreve said into the phone. He turned and shouted, "I'm in here. I'm on the phone."

"There's been another shooting. Another man got shot over on Rebecca Ridge late yesterday afternoon," Helen called out as she ran through the house to Frank's study. "Oh, you're on the phone. You should have said something."

"I did."

"I didn't hear you."

"That's obvious. You were shouting over me. Can it wait?"

"Yes, of course," Helen pouted. "Will you be long?"

"No. Just give me a minute."

"What the hell's going on?" Brost shouted over the phone loud enough for both Helen and Frank to hear.

"That awful man!" Helen said. "Why are you always on the line to him?"

"Just be quiet. He can hear you."

"Good."

"My wife," Schreve said into the handset. "She just came in with news somebody got shot out here yesterday."

"Turcotte," Brost said flatly.

"You know?" Frank asked.

"Who's Turcotte?" Helen asked.

"Can you wait until I'm done here?" Frank shouted at Helen. "Close the door on your way out."

Helen spun around and walked out of the room. Frank winced as she slammed the door behind her.

"Sorry," he said into the phone.

"I don't feel comfortable with your wife knowing what's going on," Brost said.

"She doesn't know anything. Not one damn thing."

"Good. Keep it that way."

"That's got nothing to do with us, does it? Turcotte getting shot? Isn't that the same guy you mentioned the other day . . . the guy that got picked up for selling drugs?"

"The same. It's not important. It has nothing to do with us. Just get those files to me right now. Hang up and take them to a UPS or a FedEx drop, okay?"

"Okay," Frank said. "Anything else?"

"Not now. Getting these files just pulled our chestnuts out of the fire. Everything is go. The auctions are still on a week from tomorrow, right?"

"Yes. Your guys will be the only ones bidding."

"Great."

As soon as Frank hung up the phone, Helen opened the door and walked into the room. "I can hear you, you know. You can shut me out of the room, but you talk so loud that I can still hear you."

"How can I possibly care less? I need to drive into town."

"Why?"

"I'm overnighting these files to a man I'm working with in Florida."

"I hate that little guy. That bald guy."

"What little guy?"

"That man Ramsay, who brought the black box to the house. That's where those papers came from, isn't it. That black box."

"Yes, but forget you ever saw Ramsay or that box. Just forget it."

"I couldn't make any sense out of what was in there."

"I suppose you just had to look," Frank snapped.

"It didn't have your name on the box. It's not like it was mail or something."

"As if it mattered. You should've left well enough alone. I've got to go. I'll be back in a little bit." Frank held the bundle of papers in both arms and started to walk out of the room.

"You can't take them like that, can you?" Helen said.

"They've got boxes at the UPS store," Frank snapped back at her. "I'll buy one from them."

CHAPTER 52

Raker slept comfortably through the night. Talking with Fred helped. Fred was one good thing that came out of the trouble at Heron Lake the summer before last. Fred was his first real friend since moving from Minneapolis. Fred was Raker's senior by ten years. He listened well, and Raker trusted him.

The motel and its parking lot were in shade as Raker walked to his car. The sun, well north in August, was coming up behind Mt. Jefferson. He agreed to have breakfast with Art Nichols at Hillbilly Grill, just a few blocks north of the motel on Jefferson Avenue, the main road through the center of town.

"I didn't even know my gun was missing," Art said, shaking a liberal dose of Texas Pete Hot Sauce on his scrambled eggs. "Damn Jeeps. Anyone can break into one."

"It was all staged," Raker said, looking around the narrow dining room to see if he was being overheard. "The files are missing now. Whoever has them knows you've probably read them and you know what Dennison was trying to do." Raker stopped as two men in overalls entered and walked to a table at the far end of the dining area. "When the files went missing," he continued as the two men sat down, "we lost the tie-in for everything that has happened. The only thing they need to worry about now is what you can remember, so they've put you in a questionable position by making it look like you had something to do with Turcotte's death. They want to discredit anything you might have to say. They're probably also worried Turcotte would make a deal and blow their whole scheme. They needed him out of the way."

"Yeah, and try to hang it on me," Art said.

"Sheriff's got to be pissed. He thought picking up Turcotte would break his drug case wide open. I'm headed over to see him as soon as we're done here. Turcotte was probably in on what happened at my house. We just lost out on that one too."

"You think I'm in the clear on the Turcotte shooting? Any reason why they'd haul me in?" Nichols asked.

"From what you've told me, they may want to talk to you again. You haven't held anything back. The sheriff's a savvy guy. They'll be pulling their evidence together now, building a case. I can ask about it, if you like, but I'm betting you're not under suspicion."

"It'd feel great to be sure."

"I'll get back to you then."

The sheriff's office was on the opposite side of town. Raker and Nichols parted in the parking lot, and Raker eased into the morning traffic heading north. When he arrived, he found the sheriff eager to talk to him.

"I just sent Hurdler out with a warrant to bring in Cleve Ramsay and search his place, including his truck," the sheriff said, looking up from his desk as Raker walked into his office.

"Ramsay. Why Ramsay?"

"He was below the dam the day Dennison got shot. With a rifle. That's all I needed to justify the warrant. With Turcotte dead, I'm clutching at straws," the sheriff said. "Besides, that was some hunch you played." The sheriff got up and walked over to a table that had been set up to one side in his office. "Look at this: $40,000 gets deposited into Ramsay's checking account two weeks before Dennison gets shot, long enough to clear. Ramsay draws out $15,000 in cash the day before Dennison is shot and another $25,000 the Monday after. We don't know what happened to the $15,000. Turcotte deals mostly in cash, but he's got a checking account, and he made three deposits on three different days: $9,000 on one, $6,000 on a second, and $9,000 again on a third. The first on Monday, following the shooting, and the second and third on the following days."

"Where'd the deposit come from?" Raker asked.

"The same outfit that backed Turcotte's bail. Dixie States Development Company, the same people who started the development years ago out at Lake Hannah."

"They're supposed to be broke," Raker said, recalling his conversation with Nichols on the subject.

"That's another thing. Dixie States is owned by Palmetto-Atlantic Real Estate and Development Company in Miami. Most people don't know that, but it's a fact."

"Dixie States was the company that wanted Dennison taken off as the inspector at Lake Hannah. I saw the letter their president sent to the state. So they're one and the same outfit."

"Yes, and Amy Nederveld, the woman who came up with Turcotte's bail, worked for Dixie States. It's all been a half-assed attempt at hiding the money trail," the sheriff said.

"I agree. We're missing one thing that'll tie all of this together," Raker said. "The files that got taken from my motel room."

The sheriff shrugged. "We'll just have to work around them then. It'll be interesting to see what we get out of Ramsay," he said. "When Palmetto-Atlantic came up with the money for Turcotte's bail, they also involved themselves in the drug investigation. The FBI found Amy Nederveld received the money for Turcotte's bail from Dixie States, but as it turned out, it was passed through Dixie States by Palmetto-Atlantic. The FBI requisitioned Palmetto-Atlantic's phone records and bank statements." He glanced at a sheet of paper. "It's not a big company, probably fourteen employees overall, and only a few are stationed in Miami at the home office. A guy named Vernon Brost heads it up. He's been in frequent contact with two people right here in Baden County—Cleve Ramsay and Frank Schreve."

"You've closed the circle."

"Looks like it. The FBI plans to interrogate Vernon Brost, so we need to move. We've got to get to Ramsay and Schreve before either one gets tipped off and moves out."

"How about Greg Lee, the dam inspector . . . any calls on Brost's records to him?" Raker asked. "We may have justification for talking to him. Maybe check his financial records. If Palmetto-Atlantic people were talking to him, he'd be tied in. His reports are probably false. He'd have to be nervous about Dennison's widow knowing something."

"Okay, SBI can handle that. Let's focus on what we've got right here. Hurdler will be bringing in Ramsay. Let's you and I go see Schreve."

CHAPTER 53

"I'd better get rid of this box too," Frank Schreve said out loud.

"What?" Helen called from the kitchen.

"Nothing. Just talking to myself. I may be going back out for a few minutes. I'll be back for lunch," Frank shouted as he thought feverishly about how to get rid of the box.

"Okay."

What the hell am I going to do with it? Frank thought. *People could be looking for it. Can't just dump it someplace. Break it up first so nobody'd recognize it.* "Okay, okay," he muttered, looking through the assortment of garden tools at one end of the garage. "That woman never puts anything back where it belongs." He punched the button to the garage door opener and the overhead door began to retract. He walked out across the driveway to the kitchen door.

"Don't suppose you know where the sledgehammer is, or the ax?"

"Yes. Yes, I do."

"Well?"

"They're both down by the boat ramp. You wouldn't remember, of course," Helen snipped, "but I did ask you to drive the boat ramp anchoring stakes deeper into the sand. I caught the cuff of my slacks on one last week. Remember? I almost fell. You said you'd fix it right way. Did you? I got tired of waiting and tried to do it myself. I dragged the sledgehammer down there but it was too heavy for me so I came back for the ax. It didn't work any better. I couldn't get the stakes to budge."

"And bringing the tools back here was out of the question, of course," Frank said sarcastically.

"Those bolts need to be loosened—the bolts around the stakes—or you can't get the stakes to go down farther."

"No kidding. How observant."

"If you'd have done it when I asked," Helen said, "everything would be fine now."

"So you just left the tools down there by the lake, is that it?"

"Yes. I meant to remind you. I get tired of nagging you for every little thing I want done around here. So I forgot."

"Forgot, my ass."

"I did. What's this?" Helen asked, looking past Frank to the driveway behind him. A sheriff's cruiser had pulled up and two men were getting out. "That's that same man who was here the other night," Helen said anxiously.

Frank glanced behind him and recognized Raker and the sheriff. "Afternoon," he said, turning around and stepping back out the door. "What brings you out this way?"

"That!" Raker said, pointing to the box that was sitting on the floor in the middle of the garage.

"What. That box?"

"Yes. That box. Mind if I have a look at it?" Raker asked.

"Help yourself."

Raker recognized the box as the same one that Nichols had turned over to him. He looked up at the sheriff and nodded. "The same."

"How'd you come by that box?" the sheriff asked.

"That's not his box," Helen said, walking up to Raker in the garage. "You'll just have to forgive me for eavesdropping, but you're the man who was asking my husband about the box the other afternoon. It's not my husband's. It belongs to a man named Ramsay. Cleve Ramsay. He brought it by here late one afternoon when Frank was not at home."

"Shut up, Helen," Schreve seethed.

"I think we'd better continue this conversation at my office," the sheriff told Frank.

"Oh," Helen blurted. "What is it? Frank never tells me anything. I thought that box was the same one Mr. Ramsay brought by the house, but . . . but looking at it . . . I . . . I couldn't say for sure. I . . . I don't know where it came from."

"Shut up, Helen!" Frank said.

"Let's take this conversation downtown, Mr. Schreve. Please get into the car," Sheriff Grossman said, opening the door to the back seat of his cruiser. Before driving off, the sheriff called Deputy Hurdler. "Did you find Ramsay? Good. Take him downtown." He glanced in the back seat, adding, "I'm on my way back there myself."

Once Raker and Schreve were seated opposite one another at the table in the interrogation room, the sheriff read Schreve his rights.

"Let me lay this all out for you, Mr. Schreve. We know you have been in regular, timely contact with Cleve Ramsay and a Mr. Vernon Brost at Palmetto-Atlantic Real Estate and Development in Miami. We were about to arrest Gus Turcotte for murder when he suddenly turns up dead from a shotgun blast. We know Turcotte received a considerable sum of money from Ramsay at about the time Dennison was killed. We also know Turcotte's rifle was fired below the dam the day Dennison was shot. See how all of this is coming together?"

"I don't see how any of these events involve me in the least. I want my attorney present if this is to go any farther."

"That's your right. After all, you're about to be implicated in two homicides."

"Homicides!" Frank exclaimed.

"Conspiracy to commit homicide can carry a pretty hefty sentence. Judges aren't likely to be lenient when one of the victims was a public servant acting in the line of duty."

"I had nothing at all to do with that shooting. With any shooting. I'm not saying another thing until my attorney is present."

"Fine," the sheriff said. "You call your attorney, but you're not leaving this office. You're facing several charges including conspiracy to commit murder. You can call your attorney right now if you want, and we'll wait for him."

Two hours passed and an attorney from Winston-Salem showed up to represent Schreve. The sheriff and Raker were presenting the evidence in support of the charges against Schreve when Raker's phone buzzed. Raker excused himself and stepped out into the hallway.

"I got it!" Art Nichols roared into the phone. "I figured it out. Remember when I said Dennison must've had a sense of humor because he had written 'Life is like a box of chocolates?'"

"Yes. Forrest Gump. In the motel that afternoon."

"That was my clue for the password. It just came to me out of the blue. 'Forrest Gimp.' That was Dennison's crazy nickname for me. I lived in the forest on the side of the mountain and I limped. I was a gimp. He thought that fit me for some reason. "

Raker laughed.

"Everything's here on the flash drive along with some more emails from a couple of email addresses that need to be identified."

"Did you see anything addressed to Schreve?" Raker asked. "We've got him down here right now."

"I can't tell. I know the one he uses for POA business. But if he has another one, I wouldn't know it."

"Can you bring it down here right now?"

"Give me fifteen minutes."

Raker walked back into the interrogation room. He looked directly at Schreve and said, "You and your attorney need to excuse the sheriff and me for a second." Then turning to the sheriff, "I think we just found what we're looking for. Let's step outside for a second."

Once outside the room, Raker told the sheriff about the flash drive and Art Nichols's success in finding the password. "He's on his way down here right now."

"Great. Schreve and his attorney can wait until Nichols gets here. I'd like to see what's on that file before continuing the interrogation."

When Art arrived, the sheriff plugged the flash drive into the USB port of his computer.

"It's all in PDF format," Art said. "You shouldn't have any trouble with any of the documents." Dennison had several files on the drive. Each was labeled as they had been in the file box. Within each file, documents were in chronological order and then alphabetical by author.

"God, there's a week of work in this," the sheriff exclaimed.

"Just open the file labeled 'Inspection Reports,'" Nichols suggested. "See, Jim," Art said, turning to Raker when the files appeared on the screen, "Dennison annotated every report with his own findings and opinions."

"Good thing these are all on State of North Carolina letterhead," the sheriff observed. "A smart defense attorney could question their authenticity otherwise."

"It'd be a good idea to move against Greg Lee as soon as possible and requisition his records before anyone gets wind we have this," Raker urged.

Raker and Nichols waited until the sheriff completed his call to Tim Moran of the SBI.

"He's in full agreement with us," the sheriff said, hanging up. "He's going to work on a subpoena right away and bring Greg Lee in when it's ready. Now, how about Schreve? Perhaps we should hold off until Moran and his boys have everything lined up on their end? No point in tipping our hand."

"So I'm no longer a person of interest?" Art asked, looking first at Raker and then the sheriff.

"No. Not a person of interest. But you could be a material witness. We may need you to help with these files. Let us know where you are in case we need to call you," the sheriff replied.

"No problem," Art said. He smiled, then added, "Glad I cracked the code. Nothing like knowing justice will be served . . . If you don't need me anymore, I'd like to head back. Cheryl wants to know how this is all turning out, and I'd like to tell her in person."

"I'll check with you at the end of the day," Raker said, "Great job!"

"Yes," the sheriff answered. "This makes our case. Thanks." The sheriff extended his hand. Nichols reciprocated, turned after shaking hands and left the room. "Let's tell Schreve that he can go," the sheriff directed at Raker. "We'll call him back after we've worked a little deeper into these files. Besides, the deputy is bringing Cleve Ramsay in to see us. I'd like to give that interrogation priority."

CHAPTER 54

Hurdler could tell Ramsay was hungover the minute Cleve opened the door. Still in his boxers and a badly soiled white T-shirt, Ramsay looked as if he had only gotten out of bed to answer the deputy's pounding at the door.

"Man, am I glad to see you," Ramsay said, squinting through the screen door at Hurdler.

"Get dressed. The sheriff wants to talk to you downtown. I'm taking you in."

"You arresting me? You gotta have a warrant for that, don't you."

"No, I'm not arresting you. The sheriff wants you to answer some questions downtown. Get dressed. I haven't got all day."

"This about Turcotte? 'Cause I was gonna call you guys. I was gonna call it in. I just didn't want that crazy son-of-a-bitch who shot Gus to come after me. I'm glad you showed up," Ramsay said, rubbing one bloodshot eye.

"Bullshit. Sheriff wants you downtown. Come on. No more killing time standing here." Hurdler stepped back when he caught a whiff of Ramsay's breath.

"No. Really. I need protection. That crazy Art Nichols is after me."

"Get dressed. I got a search warrant."

"Search away. I'm just glad you're here," Ramsay said and disappeared down a hallway to the back of his small home.

Hurdler checked Ramsay's truck.

✠ ✠ ✠

"Take him to the back," Sheriff Grossman said upon seeing Hurdler walk in with Ramsay. "Have someone sit with him and come back here so we can go over everything."

"Step in here and close the door," the sheriff said. "Two guys are on their way out to Ramsay's place now. Did you find anything in the truck?"

"His Winchester twelve gauge and his thirty-ought-six," Hurdler said. "The Winchester didn't have any rounds in it. The rifle had several in the magazine. There were five Federal twelve-gauge cartridges on the floor. Look like they rolled under the seat."

"What size shot?" Raker asked.

"Bird shot, number eight."

"Turcotte was killed with buckshot."

"I know," Hurdler replied.

"Anything else?" the sheriff asked.

"The other guys might find something. I didn't have a lot of time."

"Okay. Get those cartridges you found fingerprinted. Check for Art Nichols's fingerprints," the sheriff said. "You read Ramsay his rights?"

"No, sir, I didn't," Hurdler replied. "I told him you wanted to talk to him and to come in with me. He kept saying on the way he was glad I came for him and he was feeling safe."

The sheriff read Ramsay his rights as soon as Raker and he were seated.

Ramsay smiled and said he understood. "I hope Hurdler told you I'm glad one of your guys finally showed up at my place," Ramsay said.

The sheriff ignored Ramsay. "You know where you want to go with this, right?" he asked Raker.

"Yes," Raker said. "But jump in anytime you feel you need to."

"Mr. Ramsay, two witnesses said you had an item in your possession that was stolen from a Nations Inn motel room. Can you tell me how you came to possess a black plastic file case?" Raker began.

"You mean this isn't about Nichols shooting Gus Turcotte?" Ramsay made a move as if to rise out of his chair.

"Sit down," Raker said. "We'll get to that. Just answer the questions as they come up."

"No. I'm not saying anything without an attorney present, unless it's about how Nichols shot my friend."

"You'd better call you attorney then," Raker said. "There's a phone just outside the door."

"Okay, let's begin again," Raker said after Ramsay's attorney showed up and consulted briefly with his client.

The sheriff read Ramsay his rights for a second time.

"My question was about an item in your possession that was stolen from a Nations Inn motel room. Can you tell me how you came to possess a black plastic file case?"

"I found it."

"Well, that's interesting, because the cleaning lady at the motel saw you running across the parking lot with it, put it into your pickup, and drive off."

"She did like hell."

"We can always bring her in to identify you." Raker was bluffing.

"Okay, so big deal? A file box. Couldn't be worth more than ten bucks."

"Why did you take it?"

Ramsay shrugged. "I was just passing by, the door to the room was open, and I saw it. I thought I could use it. No big deal."

"But you scooped up all the papers that were in the room and took them with you also."

"Yeah. So?"

"They were in the box when you delivered it to Frank Schreve and his wife Helen."

Ramsay's attorney raised his hand to stop the proceedings. "I need a brief conference with my client," he said. "Could you grant us five minutes alone so that we can discuss a few things?"

"Of course," the sheriff replied. He and Raker left the room. When five minutes had passed, they returned.

"My client is willing to admit that he took the file box and the papers. He thought they might be valuable," the attorney said as soon as Raker and the sheriff had taken their seats at the table.

"Why did you deliver the box and the papers to Frank Schreve?" Raker asked.

"I thought he might pay something for them. They looked official, sort of," Ramsay replied.

"Did Frank Schreve pay you anything for the box and the papers?" Raker asked.

"No. He wasn't home. His wife was, but she wanted me off their property. I left the box and the papers with her and told her that her husband would be interested in everything. Then she told me to git."

"So with your admission, we can arrest you for the theft of the file box and its contents right now."

Ramsay looked at his attorney.

"Petty theft," his attorney said.

"Okay," Raker acknowledged. "We have that recorded. Now, can you tell me where you were on the morning of August 16?"

"No. I mean, I don't remember. What day was that?"

"It was a Saturday. Do you recall seeing me on that day?"

"You? No. I didn't see you on that day," Ramsay replied.

"I saw you. You were down below the Lake Hannah Dam. You parked your pickup so that it blocked traffic, and when my friend and I came down the road, we had to ask you to move it."

"Oh yeah, I remember that. I knew somebody was in the truck with Nichols, but I didn't know it was you. Yeah. That's where I was."

"You were down there with Gus Turcotte, weren't you?"

"No. I was alone. Why don't you guys want to know about yesterday and Gus getting shot—"

"We'll get to that. Just answer the question," the sheriff interjected.

"No. No, I wasn't down there with Turcotte. I don't know where Turcotte was that morning."

"Well, here's my take on that," Raker said. "I think both of you were below the dam together. You drove in separately. Turcotte walked through the woods to a site where he had a view of the dam. He had his 308 with him and took a position as a sniper. After Dennison was shot, he ran back through the woods to his truck and took off. You parked your truck to block the roadway so if anyone just happened to follow, they would be blocked."

"You think what you like," Ramsay replied. "I was checking for survey stakes down there, just like I said."

"Well, we'll just see how that might hold up in court. Now, on the following Tuesday night, you and Turcotte were caught on a traffic videotape in Charles City right after a home was burglarized and set ablaze. Where were you on the night in question? That's Tuesday, August 19."

"I . . . I guess if the video has me in Charles City, that's where I was," Ramsay stammered.

"Why were you in Charles City that night?" Raker asked.

"We had a couple of gals we took out."

"Can you give me their names? We want to call Charles City Metro Police and have your alibi checked."

Ramsay's attorney asked to interrupt the proceedings again at this point. After a brief conference with his client, he signaled the interview could begin again.

"My client's willing to admit he was in Charles City on the night in question," the attorney stated.

"So you were in Charles City the night a house was burglarized and a woman was attacked. We understand now, unless you decide to retract anything at this point," Raker said.

"My client's not retracting anything he has admitted so far in this interview," the attorney said.

"The woman in question survived the fire. She might've seen and can identify you," Raker countered.

"She couldn't see me because I wasn't there. Besides it was dark," Ramsay replied.

"It was dark in the house you entered?"

"No!" Ramsay snapped. "You're putting words in my mouth. It was night. Just as you said. I was in Charles City that night. That's all."

"The woman was left in the house to die in the fire. The blow to her head could've killed her." Raker knew Ramsay could not be certain whether Diane Welborn had seen her attacker on the night of the fire.

Ramsay shifted his weight in his chair and cleared his throat.

"I've talked to the District Attorney about this incident," Raker continued. "You see, it took place in my house. The DA is ready to prosecute the assault as an attempted homicide."

"The DA can do whatever he wants."

"The DA wants Ms. Welborn to pick you out of a lineup. She'd be on the stand at your trial. She's badly scarred from the burns. She'll make a very good witness for the prosecution," Raker persisted.

"One thing at a time, Detective," Ramsay's attorney said, holding up his hand. "One thing at a time. Mr. Ramsay's not on trial here. He has consented to this questioning. He'll have representation at a trial, if one's ever to be held. These issues can wait for the proper forum."

Ramsay slumped back into his chair and forced a smile.

"Where were you yesterday afternoon?" Raker asked.

"Okay, okay," Ramsay said, suddenly very animated. "I thought that's what this was all about. Gus and I were out looking at some property and this crazy bastard comes up on us with a gun and tells us to get the hell off his land. Gus, I guess, thought he'd call the guy's bluff, reason with him, but the son-of-a-bitch levels the shotgun at Gus and blasts him twice in the chest. Boom. Boom. Blew him away."

Ramsay paused. Raker and the sheriff looked at each other. "That automatic went off twice before Gus hit the ground," Ramsay said for emphasis.

"You took your sweet goddamn time getting around to telling us," the sheriff growled. "This happened late yesterday, for chrissake, and you want us to believe you *now*—the morning after?"

"I don't want any trouble."

"You could've called us as soon as it happened."

"Listen, all I wanted was to get the hell out of there. That crazy son-of-a-bitch with the shotgun . . . everyone knows he's not right. I ran as fast as I could down the embankment to my pickup expecting to get a load of buckshot in my back at any second."

"I don't believe this," Raker growled. "Here it's a half day later, you witness a shooting and say nothing until now. Why the hell didn't you call?"

"I panicked. I didn't have my cell phone. I didn't want to stop 'cause that fucker might've been after me too. Then I met the sheriff's cars coming out from town, and I figured someone else called it in. I just decided to go home and lie low. He saw me, too, you know. He knew I saw him. I knew you guys would get around to it. Then I'd come forward when it was safe for me."

"We don't believe Art Nichols had anything to do with the shooting," Raker said calmly. "But we do think somebody tried to make it look as though he did. Let's back up a second. Tell us again, why were you there at the site where Turcotte got shot."

"We were looking at the land."

"What about the land?"

"I don't know. Turcotte thought it was for sale or something. He wanted to check it out."

"And you just went along for the ride."

"Gus knew I owned land out there. He wanted me to help him find these lots and tell him about the place."

"The lots in question were not up for sale," the sheriff said.

"Gus thought they were. I don't know. Maybe he was mistaken."

"Tell us one more time how it happened."

"I was driving. Gus told me where he wanted to go."

"And where was that?" Raker demanded.

"Where we went."

"No, dammit. How did he identify the place, the lots he was interested in seeing?"

"Ah, he just sort of directed me as we drove."

"You just said you were along because he didn't know his way around the development. How could he give you directions? You ended up on a lot I know for a fact was not for sale," the sheriff said.

"It was his deal. I wasn't interested," Ramsay said.

"I'll tell you what I think," Raker interrupted. "You knew exactly where you were going. You knew you wanted a lot adjacent to Art Nichols's place. You wanted it to look like Nichols did the shooting."

"No. That's not so," Ramsay protested.

"Tell me this, then. Art Nichols had number eight bird shot in his gun. The victim was killed with double-ought buck."

"So. So Nichols changed the rounds in his magazine."

"If he changed ammo, then we'd find his fingerprints on the buckshot cartridges, wouldn't we," Raker continued.

"Yeah. I guess."

"Especially when the only way you can get cartridges into the magazine is push on the brass end with your thumb. Ramsay, there were no finger-prints on the cartridges."

"Maybe he used gloves."

"Right. There were no fingerprints on the cartridges in the gun that killed Turcotte because you used gloves. You used gloves handling the gun, the ammo, everything."

A smirk spread slowly across Ramsay's face. "No fingerprints," he shrugged, "so no fingerprints."

"Nichols doesn't own any double-ought buck ammunition. He never uses it. Only light loads."

"How would I know? I never hunted with the guy. I don't know the guy."

"You have buckshot in your Winchester. Magnum loads. Any reason for that?"

"Carries farther. I go after varmints out around my place. It does the job. Only need one or two pellets to knock a critter down."

"The deputy found number eight bird shot on the floor of your truck."

"Oh, yeah. Well, I use it sometimes."

"Let me put this together for you. Your Winchester has double-ought buck magnum loads in the magazine, but it hasn't been fired recently. Nichols's Browning also has double-ought buck magnum loads in it and it has been fired. We're going to find the magnum loads in the murder weapon came from your supply. They'll check out. We're also going to find Art Nichols's fingerprints on the light loads we found in your truck. We getting that done right now. The light loads don't have your fingerprints on them—only Nichols's and they came from Nichols's supply. The manu-facturer's date and lot number will be the same. You replaced the bird shot in the Browning with the buckshot because you knew it'd be more effective in killing Turcotte."

"That's crazy," Ramsay scoffed.

"Art Nichols's fingerprints are on light loads because he handled each one loading his Browning. Your fingerprints don't appear anywhere because you did use gloves, which in court will easily establish premeditation. Murder one, sir. Murder one. You replaced the bird shot with buckshot and then used Nichols's gun to kill Turcotte—"

"My client has not admitted to killing anyone," Ramsay's attorney interrupted.

"You were trying to frame Art Nichols for Turcotte's death, weren't you?" the sheriff persisted.

"This interview is over," Ramsay's attorney said. He pushed back from the table.

"Fine," the sheriff said, standing up also. "Cleve Ramsay, I'm placing you under arrest for the murder of Gus Turcotte, the assault on Ms. Diane Welborn, and other charges that will be filed in good order."

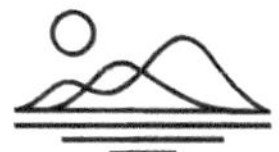

CHAPTER 55

Reviewing the documents on the flash drive did not take a full week as the sheriff expected. Dennison's strict organization made it easy to navigate through all he had accumulated. The SBI subpoenaed The Department of Natural Resources files and cross-checked them with the recorded copies on the drive to establish authenticity.

The SBI found Greg Lee eager to clear his name of any wrongdoing when they interrogated him. Copies of letters and emails proved conclusively Lee was taking direction from Brost. A review of his bank statements and the records for Brost's company also established Lee was getting paid for falsifying the inspection reports. Seeing the wiser course would be to cooperate, Lee insisted he knew nothing of the two murders and the attack on Diane Welborn.

"He's agreed to turn state's evidence," SBI Captain Moran said to Sheriff Grossman on the phone. "I'm sure some of it'll be very helpful in your jurisdiction getting to anyone involved in misleading people about the dam and coercing people about selling their property. We're passing everything along to the FBI also. This guy Vernon Brost is going to be prosecuted in Florida. Lee really gave us the goods on him."

"Thanks for everything," the sheriff replied. "We have a strong case coming together."

"Lee got in over his head. A slippery slope. Once he cooperated with Brost, even on an inconsequential matter, he was trapped," Moran continued. "All Brost needed to do was get someone like Schreve to report Lee to his boss. The prosecutor here thinks Lee will plead guilty to one count of conspiracy to defraud. He'll lose his job, his benefits, and have a record as a felon."

Frank Schreve asked his attorney to return from Winston-Salem so the man would be present when the sheriff and Raker called Schreve to complete their session.

"You've got a number of choices," the sheriff said. "We can go with the charge of conspiracy to commit murder and conspiracy to defraud. If we don't get you on one charge, we will on the others. Things'll go a whole lot easier for you if you'll help us move against the people more directly involved in this scheme than you are. I've spoken to the district attorney, and he's prepared to consider my recommendation when he files charges. My recommendation will depend on what you decide."

Schreve cleared his throat and turned to his attorney who nodded. "Okay, yes. I know Vernon Brost. I worked with him and got paid for my consulting services. But I didn't know this man Turcotte. Brost may have mentioned his name once or twice, but I told him I didn't know the man. As for Dennison . . . of course, I knew him. I knew him through the property owners' association. But that doesn't mean I knew anything about plans to have him killed. Until all of this broke wide open, I thought he was the victim of an accidental shooting."

"It doesn't matter what we believe. Your attorney will need to convince a jury in federal court. This agency is putting the case together against you and everyone else involved in the scheme to defraud the property owners around Lake Hannah. We're going to prove the murders were part of the scheme. You're implicated. You played a big part. One final note, when we subpoenaed the records at Brost's office, we found your signature on a UPS parcel that contained all of the files that were stolen from Officer Raker's motel room. That's grounds for accessory after the fact and impeding an investigation."

"I didn't know anything about an investigation. I . . . only did as I was told. Brost told Ramsay to get them to me. I was supposed to check to see what information they contained. I wanted to protect the members of the property owners' association. Those files were threatening with regard to their interests."

"But you knew the inspection reports were false. You conducted the meeting to inform the property owners of what was going to take place," the sheriff said. "Hell's bells, Mr. Schreve, we don't need to debate this. This was a conspiracy that involved parties across state lines and probably the U.S. Mail service. Because of that, your attorney will be allowed to see all of the evidence that has been compiled against you. This will hit the papers. You can spend a lot of money on a trial that risks producing a verdict far worse than an agreement the Baden County Prosecutor may offer if you cooperate with us and the FBI."

After a brief consultation with his attorney, Frank Schreve agreed he would enter a plea of guilty to a charge of conspiracy to defraud. The magistrate set bail at $100,000. Helen Schreve showed up with the funds later that day to get her husband out of jail.

"I told you I didn't like that man Brost. Would you let me listen in on his phone calls? Oh no! Close the door. Turn your back. If you'd just once let me know what was going on, we wouldn't be faced with this humiliation. You realize how degrading this it is going to be. You, in prison! A convicted felon, Frank. Do you realize?"

In Miami, the FBI interrogation of Vernon Brost ended with Brost's arrest on several charges, including conspiracy to defraud, bribing an officer of the state, and conspiracy to commit murder.

"They ought to throw in conspiracy to defraud Medicare," Diane said, recalling her experiences as an employee when Raker reported to her over the phone about the action authorities had taken.

"That would probably fall pretty far down on their list," Raker said with a chuckle. "Brost is in so much hot water, they may not get around to trying him on that for a very long time."

"If they do, do you think I'll be called as a witness? I'd love to help put him away."

"Careful, you could be implicated also. You need to remember that."

"But I quit because he was asking me to do something illegal."

"I know. Just remember, attorneys can twist things around. Keep your head down. I remember you saying you were glad you'd never have anything to do with Brost again."

"Okay, I won't volunteer anything. I think I have a good chance at a job, Jim, not to change the subject."

"What's that?"

"There's an opening at Presbyterian Hospital in the burn unit. I interviewed for it, and I think it went really well. The fact that I'm a burn victim was something the people liked. It gives me credibility."

"Something you'd like? Day in and day out?"

"Yes. I'm positively enthusiastic about it. The man who interviewed me all but promised me I'd be getting the job. After all, I'm not just another pretty face." Diane laughed.

"You're something. Keep that attitude—that sense of humor—and I don't see anything stopping you."

"You're sweet."

"Oh boy. That's my signal to hang up."

"For now."

"For now."

CHAPTER 56

Days later, Raker heard from Howard Brooks that Diane was going to be discharged from the hospital. The detective promised to visit her when he returned from Baden County. It would be the last time they would meet at the hospital. He was pleased to see she was out of bed and relaxing with a book in a chair beside the bed.

"You've been a good friend," Diane said, extending her hand to Raker. "Honestly, you could've walked away from all of this at any time, and I wouldn't have blamed you one bit."

"I'd never have done that. You were in *my* house," Raker replied.

"Yes. Because I invited myself. You had nothing to do with my getting hurt. And don't stand there. Pull up that chair from the window."

"Well, I just didn't feel that way," Raker said, grasping the side chair by its back and carrying it over near Diane. "When I realized you didn't have any friends or family nearby, it just seemed like the right thing to do."

"You've been great about it," Diane said and looked away. "I was really disappointed we broke up. I wanted desperately for things to work out between us. But that's me. Good ol' desperate Diane. I'm sick and tired of being desperate, Jim. It's as if I really believed the only way I'd get what

I wanted was to be less. This has all been a blessing in disguise. So much came back to me while I was recovering . . . while I was in bed. Sometimes I didn't know whether I was conscious or not . . . like a hypnotic state. I wasn't awake, but I wasn't asleep either. Things kept coming back. Some like ghosts. Others, so very real, as if they were in the room with me. My father. My awful father. How could I have kept on loving him? And Mother. So weak. So spineless. But they were all I had—"

"You don't need to go into all of this," Raker interrupted. He shifted in his chair. "You're going to be fine."

"No, no. I do need to go into it. Can't you see, Jim? I wanted their love, and the only way I thought I could get it was to be less. To give in to Daddy. To pretend with Mother. None of it was real." Diane stopped but continued to look at Raker. She could see his discomfort. *He's been a better friend to me than I've been to him. He means it,* she thought. *He doesn't want an explanation.* She smiled.

"I . . . I think it's wonderful you've gained some insights, Diane," Raker said, accepting the moment of silence as an opportunity. "Really. You've done that on your own. I didn't help with any of it. I was just here . . . just doing what I could."

"But you did what you did," Diane insisted. "Was that difficult?"

"I'm not saying that. I did what any other guy would do. You . . . you're the one who found the way out. You cleared your own way to reach the point that you have now. I've never been good at psychology, but I believe in what you're saying . . . that it's true for you. I can see a change in you."

"I have to say this, Jim. I want you to understand. I wanted to take on our relationship in the same old way. Little me. Great big wonderful you." Diane was pleased to see Raker chuckle. "That's never worked. It wouldn't have worked for us."

"No," Raker said, letting his head drop, and he studied the floor under his feet. "I know."

"Ha!" Diane blurted. "You knew that days, maybe weeks, before you told me. You're not good at this kind of thing, Jim. You really aren't. Did you think I'd get tired of tagging along and call it off myself?"

"Yeah. Well, maybe." Raker looked up and grinned.

"Well, I tell you what, okay? I'm calling it off. The Diane who followed you around isn't here anymore. I feel really shaky. I've a lot of scary decisions to make, but I'm not going to make them from a place where I feel weak and unwanted."

"I never wanted to say you were 'unwanted.' I only meant I couldn't see things working out for us," Raker said, struggling to explain.

"I know. I really do know. I'm talking about me. How I feel. And . . . and I'm not asking for a second chance. No way. Suppose . . . suppose we did try again? I'd be afraid every minute I'd fall back into my old ways of doing things. I don't want that. Not now! I want to find out, now that I'm in a different place, what it's like to feel wanted . . . to believe there's something in me, strong and beautiful . . . something I can trust that would hold someone I loved to me, so I wouldn't worry about being good enough."

She took a deep breath, then continued. "I can only imagine it now. Sometimes, I get a glimpse, just a glimpse of who I'd be as my better self. Just telling you makes that seem possible. I'd be confident in my partner. My confidence would come from being valued and treasured because of who I am. I have a long way to go. And the first thing I'm going to do for myself is take time to build on what I've been through . . . with the visions from my coma and with what I've been going through all of my life. Does that make sense?"

"Absolutely," Raker replied. "I like seeing you enthusiastic and confident. I believe you'll do whatever you need to do. I want only the best for you. I want you to be happy. You'll make it. You'll make it just fine."

"I think I will too."

"I . . . ah, just don't know what else to say, Diane. I think that's a good note for me to leave on."

Diane smiled and giggled.

"What's funny?" Raker asked, smiling back and standing up as if to say goodbye.

"Sounded Gary Cooperish. I loved it," she said, stifling another giggle.

"Gary Cooper? Okay . . . That's a good thing, right?" Raker asked.

"Definitely a good thing," Diane said, grinning. "Now take care of yourself, Mr. Cooper. Friends, right?"

"Always." Raker stepped forward and gently kissed Diane on the cheek. He pulled back and looked directly into her eyes. "Take care of yourself."

"I will," Diane said. "Call me when you get a chance."

"When I get a chance," he said with a smile.

CHAPTER 57

Upon leaving the hospital, Raker decided to drive by his home to see how work was progressing on the repairs. He was disappointed there was no activity as he drove up. He pulled over to the curb and parked, letting the motor run to keep the air-conditioning system working.

August always was a dead month, he thought. Nothing special ever happened. No holidays. Just unrelenting heat and humidity. Both he and Susan were surprised by how restricted their activities were in August after they moved from Minneapolis to Charles City.

"Like living in a hair dryer," Susan exclaimed one day after working a few minutes in the yard. "I can sweat and sweat, and all it does is run down my blouse. It's too humid for anything to dry of its own accord."

Cicadas, Raker thought. August belonged to the cicadas. They had followed him throughout his life. Their reedy pulsating shrill sliced through the late summer heat until, like a siren winding down, each searing attack died away, succumbing as if surrendering to despair. He remembered finding the fragile golden shells on the bark of the huge Mulberry tree in the yard across the alley from his boyhood home. He always heard them. But he never saw one emerge from the shell, break out of it, and take flight.

He turned off the engine and stepped out onto the lawn. The humidity wrapped around him. He caught his breath. The house looked much as it did the day after the fire—a yellow and black cordoning ribbon stretched across the front porch—but other than that, the exposed rafters and gaping hole in the roof looked like the rib cage to a rotting animal abandoned on the floor of the forest. He took a tentative step toward the house and then stopped.

Diane had changed. *On the verge of taking flight*, he thought. The house was not his anymore. He did not want to go back into it. The fire had released him from it—from the quiet afternoons with Susan that had faded away over the months, from the soft dusky evenings that spread across the lawn after their last meal of the day. He lived those days as if they would go on forever. He felt detached from them now, almost as if they had happened to someone else. He was looking, if only for the moment, at the empty carcass of a house that was once his home, his shell.

He was never going to go back. He got into his Camry and drove away.

EPILOGUE

When the conspiracy came to light, the Lake Hannah Property Owners' Association took immediate action to gain control of their development. They launched a campaign to secure the two-thirds of the owners needed to ratify new bylaws that complied with the model the state made available.

Sheriff Grossman had several weeks to compile evidence on the cases for the county prosecutor against the conspirators arrested in Baden Country. Those charged, to a man, opted to plea bargain rather than go to trial.

Cleve Ramsay admitted to being the contact man for Palmetto-Atlantic Real Estate and Development Company in Baden County. He carried out the plans, as directed by Vernon Brost. He was charged with first-degree murder when the twelve-gauge shotgun cartridges of number eight shot found in his pickup had Art Nichols's fingerprints on them, proving Ramsay substituted the ammunition used in the gun prior to using it. Ramsay had stolen Art's gun and replaced the ammunition, an act that established Ramsay acted with premeditation.

The prosecutor promised to request a life sentence with eligibility for parole after thirty years if Ramsay pleaded guilty to first-degree murder in

Turcotte's death, accessory to murder in Dennison's death, and conspiracy to defraud. Ramsay gave evidence against all of the other conspirators except for Greg Lee, the state employee who was not known to Ramsay.

The FBI looked into the financial standing of Dixie States Development and found the company was wholly owned by Palmetto-Atlantic Real Estate and Development. The bank records for both companies revealed Ramsay had received funds forwarded by Dixie States on behalf of Palmetto-Atlantic. The timing of these payments was highly incriminating, as the transactions took place at the time of Dennison's murder; the first on the day before the shooting and the second on the following Monday, representing a total of $40,000. Telephone records also documented Turcotte and Ramsay had been in frequent communication with each other at the time of the killing.

Videotape of the city traffic established Turcotte and Ramsay were in Charles City the night that Diane Welborn was assaulted. The pair were traveling in Turcotte's truck. The only witness at the scene of the fire, however, was unable to identify Ramsay as one of the men who fled Raker's house. No arrest was ever made for the assault against Diane Welborn. She did not see her assailant; the case is still open with Charles City Metro law enforcement.

Records also showed payments were being made, on a regular basis, to Greg Lee, the dam inspector for the state. Lee—suspicious Dennison had been building a file on the Lake Hannah Dam—passed the word to Vernon Brost that Dennison's widow might be delivering the dead man's files to someone with an interest in Lake Hannah.

Evidence pointed to Gus Turcotte as the man who shot Norm Dennison. The spent casings matched with Turcotte's 308. Turcotte was the only person among the suspects who was a trained sniper. The payments Turcotte received from Ramsay, in absence of any other service performed or transaction between the two men, was also highly incriminating. Epithelial tissue found on Turcotte's crowbar pointed to him as Welborn's assailant.

Brost was charged with several crimes, including the Dennison murder, conspiracy to commit murder, and conspiracy to defraud. Brost funded Ramsay's activities which directly implicated him in the Dennison and Turcotte murders, the Diane Welborn assault, and the Raker home arson.

Brost denied all involvement with the killings of Dennison and Turcotte, but Ramsay's evidence against him was too strong. In retaliation, Brost gave evidence against Ramsay that strengthened the charges against him. Just before going to trial, Brost admitted guilt on all counts in exchange for the prosecutor's offer to ask for a life sentence with parole eligibility after thirty years.

Frank Schreve was charged with conspiracy to defraud the property owners. The testimony from Ramsay and Brost established he did not know about either Dennison's or Turcotte's death. Schreve's attorney argued the conspiracy was foiled by the swift action of the local sheriff's office, and while the trial proved Schreve was guilty, the consequences of his participation in the conspiracy did not result in losses to the property owners.

Schreve was sentenced to one year in prison, stripped of his realtor's license and barred from the profession for the rest of his life. After serving his sentence, he and his wife Helen continued to occupy their lakeside home, during the summer season.

AUTHOR'S NOTES

Readers familiar with the North Carolina community of West Jefferson in the northwest corner of the state will recognize the setting for *Breached*. When I wrote *Deadly Portfolio: A Killing in Hedge Funds*, I modeled the setting after the Lake Norman and Charlotte areas. When the book came out, many readers expressed disappointment that I did not put the story into its real life setting.

With *Breached*, I compromised. To readers who know the area, many of the landmarks will be easy to identify. That said, however, there is no town of Riley's Creek in North Carolina. Lake Hannah is not a real lake, and the Lake Hannah Property Owners' Association is a fictitious organization. Any similarity in the characters depicted and actual persons, living or dead, is purely coincidental.

One psychologist described child sexual abuse as "murder of the soul," because coping with it leads a victim to dissociate, which in its simplest terms means the child's psyche becomes fragmented or splintered. The dissociative personality fails to integrate various aspects of identity, memory and consciousness in a single multidimensional self. Usually, a primary identity carries the individual's given name and tends to be passive, dependent, guilty, and depressed. When in control, each personality state may be experienced as if it has a distinct history, self-image, and identity.

Unlike the split personality, in the dissociated person the separate states do not act independently of the primary identity. Usually, the function of the alter state is limited and specified. The alter state is a coping strategy. It intervenes to protect the primary identity. The alter state does not take on a full personality, discreet and separate from the primary identity. Alter personalities do not grow as persons in their own right in the dissociated mind, as may be true of the personalities in a split personality patient. The disorder is called dissociated identity disorder, or DID.

The dissociative personality can result from an early trauma such as sexual abuse. The primary identity delegates enduring the abuse and may see what is happening almost as if it is happening to someone else. Adaption later in life may lead to delegating other alter identities to participate in adult sexual relationships, parenting of children, and other life roles. The dissociative personality fails to integrate the life experience into a single strong core. The damage done to the victim is indeed tragic. The damage is amplified in the pain that the dissociative adult introduces into the lives of those who seek to be close to the victim.

ABOUT THE AUTHOR

John J. Hohn grew up in Yankton, South Dakota, the last upstream steamboat stop on the Missouri River. His family is intimately tied to the history of South Dakota. His grandfather homesteaded north and west of Yankton, staking out 360 acres that remain in John's family today.

John has been interested in the arts his entire life, first publishing at age ten in the nationally circulated *Pilot* magazine. In 1972, he was instrumental in combining the student symphonies of Minneapolis and St. Paul in the founding of the Student Symphonies of the Great Twin Cities area. In 2016, he co-founded 40+ Stage Company in Winston-Salem, North Carolina.

John graduated from Yankton High School, turned down a Navy ROTC scholarship to marry his high school sweetheart, and earned a degree in English from St. John's University in Minnesota. Upon graduating, he taught at St. John's Prep School before beginning a forty-year career in the financial services industry.

John and his wife Melinda divide their time each year between their cottage near West Jefferson, North Carolina, and a home in Winston-Salem, where they spend the winter months. He has six wonderful children, five boys and a girl. He is proud of each one of them and grateful for their friendship and love.